HOUSE
OF
MONSTROUS
WOMEN

HOUSE OF MONSTROUS WOMEN

DAPHNE FAMA

BERKLEY | NEW YORK

BERKLEY
An imprint of Penguin Random House LLC
1745 Broadway, New York, NY 10019
penguinrandomhouse.com

Copyright © 2025 by Daphne Fama
Penguin Random House values and supports copyright. Copyright fuels creativity,
encourages diverse voices, promotes free speech, and creates a vibrant culture.
Thank you for buying an authorized edition of this book and for complying
with copyright laws by not reproducing, scanning, or distributing any part of it
in any form without permission. You are supporting writers and allowing
Penguin Random House to continue to publish books for every reader.
Please note that no part of this book may be used or reproduced in any manner
for the purpose of training artificial intelligence technologies or systems.

BERKLEY and the BERKLEY & B colophon are registered trademarks of
Penguin Random House LLC.

Book design by Kristin del Rosario
Title page art: tree by Hale Wistantama / Shutterstock

Export edition ISBN: 9780593956762

Library of Congress Cataloging-in-Publication Data

Names: Fama, Daphne, author.
Title: House of monstrous women / Daphne Fama.
Description: New York : Berkley, 2025.
Identifiers: LCCN 2024040541 (print) | LCCN 2024040542 (ebook) |
ISBN 9780593817582 (hardcover) | ISBN 9780593817599 (ebook)
Subjects: LCGFT: Gothic fiction. | Novels.
Classification: LCC PS3606.A499 H68 2025 (print) |
LCC PS3606.A499 (ebook) | DDC 813/.6--dc23/eng/20241023
LC record available at https://lccn.loc.gov/2024040541
LC ebook record available at https://lccn.loc.gov/2024040542

Printed in the United States of America
1st Printing

The authorized representative in the EU for product safety and compliance is
Penguin Random House Ireland, Morrison Chambers, 32 Nassau Street,
Dublin D02 YH68, Ireland, https://eu-contact.penguin.ie.

To my mother.
Without you this book wouldn't exist.

To Harry Milton.
Thank you for believing in me.

To my father.
Who passed on his love of words.

And to you.
I dreamt of you and here you are.

HOUSE
OF
MONSTROUS
WOMEN

ONE

February 23, 1986

TWENTY-FIVE years in Carigara and yet she still felt like a stranger in the plaza where she'd grown up. Women who should have been her friends leaned together, their eyes bright, their lips the same shade of rose red, given bloom by the communal lipsticks they'd swapped multiple times a day. Dirt-streaked children ran circles around one another. Men rolled dice on the street, throwing down coins as they made bets.

But all of them were watching her. She could see the way their dark eyes flitted to their peripheries, glancing at her again and again. She could almost see their mouths shaping around her name. *Josephine del Rosario.* The daughter of dissidents. A political orphan. The heir to a crumbling house and a legacy of blood. Perhaps even worse than all that, a spinster in her midtwenties.

She was so sick of it.

The same rumors floated over the courtyard walls into her

house, month after month, year after year. Even the maids she'd grown up with, girls she'd always thought of as practically family, had started to speak with low, husky whispers. As if they were afraid their voices would carry in the dark del Rosario halls and worm their way into Josephine's ears. But not once had anyone ever had the spine to say a word to her about it. Everyone in town seemed hell-bent on pretending she didn't exist at all.

But today they were having a hard time of it, and Josephine smiled bitterly. She sat alone on the concrete bench of the jeepney stop, her long hair pulled back into a low bun, made shiny with coconut oil. Her father's old suitcase sat beside her, and she wore her mother's clothes. An ostentatious dress with bell-like sleeves and a long skirt, made of muslin dyed a subdued emerald. A decade out of fashion and a little too over-the-top for a ride deep into the countryside.

She could almost hear the wheels in their heads turning as they tried to find out where she was going. It was rare for her to leave the del Rosario house unguarded. And with her brother in Manila, she didn't have a single person to chaperone her out of town.

Her gaze skipped over the plaza, across the women slowly turning pork on iron skewers in market stalls, filling the air with the scent of sizzling meat. It was a smart business tactic to set up shop close to jeepney stops, when jeepneys were perpetually late and timetables were only vague promises. Plastic chairs scraped across the concrete nearby, and she glanced to her side to see the mayor of Carigara, flanked by his sons, settle at a white table only a few yards away. Eduardo Reyes held her stare as he leaned back in his chair, its plastic groaning, a satisfied smirk creeping across his wet lips. The woman at the stall rushed to put sweating glass bottles of San Miguel beer in front of him and his boys, popping their metal caps before rushing off to fetch a fistful of pork skewers.

A decade's worth of nightmares crept into Josephine's throat, but she refused to be the first to blink. *He* was the reason the del Rosario name was pronounced like a curse. In the light of a sweltering afternoon, he looked like any other old man on the plaza. Just a man grown round with age and luxury, his white shirt pulled taut over a sloping stomach, tucked into his black slacks.

He'd been lean when he orchestrated the death of her family eleven years ago. When her father had run against him on a platform that promised to push back against President Marcos's martial law and oppressive taxation. The combination had proved to be a potent threat to the incumbent Eduardo. For weeks during the campaign, her father and mother, and their cousins and aunts and uncles, had all piled into a caravan of open-air trucks to drum up support in the neighboring barrios. Music would pulse out of their speakers, filling the streets. Her father would shout out his joyful promises to the crowds that gathered around the trucks, and her family would distribute bottles of beer and bags of rice. The bright promises and gifts garnered them enough goodwill to win the votes of the people, and every poll pointed to a del Rosario landslide victory.

But a week before the election, her father's convoy had been rerouted by police cars and led outside town. The fine details of what happened next had never passed through anyone's lips, but the gunfire ended an hour after it started, and it left the sole coffin maker of Carigara hunched and solemn for days. Josephine's parents, her family, everyone who'd had the bad luck to be part of the convoy that day, were tossed into a pit that'd been dug days before, their bodies covered in a thin layer of dirt. It was almost insulting, how little they tried to cover it up. But the police were bought and paid for by Eduardo, and rumors swirled that it'd been Marcos himself who'd funded the guns and bullets that had torn her family

3

apart. She and her brother, Alejandro, had avoided the execution only because their mother had demanded they stay home to study.

A cursory investigation had taken place, and a few triggermen had taken the fall. But Eduardo ran unopposed, and the roots of his political dynasty had only deepened since then. He and his sons filled the seats of the local office, following Marcos's word like biblical law. She couldn't tell if he just delighted in watching her squirm or if he was using her as a living warning to everyone else. Either way, no one had dared to run against him since.

Eduardo was a wart, but Marcos had been a cancer rotting the country from the inside out for the past two decades as he grew round and smug on his presidential throne. She could scarcely remember a time before he'd been in power—or a time when the world was still in love with the young and decorated war hero dripping with charisma and medals.

But with each passing year, the effect of his rule had only become more prominent. The country had become lean beneath rampant inflation and taxes. The dissidents, once loud and proud like her parents, had been silenced by death, coercion, or greed. But now hundreds of protesters, emboldened by Cory Aquino, were gathering in the streets in Manila, demanding that Marcos end his dictatorship. Aquino was the widow of Marcos's most prominent political opponent, a man who'd been assassinated in full view of reporters. The protesters and the church had rallied around Cory after that, as if she were the Holy Mother given flesh, in the hopes that she'd deliver them from Marcos's evil.

And yet that ferocious, hopeful spirit still hadn't reached Carigara. Their little village, tucked between sea and mountains, was caught in the web of the past, drowning in the long shadows of Eduardo and Marcos.

There's no way those protests will end without bloodshed, Josephine thought. President Marcos and his cronies like Eduardo had proven time and time again that a bullet could be an easy, consequence-free solution to most problems. It terrified her to think that Cory, small and always dressed in yellow, with a big perm and bookish glasses, might end up like her parents. Cory was too tender, too full of bright aspirations that the country could find some happiness after so much pain.

"Josephine? What in the world are you doing out here?"

Josephine blinked and looked up to see a middle-aged man with a stooped back standing beside her. His age-softened face mirrored her surprise, and like her he was dressed too well for Carigara's plaza. His thick polo, while perfectly becoming for a doctor educated in the city, didn't suit the humidity of the day.

"Oh, Roberto. Good morning." Her tongue stumbled over the greeting. If there were a list of people she didn't want to see this afternoon, Roberto undoubtedly would have been second. He was the only person who seemed unfazed by the gossip that swirled around her, which kept everyone a lonesome but safe distance away. In fact, he seemed to have taken on a new, vigorous interest the moment she turned twenty. But any goodwill was lost by how close he insisted on standing beside her, how intent he was on trying to guide her life.

His fixation made her anxious in a way that Eduardo simply did not.

She struggled to push the exasperation off her face. The older man clucked his tongue. "I wouldn't goad him, Josephine," Roberto warned, without once looking at the mayor, who watched them over a fresh beer. "It's been a long time since that awful tragedy. But his sons seem quite content to follow in his footsteps."

Josephine glanced again at the table, and at the two boys flanking their father. They weren't much older than her, but they stared back at her with a stony coldness, like the cobras that made their homes in the graveyard.

"I wouldn't dream of it," she muttered.

"Good, good. Now . . . why are you dressed so lovely today?" His eyes flickered appreciatively over her, and she clenched her fist around her suitcase's handle.

Where is that jeepney? This was the absolute last conversation she wanted to have. And she hated the feeling of his eyes on her.

"I'm going to see my brother and an old friend."

"Your brother? A friend?" There was a disbelieving emphasis on that last word, as if it was hard to believe that Josephine del Rosario still had a single friend left in the world. "Not Gabriella Santos? I thought you hadn't spoken to her since high school."

The disbelief in his voice was palpable, and she couldn't blame him. Gabriella and she had been close as girls, but after the way things ended in high school, the two had barely spoken.

"Oh, she'll be there, too. It's someone I haven't seen in a long time." She chose her tone carefully, refusing to let the anticipation of seeing this old friend permeate her voice. She couldn't let him know who else she was going to see. She was almost certain that he'd forbid it—as if he had the right to do so. It made her blood boil, the way everyone thought they could control her life, just because she was a young, unmarried woman. If she hadn't been insistent on keeping the del Rosario house standing, a memorial and proud testament to her family and their legacy, she would have left long ago to join her brother Alejandro and Gabriella in Manila. But if she left, Eduardo would win. She could never accept that.

"Well, surely they don't expect you to go to them by yourself?

Not without a chaperone?" Roberto asked, but it wasn't a question. He sounded unconvinced, and his eyes narrowed as if trying to catch her in a lie.

Josephine tried to smile, but it came out strained and thin. If her brother were here, she was certain that he'd have sent the old man packing by now. But she could feel eyes on her, and the weight of her mother's prim and strict upbringing. It was unacceptable for a young woman to raise her voice to her elders, especially to a man. More than anything, she wanted to snap. Instead, she reassured him. "It's not far. I'm not going to Manila, just an hour or two north—"

"It's not safe for a girl to travel by herself. I'm sure your brother didn't ask you to come visit him all on your own," Roberto protested. "You certainly can't travel in such a dress by yourself. What will people think? What will they say? I can arrange for someone to accompany you. My nieces are around your age—"

Down the road, the jeepney rolled into view. An image of Jesus wearing a thorned crown had been painted across its side, his weeping face Josephine's salvation. The jeepney pulled up to Josephine's stone bench, and a line of people slowly disembarked from its open back door. Hope surged through her chest. Her hands tightened around the handle of her suitcase as she waited for her chance to flee.

"Here, we'll go to the grocery store and call your brother together. He'll understand," Roberto continued, straightening, as if the decision had already been made. He laid a firm hand on her shoulder, fully prepared to lead her to where she needed to be. Josephine watched as the last passenger disembarked—a short, wiry old woman carrying a woven bamboo basket that contained two live chickens. The hens crooned softly, their eyes glassy and unblinking.

Looking at them filled her with a wild surge of panic. If she stayed, if she listened, she'd be trapped here. The moment the old woman was out of the way, Josephine pulled away from Roberto, darting away from his grip. Her free hand fumbled through her purse for a fistful of centavos and silver pesos. She shoved the payment toward the driver.

"Please, *kuja*, take me to Biliran."

The driver's dark nose crinkled, but he took the handful of coins and dumped them into a cut-open Coke can, where they clattered with a dull symphony.

Roberto stood, open-mouthed, beside the stone bench she'd been on just a moment before. He approached the long, rectangular window of the jeepney, his eyes not quite comprehending that she'd simply gotten up and left.

"You can't be serious, Josephine. This isn't safe. Be reasonable."

"I'm very sorry, Roberto, but I have to go," Josephine replied. She wasn't the least bit sorry. Instead, she prayed to every saint that the driver would push the pedal to the floor and leave him in the dust.

Roberto scowled and turned to approach the jeepney's door in the back, as if he meant to drag her out with limp-handed force. In the front seat, the driver leaned out his window and spat betel nut juice onto the street before revving the engine of the old, repurposed military jeep. The jeepney lurched forward, sending up a puff of exhaust, and Roberto was fading into the distance by the yard.

He called out after her, but the driver had already switched on the radio. Bing Rodrigo's mournful voice drowned out his shouts. Since Marcos had come into power, it'd seemed like every song on the radio was a sweet, melancholy dirge. And for once, Josephine found them tender, even welcoming.

Relief swept through her, and Josephine collapsed into the narrow leather seats, her shoulders slumping as if the weight of the world had finally slipped off her shoulders. Carigara rolled past the open window. First the markets, then the church, and finally the farms and their fields of rice. A new, buzzing excitement grew in her chest. It'd been years since she'd left Carigara, and she cherished every mile that grew between her and her hometown.

But more than that, she was excited, *ecstatic*, about her destination.

Gently, she pulled the letter from her suitcase. Its fine paper was already creased from how many times she'd read it. Her lips grazed tenderly across the letter. It smelled of fertile earth, of santol rotting between roots, of honey thick enough to drown in. She unfolded the letter, just to read it again.

> *Dear Josephine,*
>
> *I've missed you so much. Nothing would make me happier than a reunion. Why don't you come visit, and we can play games like we used to? And if you do, and you win, I promise to help you claim the future you've always hoped for. Alejandro and Gabriella have already accepted, and I deeply hope you will, too.*
>
> *With tenderness,*
> *Hiraya Ranoco*

It was taken as fact that the Ranoco family were witches capable of cursing and doling out blessings in equal measure. But there were darker, persistent rumors that they were more than that. That they were *aswang*, creatures who looked like beautiful women during the day, and at night turned into shape-shifting monsters who hungered for corpses and blood. She was certain that the rumors were unfounded, though a soft dread in the recesses of her mind told her that something wasn't quite right with the Ranoco family. They were secretive and strange, sometimes even cruel. And Hiraya had led a parade of broken hearts through Carigara until a fire sent the whole family fleeing back to Biliran. Josephine's own broken heart had followed Hiraya there, and she wasn't certain she'd ever gotten it back.

But there was more in the Ranoco house than her heart. Every letter she'd received from Alejandro in the past few months was scarce on details, bordering on skittish. He was so determined to be the man of the family, to strike out and turn their miserable legacy into gold. But she suspected things had not gone to plan in Manila, and neither he nor Gabriella seemed willing to tell her precisely what had happened. If she cornered him in Hiraya's home, he'd finally have to answer her, and no amount of machismo and pride was going to stop her.

He couldn't leave her alone and waiting in Carigara forever, guarding the del Rosario house by herself. She wouldn't let him.

TWO

ONCE Josephine was free of Eduardo's and Roberto's dissecting stares, the tension in her shoulders fell away. Her hands fumbled for her mother's silver compact mirror, and carefully she took in her own face. Her father's dour eyes stared back, a harsh juxtaposition to her mother's high, almost gaunt cheekbones. Carefully, she twisted the silver bullet of the half-used lipstick and painted her lips bright red. The lipstick was old—twenty years old at least. But like the compact mirror, it was more charm than cosmetic. It made her feel safer, braver. Like her mother was in the mirror with her.

But as she smacked her lips, her reflection shook with her hands. She was full of frayed nerves. Eduardo and Roberto had unsettled her, but Hiraya. The thought of Hiraya made her second-guess everything.

Lipstick, her hair, the dress. Was it too much? She'd never seen

Hiraya wear makeup. But she could remember vividly how Hiraya loved the singing starlet Elsa Oria, with her bold, pouty smirk. She'd cut out her picture from a magazine and pasted her image onto the wall, claiming the image to be "aspirational."

Josephine snapped the compact shut and new passengers filtered on and off. Fashion meant something different here in these towns with vast swaths of rice fields and forest stretching between them. Styles that had been popular ten years earlier were gaining traction, and all around her were different iterations of T-shirts and harem pants, shorts and skirts. Bright jewel-toned emeralds and ochers. Little touches of America's occupation interweaving with a national love for all things bright and colorful.

But if Hiraya's letter was anything to go by, Josephine would bet money that the Ranoco house would have rejected most aspects of modern life. Even when the girls were children, Hiraya's mother and aunt favored traditional remedies and hand-stitched clothes, their hands repeating for years the intricate geometric patterns that had been native to the Visayan islands tucked in the center of the Philippines. And some part of that seemed to have taken root in Hiraya, because it hardly made sense that she was enamored of their childhood games now that they were all well into adulthood.

But tagu-tagu had always had a certain allure to Hiraya. The game was nothing more complicated than hide-and-seek at night. And yet, even when they were children, it'd never really felt like a game at all. More like . . . practice. A rehearsal Hiraya would goad her and Gabriella and Alejandro into playing, as if they each had their role. They'd been barely seven when Hiraya had dragged them into it.

Josephine could almost *taste* the heady scent of rotten santol fruit, thick and sour-sweet on her tongue. The way the broken stems on that old jungle path had dug into her bare feet. Gabriella's screams jolting between the trees as Hiraya hunted her through the forest.

The game had terrified her as a child. It'd felt like life or death. And yet she almost missed it. They'd been so innocent then, and all too happy to follow Hiraya into the woods. Even Sidapa, Hiraya's little sister, had tromped dutifully after them. Though she hadn't been allowed to play.

"The way my family plays tagu-tagu is different," Hiraya had explained, her mouth a serious arc, as she and the rest gathered beneath the ancient branches of a santol tree. In the distance, the Angelus bells rang, calling the faithful to church, and the sun had begun to slide beneath the horizon. A nervous thrill gripped Josephine's heart. She knew her mother would beat her if she found her daughter had stayed out past her curfew to spend time with *them*.

"This is the Ranoco version," Hiraya pronounced, full of swelling pride. "There will be two seekers, who will be the aswang. And two hiders, who will be prey. Sidapa can watch, since she shouldn't even be here." Hiraya shot an annoyed look at Sidapa, and Sidapa bent her head, hiding her face beneath her long sheets of black hair.

Sidapa had scarcely seemed like Hiraya's sister at all. She had been too mousy, with narrow shoulders and lank hair. A shadow of her older sister. No one had stepped in to defend her.

"If the seekers are aswang, does that mean they get to suck the blood out of losers' necks?" Alejandro had asked. He grinned at Hiraya, his voice flippant and teasing, his shoulders slouched. He was older than they were by a few years, and already too mature and grown-up for their games. He'd come only because Josephine had begged him. But Josephine could still recall, vividly, how she and Gabriella exchanged glances upon hearing his question. Even when she was a child, the rumors that the Ranocos were aswang were omnipresent. But she'd never been brave enough to ask Hiraya outright what that meant. And, more importantly, if it was true.

"Aswang don't drink living blood," Hiraya had chided, rolling her eyes. "Don't be stupid. They eat the living and the dead. But if you beat an aswang at their game, you get a gift. If the aswang catches you, you have to give them something in return. That sounds fair, right?" She didn't wait for them to answer. Instead, they drew lots from broken twigs and the roles were picked. Alejandro and Hiraya would be aswang, and she and Gabriella would be the hunted. Gabriella had heaved a deep, bone-weary sigh that hadn't suited her princess-soft face and looked at her.

"I'm not sure about this," Gabriella muttered.

"It'll be fun," Josephine whispered, grabbing her hand. "Let's hide together."

Since that first game, they'd played tagu-tagu countless nights in the forest, tumbling through the dark as if they were spirits tumbling across the land.

Her mother hated how much she adored that game, and how much time she spent with the Ranoco daughters. Perhaps she could sense the deep fascination her daughter already had with Hiraya and recoiled at the thought that Josephine might be a tomboy—a girl who liked girls. And yet, as much as Josephine admired her mother, as much as it wounded her to see the anger and panic in her mother's eyes, she couldn't bring herself to keep away. Perhaps the infatuation was genetic.

A dark memory twisted in the back of Josephine's head. One she'd spent most of her life keeping away, so that it had a sort of dreamy, half-remembered quality. She'd seen her mother on more than one occasion with Hiraya's aunt, the healer and fortune teller Tadhana. Tadhana was a stern woman with black plaited hair, and she was handsome, even with the deep, sunken hollows where her eyes should have been.

Tadhana would come every full moon, and Josephine's mother would welcome her into the backyard. From her room upstairs, Josephine could see everything. She'd stare through the window and watch Tadhana bathe her mother in herbal water. Water full of vines and leaves, tinted brown, as if it'd been taken from a swamp.

It felt wrong to recall how Tadhana's firm, calloused hands would read the leaves stuck to her mother's skin as if they were braille, and how her mother seemed to melt beneath her hands.

It was witchcraft. Tadhana was renowned throughout the coast as a talented *manghuhula*, a soothsayer who could read fortunes. But unlike the fortune tellers who clogged Manila's Quiapo district, Tadhana didn't lean on dog-eared tarot cards. She read the knots in animal entrails with her bare hands, prodded the recesses of scars that lay across arms and legs, divined meaning from broken bones scattered across tables. The blind, it was said, were the most talented at these arts. And it was rumored that Tadhana's eyes had been taken so she'd be even closer to the spirits that helped her divine the future.

But this strange reading of water and earth seemed to be reserved for Josephine's mother alone. And no one in the del Rosario family ever acknowledged it. Certainly not her mother, who put on bold airs of hating Tadhana and the Ranoco daughters while in public, and certainly not her father, who would refuse to look at her mother the day after a full moon.

She was certain her mother would be furious to see her in this jeepney, wearing her lipstick, her clothes, to see Hiraya Ranoco. Or perhaps she'd be jealous that her daughter would see Tadhana and she would not.

"Miss, when are you getting off?" the driver called back, his voice clipped and rough, as if he'd asked the same question several times in a row.

Josephine lifted her head abruptly and only then realized how far they'd come. The pockmarks of civilization were gone, and now they traveled along a narrow road, with dark trees pressing in on them from either side. She was the last person on the jeepney.

"Kawayan, *kuja*. Is it far?"

The driver stole another glance, and this time she could see his brow wrinkle, his eyes narrowing into an expression she couldn't read.

"You don't look like you fish." He said it like an accusation, and Josephine gave him a thin smile.

"I don't. I don't think I've ever touched a fillet knife."

"You're going to the old Ranoco house, then." It was a statement, not a question.

"You know them?" Her heart fell, even as she kept her smile afloat. Even after all these years, rumors shadowed Hiraya and her family like a persistent wraith.

"Everyone here knows them. You've got some future you're chasing?"

So I'm not the first to get that letter, Josephine mused.

"Don't we all?" she asked.

"Sure, we all do. It's human to sin. To covet and want. But everyone I've seen who goes to that house? They either go in and come back different or they don't come back at all."

Josephine barely prevented her eyes from rolling to the tops of their sockets. Small-town superstitions and urban myths. She forced a smile instead, offering teeth and feigned confidence.

"I go with God, and God protects me," she reassured him, her eyes drifting toward the mournful expression of the Virgin Mary hanging from his mirror like a Christmas ornament. And just to lay it on a little thicker, she placed a hand on the rosary around her neck, silver and tarnished by her mother's fidgeting.

"I'd question if it's God that put you on this path, miss."

She laughed, but the driver didn't return it. He turned back to the road, but she caught him sneaking periodic glances at her in his mirror, as if she'd turned into a brief, ephemeral exhibit instead of a passenger.

Silence traveled with them until they reached the stop outside Kawayan. He didn't respond to her thank-you, and the moment she stepped out he was gone, the jeepney spitting dirt up into the air as it spun around and headed back toward civilization.

She was happy to see him go, and took stock of her surroundings. She could see Marcos in every road and house before her. Carigara had grown thin, but Kawayan was at death's door.

The fishing village was just a fraction of the size of Carigara, and it was sustained only by the fact that the ocean and its bounty were plentiful. But the cement houses were topped with rusted roofs, and the sari-sari corner stores were all closed. No one could afford to stock the shelves, with inflation making even basic goods nigh inaccessible.

If Marcos stayed in power, the town would collapse to its bare bones. But tied around the cement pillar of the jeepney stop was a yellow ribbon. The hallmark of Cory Aquino and her followers. It was a bold statement, especially in a town small enough where nothing was ever truly anonymous. A small spark of hope lit in her heart.

Josephine moved toward the ocean, following the languid, irregular screeches of ocean birds. The ocean waves beat against a narrow comma of a shore, its sands dark and kelp-lined. A stubby cement pier stretched out beyond the reach of the town.

But Josephine's eyes were drawn to the craggy rock cliff and the alcove carved into it. Within it, a statue of the Virgin Mary stood. Decades standing beside the sea had caused the statue's face to be worn away, leaving craters along her eyes and cheeks, smearing it until the divine mother's visage was a mass of mottled stone. Her hands, which Josephine was certain would have been pressed together in prayer, were gone. Lost to the elements or worse.

Grotto shrines were common, but she'd never seen one so old or so decorated. Votive candles had been burned nearly to their bases. Piles of flowers, their petals spilling across the stone floor, covered the bottom of the shrine's alcove. Coins glittered among the darkened splashes of color, along with bits of tack.

I should offer something. Anything.

The thought rang out in her head, tinged by something desperate and superstitious. She fumbled through her pockets and mentally kicked herself for giving the driver every last peso. But she felt certain that leaving without giving the statue an offering would be a terrible mistake. She fumbled at her fingers and took off an old gold ring. It had belonged to her mother, the way almost everything she owned did.

And it was with reverence and reluctance in equal measure that she laid it at the statue's feet, on the bed of wilting flowers.

"O Mother of God, I stand before you sinful and sorrowful. I seek refuge under your protection. Don't despise my pleas, we who are put to the test, and deliver us from every danger. Amen."

Even as the old prayer fell from her lips, it felt shallow. It'd been years since her heart had been moved by the glory of God. Not since her parents had been gunned down all those years ago. Not since the day she'd seen them laid to rest in twin white coffins flanked by half a dozen more. She could recall vividly the eyes of her brother as they followed the procession to the graveyard. His dark eyes were wet with unwept tears, black and determined. That was the day he'd become a man. It'd been thrust on him all at once, and he had taken on the role with a solemn dignity, rising to become the man of the house.

How could God lay such a burden on him? How could God steal their parents and refuse them any hope for justice? But still she lifted her eyes to the hollowed-out crevices of the Virgin Mary's face and tried to find solace in it. There were too many blessings here for a fishing town. Especially one so desolate as this.

Had they all come here asking the Virgin for blessing and protection before making the trip to the Ranoco house? How many games had Hiraya and her family held in the time since they'd left Carigara? The driver had made it seem like there was an endless stream of people playing the Ranoco game for wishes. And these offerings, abundant as they were, seemed tinged with desperation.

Questions swirled in her head as she turned back to the pier. Its stone was battered and chipped from countless storms. But there, tied to a thin rope, was the small, motorized *bangka* boat Hiraya had promised.

She'd seen the fishermen in Carigara gliding through the still morning waters on these boats, using nothing but the sputtering engine and an oar to steer. And, while she had no experience, Ranoco Island was only a mile from Kawayan. With a hand shielding her eyes from the glare on the waves, she could see it from the pier.

The island rose from the dark waters, precisely as Hiraya had described it to her when they were children. Just a few miles across, with thick trees covering it, so that it looked like a turtle's seaweed-covered back. Its craggy, black-rock edges made it a hostile-looking jut of land. But if she squinted, she could see another pier abutting a dark beach.

"God help me not drown in these still waters," she muttered as she laid her bag on the bench. She unmoored the boat and, after some scrambling, managed to tilt it in the island's direction with the single oar. Once she got the motor going, she was zipping across the waters, salt spray stinging her face. And for a brief, terrifying moment, between the islands, on the dark waters, she felt free.

She reached the beach faster than she expected and gracelessly disembarked, the shallow waters turning the edges of her dress heavy. Grunting, she tugged the boat by its rope onto shore, bringing it to rest by a twin boat laid out on the sand, a yard away. Two sets of footprints led away from the boat to the beach, dulled and swept a little by wind.

She stared at the set of prints for a moment, a rush of excitement and anxiety and anger tangling in her chest. She hadn't heard from Alejandro or Gabriella for the last few months, though that wasn't so unusual. The protests had slowed letters and packages down to a trickle—if they ever made it to their recipients. She was lucky to get updates from Manila at all, with the protests and blockades that stretched between the capital and her little tucked-away town.

But it still struck her as strange that they'd come to the Ranoco house now, after all this time. Gabriella had always been a skeptic about traditional medicines, the spells and curses, but Alejandro waffled between believing in the superstitions their mother had taught them and pushing it all away.

He must be desperate, to drag Gabriella all the way out here. What could have happened in Manila?

She knew the answer wasn't anything good. When Alejandro

had left for Manila all those years ago, he had the firm, indomitable look of their father. But through his and Gabriella's periodic letters to Carigara, she'd pieced together the truth. He'd spent an untold fortune of their shared inheritance trying to follow in their father's legacy, going to law school and eventually trying to become a politician.

What followed that was business after failed business, and letters that had become increasingly cryptic. No one wanted to worry her, and her increasingly insistent demands to know what was going on had been danced around if not outright ignored. She didn't care if her brother was trying to protect her. He was the last family member she had, and she hated knowing that he was enduring the worst of Manila without her. And no matter how she begged, he seemed insistent on staying.

This is where the money is was all that he'd write. *I'll stay until I make back everything I lost.*

She trod toward the thick, encroaching jungle, the gray sand giving way to dirt, her hand tight around her suitcase handle. A well-worn path stretched out in front of her. A dark, empty corridor of matted leaves and creeping vines that unraveled into the shadowed corners of the island. This was the only mark of humanity. The rest was untamed and wild.

Gnats accompanied her intrepid steps into the jungle like a halo around her head, but through their mist she spied the shiny black gleam of beetles through the leaves. Bees, more black than yellow, crawled across rotting wood, carrying pink morsels in their mouths.

She was no stranger to insects—how could you live in the Philippines and be a stranger to them? But there were so *many* here. The forest squirmed with them. And they seemed to have no fear of her as she dragged herself up the well-worn path. Instead, they seemed to watch her with dark, almost intelligent eyes. Like shards of clever obsidian. It unsettled her. It almost made her yearn for the stares in the plaza. She hated Eduardo and Roberto, but at least she knew what they were thinking.

The gnats grew bolder the farther up the trail she went. But there was no swatting them away. They were persistent, feasting on the sweat of her nape, taking sly kisses where they wanted them. She didn't dare open her mouth for fear they'd crawl inside.

The trail swept upward, the jungle thinned, and the path widened. She could see the first few shards of blue sky and, beneath it, Hiraya's home. The Ranoco house.

This? This is where Hiraya lives? The shock of the place was enough to root her where she stood, the unease of the insects for a moment forgotten.

She'd seen pictures of President Marcos's house, the ostentatiously named Malacañang of the North, and had thought that a decadent affair bordering on gaudy. And yet here before her was a house more grandiose, more sprawling than anything Marcos and his insatiable appetite could even dream of.

The Ranoco house should have been ostentatious, but it wasn't. You wouldn't call an animal vulgar, and the house seemed as if it'd been born of the blackened soil of the island, though it was structured in the style of a *bahay na bato*, like Josephine's own home. Its first floor was volcanic stone covered in lichen and fat moss. The second floor was dark wood, complete with generous baroque wood carvings flanking the windows.

But where the wood and stone were ageless, the window lattices were filled with yellowed capiz shells that turned them into countless jaundiced eyes. Dozens upon dozens of eyes, like an obese, ancient spider, its gaze unblinking and patient upon her. Josephine shook the sticky, foreboding thought out of her head and bit her lip hard when the feeling refused to leave her. Instead, she tried to see where the house ended.

But it stretched to either side, its dark wood blending with the shadows and vanishing into the jungle, as if it had no end. Aging stone walls marked the edges of what might have made up a court-yard. But beyond them were the remnants of charred, rotting wood. The house had somehow been bigger once. A fire had razed it to the ground. Josephine bit her lip again. Fire and the Ranoco family. They seemed to chase each other.

Gently, she edged toward the house, following the trail of burnt, charred wood along its perimeter. The night the Ranoco women had left Carigara for good had been seared into her mem-ory. It'd been only a week after she and Alejandro had laid her parents to rest. She'd been sleeping fitfully, her dreams haunted by gunfire and shallow tombs, and lungs full of dirt and blood. But Alejandro had woken her up with a knock at the door, telling her not to leave her room. There'd been a fire at the edge of town, and he was going to see if he could help. He was still just a boy, but he'd already taken on the mantle of the man of the del Rosario house, and he'd locked her in her room for good measure.

But that had done nothing to stop her. She'd gotten up in an instant and slid open her window to look out over town. A black, angry plume of smoke rose miles away, and she'd known instinctu-ally that it was the Ranoco house.

Someone had set it ablaze. She had no doubt about that. The fear that had shook her in that moment was so deep that it worked its way into her soul, and she'd broken out in a cold sweat. Her world had shrunk so viciously in the span of days. She couldn't bear to lose Hiraya, too.

She'd thrown her leg over the ledge, determined to find Hiraya herself, and scrambled down the wood and coral-stone rock of her family home. She reached the earth and, barefoot, she had run into the empty streets. There, two silhouettes stood at the del Rosario gate as if they'd been waiting for her.

"Hiraya? Sidapa?" Her voice croaked, surprised and full of relief as she stared at them through the metal bars.

But something about the sisters kept her rooted in place on the other side of the gate. Hiraya stood rigid, her shoulders squared. Sidapa stood limp beside her sister, Hiraya's hand a vise that kept her in place. Sidapa's clothes were singed, her hands pink with fresh blisters, and she smelled undeniably of kerosene. The pity that Josephine had always nursed in her heart for Sidapa twisted. A small thought had kicked in the back of her head as she stared at the younger Ranoco sister.

She's done something awful. "Is everything—is everyone okay? Is Aunt Tadhana, your mom—" Josephine asked, uncertain if she wanted the answer.

"Aunt Tadhana is fine." Hiraya cut her off, her voice clipped and struggling to pass through her clenched jaw. "Mom is . . . Aunt Tadhana is going to help her. She'll make it okay."

The silence that stretched on for a moment longer told Josephine everything she needed to know about Hiraya and Sidapa's mother.

"Sidapa and I have to go," Hiraya whispered, and her voice had turned soft and wet. She laid a hand against the bars, then rested her forehead against it, staring at Josephine through them. She looked lost and terribly alone. "We're leaving for Biliran tonight. Now. We can't stay here. But I wanted to see you before we go. I wanted at least to say goodbye."

That was enough to cut the roots that bound Josephine in place. She took a step forward and tossed open the gate, and felt hot, bitter tears start at the edge of her eyes. She desperately fought them down. It wasn't fair to lash out at Hiraya.

"Why? Can't you stay? You can all live with us. With Alejandro and me. We have enough room—" she pleaded.

"I wish I could. I really wish I could. But Carigara was never forever. We have to go back home. To Biliran. To the Ranoco house."

"Then . . . let me visit you. Let me come and stay with you. Biliran isn't far—"

"No," Sidapa said, her voice almost violent with the force of the rejection, her limp body suddenly turning taut. Her dark eyes stared at Josephine through the shards of black hair plastered to her sweat-slicked face. "You're not invited. You can't come."

Hiraya tugged hard at her sister's wrist, but Sidapa stared back at Hiraya, her eyes catching the light of the moon. Hiraya broke the stare, her face softening as she turned back to Josephine. Some unseen words passed between the two sisters. A silent, tense understanding settled over them.

"It's better you don't come." Hiraya sighed. "But I wish one day you would. I'm really going to miss you. More than . . . more than anything."

Hiraya let go of her grip on Sidapa, just long enough to wrap Josephine in a tight hug that squeezed the air out of Josephine's lungs. Smoke filled Josephine's mouth as she buried her face in Hiraya's hair. But she still clung to her, refusing to be the first to let go.

"Please don't go," she begged. But Hiraya had gently pried her hands off her, and in silence the Ranoco sisters had walked away into the dark.

That was the first time Hiraya had left her. Since that fire-tinged embrace, she seemed to appear every decade, flitting into Josephine's life before vanishing, leaving a tender wound in Josephine's heart each time.

Josephine stared out into the ruins of the courtyard, at the thick balete trees that had broken through the stone, their twisted trunks and stretching branches leaning toward the house.

A breeze whispered cool air across the back of Josephine's neck, comforting, but it was accompanied by a touch at her back. Josephine flinched and turned to see one of the balete tree's aerial roots grazing against her, like thick hair. She slapped it away and skittered closer to the house, a rash of goose bumps springing to life on her arms.

She hated balete trees. They reminded her of the stories her mother used to tell her about how the hollows in their trunks were the homes of *diri sugad ha aton*. Those Who Aren't Like Us. Spirits that skewed malicious, who were to be avoided at all costs. Her mouth formed around a superstitious prayer: *"Tabi tabi paagi-a ako."* Please, stand aside, let me pass.

And as if the vines could hear her, they seemed to fall away from her shoulders, swinging harmlessly like curtains behind her. Of course she was being stupid and superstitious. She was letting her thoughts get the better of her, twisting harmless things into monsters. The trees, the bees. Even a house.

Still, she moved quickly away from the trees, her gaze set determinedly on the doors of the house, as a new, foreign noise caught her ear. Something wet and squelching.

She twisted her head toward the noise and saw several yards away a servant crouched by the roots of a balete tree. Beside her was a bucket, its metal edges rusted and scarlet-stained. Flies orbited it in a dark, hungry mass, sometimes landing to cling to the long white veil that covered her face.

Josephine watched for a moment as the woman reached into the bucket, then squeezed something within. It popped, an unpleasant noise that stirred nausea in the pit of Josephine's stomach. The woman took a dark mass from the bucket and dropped it through a hole between the roots of the tree.

Even without seeing it, she could smell the stench of whatever had drawn the flies. Like pennies and morning markets. A wave of nausea washed through her as she narrowed her eyes, trying to see what the maid crushed in her gloved hands.

Is it meat? The shadows were too thick. She couldn't quite see. She edged forward toward the maid and the stained roots of the balete tree.

"Josephine? Is that you?" A voice like copper bells rang out over the courtyard. Josephine tore her gaze away from the maid to see a familiar silhouette beneath a balete tree on the other side of the courtyard.

Hiraya lifted herself from the roots, where she'd been curled with a novel clutched in her hand. The aerial roots of the balete tree seemed to cling to her for a moment before falling away as Hiraya pushed past them to sprint to Josephine, her hands clutching fistfuls of her red skirt, the hems of which were stained with mud.

Josephine dropped the suitcase at her feet, the maid all but forgotten as she tossed her arms outward. Hiraya threw herself at her, her arms wrapping so tightly around Josephine's waist that the breath was squeezed out of her chest.

Laughter sprang out of Josephine's mouth, and for a moment she felt like a child. "Oh God, Hiraya, you're really here. I missed you!" The smell of rotting santol fruit and fresh, fertile earth filled

Josephine's lungs as she buried her face in Hiraya's hair and met her hug with the same ferocity. She'd missed her so much.

Gently, Hiraya pulled herself out of the embrace, and she looked Josephine over, her gaze tender, resting first on her eyes, then her lips, then Josephine's dress. "You're a dream. Look at how beautiful you are, Josephine del Rosario. The belle of Carigara, here at my house."

"Oh, shut up. I know Gabriella's here, and she won that title the moment they made her Reyna Elena." Josephine rolled her eyes, but she could feel her face burning. She'd been called pretty things by a handful of suitors, Roberto chief among them. But this was the first time it felt like it mattered.

"But look at *you*. You look like a forest *diwata*, wild-haired and pretty, like I've stumbled upon your fairy kingdom," Josephine teased, reaching to playfully brush aside a flyaway lock of Hiraya's wavy hair. "I feel like you might spirit me away."

The years had been sweet to Hiraya. They'd carved the last remnants of baby softness from Hiraya's cheeks, leaving them high-arching and elegant. Hiraya's eyes had always been dark and heavily hooded, giving her a permanently melancholy look that had always been at odds with her mischievous mouth.

Now only one eye stared back at Josephine. Still melancholy, still velvet black. But the skin around the other eye was shiny and puckered, the eyelid sunk inward, limp without flesh to fill it out.

"What happened? An accident?" Josephine asked. She barely resisted the urge to touch the darkened skin around the eye, which had the vague impression of roots across soil. Even this old scar looked pretty on her. Like a Japanese kintsugi bowl, once broken and repaired with gold.

Hiraya laid self-conscious fingertips against her eyelid, shielding it from view. "Oh, that. I forget, sometimes, that it's not there." Hiraya murmured, her earnest grin falling into a sheepish line. "Ugly, isn't it?"

Josephine blinked, then grimaced, horror lancing through her chest as she realized she'd made Hiraya uncomfortable.

"Oh no, of course not. That's so rude of me, to stare." Josephine stammered over her words, embarrassment and shame turning her face hot. How could she be so stupid? "You're beautiful, with or without it. It just surprised me. I'm so sorry."

"Oh, don't apologize. Of course it's ugly—you don't have to pretend. But thank you. That's . . . kind of you to say. It happened a few years ago, and now it's all healed. I've come to terms with it, for the most part. Here, let me get your bag out of the mud." Hiraya reached for her suitcase without waiting for Josephine to answer. "Thank you for coming, by the way. I know it was out of the blue, and that this island isn't exactly easy to reach. But it means the whole world to me that you're here," Hiraya said, and she smiled, almost shy.

Josephine shook her head. "I'm so happy you wrote. After you left that last time, when we were teenagers . . . I thought that was it. You'd get married, have children, forget all about me. I was so happy to get your letter."

"As if I could ever forget you!" Hiraya laughed. "You're my best friend. It doesn't matter how long it's been, how many years have gone by. And it's wonderful to have everyone back in the same place. You, Alejandro, Gabriella, just like old times. I feel like a kid again."

"I can't believe my brother and Gabriella are here. My brother's been avoiding Carigara like the plague, like he has something to prove before he comes back. And Gabriella—"

"Hates me," Hiraya finished.

"She doesn't hate you," Josephine protested. "She's never *hated* you. She's just . . ." Josephine couldn't find the words. For whatever reason, since they'd been children Gabriella had always been icy to Hiraya. Josephine had never understood why.

"It's okay if she does. I like her just fine, and she's civil to my face. Shall we head inside?" Hiraya offered.

Hiraya walked toward the grand double doors of the house, and Josephine paused to glance over her shoulder. The maid and her bucket of viscera were gone. And if not for the soft footprints leading into the woods, Josephine would have been certain that she'd never been there at all. Just a strange figment of anxiety, a nightmarish hallucination in the shadows.

She glanced toward the doors as Hiraya pulled them open. Inside, the house was dark, despite the dozens of windows that lined the outer walls. It looked like a mouth, toothless and hungry.

"My mother always told me to stay away from your house. She was so superstitious," Josephine murmured.

"She really didn't like us. I guess most people don't. But if you stay out there, the mosquitoes will eat you up before nightfall." Hiraya's mouth twisted in a mischievous, almost catlike curl, and she extended a hand to Josephine.

Her fingers tangled with Hiraya's, and with the dread still thrumming in her chest, she passed into the house, its heavy doors closing behind her.

THREE

THE Ranoco house wasn't a normal house, by anyone's definition. It sprawled on the outside. But inside? Josephine felt like she was in the stomach of a monster. Heavy wooden trusses ran along the edges of the room, ornately carved and separating the foyer from the hall. It gave the impression of a rib cage, and the corridors that stretched to her right and left scarcely helped the effect.

Even the foyer was so much grander than Josephine's house. Tiles all shades of a citrine sunset lined the floor, forming geometric patterns as they spiraled toward the mahogany stairs directly opposite the doors. But there were ample signs of wear and tear. The wood of the stairs was chipped and scuffed, and even the tile had been cracked.

Two corridors flanked the imperial staircase on either side, each lined with doors. Tiles that tapered yellow distinguished the leftmost corridor. The right's tiles faded from vermillion to a cerulean green. From the far left, down the golden corridor, came the rhythmic sounds of chopping, of metal on wood. But beneath the aroma of someone cooking dinner was the bitterness of charred meat.

"I think something's burning," Josephine said. Hiraya, mounting the first few steps of the imperial staircase, paused. Her hand rested on the railing. Her brow furrowed as she stared down at Josephine with her single eye, which had turned an obsidian black in the shadows of the staircase.

"You smell something burning?" she asked, her voice soft.

"Don't you?" Josephine waved her hand in front of her nose, but the scent only grew stronger, as if a fire crept toward them.

"No. Not at all. Our chef is an expert at what he does. I doubt he'd ever burn anything. Perhaps you're tired? It's been a long trip."

Josephine hesitated, staring down the hall toward the dim sounds of cutlery. The taste of burned meat filled her mouth, twisting her tongue. But she nodded. Hiraya was right. She was tired. And her imagination tended to take hold of her when she was tired.

"Tired and hungry, I think. I can't even recall the last time I sat down to dinner with everyone. And I don't think I've ever had dinner with Aunt Tadhana or Sidapa. That'll be a treat."

"Sidapa won't be joining us. Nor will Aunt Tadhana, I think. She's already eaten, and she's not all that fond of company," Hiraya replied.

"Oh," Josephine murmured. She was disappointed, though she wasn't sure why. "It'd be nice to see Sidapa again. I'm sure she's changed so much."

"She's here somewhere," Hiraya said, her voice clipped. "But she's just as skittish as when we were children. She takes great pains to avoid both Tadhana and me. And with luck, you too."

"Oh?" There was so much that Hiraya wasn't saying. Josephine could read it in her shoulders, which had tightened and squared. "That's a shame. I always felt like Sidapa wanted to be our friend but wasn't brave enough to ask."

They reached the first landing, and Josephine fell silent, her gaze drawn upward, her eyes wide. The first floor had been dark and almost organic. The second floor was another beast altogether, and the longer she stared, the more outlandish it became.

A grand chandelier hung over the stairs, three-tiered, its pendeloques dull and dust-choked. But among the shards, necklaces hung like Christmas ornaments, catching the light that filtered in through the open windows. Diamonds and crystals, red-stained glass, bits of copper. Baubles you could find in the open-air market by the sea, or heirlooms that should be treasured and well guarded in a lacquered box.

It was a gaudy, chaotic display that reminded her of a magpie's nest. As if the only standard was to capture what gleamed. She touched the small golden crucifix on her chest. Countless rosaries just like hers dangled in the branches of the chandelier above. It unsettled her. Hiraya and her family had never attended mass, and yet Josephine had never seen so many crosses. An entire church's worth of rosaries hung from that chandelier.

But she tore her eyes away from the tangle of jewelry and crystal to the landing. The landing was square, with thick wooden columns lining it. The one in the del Rosario house, where she'd spent her entire life, was similar. But on each wall of the corridor were countless doors, not all of which were suited to the dark wooden walls. Some were brighter, more brittle. Others scarcely seemed to fit in their moldings.

"It's like they've come from all different houses," Josephine

murmured. She didn't care for it. It was a Frankenstein amalgamation, as if pieces of houses had been chopped up and stitched to
this one.

"Oh, the doors? We replace them as needed. But it's difficult to
get the same wood. So here we are. I like the splash of colors. It adds
a little light to the place," Hiraya said, tapping her bottom lip with
a fingertip. She said it airily, as if there were nothing odd about the
house at all.

"And the . . . décor?" Josephine pressed, not quite certain if that
was the right word for it. The walls that stretched between the
hodgepodge of doors were a gallery of odds and ends. Most of the
collection were paintings and photographs, the vast majority sepia
and yellow. But among them were more disorienting items, almost
disturbing. Old ritual masks, but none like she'd ever seen in her
grandmother's house. The mouths were ugly, jagged lines, and rotting cloth covered the eyes. Taxidermy insects, like the beetles and
bees she'd seen on her way to the house, were nailed directly to the
wooden panels in the space between the frames, as if they'd been
caught and killed there, and now dust lay over them in a thin blanket.

"The décor. Of course, that's always the question, isn't it?" Hiraya chuckled, but the amusement didn't reach her eyes. "Whenever we have guests, they always stand right where you're standing.
They ogle as if they've seen nothing like it."

"Well, it's true I've seen nothing like it." Josephine forced a polite smile that came out crooked and frayed. "It's like combining a
dozen houses into one. A chimera."

"I think it's only natural in a house like this. The Ranocos have
been in this house for years. For generations. And I suppose each
woman who's born here wants to leave her mark. Even if her vision
doesn't necessarily match with the aesthetic."

Hiraya glanced at the walls and laughed before turning to stroll down the corridor, and Josephine followed, keeping close to her shadow. She didn't want to be left behind in this strange house with its strange designs.

"Aunt Tadhana claims that the women who've lived in this house, who've decorated it, were pulled by *divine inspiration*," Hiraya explained. "And it manifests differently in each of us. So, of course, there is no guarantee of a cohesive vision. That's a family secret, by the way. The divine inspiration. So don't tell her I told you."

"I promise not to," Josephine said solemnly, though she suspected Hiraya was just teasing her. "Have you been pulled by . . . divine inspiration to decorate as well? None of this looks like . . . you. Or, maybe, the you I knew when we were children."

Though what did she really know of Hiraya? The last time she'd seen her, they'd been sixteen and on the beach. They'd spent a few hours collecting seaweed, sand dollars, and shells, and Hiraya had been quiet, almost drowning in melancholy.

"Oh." Hiraya laughed. "Don't worry, I haven't changed so much. I've left my mark here, but nowhere you've seen. I didn't want the walls, the landings, the obvious spots where everyone's chipped away and scribbled. I wanted a secret place. But Aunt Tadhana, and my mother—you've seen bits of them embedded into the wall. My grandmother and her sister, and their mother and sisters as well. This family—they're obsessed with living forever. With immortality, in whatever form they can get it. I suppose that's just being human, isn't it?"

And what about Sidapa? Is she somewhere in these walls? Josephine mused.

"I think I'd rather have one life, so long as it was worth living,"

Josephine murmured. "But it's hard to think that this place is cen-turies old." She glanced at the ornate doorframes, the walls, the floors. "It's so very Spanish, isn't it?"

Hiraya stared through the open window, down onto the grounds, at the branches of the balete trees, her gaze misty and thoughtful. Something about the stance, the comfortable way she leaned against the wall, made Josephine certain that she'd stood here many times before, looking out over the courtyard and into the dark forest.

"Occasionally . . . we have to rebuild. I think you know how much people hated us in Carigara. Sometimes those types of people find us, even out here. Or sometimes it's something simpler, like a fire. Fire seems to come every generation or so, and it seems like it'll destroy this house and our family once and for all. But it doesn't. It never, ever does. We just emerge from the soil and grow again. But if this house burns down again, I think I'd do something more modern. More colorful."

Hiraya's hands came to trace the bronze amulets hammered into the wooden frames of the window, and Josephine leaned close to her. She seemed so desperately sad.

"I think I'd like to see a house you'd make," Josephine mur-mured. "The del Rosario house has gotten so drab since you've seen it last. I can't keep my mother's flowers alive, and the paint is all peeled."

There were half a dozen amulets hammered into the wood of the window, and as she looked closer, she found them familiar. Her mother had hung similar ones around the del Rosario house with bright red and gold cords. One amulet per window hung on an old, rusted nail. But the images on the amulets her mother had hung had all shared the same motifs: women with outstretched hands, trees with abundant fruit. But here, in the Ranoco house, the images were different. They were of insects and eyes, carved into copper and gold.

Josephine traced her fingertips over one of the amulets in the windowsill. It was slick to the touch, as if it had been tenderly and meticulously oiled.

"My mother had a few of these in the house. They still hang there," Josephine said. "I've . . . let them hang there all this time. It's silly, but it feels like it keeps me safe."

Hiraya's gaze followed Josephine's hand. She laid her own fingertips across the molded shape of a coiled centipede on an amulet, her calloused fingertips running across the scale-like grooves. "I'm sure Aunt Tadhana would be happy to hear that. She made them for your mother especially."

"Did she?" Josephine asked, her brows rising. The memory of her mother in moonlight, glistening as Tadhana caressed her bare back, flickered into her memory.

"Oh yes. Tadhana hated Carigara. But she loved your mother, and your mother was her biggest customer. She'd make your mother amulets, trinkets, oils, and potions. Anything she wanted. Tadhana's nothing but bristles and spit for Sidapa and me, but for your mother? She absolutely purred."

Hiraya drew away from the window, closing it against the golden afternoon and the dark, encroaching trees. "Let's join the others. I've kept you to myself long enough."

They drew closer to the parlor, and voices joined the dull chorus of their footfalls.

"You can't mean that?" a man asked, his voice stricken with disbelief. It felt like it'd been years, but the voice of her brother was unmistakable.

"I'm sorry, Alejandro. With the taxes they've put on the farms, my father doesn't have the funds for another venture."

And Gabriella. Her voice was placating and diamond clear, and Josephine's heart thudded in her chest. Now that she was just outside the door, she wasn't certain if she was ready to meet them again. But it was too late for second thoughts.

"That's ridiculous. Exports are at an all-time high. Your father should be making profit hand over fist—" Alejandro pressed.

"He's not," Gabriella protested. "The protection fees Eduardo's imposed means that it's a record loss. Just like the year before, and the year before that. Not to mention how awful inflation's become. It's fifty percent now, the highest it's ever been. I'm sorry I can't help. But Father's written to say that he has a job in his store in Carigara—"

Alejandro cut her off. "Eduardo would piss himself to see the del Rosario son be reduced to a gopher for his girlfriend's father. God damn Eduardo and may hell take Marcos. How deep into our throats are they going to kick their blood-slicked boots? How can anyone survive this?"

"I know, I know. Believe me, I know. But the protests in Manila . . . I really think there might be something happening, maybe we can really make a change. If enough of us try, if enough of us stand together—"

"You're fooling yourself, Gabriella. Even if Marcos steps down, his cronies will kill each other to fill the vacuum he leaves behind. There's no way to escape the corruption here. It's in the soil, the air. It's built into the laws that the Spanish gave us, cemented by the American occupation."

"So, what? You give up? You won't even consider that it's possible things might get better?" Gabriella persisted.

"I've *tried*, Gabriella. God knows, you've seen me try. And what has it gotten me?" His voice swung low and defeated, and a valley of silence followed.

Hiraya didn't hesitate to push the door open the moment she reached it. Doing so revealed a sitting room like any to be found in one of the old manors in Carigara. Rattan chairs encircled a mahogany coffee table, where a pitcher of water perspired. Beside it, a bottle of *bahalina* coconut red wine had already been uncorked, and two wineglasses were balanced in the hands of Alejandro del Rosario and Gabriella Santos. Alejandro's glass was emptied to its dregs, while Gabriella's remained full and practically untouched.

Surprised, they turned to stare at the open door, and Josephine could feel the tense energy in the room shift. As if they were grateful someone had come to interrupt an old argument that both of them knew would have no victor.

"Ah! Josephine, I can't believe it." Gabriella gasped. In a breath she was up, and in the next her hands were on Josephine, as if the years that had snuck up between them hadn't mattered at all. Gabriella's soft hands pulled her close, and she kissed each of Josephine's cheeks the way they did in foreign films. Perfume wafted off her, chemical and sweet, and a wave of nostalgia shook Josephine to the core. She couldn't tell if the scent warmed or broke her heart—it was familiar enough to be tender, different enough to hurt.

"When Hiraya wrote that you'd be here, I didn't think you'd *actually* come." Josephine laughed, pulling back from Gabriella. But even as she said it, she could feel herself tensing up. She'd been afraid that Gabriella might still hate her after she had failed to manifest during Gabriella's coronation as Reyna Elena during the fiesta.

Shortly after, Gabriella had left for college, and they'd only spoken in letters since. Friendly, sweet letters, of course. But there was a distance in the way Gabriella wrote to her, and a distance in which she replied, that proved that the failure had wounded their friendship.

But Gabriella grinned, as if any bad blood had long since been forgotten. Her hair was styled into a trendy bob, and she stared at Josephine through eyelashes thick with mascara. Those heavy lashes around her bright black eyes made her look like a starlet. It was no wonder that she had left their provincial town for the big, glamorous city.

"Oh Lord, Josephine, *I* can't believe I'm here. Alejandro begged me for days. Apparently, in the Ranoco version of the game, you need even numbers to play. Let's just say he owes me once this is all over." Gabriella rolled her eyes, but her initial excitement dimmed, as if coming back to the reality of where, and with whom, they were. She didn't look at Hiraya standing beside them, as if she was pointedly ignoring her.

"But . . . at least this game gets Alejandro and me away from the city. And it gives us a chance to reconnect." Gabriella's voice swung low and intimate, and she squeezed Josephine's hands. "I've missed Carigara. I missed you."

"And I've missed you. It's been devastatingly lonely and boring in Carigara, with everyone gone," Josephine agreed. But she lifted her gaze over Gabriella's shoulder to where Alejandro was sitting. Like Gabriella, he dressed fashionably, his hair gelled. But, unlike Gabriella, there was clear wear in his clothes. The hemming on his pants was frayed, and his shirt was missing a button. Gabriella had parents to sustain her pursuits, but Alejandro had clearly stretched their inheritance thin.

"Alejandro, I was starting to worry you were getting someone else to write your letters to me. They've been so curt and secretive," Josephine said. She tried to keep her tone cool and civil, but some of the hurt bled into her voice.

Alejandro stood and Gabriella unanchored herself from Josephine, allowing the del Rosario siblings to get a long, hard look at each other.

"It's . . . been a while, hasn't it, Josie? Letters are just words on paper, but there's nothing quite like the real thing." Alejandro sighed around a bone-weary smile. There were new lines around her brother's eyes and deep wrinkles embedded in his forehead. She didn't care for them, or how much they made him look like their father.

And like their father he bore the scars of a failed campaign. The last two knuckles of his ring finger were missing. It was a rough, angled chop, with a hard callus of healed skin over the bone. Without a word, she took his damaged hand in hers.

"They're monsters. I can't believe they really—"

She didn't finish the sentence. He hadn't told her what happened, but Gabriella had outlined the bare facts in a letter to her. A late-night visit from one of Marcos's cronies had ended Alejandro's campaign to join the barangay's council. It'd been a small position, nothing of note. And yet only days after he'd registered to run, he'd been visited in the middle of the night. It chilled her to see that gap in his hand, to think of what had happened to her brother. To know that, so easily, he could have joined their father in an early grave.

Alejandro pulled back his hand, and with the other he rubbed the remaining fingers, as if a phantom pain had struck them. "Yeah, well. Turns out they don't want me in business, either. Had a . . . visit, recently, from another associate of Marcos. Or someone who's trying to get in Marcos's good graces, anyway. Had to shutter the pharmacy before we could even stock the shelves. The del Rosario name carries the wrong type of weight with it in Manila."

"I'm sorry. Maybe it's time to come back to Carigara? I've had to sell off our carabao and coconut groves to keep our maids paid. But if you're back—" Josephine offered.

"No, no. Let's not talk about that right now. Not after how long it's been," Alejandro replied, cutting her off. "I just . . . I just want to enjoy today, this little reunion. And we'll figure everything else out later." He smiled at her, but there was none of his trademark charm in it. He looked exhausted; the anger and passion he had moments ago with Gabriella had washed away.

She opened her mouth instinctually to protest but swallowed the breath instead. There were ten thousand things she wanted to say to him, most of them fueled by frustration at years of being left in Carigara to care for the house and their legacy herself. But he was right: there'd be plenty of time for her to corner him. He couldn't very well escape her in this house, no matter how sprawling it was.

"All right, Alejandro. I understand. But it's a conversation we're going to have to have. You know it's inevitable," Josephine said. "Maybe it's even good for you. Our inheritance will go further in Carigara than in Manila. There's still plenty to invest in there. People will always need to eat, and we've still got plenty of farmland. Just . . . no one to plow it or seed it."

"You're relentless. Mother would be so proud to see how much you've grown up to be just like her. You even look like her." Alejandro laughed weakly. "Same dress and everything." His gaze lingered on her for a second, and if it was possible, he seemed even sadder, his shoulders slumping. "I wish I could have done the same. Followed Father a little closer, maybe even edged out of that long, proud shadow and seen the sun. But Marcos and his goons, damn them . . ." He took the bottle of coconut wine and filled the glass until it was heavy, the lights of the room turning the liquid garnet. He drank heavily and Gabriella flinched, but she didn't protest. Josephine could almost feel the long arguments that had stretched between them, likely regarding her brother's overindulgence.

"Well, now that we're all together, what do you think of a game? To help you get acquainted with the house, and give you all a chance to properly prepare for the big event tomorrow night," Hiraya said, her smile sprightly and eager. The dour, tense mood that lay over the lounge seemed to have no effect on her.

"That . . . might actually be a good idea." Gabriella sighed, leaning back in her chair with her full glass of wine. "Something to get our minds off everything."

Hiraya lifted from the coffee table a lacquer container the size and shape of a cup with a lid. "Tonight's game will be a little similar to tagu-tagu, but in reverse. There will be three seekers, one hider. Once the hider is discovered, the person who was hiding joins them in their hiding spot. Once the second seeker finds the two hiders, they must also join them. Until the three hiders are discovered by the last."

Gabriella's nose crinkled. "How in the world are you expected to hide with three people in one spot?"

"That's the fun of it. It's silliness for silliness's sake," Hiraya answered, and she shook the lacquered box so that the dice inside clattered together. "But I'll admit, we're also playing it so I don't have to give you the house tour. It'd be so utterly tedious to tramp through all these hundreds of rooms when you could discover its nooks and passages yourself."

Hiraya lifted the lid off the container and offered it to Alejandro. He reached within and plucked out a wooden die painted black.

"Seeker," Hiraya stated.

Hiraya extended it to Gabriella. Gabriella reached in, but she hesitated, her fingertips probing the depths, as if she might discern the colors within. But when she pulled it out, she, too, had a black die.

"Josephine?" Hiraya offered it to her, and she stuck her hand in. There were only two left, and she plucked one immediately.

A die painted white. *Of course it'd be me,* she thought.

"So no need for me to pull. It seems we have our hider. You have ten minutes, Josephine," Hiraya pronounced, her barely restrained grin widening.

"Ten minutes?" Josephine repeated, her brows reaching high. "I don't know this place at all. How am I—"

"You're wasting time," Alejandro teased, his smile gentle but just wide enough to show the glint of his canines. The game seemed to perk him up a bit, or perhaps it was just seeing his sister have to scramble on a time limit. "Give us a good game, at least."

Hiraya flipped over a small hourglass, placing it on the table. She looked expectantly at Josephine as the sand began pouring, quickly covering the bottom.

Josephine sucked at her teeth in irritation. She wasn't going to win this debate. Even Gabriella seemed to warm to the idea, her hands rolling her black die in her palm, her smile turning impish.

"Fine, fine. I've just gotten here, without a chance to rest, but here I go. I'm hiding." Josephine stood. "But I'm going to make you work for it."

FOUR

WHY is it always me? For once, I'd like to be the one on the hunt," Josephine muttered. Bitterness clung to her voice as she shut the door behind her. She'd ridden on a rough jeepney seat for hours; she'd learned to use a *bangka*; she'd hiked. And now here she was, running around a house while Alejandro and Gabriella sank into their glasses, as if they hadn't already had all the time in the world to chat and rest their blistered feet.

Josephine deliberated outside the door, staring down the hall that stretched on either side of her, her mouth an irritated bow.

If I go left, I'll be back at the stairwell, which leads to the foyer, Josephine mused. She thought so, anyway. But Alejandro would expect that. He'd be on her in minutes, like a hound after a rat.

No. She'd pick someplace they'd never find. The last place anyone would think to look.

Josephine turned to the door immediately next to the sitting room, her hand firm on the copper handle to ensure it made no noise. The door swung open on soft-creaking hinges. Behind it, she expected another parlor. A storage room, even.

Instead, the door swung open to reveal a hall that narrowed as it went, so that there was barely enough room for a young woman to walk straight ahead. It went half a dozen yards back, with doors offered at its end and to its sides. She was certain that one door led right back into the sitting room Alejandro and the rest sat in.

It was claustrophobic, dark. And far too close to where she started. No one would ever expect it. She crept inward a few feet, letting the door shut behind her. Darkness followed after her, drowning her shadows, so that they all blended into one.

Josephine hesitated. Her heart pounded in her ears. She hated tight places like this. It was too reminiscent of the cement catacomb she'd watched her parents' coffins slide into. Two pristine white coffins that had been shoved inch by inch into boxes of stone, where the wood would rot, and her parents' bones would one day mingle with the dust of her grandparents'. If she never married, she too would disintegrate and become part of the dust that lay in the bottom of that mausoleum, her ashes inseparable from her parents' and of all who'd come before her.

Her shaking hands traced the wall, dust catching on her fingertips, and she willed the floorboards beneath her feet to be quiet. They groaned softly anyway. But through the wood beside her, she could hear Alejandro and the rest falling back to their soft chatter. A radio flicked on with a whine, and the audio crackled around the voices of newscasters talking about events unfolding in Manila.

She inched along as the newscasters spoke quickly, as if their tongues couldn't paint the scene fast enough. People were taking to the streets, filling the highways in Manila to protest the election two weeks earlier. The vanity election President Marcos had forced on them to impress a distant American president and a slew of foreign reporters had been too much of a blatant sham.

The newscasters cut to a live interview with one of the poll workers, who had discovered cheating in the election and taken sanctuary in Baclaran Church with the rest. The tabulator shouted to be heard over the noise of the crowd gathered in the church's nave.

"When the discrepancy between the computer tabulation reports and the figures on the tally board was detected, the immediate reaction was one of indignation and utter frustration. It hurt us to see a deliberate betrayal of trust. It did not matter who was winning or losing; cheating whether by one vote or one hundred thousand is still cheating. It was an insult to our most basic sensibilities, both moral and professional. And we did not want to have anything to do with it.

"The walkout was an escape from an intolerable situation. We just wanted to leave the place and go someplace where we can 'drink our blues away'! But as we left the Plenary Hall, we were mobbed by people whom we didn't know, and we didn't have a choice but to let ourselves be led to Baclaran Church in the confusion that followed. Shocked and scared, we are helpless."

Since the walkout, footage of Marcos's thugs destroying votes had surfaced. The interview was cut off, and the reporters began speaking with new vigor about a recent killing. One of Marcos's detractors was murdered in front of his city's capital, 370 miles away from Manila. Journalists uncovered a ledger showing that Marcos paid the assassin one million pesos to get the job done. The news reporters shouted the list of Marcos's sins, the countless deaths fueled by taxpayer money, spilling out an endless list of victims through tinny speakers.

The parlor had grown deathly silent. Every name contributed to the dirge of countless lives lost in a war waged by one man against an entire country. Marcos had been killing them for years, and only now were people starting to acknowledge it.

Fourteen years. It took fourteen years for people to start fighting back, Josephine thought bitterly.

"Marcos would kill the whole world if it meant he kept power. Give him a gun, and he'd personally shoot every person protesting. It doesn't matter how much they shout, or pray, or sing. He's not leaving the presidential palace," Alejandro said, his words dulled by the wall between them.

It comforted Josephine to know that even after all these years, he was still suffering, too. That they shared the same twin wound. In the next room, she could hear the *thunk* of a wineglass on a hard surface. In near total darkness, Josephine pressed her way through the corridor.

"Hiraya, another bottle, please," Alejandro asked, defeat turning his voice heavy.

"Don't you think you've had enough?" Gabriella protested.

"We don't practice moderation here," Hiraya chirped. A cork popped, and soon came the glugging of liquid spilled lavishly into a glass. "You've barely touched yours, Gabriella. God isn't watching. Sin a little."

There was a pause. "I don't drink on Lent. And even if I did, I don't like to drink in strange places."

"It's not that strange, is it?" Hiraya asked. There was a long pause that followed, and Josephine could only imagine the look on Gabriella's face.

Josephine's fingers touched the first door on her left. She couldn't remember how many doors had been on her left or right before things went dark. She edged past the frame, waiting until her hands tripped across the second.

Beside her, she could hear clapping and Hiraya's muffled voice. "Well, if you're not going to drink, we might as well hunt. Add a little excitement to the night, and a little exercise might distract you from all those dreary thoughts."

"It's not been ten minutes, though," Gabriella said. "Perhaps five, six at most? The hourglass is barely half filled. How far could Josephine have gotten?"

"Oh, but aren't you bored with sitting? I am. You can bring your glass, Alejandro. Let it not be said that I'm not a good host," Hiraya chirped.

A chair was pushed back, and the radio was shut off with an aggressive click. "Yeah, I think I want out of this room. And at best she's downstairs, already lost," Alejandro stated. "Let's put her out of her misery and give her a chance to sit."

"You're both ruthless. I wouldn't want either of you hunting me tomorrow." Gabriella sighed. But more chairs scraped against wood, and Josephine grasped the knob and slid into the next room without waiting to see what was within. They were right: she hadn't gotten very far at all. She'd been too busy eavesdropping. But still, she was confident they'd never think to check the door right beside them.

She was relieved to find that the room was lit. A kerosene lamp burned a low flame on a nightstand beside a narrow cot, with a thin, tattered quilt stretched across it. A bedroom? It felt more like a prison cell.

But who slept here, in this windowless room, wedged between the walls? There was almost no décor, save for passages of the Bible meticulously nailed to the wall, so that they completely covered the space around the bed like a protective halo. Around the foot of the bed, a thick line of ants made their march into a hole in the wall. The room offered two other doors, and she could hear her friends now. The opening of doors, the creaking of steps. They'd scattered in all directions, it seemed, so it was like they were all around her. The house twitched with new life.

It's excited, Josephine thought, then pushed the notion away. The house wasn't anything, of course. It was just a house.

Josephine hesitated before grabbing the lantern. It felt like stealing, but she was certain that Hiraya would understand. She slipped through three more doors and wandered through a labyrinth of strange, hodgepodge rooms. There was no rhyme or reason to this place. No room was the same size, nor did the doors offer any sort of hint of what lay beyond.

Oh God, what is this place? This is why Hiraya wanted us to play. She wants us to see how ridiculous this place is. It's a maze, a knot. I'm not even sure I could make it back to them if I wanted to.

Whatever architect had first laid the plans must have had their head bent by madness, their hands guided by an alien inspiration. Josephine felt stupid for thinking that this place was like the del Rosario house at all. Its outer façade was just a mask of normalcy, hiding what lay within.

Josephine flitted from room to room, no longer bothering to be quiet. She doubted that anyone but Hiraya could track her down now, even if they realized it was her and not one of her other seekers. She pushed open another door to a long corridor, but this one was grander. There was no light in this great corridor. No windows, no chandeliers. Electricity simply wasn't a concept this far from the mainland. It'd barely touched Carigara, and even the del Rosario house, as stately as it was, didn't have the budget to have it installed yet. Perhaps once she dragged Alejandro home, that would all change.

She swung her lantern left, then right, not quite sure which direction she should take.

"Josephine. Why are you here?" a voice sighed, just beyond the light of her lantern. Josephine hissed around a sharp inhale of surprise. She lifted the lantern higher, casting its golden light toward the end of the hall. Just at the edges of it, she could see blackened bare feet, which might have been covered with dried mud or soot. The light traced upward, toward the frayed, graying hem of a white dress.

The dress flickered, and the girl slid away, back into the dark, away from Josephine and down the hall.

"I'm sorry? Have we met?" Josephine called after her, her shoulders squaring instinctually. A flicker of nervous energy had put her on the defensive. She didn't like how dark the hall was. But she followed after the girl.

"Sidapa? Is that . . . you?" she asked, and took a few tentative steps after her. She could hear the girl's footsteps retreating, and she followed after her, the lantern swinging and casting long shadows along the wall. At the far end of the hall, she could see a door open in the blackness, and the girl slid inside, closing the door with a soft click.

"Hey, come on—" Josephine called.

Grabbing her skirts in her free hand, Josephine chased after her, straight down the hall toward the door the woman vanished through. But as Josephine took the handle, she recoiled. The copper handle was soot-slick, staining her fingertips a lead-gray. Disgust rose in the pit of her stomach as she looked at her blackened fingertips. But she forced herself to turn the knob.

The door slid inward, creeping into a room that was blacker

than the hall Josephine stood in. She pushed the lantern in, her eyes searching for the girl. Unlike all the other rooms she'd slipped through, there were no doors, no furniture, no knickknacks. But the walls—the walls were covered in masks. Like the ones in the foyer, staggering in their number.

Some of them were wooden, others made of tin or copper, hammered into place. Real hair spilled off the tops, framing their artificial faces. The light of the lantern made the shadows along their soft curves and hard edges jump. The longer she stared, the more she was certain that the mouths curled in grins and snarls. Their lips twitched as if speaking to her.

"Josephine." Her name filled the room, whispered on the back of a sigh. Josephine jumped, her heart jolting in her chest.

The strange girl stood on the other side of the room. She stood so still, Josephine hadn't seen her at all.

"You frightened me," Josephine gasped, pressing her fist hard against her chest. She could feel her heart pounding beneath her sternum, like a bird that wanted to leap free of its cage.

The girl wore a wooden mask that seemed to have been taken straight from the trunk of a balete tree, its shape warped and braided. Her black hair fell to either side in thick, ropy strands, like the aerial roots of the trees outside. But she knew without a doubt that the woman who stared at her from the blackened hollows of that mask was Sidapa. It'd been years since she'd seen the tagalong Ranoco sister, who occasionally followed them into the woods to play tagu-tagu. The last time she'd seen Sidapa was eleven years ago, just a week after her parents' funeral. Sidapa had smelled of soot and fire and kerosene, and her hands had been pink and blistered. But now they hung limply at her side, hidden in shadows that the light of Josephine's lantern wouldn't touch.

"Sidapa." Josephine smiled, relieved. "It really is you, isn't it? It's been years. How have . . . how have you been?" The question sounded stupid the moment it fell off her lips. Nothing about this situation felt normal. The mask, the room, the taste of smoke in the air—it made her skin crawl. She felt like a pig that had been led to the killing pen but wasn't yet aware of the farmer creeping up behind it.

"Why are you here, Josephine? I told you not to come," Sidapa said. Her voice had been meek when they were children, but now it was like darkened honey. Melancholy and mellow and slow.

She did, didn't she? She told me to stay away. The thought came unbidden, and the last memory she had of Sidapa flashed into her mind. Hiraya had invited her to the Ranoco house, but Sidapa had been viciously vehement when she said no.

Both she and Hiraya had been shocked by Sidapa's insistence. But rather than shut her little sister down, as she'd done dozens of times before, Hiraya had shrugged. Something significant had shifted that night. Some transfer of power that Josephine hadn't understood then and still didn't understand now.

But the anger Sidapa had had as a child seemed dulled and dimmed. Josephine preferred that rage to the slow ice in Sidapa's voice now.

"I'm sorry," Josephine offered. Though she wasn't at all. She stepped forward, and the door shut behind her with a soft click. In the back of her head, warning bells chimed, sharp and panicked, but she quashed them. She'd spent too much of today feeling paranoid when there was nothing to be afraid of at all. Sidapa had been her friend once.

But now that she was closer, the soft smell of smoke turned bitter and harsh. Her mind filled with images of burned, blackened things, twisted and turned brittle and frail. She could only stare at the edges of Sidapa's body, the way they blended into the shadow, almost as if there were nothing to separate the two.

"I don't know what I did to upset you, or why you don't want me here . . . but can't we make amends? Just tell me what I did wrong."

She edged closer, but Sidapa seemed to bristle, the ends of her fingers tapping and chattering against the wall in an erratic rhythm. "You're so stupid. You, Alejandro, and Gabriella," Sidapa muttered. "Is she really that beautiful? Are her promises that seductive? Why couldn't you just stay away?"

"I'm sorry? Are you talking about Hiraya? Of course she's pretty, but it's more than all that, more than the promise of a wish. I missed her. I missed Alejandro and Gabriella. I missed you, too," Josephine persisted.

From the hall came the creak of floorboards, and Josephine turned toward the door at her back, startled. She'd completely forgotten that she'd been playing a game, and she lifted the lantern in time to see Gabriella push open the door, bringing in with her the glow of the hallway lanterns, bright and shining.

Josephine flinched at the light, disoriented. She'd been certain they'd been out before.

"There you are, Josephine. Looks like I'm the first winner. I thought I'd never find you in this maze, but your chatter led me right to you. Who were you talking to?" Gabriella tilted her head, a teasing smile on her mouth.

But Josephine lifted a hand toward the wall and Sidapa. "You remember Sidapa, don't you? I got a little waylaid when I saw her." She was happy to have Gabriella break the somber, brittle tension that held the room in such a choke hold.

Gabriella glanced over Josephine's shoulder, toward the far wall, and her gaze slid back to Josephine. Her smile faltered, and her eyebrows pushed together in concern.

"Sidapa was here with you?" Gabriella asked. "Hiraya's little sister?"

Josephine turned back toward Sidapa, but no one stood against the wall. Only the countless eyes of the strange, handcrafted masks stared back at her, their sockets empty and shadowed. The mask Sidapa had worn against her face, the rough cut of the balete tree, chipped and carved into a human face, lay against the wall, too.

Gabriella made a small, uncomfortable noise of disgust as her gaze ran over the dozens of faces. "Is it possible you mistook her? It'd be easy to, with all these masks. There isn't another door, is there?"

Gabriella waved her hand vaguely at the other walls. But it was obvious to both of them there were no other doors.

A numb confusion lay over Josephine. How had Sidapa slid past her? A trapdoor? A secret passage? "She was here. Right there, just a moment ago."

She reached for the mask but didn't dare to touch it. Instead, she pressed her hand against the wall. It didn't move. But as she rapped her knuckles against it, she was almost certain that the space behind it sounded hollow.

Of course. Another corridor, likely the one she'd used to get here. But the knowledge of it didn't settle her nerves. Sidapa's words clung to the inside of her skull, rooting inside her brain. There was something *wrong* with Sidapa. And Hiraya knew what.

"I'm sure she was there, darling. Perhaps she slipped away while we were talking? This house is strange. But, Mother Mary, I hate this room," Gabriella said, her hands rubbing her upper arms.

"I hate it, too," Josephine muttered as she looked into the empty eye sockets of the mask. Gabriella didn't seem to hear her.

"Why did you pick this room and not someplace more pleasant? Someplace with chairs? There were rooms full of dried flowers, half-empty perfume bottles, and books. But no, here we are in a bizarre shrine. How utterly Hiraya. How utterly Ranoco."

Josephine's lips pressed into a thin line, her mind still tangled up in Sidapa's vanishing. But she'd felt a little kick of heat in her chest at Gabriella's remark, and she turned to confront her.

"Hiraya isn't *bizarre*," she protested.

Gabriella rolled her eyes as if she'd been expecting that protest. "Oh please. She's been an odd little duck since we were children. Her and her sister both. You can't tell me any of this"—Gabriella waved a hand at the surrounding walls—"is normal."

"I admit it's a little disorienting," Josephine conceded. And she knew that was the understatement of the century. "But we're all strange, aren't we? Hiraya just doesn't mind being strange where others can see it. I admire her bravery. Her willingness to not compromise herself for anyone else's vision."

"Yes, yes. I know. You adore her. She hung the stars in the sky and moves the sun with her breath. But come on, Josephine. Disorienting? You think this place is just disorienting? That barely comes close to describing this place," Gabriella muttered.

But she turned to Josephine and sighed, waving her hands again, as if she could shoo away the tension building between them. "God, but I'm getting off track. That's not the point. Forget her for just a second. I wanted a chance to talk to you alone. To check in."

"Really? But we've written so much. I could wallpaper a room with our letters." She smiled, but she knew precisely what Gabriella meant. Every letter they'd swapped for the past few years had felt stale and superficial. The friendship they'd had before was on life support, and neither one of them seemed willing to let it die.

"I know. But I miss what we had when we were girls. We used to be so close." Gabriella's voice turned soft, almost tender. But guilt kicked at Josephine's heart, and she turned away, her eyes coming to focus on the empty gaze of a mask instead.

"What's there even to say? And it's not like you or Alejandro are much better. You're both living in the city, with your degrees and parties and business ventures. And you're writing me scraps about what's playing in the cinema or whatever you last read. Nothing real, nothing about *you*." She could hear the sourness in her own voice; she could feel herself turning defensive. But she couldn't seem to stop herself. The resentment and jealousy and guilt that had been building in her heart for the past decade was too hard to keep down.

"But I guess I shouldn't complain to you. You're still leagues better than Alejandro. He barely tells me anything at all. I've got to learn all the gossip from the maids and pretend like I already knew. Worse, he's refused to answer me about my allowance. It's been months since he last sent us anything, and the del Rosario house is practically falling apart. It's humiliating."

Gabriella's shoulders tensed into a tight square, and she paused before she spoke. "I'm sorry, I can't imagine how hard it's been to be there by yourself, trying to keep everything together. Alejandro's . . . been stressed about money. We both have. Every single venture we've tried has failed. I can't even mention it without him shutting down or starting some huge rant about how we're being targeted by Marcos's men, and it's a huge conspiracy to see him fail."

Gabriella wrapped her arms around her chest. "I know that I

might not have been the best friend these past few years. But I'd like to change that, if you'd let me? How have you been? What have you been up to all these years?" Her gaze slid back to Josephine's face, but her smile seemed strained.

"It's really no different than what I've written. Everything's precisely the same as it always was. Carigara hasn't changed. I haven't changed. The days haven't changed. It's the same Carigara you knew from when we were children."

Gabriella's eyes rolled. "You're being ridiculous. It's not like you're dead. Something must have happened. You can't tell me after all this time you haven't gotten a boyfriend." Gabriella hesitated for a beat and then ventured to say, "A girlfriend, even." There was a long pause, and Josephine could feel Gabriella's gaze drilling into the side of her head.

She refused to take the bait. "There is nothing and no one. Except for old man Roberto, of course. It seems like I can't go three yards without tripping over him and that fog of musk he calls cologne."

"Roberto?" Gabriella echoed. "Well . . . he's not so awful, is he?"

"He's three times my age, Gabriella," Josephine retorted, unable to keep the disgust from crinkling her mouth.

"He's not! Twice your age, maybe. But he's a good man, isn't he? Patient, kind. That's leagues better than ninety percent of the men in Manila."

"Oh, so kindness is enough for marriage now, is it? Not love or attraction or compatibility?" Josephine asked.

"Well, you're certainly not getting any younger," Gabriella protested. "And you could do worse. Much worse."

"Oh, please spare me. I'm twenty-six, not a corpse. What about you, then? Are you and Alejandro going to be marching down the church aisle anytime soon, declaring your unending love?"

It was Gabriella's turn to sigh, and she did it with a dramatic, exhausted flourish. "You know your brother. He can commit to a business venture if it looks the least bit promising. But marriage? Children? He looks at me like I'm insane. You can go ahead and say it; I know it's been years."

"Then I'll say it. You can do better than my brother. So much better." She softened. She knew her brother had never been the romantic type. Neither had their taciturn and reserved father. But still, she couldn't even imagine Gabriella with another man. She'd been carrying a torch for him since they were children, and the flame hadn't flickered or dimmed once. "Has something happened between the two of you? Things seem . . . tense."

But before Gabriella could answer, the door beside them cracked open.

"Am I interrupting something?" Hiraya asked as she peered inside, her smile tentative. Alejandro stood behind her, disappointment on his face. Though Josephine wasn't certain if it was because he'd lost or because they'd been so easy to find.

"Just chatting. I'm shocked you found us at all," Josephine answered.

"It was easy to find you, actually. The way the floors creak and groan, it gives you away. Did you enjoy your tour of the house? I hope you found something of interest." Hiraya's gaze flickered toward the walls, covered in masks.

"Tour? It's not really a tour, is it? I saw at least two dozen rooms and I know that's just a fraction of this place. I don't think I'd be able to make it back to the foyer at this rate," Gabriella scoffed.

Hiraya chuckled. "Yes. Most of our visitors spend their time lost. But finding each other—that's the basis of everything. Reunion. Desire. Choice and sacrifice. But of all the places you could find yourself, I'm glad you found this room. Here, on these walls, you can see each one of my ancestors. My mother, my grandmothers, my aunts and great-aunts."

Hiraya lifted her own lantern upward, her flame strong. She wore a half smile as she gazed upon the dozens of staring faces with their cracked cheeks and flaking paint.

"Before a Ranoco dies, we make a cast of our face. We paint it ourselves. And when we pass, our survivors hang it here."

"And the hair?" Josephine asked. She hated the hair the most. The way it hung in long curtains on either side, brittle and stringy. Some were jet-black, others shades of gray or yellow-tinged white.

"We give up our hair when we're dressed for death, and it's woven into our masks. A temporary thing in life turned immortal."

Gabriella shuddered. "It's like a cemetery."

"No, no. We don't keep our dead here," Hiraya chirped, letting the lantern drop. "Just their memories."

"That's so much more reassuring. I think I'd like to leave," Gabriella said, already edging out the door.

"Excellent idea." Hiraya clapped her fingertips together. "Dinner?"

FIVE

HIRAYA led them from the room of empty-eyed masks, and they kept close to her, like ducklings nipping at the heels of their mother. Losing track of Hiraya meant getting viciously lost, and Josephine tried to count the twists and turns, cobbling together a broken map in her head. It was a pointless effort. There were too many rooms and halls, too many narrow passages.

Their caravan passed through stately halls and well-furnished rooms. Rooms filled with antique gold-tarnished treasures, glass-eyed stuffed predators from lands far away, their once vibrant furs haggard and grayed with dust. Past a room dedicated purely to mirrors, which reflected Josephine's face back at her dozens of times.

She could see the apprehension lined there in her furrowed brows and narrowed eyes. She couldn't get the youngest Ranoco out of her head, and it showed.

Hiraya glanced over her shoulder periodically, a smile tugging at the edge of her mouth. She was flaunting her knowledge of the house now, and the eccentric trove that its rooms possessed.

They slipped into a large hall, well-lit and spacious. "It might not seem like it at first, but the Ranoco house is like a heart. It has veins, which pump life into its chambers. But it also has its major arteries. This is one of them." Hiraya's hands fluttered at her sides like heavy moths, drawing their eyes to the floor, where a thread-bare floor runner with an oriental design stretched the entire length of the corridor.

"It's scarlet, see? So this is the Scarlet Hall. If we follow it, it will lead you to the banquet hall. Then sitting rooms, the smoking room, the bars."

"Everything to do with entertaining guests, then," Josephine surmised. *So there* is *a rhythm to the house. A skeleton of logic that keeps things in order. Or perhaps it's the one thing they won't let their renovations interfere with.*

Hiraya nodded. "Yes, exactly. Guests are everything to us. Let's be honest, this island is a lonely black rock in the middle of the ocean, and without guests we'd be starved for company. So we try to keep them coming any way we can. Tadhana's divinations, oils, and healing massages have done the job well enough for the past decade. And for the past few years, she's been training me to do the same. I bet I could read your palm like it's an open book. What do you think, Gabriella? Interested?"

Gabriella balked, her fists clenching. "I'd like to keep the cover on that book closed, thank you. But I'm shocked to see you so . . . enthused about guests now. Tadhana always seemed like she hated people, if that's not too blunt. And you and Sidapa were always skittish."

Hiraya shrugged. "Well, we all have to survive somehow. You

and Alejandro, with your business escapades in Manila. And the Ranoco family, we've always used what our grandmothers taught us. You wouldn't believe how far people will go to know their future, to try and influence it even a little."

"I've no doubt," Gabriella muttered. "I've seen the lines for fortune tellers in Quiapo. People go to church to see the Black Nazarene and then head right outside to have their fortunes read on dog-eared tarot cards. Though I'm not sure I've ever seen a fortune teller do more than give it their best guess. What are the other halls, then? Should we assume there are four of them, for each of the heart's arteries?" Gabriella stared pointedly at the ragged carpet beneath their feet. Dirt had been trod deep into the fabric of the rug. At one point, the carpet might have been scarlet. But now it was a muddy ocher.

"The Emerald Hall on the first floor will lead you to the guest rooms and the guest baths. The Golden Hall, to the servants' quarters and kitchen. The Cerulean Hall, to the family rooms."

"Oh, speaking of family," Josephine said, "I saw Sidapa earlier. She's the one who led me to that mask room. Will she be joining us for dinner? I want to clear the air with her, if possible."

Hiraya's stride stuttered, but she recovered half a beat later. So fast that Josephine wasn't even sure she'd seen it. "Sidapa won't be joining us. She doesn't care for crowds."

Alejandro clucked his tongue. "After all these years, she's still shy? She was always watching us from the sidelines. I'd love to pick her brain sometime. It's the quiet ones that always turn out to be the most interesting, if you care to probe them a bit."

"I doubt Sidapa will take you up on that offer. I'm surprised she even appeared at all," Hiraya said. There was a heavy displeasure in Hiraya's voice, a stiffness to her shoulders.

"Oh, that's a shame," Josephine said. "She really seemed upset that I was here. That warning she gave me when we were kids, to stay away? I had no idea that she meant it so seriously."

Ahead of her, Alejandro and Gabriella shared a quick glance. Neither of them had known that she'd met with the Ranoco sisters the night of the fire, the night they'd fled from Carigara. But they were quiet, intently listening.

Hiraya sighed and rolled her shoulders, the motion reaching her wrists and hands, which splayed outward dismissively. "It's complicated. Just before we left Carigara, Mother declared Sidapa her favorite, and the one she wanted to succeed her in her craft. Which means that, once Mother passed, it'd be up to Sidapa to decide who was invited and who came to the house. But Mother died a few years ago, and Tadhana decided that Sidapa wasn't fit to lead our house. Instead, she declared me the heir. Which is why I invited the three of you. Sidapa's unhappy about the change in direction, and so she's sulking somewhere in the corners of the house. Just ignore her."

The words came out silken and nonchalant, but Josephine caught the sharpness of a warning, like a dog baring the first white sliver of fang. Asking another question would invite a bite. But she couldn't help herself.

"So, are you two not on good terms, then?" Josephine persisted. "She must be frustrated that you took her spot. But why is she hiding when she could just—"

"It really doesn't matter." Hiraya cut her off, her voice crisp. "She's always been stubborn and argumentative, and she's only gotten worse over the years. It's for the best if you pretend she doesn't even exist."

A door stood at the end of the hall, and Hiraya stopped before it. Unlike the rest of the doors in the hall, it was imperial and distinct, its wooden frame carved with flowers and leaves. Through it, Josephine could smell the meat, the thick stench rolling out from underneath the door. Her throat constricted and tears pricked at the edges of her eyes, as if an allergic reaction had seized her. The response was automatic, but her heart twisted with that old childhood grief.

"Oh, it smells divine. Is that lechon?" Gabriella asked. Her enthusiasm made her tone sparkle, and the rough tension that had settled over the group fractured.

"It's our version, distinct to this island. I hope you like it," Hiraya said as she pushed open the door.

Light flooded across them, and Alejandro and Gabriella swept after Hiraya into the dining hall. Josephine took her time, breathing through her nose as she hovered in the doorway, clutching at the skirts of her dress. She hated, hated, *hated* the smell of meat.

Three hanging candelabras kept the room in a state of dim gold, their smoky glass flickering with candlelight. Beneath them, a table long enough to fit twenty guests stretched down the middle of the room. It was a *kinamot* feast decadent enough to be fit for a family reunion, with more food than the four of them could possibly eat.

Plantain leaves lay across the center of the table in vibrant stripes of emerald. Hiraya sauntered to a chair at the table's center and a shadow at the edge of the room flickered. A man detached himself from the wall.

Josephine couldn't help but stare at him from her post by the door. His uniform, dark navy linen pants and a *barong tagalog* shirt, was pressed and formal. But a lacy mantilla was draped over his head, the kind worn by particularly pious women in church, its edges flowery and feminine. But it didn't just cover his hair. It was laid so that it covered his face, draping halfway down his chest like a funeral veil, but almost entirely opaque, so that the features of his face were impossible to see in the dim light of the banquet hall. She'd seen this type of veil before, worn by the woman in the courtyard.

Gabriella laughed as she stared at him, the noise a snort that mingled amusement and befuddlement before her hand flew to her mouth to suppress the sound. But the man was unperturbed. He pulled the chair out for Hiraya in an elegant movement so precise it was obvious he'd done it dozens, if not hundreds, of times before. Hiraya sat, and he melted back into the shadows.

But now Josephine could see that he wasn't alone. An unbroken line of staff stood pressed against the wall, militant in their rigidness and uniformity. Their hands lay folded in front of them, and each wore a veil, so that there was nothing to distinguish them from one another but their heights and uniforms. Men wore cassocks like priests; the women wore black dresses that seemed almost identical to the habits of the nuns who had taught them in school. The sight was ridiculous, fever-dream surreal. But she couldn't find the humor in it as easily as Gabriella. She hadn't liked the maid at the edge of the courtyard. And these servants, like dolls pressed against the wall like tin soldiers, filled her with unease. She couldn't tell if they were watching her or not, and yet she felt inexplicably that every set of eyes was on her, staring. Gauging her every movement, weighing her worth.

But no. That was stupid. She was being stupid, and paranoid, and ridiculous. Alejandro seemed, at most, amused, and he stared at them with an open, frank curiosity.

"Such a robust staff, Hiraya," he observed. "You know, please don't take offense, but I always thought the Ranocos were flirting with destitution when we were kids. That rough nipa shack you called a house in Carigara barely kept the rain out. But all that time, you had servants and a mansion here in Biliran. Why would you ever leave this place?"

"Oh well. Tadhana was insistent. She'd heard lovely things about Carigara, and she wanted to see it for herself. But once our house caught fire . . . it seemed like a good time to leave. But please, sit. You must be hungry," Hiraya said from her chair. Her black eye remained fixated on Josephine, who still hovered in the doorway. Hiraya leaned her elbows against the gleaming varnish of the table, balancing her chin in the palms of her hands.

Alejandro and Gabriella took their seats, their shoulders a little tenser for their masked audience. Alejandro sat beside Hiraya, Gabriella across from him.

Josephine followed and stood beside the chair in front of Hiraya, automatically gathering her skirts in her hand. A servant seated her, and Josephine sat rod straight in the chair, staring at the table. Lechon dominated the table, its skin crisped and dark. But its head had been removed, along with its legs, so all that remained was the torso. A small blessing, to neuter it and make it more contoured mass than body.

"Well, thank you for having us. And I'm not one to complain about free food, especially food as nice as this, but no head, Hiraya? The face is the best part." Alejandro grinned, his teeth gleaming with saliva.

"Oh, it's Tadhana's preference. She doesn't like eyes. Especially of dead things," Hiraya explained.

"But she's blind, isn't she?" Gabriella asked.

"Yes. Perhaps she's jealous of them," Hiraya murmured.

Josephine couldn't help but stare at the crisped skin of the slab of meat between them. It smelled so much like the stuck, barbecued pig that they'd been cooking in their backyard the day she and Alejandro had learned that her parents, and every last member of their family, had been slaughtered.

Her father had brought everyone with him on that final day on the campaign trail. Her mother, her aunts and uncles, her cousins. Even their attorneys and a group of bright-eyed, ambitious journalists who were excited to pen a story about the upstart in Carigara who was brave enough to voice dissent against Marcos's policies. But she and Alejandro had been left behind to study, and watch the servants slowly roast a lechon in the backyard. The lechon would have been the centerpiece of the feast when her parents and their convoy returned.

Instead, it'd been pulled apart and served cold on the night that she learned her parents had died. Now the smell of it made her sick to her stomach. It made her feel like a child, lost and powerless.

A cold wave of nausea rushed through her. She gripped the cloth of her skirts in a death vise. No one seemed to notice. She grasped at something to distract herself.

"Will Tadhana be joining us, then?" Josephine interrupted as she tried to ignore the massive hulk of flesh between them, and that old childhood wound. It was cruel that Alejandro seemed so wholly unaffected, his eyes bright and hungry.

Hiraya gave her a thin smile. "I wouldn't hold your breath. Aunt Tadhana's gotten fickler with age. But she took special care to treat the lechon. It's her touch that makes it a Ranoco special. Likewise, the honey is freshly harvested." Hiraya gestured at the spread of food, and to the pot of honey with a ladle at the center. "Please, try it. I'd hate it if you went to bed on an empty stomach."

Surrounding the lechon was tocino, gleaming sweet and sour meat anointed with sauces and spices aplenty. Two dozen dried slender fish, headless. Skewers of barbecue, bowls of adobo, golden curled shrimp, pancit noodles with speckles of green and orange. Flies hovered over all of it in wide circles. But they never dared to land, feeding themselves off the aroma alone.

She wanted to vomit. The smell of meat was cloying, sticking to every corner of her mouth. And yet she couldn't tear her eyes off the precisely cut neck of the lechon. The rings of white and pink meat, radiating out from the spine.

Gabriella and Alejandro took handfuls of food as if they hadn't eaten in days. As if the game of tagu-tagu they'd played had famished them.

In the room's corner, a radio hummed to life. A servant twisted the knob, flipping through stations until Freddie Aguilar's "Anak" filled the room, his voice velvety and smooth as he slunk into a song of remorse and grief for his parents.

It was like she was being mocked. But beside her, Alejandro's laugh broke through the dark web of her thoughts. Gabriella had said something witty or charming, something about how they hadn't had a feast like this since Gabriella graduated from Santo Tomas, and how they'd all gone to Taal after, to the resort by the crater. Josephine stared at them, her hands still on her lap, as a cold feeling of loneliness swept through her. How much of life had she missed, safeguarding her family home in Carigara? A part of her felt stupid for standing like a stone wall around her family's legacy while Alejandro sipped San Miguel by the pool with a woman most men would have killed for.

"Oh God. You were so drunk! Do you remember, you almost fell into the canal—" Gabriella chuckled, peeling the skin off the lechon's dark back with her fingertips. The meat below was pale and soft and Josephine's mouth filled with bile. Her mind turned to soft static, but she could almost feel the rain-heavy breeze from the day her parents died.

"*I* was drunk? I'm shocked you can remember anything," Alejandro retorted. He was rougher with the meat, digging his fingertips into its side. "If I remember correctly, you were so drunk you kicked off your heels and demanded I carry you down the mountain."

"I had blisters!" Gabriella retorted, with mock anger. "Would you really make a woman walk down a hill with blisters?"

"Why were you even wearing heels in the first place? It's a *mountain*."

"You don't have to eat the meat if you don't want," Hiraya said, her voice so soft it almost slid beneath Alejandro's and Gabriella's laughter, fitting nicely beneath Freddie Aguilar's song and Josephine's humming brain.

"What?" Josephine blinked across the table at her, struggling to return to the present.

Hiraya didn't repeat herself. She plucked a rambutan from the edges of the spread. With her fingertips, she split open its thick skin, revealing the milky-white center within. She rolled the soft pearl in front of Josephine. "Just as tender. Just as white. But perhaps it'll suit you better than meat and honey."

The gesture caught Alejandro's attention, and the smile dulled on his lips. His gaze slid toward the fruit, then to Josephine. "Oh . . . still? Are you still refusing to eat meat? I know it upsets you, but you can't go your whole life without eating meat, Josie. It's unhealthy."

The disappointment on Alejandro's face felt like a slap. It was strange how her brother could still make her feel small and immature after all these years. How he could make the gulf between them feel as deep and dark as an ocean.

"I just . . . don't like the smell," she muttered.

Gabriella tutted at Alejandro. "Don't tease her. She's had it hard. And we all cope with grief in different ways," Gabriella scolded, her hand coming to briefly squeeze Josephine's beneath the table. Somehow, that sweet gesture only made Josephine feel worse.

"C'mon, Gabriella. You don't have to coddle her anymore," Alejandro sighed. "You're not schoolgirls. She's not a child."

Josephine pulled her hands away from Gabriella and set them on the table. She arranged her words into a series of calm, measured syllables.

"I've been living on my own for the past eight years, Alejandro, as the head of the del Rosario house. I'll eat what I please." Each word was soft, but there was molten anger beneath them. And beneath that anger, an agonizing hurt. She smiled, but it was strained, and he didn't return it. She'd never felt more alone.

"Oh God. Please, Josephine." Alejandro rolled his eyes. "Are you really throwing the house in my face right now? We can't even get through one dinner without talking about it? You're not the head of the house. Though I *do* appreciate you keeping it standing while I'm away rebuilding our family legacy. And before you get angry, I'm not saying you aren't a woman in your own right, that you can't make your own decisions. I'm just worried. It's my place as your brother to be worried about you." The joy he'd shared with Gabriella moments ago was gone, and what was left was exhaustion and irritation.

Hiraya's gaze slid between Alejandro and Josephine. "Worrying is such a waste of time. But what matters is happiness. Are you happy, Alejandro? Are you happy, Josephine?" Hiraya asked, her voice breaking through the strain that had settled over the table. She leaned forward, her singular eye gleaming with what might have been joy or curiosity, as if this were a show to which she had front-row seats.

Alejandro scoffed and leaned heavily back into his chair. "Of course, Hiraya. I'm thrilled. Just spilling over with joy."

Three sets of eyes settled on Josephine, and embarrassment bit at the back of her neck, turning her entire face hot.

"I'm happy," Josephine answered. It was clear that she was not. It killed her that she felt so alone at the table. That Alejandro and Gabriella had built lives side by side in Manila, full of memories and laughter, while she'd guarded what was left of their parents in Carigara. It killed her that her food, one of the few things she had control over, was so open to examination and ridicule. That it was even up for debate.

Gabriella waved her hands, as if trying to physically disperse the heavy atmosphere in the room. "Perfect. You're happy, she's happy. No one cares who eats what, so let's focus on why we're here, hm? You invited us here because of a game. Is that right, Hiraya? I didn't see the letter myself, but Alejandro told me. And I'll be honest, I was surprised. We haven't spoken in years, so it felt out of the blue."

Hiraya's stare slid with a reluctant slowness to Gabriella's face, her mouth falling briefly into a crescent of displeasure. "It was at Tadhana's suggestion, believe it or not. I asked her to divine my future, and she found that my future would be brightest if I invited the three of you. But it was my decision to reach out to you three. I miss those long evenings in Carigara, all those games we played, the memories we made. Those were some of the best moments of my life."

Hiraya said it so frankly, so honestly, that all attention fell onto her. And Josephine let out the tense breath that had been building up in her lungs, her shoulders slumping. It was good to be off the operating table, no longer dissected by her friends and found wanting. Hiraya endured the spotlight so much better than she did.

Hiraya plucked another rambutan from the table and broke open its pink skin with her short nails. She inspected the white fruit for a moment, then laid it tenderly in front of Josephine again, as if making a statement.

"But you're right, Gabriella. I called each of you for a reason. You all know that my family comes from a long line of *mananambals*. For generations, we have been healers and sorcerers, passing the old beliefs and rituals from mother to daughter and protecting them. Our most famous and powerful ritual is a game similar to tagu-tagu. Tadhana was the facilitator of that game for decades. Now Tadhana is reaching the end of her life, and it falls to me to inherit the game, to be its conductor and maintain our tradition. And to celebrate my inheritance, I get to play the game myself, just once. It's my pleasure and privilege to choose who I play it with. And the only people I wanted to play with were the three of you."

A silence fell over the table, and Josephine glanced at Gabriella and Alejandro. She could see her own hesitance mirrored in their faces. Hiraya spoke with sunshine in her voice, but there was something beneath the surface. Josephine knew she was the only one who had ever really been close to Hiraya. And even she had always felt like Hiraya was more of a stray cat, secretive and independent, only allowing you to get close when the mood struck her. But she'd kept both Alejandro and Gabriella at arm's length their entire childhood.

Alejandro rolled his wrist as if trying to pull more from Hiraya by force. "This game, then. It's a gamble, isn't it? A little hide-and-seek, with the winners taking—"

"The three of you . . . you're all at a crossroads, with the uncertain future a grim specter leering from the shadows. Each day, that specter draws closer. Each day, you wake with the weight of anxiety in your chest. But the future doesn't have to be uncertain. Win this game, and I will call on the spirits to divine your future and tell you precisely how to mold it to your liking. How to avoid the fate that you're most frightened of."

"What does that even mean?" Alejandro laughed. It didn't reach his eyes, which were dark and deadly serious. He leaned forward on his elbows.

Josephine tilted her head as she stared long and hard at her brother. She hadn't seen it before, but she could see it now. *Desperation.* Desperation and fear. Hiraya was right. Alejandro was up against a wall. He was afraid of the future. There was something dark there that terrified him. And he'd been keeping it from her.

"I mean exactly what I said. The future is a malleable thing. If you play, and pour your body and soul into winning, the future you hope for will be arranged. Be it for love, or victory, or freedom. Whatever it is your heart desires."

Gabriella scoffed, her mouth a skeptical smirk. "And you? What do you get, Hiraya?"

"If I play well, I get the same reward as you. The spirits will help me manifest the future I want. Though I suppose when it comes to playing, I have home-court advantage." She flashed Gabriella a vulpine smile, her pointed canines on full display.

"Do many people come here, then, to play the Ranoco game? To try and win a future where they're happy?" Josephine asked. She still recalled the dozens of trinkets and coins at the foot of the Virgin Mary at Kawayan's pier. The heavy warning the jeepney driver had given her.

"Oh yes," Hiraya said brightly. "People come all year just to play. Sometimes just four at a time, or even up to a dozen. That's why the house was built the way it is. Why it keeps expanding. It keeps the game challenging and fresh."

"Well, it's an absolute maze. I don't know how you ever find anyone," Alejandro said, and took a deep sip from his wineglass. A servant filled it again immediately. He was drinking too quickly, but Josephine kept the opinion to herself. She wasn't his keeper, and she could tell by the hard lines on his face that he needed it.

"True, it's a hard game. The aswang, the hunters, have until dawn to find the hunted. And the hunted can find Sanctuary and end their game early. But most games end just after midnight. I expect better from you three, though," Hiraya said, tilting her glass toward them.

"So do the Ranocos ever lose?" Gabriella asked. "Since you all know the house so well."

"Each Ranoco woman only plays once: right before she inherits the role as matriarch of the family. The game I'll play with you will be the only game I've ever played. It's possible I might not even be a hunter. I might be the hunted. But you're right: I'll probably win. Though you'll have a fighting chance."

The radio hummed and sparked as the song ended and the radio hosts took to the air. *"A new report from Manila! Hundreds of thousands of people are flooding the streets. They have taken over Epifanio de los Santos Avenue, spurred on by Cardinal Sin. They are going unarmed, carrying statues of Our Lady of Fátima. The priests and nuns go with them, calling for peace—"*

"Oh God. Can someone please turn that off? I don't want to

hear how beautiful they are today and learn how many died tomorrow," Alejandro murmured, dragging a heavy hand over his face. Hiraya gestured, and a servant twisted the knob of the radio until a new song Josephine wasn't familiar with hummed placidly through the room.

"They're doing a good thing, Alejandro. It might not work, but now, at least, it's out in the open. Everyone knows what Marcos is. He can't hide anymore," Josephine said, taking a delicate sip of her wine.

"God, I'm sorry, Josephine, but what would you know? You have no idea how brutal they are. Everything good and pure in this world, they're hell-bent on destroying. All to make a handful of pesos and to keep the people in line. It really doesn't matter. You should be happy you're in Carigara. At least there, you're somewhat protected."

"I should be happy to live in Carigara? Where I'm *protected*?" Josephine snorted. "I live three blocks from our parents' killer. Our house is falling apart. The roof is leaking, I've sold the rice fields, the coconut groves. And still it's not enough. It's like trying to fight the ocean with a bucket. I've spent the better part of a decade trying to keep our parents' home standing, to keep our parents' legacy alive. And I've done it all without you, and months without seeing a single centavo of our inheritance and my allowance. When are you coming home?"

Alejandro grew deathly still. His head was bowed toward the table, and his hand was tight around his glass. Josephine couldn't see his face, but she knew she'd stumbled upon a weeping, infected wound. The radio sizzled and Martin Nievera's crooning filled the room, happy and wistful.

Gabriella, wearing the brightest, fakest smile Josephine had ever seen, clapped her hands. "Oh, I love this song. Go on, then, Alejandro. Let's drop all this grim talk and dance. If we're having such a grand dinner, let's make it a party."

Gabriella twisted the knob until the radio boomed and it felt like Martin Nievera was in the room with them, but it was impossible to drown out the words bouncing around in Josephine's head. Gabriella sashayed to Alejandro and took his arm, pulling him onto the impromptu dance floor. He was briefly robotic in her arms, but in moments he thawed, as if she were his life raft. Neither Gabriella nor Alejandro looked at Josephine.

Josephine stared after them, feeling like she'd missed a step on a staircase. She knew that Alejandro was struggling in Manila, that he was trying in his own way to rebuild the del Rosario legacy. But the real legacy of their family was in Carigara, and she desperately wanted him to realize that.

"Am I in the wrong here?" she murmured.

Hiraya nodded, tearing a piece of the white meat of the lechon by hand. "We cope however we can. You're both suffering. It's a shame that suffering doesn't always bring us together." Hiraya flicked her hand toward the wall, and a servant appeared, this time bearing a round glass of bourbon. "Here, would you like to try something new? It's awful and it burns. But it's a good type of burn. An American soldier came by with a bottle of it, and I find that it's perfect for making painful emotions a little less sharp."

Josephine said nothing, and that was all the answer Hiraya needed. A servant poured the drink and set it in front of her. Josephine contemplated the amber pool, the crystalline glass, its shards of light. It was the prettiest, cleanest thing at the table, in the mess of oil and torn-apart meat. It would hurt, and yet it still somehow looked like a refuge.

Hiraya lifted her own glass, tipping it toward Josephine. "Go on, then, a toast for just the two of us. To old friends and new roads."

Josephine lifted the glass, peering at Hiraya over its rim. Alejandro and Gabriella had each other, but at least she had Hiraya. That hadn't changed. She tapped her glass against Hiraya's. With novice enthusiasm, she knocked a deep swig back, the way they did in Western movies, and immediately regretted it. Her face crumpled in disgust. It tasted awful, and it bit as it slid down her throat. She gagged and sputtered, and Hiraya giggled.

"I think it's one of those things you acclimate to. I wouldn't know. I only drink wine," Hiraya reassured her, swirling her drink in its glass.

"It's awful," Josephine muttered, once she got her voice back. "Alejandro can't actually like this."

"I'm sure he's learned to like a lot of terrible things in Manila," Hiraya said, her tone lush and teasing, weighted with a secret knowing. For a moment Josephine stared back at her, trying to discern something in Hiraya's face. Had Hiraya and Alejandro spoken about the games before she received her invitation?

Something in her gut said yes. Alejandro had been the first to be invited, followed by Gabriella, and finally her. Was it because Hiraya knew that she'd come no matter what? Or for some other reason? She drowned the thought in another tight sip of bourbon, the foreign burn on her tongue a bitter salve.

Instinctually, her gaze swung to Alejandro and Gabriella on the makeshift dance floor. They'd slid deeper into each other's arms and rocked back and forth in slow circles as they spoke. Alejandro said something and Gabriella laughed. In Carigara, she'd felt like an island at sea. Alone, waiting for any letter to let her know the events unfolding in the unseen horizon of her family and friends' lives. But now that she was here, among the people who had once been her closest friends, her best confidants, the people who knew her before disaster and tragedy had melded within her to form something new, she still felt utterly alone.

Across from her, Hiraya regarded her solemnly, as if she could read the thoughts in Josephine's head like they were tea leaves. Without a word, Hiraya reached across the table and gently squeezed Josephine's hand. It was a small, soft reassurance, and Josephine felt herself melting.

She wasn't alone. Hiraya was here, and no one could understand how she felt better than Hiraya. By the very nature of her name and lineage, Hiraya had been set apart since they were children. The entire town seemed to hold her at arm's length, and Hiraya, in response, had only grown more distant and secretive. To the point that she no longer attempted to make friends with the other children, and instead visited Josephine in the hours before dusk, intercepting her on the way back from class when they were just girls.

And as a child, she'd found a kinship and comfort in Hiraya's presence that she could find nowhere else. They'd bonded in silence and solitude in the feeling that neither of them was wanted in Carigara. The townspeople hated the Ranocos, and Eduardo hated the del Rosarios. But beyond that, she and Hiraya shared an introverted intenseness, a melancholic cloud that didn't quite suit the vibrancy of the town but suited each other just fine. And that feeling of kinship hadn't changed, despite the years.

Josephine was wildly grateful for that in this moment. Alejandro and Gabriella had built their own separate life in Manila, far away from her. But the friendship and affection she'd created with

Hiraya was just as real, and now she leaned into it, seeking solace in it.

"I missed you," Josephine murmured, ducking her head. She didn't want to see the look on Hiraya's face. But she didn't need to. She could hear the warmth in Hiraya's voice, the smile along the edges of her words.

"I missed you, too. I thought . . . maybe, as you got older, your feelings about me and my family might change. I was so happy to see you walk up that path to the house," Hiraya said.

"Oh please. I think I've spent a better part of a decade wishing you'd come back to Carigara. That you had accepted my invitation to come live with me, all those years ago."

"To be honest . . . I wish I had, too," Hiraya admitted, her voice swinging low. "I've thought about it more times than I can count. And how different my life might have been if I'd been brave enough to say yes."

The song ended, and Alejandro turned off the radio with a snap. His and Gabriella's faces were flushed, with dancing or conversation, Josephine wasn't sure which. But they were both smiling, their arms wrapped around each other.

"I'm sorry to cut the party short, ladies, but I think Gabriella and I are going to turn in for the night. It was a long trip here, and we're both absolutely exhausted."

"Oh, of course," Hiraya said, her back straightening. "Let me take you to your rooms."

Alejandro laughed and held up a hand. "That really won't be necessary. I think I saw no less than two dozen bedrooms while I was searching for Josephine. Gabriella and I will be just fine."

His gaze slid toward Josephine, and his smile tightened. "I know we haven't had a chance to really sit down and talk, Josie. But

I'm sorry I was so stern with you earlier. It's been a hard few months. Scratch that. A hard few years. But it was really good to see you again. We'll catch up in the morning."

It wasn't *quite* an apology, but Josephine knew that was as close to one as she was going to get from him. She nodded. "We'll talk more in the morning," she agreed. No matter what tomorrow brought, she was going to convince him to come back to Carigara. She couldn't protect the del Rosario legacy, and their family home, alone for much longer. And she wasn't going to let him waste another year in Manila if she could help it.

Gabriella petted Alejandro's chest with soft reassurance.

"We know things have been rough, darling. I'm sure they will get better once the protests in Manila settle down," Gabriella murmured.

He didn't respond but guided Gabriella to the banquet hall door. "Good night, everyone." The two of them slid into the corridor, and the door shut firmly behind them.

When their cheerful voices faded to nothing, Josephine was left alone with Hiraya in the grand emptiness of the dining hall.

SIX

OW that they were alone, just them and a room full of servants, Josephine's breath felt awkward in her mouth. Oil and
meat still tainted the taste of the air, and the well-picked corpse of
the lechon stretched between them, showing off its strange spine.
Its odd, flat shoulders.

The haze of alcohol made everything feel so strange, detached
and distorted. It was easy to imagine it was her own body laid out
on the table. Her skin peeled away, her muscles and fat plucked and
gobbled, until she was nothing but scraps and bones, no longer
worth consuming. And yet beneath this sick daydream was the
weight of Hiraya's gaze on her, patient and unblinking.

Josephine's stomach flipped, and her fingers twitched in her
lap. After all these years, Hiraya still made her nervous. She couldn't
bring herself to meet her gaze. "Thank you for dinner," Josephine
managed to say, desperate to break the silence.

Hiraya's stare fell to the stretch of plantain leaves in front of Josephine. Sticky rice grains and the hard husks of fruits lay stacked in front of her, and nothing else. It'd been a meager meal, but Josephine couldn't have stomached anything else.

Hiraya shook her head. "No, I should apologize. I'm sure our fruit is less fragrant and sweet than what you're used to. They don't grow well on the island. The bees here are not really pollinators . . . they have other interests. And their honey, it has depth, but I'm glad you didn't have it, though Tadhana insisted it be served just in case."

"Oh, don't say that. The fruit was sweet. Sweeter than anything in Carigara," Josephine protested. But it was also true, and Hiraya beamed.

"Do you really mean it? If it is sweeter, I suspect it's the soil. The bees might not care for flowers, but the loam is thick and nutritious, and maybe that makes up for it. Our trees grow well here. I'm quite proud of them."

The balete trees that had stretched their branches across the courtyard filled Josephine's head. "The jungle I had to climb through to get here was so thick with vegetation, ferns, and trees. But I've never seen so many balete trees in one place, with such thick trunks and wide canopies. They're massive." *And creepy,* she thought but didn't say.

"They are impressive, aren't they?" Hiraya grinned. "But there weren't always so many here. Balete trees are parasitic. They slowly overcome the host tree and grow around it, strangling the original tree to death. Supposedly, my great-great-grandmother and her sister helped cultivate the trees around the house, meticulously selecting good hosts. And since then, every generation that's followed has done their best to keep the grove alive. Everyone thinks the Ranocos are fortune tellers, healers, spell workers. But really, our most important work is gardening. And we teach our servants to follow those old traditions as well."

Hiraya placed her wineglass on the table and leaned forward, her hands reaching halfway across the table, her fingers splayed out toward Josephine. Josephine couldn't help but stare. Hiraya's nails were short and neat, her fingers long and elegant. She could imagine those fingers tenderly planting seeds, pruning away dead leaves. She could imagine those fingers doing all sorts of things.

"But to be honest, I'm sick to death of gardening. Of digging my hands in the dirt, of following the same monotonous rhythm that every woman in my family followed before me. Seeing you reminds me of the world off this island. Of Carigara, and the plaza, and the beach. The evenings we'd buy bags of soda from the market stand, the golden afternoons when we read comics in the shade of the church. I bet that sounds silly, doesn't it? It was silly and trivial even then, when we were kids. But those were the best days of my life. And I wish more than anything I could go back to them. I wish I could do silly, trivial things. That I could do them with you."

The utter vulnerability of the statement, and the hushed tones that carried it, forced Josephine to meet Hiraya's gaze.

Time had marked Hiraya's face early. Even in the forgiving light of the candelabra above, she could see the start of crow's feet around Hiraya's intact eye. A thin crease cut between her brows, as if she'd spent years deep in thought, trying to scry a happier life. But she was still the Hiraya who Josephine had known beneath the santol trees. Still beautiful, and hopeful, and desperate to be free.

"Don't put Carigara on a pedestal." Josephine laughed, reaching out to touch Hiraya's fingertips. "It's not paradise by any stretch, and it feels like each year it gets a little uglier, a little more claustrophobic.

It's—" She hesitated. Carigara was many things. But seeing Hiraya's face, she knew what it was most of all. "It's lonely. It's so incredibly lonely. But maybe if you'd stayed, if Alejandro and Gabriella would come back, it'd be different. I think that's what I want more than anything. A chance to . . . start over. To have the Carigara of my childhood back, before Marcos bathed it all in blood and death, curfews, and men with guns."

Hiraya sighed and nodded. "Yes, if I had stayed . . . maybe it would have been different. If I could, I'd row back to Carigara with you tonight. I adore my family, our legacy, the sacrifices they made to give me the life I live now. But each year, I feel myself being crushed by the walls of this place. Pressed thin, until the face in the mirror no longer seems like my own but an amalgamation of things that my aunt, and my mother, and all those who came before me *want* me to be. Or is that dramatic?" Hiraya laughed and buried her face in her hands. She was still smiling, but it was strained now, with enough teeth to appear like a grimace.

"It's so quiet here. No one talks; no one laughs. I'm just alone in my head, so it's hard not to let my thoughts get out of control," Hiraya muttered, pressing the balls of her palms into her eye sockets.

Josephine nodded. "I . . . I know that silence. I know how evil it can be. The del Rosario house is like a crypt most days. I know the maids are there, that they talk to each other, but I think they've gotten to the point that they're scared to talk to *me*. Like friendship might mean that Eduardo and his family come down and crush them next, to make an example of them. It feels like I'm cursed sometimes. But if Alejandro came back, if he'd just show them we're not afraid, that we can't be pushed around—" She floundered for words.

She wasn't even certain if she believed what she was saying. Would Alejandro's presence in the house really change things, or did she just not want to be alone in the fight? "I wish that I could have my family back in Carigara. I'm so tired of being alone there."

"It's terrible, isn't it? How silence and looks can slowly rot your soul away."

I'm almost certain the looks we get are nothing alike, Josephine thought. She'd been dealing with pity and apprehension for most of her life. But Hiraya? It'd always been judgment and distrust, like she was a cobra in the grass. But the sentiment was the same, and she nodded.

"I suppose you've been dealing with that your entire life," Josephine murmured. She couldn't think of a time that Hiraya hadn't been looked at with distrust. The rumors that Hiraya and her family were aswang, beautiful women who cursed the living and ate the dead, had been trailing her since they were children. It was cruel.

"Oh Lord, yes. But that's the reason I wrote to you, why I invited you here to play the game. If I win, I have a future I could be happy to live, one full of choices. But if I lost and you won, I think I'd still be happy. You deserve to have whatever future you want. One where you're happy, where you're not alone. And maybe I could live vicariously through you," Hiraya said, lowering her hands.

Josephine's smile turned wry, bordering on skeptical. "But it's not guaranteed, though, is it? The prize of your game."

"It is," Hiraya insisted. "If you win the game, your heart's wish is guaranteed. But you have to offer a sacrifice that fits the prize. So many people aren't willing to sacrifice to get the future that they really want. God, I can't help but get so serious and somber with you. Have a glass of wine; maybe you'll like me better."

Hiraya nodded toward Josephine's glass, which showed only the thinnest amber circle of bourbon at the bottom. Without waiting for an answer, she gestured, and a servant presented a glass each to Josephine and Hiraya. Hiraya sipped delicately, her eyes locked onto Josephine's.

"You know I already like you." Josephine chuckled. But she lifted the glass to her lips and took in the bouquet of wine. It smelled like the fruit she'd dined on, sickly sweet and earthy. As if the grapes had grown in between the roots of the balete trees surrounding the estates rather than on some pristine vine.

"I don't know if I'm prepared to make any grand sacrifice," Josephine admitted. "I'm not like my brother. I couldn't sacrifice half a finger just to become some barangay captain. And I don't have anything else to give."

"I think you truly underestimate yourself," Hiraya returned. "It takes mettle to stay in Carigara and face down an entire town when everyone around you has fled. You just think you're different from Alejandro because he left for the city, and you think that's brave. I think what you've done is braver. Would you like me to take you to your room? I hope I haven't been holding you hostage."

"No, I don't think I could sleep," Josephine said. "It's embarrassing to admit, but this is my first time sleeping away from home. And I don't mean to offend you, but as lovely as your house is, it's a little . . . odd."

Josephine's choice of words seemed to tickle Hiraya, who nodded. "*Odd* is surely an understatement, and I know you're only saying it to be polite. And I imagine you're only talking about what you've seen so far. The twists and curves. The rooms within rooms."

"There's something odder than its architecture, then?" Josephine asked.

"Oh, of course. The first Ranoco woman, the primogenitor of

eccentricity and strangeness, crafted the walls of this house to reflect her own body. Halls like the networks of her veins, rooms that overlap like muscles on bones. It's only natural for a body to hide secrets. Little scars, growths benign and cancerous. And each generation of Ranoco has added their own bodies to it. Tokens of memory, for the Ranoco girls that will come after." Hiraya grinned, and she ran a hand over her arm as if using her own body as an example. "I know Gabriella hates this place. But I find the house's complexity, its organic nature, to be beautiful."

"I understand why," Josephine said. "It's . . . like an heirloom. A living family tree, a living legacy. It must be comforting to feel your family all around you."

"It's a comfort, yes. But . . . it's still so devastatingly lonely. So lonely I ache. My mother, my aunts, my grandmothers, they're here but they're not. But it *is* nice to be reminded of them when I walk through the house. To feel like I'm part of something bigger than myself," Hiraya replied, her eyes turning up toward the grand ceiling with its bare rafters. "If there's anything we ever did right, it's building this house."

Half-full glass still in hand, Hiraya stood, her body listing ever so slightly to the side. She was drunker than she'd seemed when she was sitting, but that only endeared her to Josephine. She loved seeing Hiraya this vulnerable, so soft and sweet.

"If you like, Josephine . . . I could make you one of us, just for the night. You could be my sister, or my cousin. And I could be yours." She extended a hand toward Josephine, palm up, fingers curled.

Electricity sparked in Josephine's heart, running down the length of her spine. She slid her hand into Hiraya's, feeling the warm ridges of her palm. Even with a touch, she could tell that

Hiraya had lived a life different from her own. She could feel the calluses on the lines of Hiraya's hands, the shiny smooth spots where burns had healed across her palms. A wicked impulse bloomed in the pit of Josephine's stomach. A desire to spread open Hiraya's hands and gently kiss the calluses tender, to lick the smooth planes of her burnt skin. No part of her wanted to be Hiraya's sister or cousin. She wanted something deeper, something *more*. But she buried the feeling, her face burning with bourbon and the silliness of unrequited fantasies.

"I think I'd like that. Josephine del Rosario–Ranoco. It has a ring to it."

"It's a beautiful name." Hiraya took a lantern from the side table beside the radio and lifted her chin, using her lips to point toward the door. "Be my doorman, dear sister, and I'll show you a few of my favorite places in the house."

"A fair trade for a personal tour," Josephine agreed.

"The fairest of trades. I've not shown anyone else. Other than Tadhana and Sidapa, of course. You're among the most esteemed and exclusive company."

Josephine opened the door and Hiraya led the way back into the hall. But she selected a side door, which opened first to an archive with thick books on the shelves.

"My great-aunt's personal library," Hiraya stated.

The next room was full of old copper knickknacks, and Hiraya's nose crinkled. "Trash. I'm not even sure who it belongs to. But I'm forbidden from throwing it away. I suppose bodies have their ugly bits, too. The skin tags and hidden dirt."

"Are there rooms that are just yours? Yours and Sidapa's?" Josephine asked as she picked her way across the trash, trying to avoid stepping on hard, strange bits and bobs.

"Yes, but I like to think I'm not nearly as big an accumulator as my predecessors. I, at least, exert a little order over my rooms. I'm not sure I could say the same for Sidapa or Tadhana."

"What about your grandfather? Are there ever any brothers?" Josephine mused as she pushed into another room, holding it open for Hiraya.

Hiraya chuckled. "Oh no. We don't keep men here. Not for very long, anyway."

"*Not for very long?* What does that mean?" Josephine asked, her brows arching.

"Oh, I don't know. They just come and go, men. Like stray cats or wild birds. They leave when the weather is good and return when things get bad. But it's not as if others can't live here. We have so many servants who have spent years with us. And periodically someone stays. They choose to become part of this house. Or they're made part of it."

"Like husbands?" Josephine asked, still not comprehending. It seemed impossible to live without men, though the idea had a strange, foreign appeal.

"Oh gods, no. Jesus, Josephine. Imagine a husband. Could you even picture yourself married? Handcuffed to someone who thinks they own you? Lording around a house they didn't help build? I'd kill him then myself."

Josephine fought back a thin grin. "That's so dramatic. I've heard there are some lovely men out there. Kind and sweet."

"I've no doubt," Hiraya murmured, clearly unconvinced. "But the Ranocos aren't inclined toward husbands. We prefer sisters. My great-aunt was adopted into the Ranoco family. She came, I think, from Bohol. But she liked it here better."

The thought of such a life intrigued Josephine. She'd struggled to imagine a life where she woke up every day beside a man. But seeing the dawn's light falling across Hiraya's face? To learn the way she liked her coffee, to learn the titles of the books she loved the most, to slowly uncover the ways to make her smile? That had its own charm, the way playing house with a man did not.

"Is that why we're playing this game of siblings?" Josephine asked, her mouth stumbling around the desire to ask if it was something more.

Hiraya shrugged. "Maybe. It just . . . feels right."

God, put me out of my misery. Does she want me like I want her? Or is this just another game? Josephine thought, but her heart thudded in her throat. She wasn't brave enough to ask. No, more than that, she didn't want to know the answer. Even pretending for just one more night was sweeter than learning it'd all been in her head from the start.

Silence fell between them as Hiraya guided her through corridors, bedrooms, storage rooms. Rooms without purpose, rooms that shouldn't exist. Rooms that made no sense at all.

It was in one of these latter rooms that a shadow flickered upon their arrival, at the edge of the lantern's light. A maid shifted sluggishly against the wall, her head hung low, chin close to her chest, as if she'd fallen asleep standing. Hiraya passed by the woman without a second glance. But Josephine's gaze lingered on the woman for a minute longer. The maid's fingers twitched as if she were in the thralls of a terrible nightmare.

The farther they went into the house, the more maids and servants they stumbled across. In nearly every room, Josephine caught sight of them standing in corners or among the debris of the house, curled in on themselves like wilted flowers or the empty husk of a snake's skin. As if they'd fallen asleep on the spot.

"Don't mind them. They won't hurt you," Hiraya whispered.

Josephine stared at Hiraya's back, her mouth pressed into a thin, hard line. She hadn't liked the reassurance; it only made her think they would. And it unsettled her to see them crouched among the shadows, only revealed because the white veils lay across their faces, streaks of dull ivory in the darkness.

"Why do they sleep there? Don't they have rooms?" Josephine whispered back.

"They do. But sometimes they don't make it back before night-fall. So they just settle down wherever they find themselves. It's a hard job tending to this house. Even with dozens of them, it's never, ever clean. But they are our good little worker ants."

Josephine couldn't argue about the state of the house. A fine layer of dust covered half the rooms she'd been through. "Ah, I see. You're their queen, then? Queen of the anthill." She was joking, but Hiraya hesitated for a moment. As if the throwaway tease had caught on the root of a thought.

"Not yet. But I will be, I suppose. Once the game is over and Tadhana finally retires from her matriarchal throne."

From behind the next door came the soft splash of water, and Hiraya lifted the lantern so that its glow fell upon the copper knob. Carved flowers and trees laced the door's wood, stained dark like an antique camphor chest.

"Here we are. My favorite place in the house." Hiraya squeezed Josephine's hand, her giddiness infectious. "Go on, then, open it. Open it."

Josephine pressed on the door, and it swung outward in a silent arc. Warm air washed over her, and she breathed deep. Crisp, floral-steeped air flooded her lungs. She hadn't realized how dank and stagnant the air in the house was until she'd escaped it.

The night sky stretched above them, half-shrouded in clouds, but countless opaline stars glittered in the velvet black where they broke. The moon, already descending, cast a silver light onto the open courtyard before them, bathing the lushest garden Josephine had ever seen.

"A garden? Here?" she asked, not quite believing what she was seeing.

Hiraya laughed, clearly delighted at Josephine's bewilderment. "It took ages to carve this courtyard out of the house. All the other rooms had to be shifted to accommodate it. It was like pushing a living womb into a corpse. But look, it was worth it, wasn't it? I planted everything here by hand. I filled it with life. It's the one thing I'll miss if I ever escape this place."

She let go of Josephine's hands to step deeper into the garden. The growth here was thick, as if it'd always been part of this house. And Hiraya was right: it did feel like a womb. Hot and throbbing with life, in stark contrast to the stifling bones of the house that surrounded it.

Ylang-ylang trees in full bloom stretched their branches out. Bushes of rose grape blushed with their soft, orchidlike blooms. Flowers that shouldn't be in bloom yet were sparks of color in the dark, larger and brighter than anything she'd ever glimpsed in the wild or in the curated gardens of Carigara.

But behind all of it, hidden against the walls of the courtyard, Josephine glimpsed thick ivy that climbed up each wall like count-less serpents. In between these thick braids of vines were windows, their panels pushed to the side, so that the dark rooms squinted down at her. Too black for her to see in, too easy for anyone within to see out. She tore her gaze away from the windows, back to the amputated paradise that Hiraya had lovingly crafted. Stone tiles led to an alabaster fountain, and Hiraya sat upon the rim of the fountain, her hands laid primly in her lap, her face golden and grinning.

Behind her, two stone statues stood in the center of the fountain. The figure of a woman was caught in midflight, pushing away a man, her body half-transformed into a tree. Her fingers already branches, her feet already roots.

"Have you ever heard the story of Daphne?" Hiraya asked. "A woman relentlessly pursued by a man, a god. To escape him, she sacrificed her body and became a tree. The ultimate defiance, the ultimate sacrifice."

Josephine stared up at the stone woman's face, ripples of anxiety washing over her. She couldn't help but think of Roberto. Of his hand descending onto her shoulder at the bus stop. Or Eduardo and his sons, slowly circling her like vultures.

"How tragic. She must have been desperate," Josephine murmured.

The statue's jaw was set, her teeth bared, her mouth open, as if shouting him down. But her pursuer grinned back at her, utterly unperturbed by the hate carved into her face. Perhaps he even delighted in it, as if her anger were something to laugh at.

"It takes courage to refuse a god," Hiraya replied. "Courage to give up your world for something entirely new. But I wonder what it's like to be a tree. To be eternal, free of all worries. But unmoving, unspeaking."

Josephine could think of nothing worse. Her gaze drifted to the statue's feet, where water sprang and trickled from between her rooted toes. She'd never take another step. Never make another decision. She might as well be dead, immortalized as a tree or not.

But Hiraya seemed oblivious to Josephine's hesitance. "What do you think? This place belongs only to me. No one else comes here. No servants, no sisters. Just me . . . and now you."

"It's lovely," Josephine murmured, dragging her gaze away from the tree and trying to pour her focus back into the moment, onto Hiraya. In this beautiful place, Hiraya seemed the most herself. Her shoulders were rounded, her single eye bright and wide, glittering with the dim reflection of stars and moonlight. And her smile seemed frank and open. Not carrying that vulpine mischief that she seemed to wield like a knife, keeping everyone at a safe distance.

If Josephine had any chance of cutting through the smoke that cloaked the Ranoco girl, it was now. She wasn't sure there'd be a next time.

"Hiraya . . . would you be honest with me?" she asked, her voice quiet.

Hiraya tilted her head, but she seemed unsurprised, as if she'd expected the question all along. "I'll try to be."

"What is all this? Really. The game, the promises of futures, the secretiveness. It feels like there's something you haven't been telling me."

"I haven't lied to you about anything, if that's what you're thinking. And it's really just like I said in the letter. You know what everyone in town called my family. They knew us as readers of *kapalaran*, who could read their fates through bones or the bumps on their bodies. They knew us as *mananambal*s, who could heal or hex. And that's all true. Tadhana and my mother sustained us by making *lana* oil and *anting-anting* amulets, by breaking and returning curses. But we're more than just healers, fortune readers, and trinket makers. This game . . . has been the heart of our family since the very beginning. It's like a long ritual that the four of us will take part in. Each of us has a role to play, and only two of us will emerge victorious. The two who win will be told precisely what they need to do to have the future they want. Maybe it's marrying a certain person or being in a certain place at a certain time. Either way, if the winner does as they're instructed, the future they want is guaranteed. It's as simple as that."

Josephine chuckled. "It doesn't sound simple. But is it real, then? Wishes you can turn into perfect futures, the rumors?" she asked.

"Do you think it's real?" Hiraya retorted. Her expression flattened and her voice turned serious, almost cutting. The smile died on Josephine's lips and her brows arched. Hiraya had never been so sharp with her.

"I don't know," Josephine admitted. "My mother believed in Tadhana's abilities. And maybe I want to believe in the Ranoco family, too." But even as she said it, she knew that wasn't quite right. She wanted to believe in Hiraya.

"Of course your mother believed Tadhana. Because it *is* real. And you wouldn't have come if you didn't believe it. You would have seen my letter and laughed and thrown it away. But you didn't. Because there's a future you'd do anything for."

Hiraya was more than half wrong. Josephine would have come anyway, even if there hadn't been a wish attached. Just to see Hiraya. To be free of Eduardo's and Roberto's stares. To be closer to Alejandro and Gabriella, and the hope that her words would be enough to draw her brother back home. But the certainty in Hiraya's voice about her mother's faith stirred something in her.

"Did the Ranoco family . . . ever grant a wish for my parents?" Josephine asked.

Hiraya hesitated, her eye widening for a moment. Her gaze

flashed toward a window on the second floor. Josephine followed her gaze, but all she could see was shadows. An empty room, where something against the blackness might have flickered. She wet her lips and lowered her voice, as if she was nervous about being overheard.

"I've granted no wish. Tadhana, though. She called on the spirits to read the del Rosario future, once."

"Here? In this house?" Josephine asked, leaning closer, her voice rising.

Hiraya grimaced and raised her palm, as if begging Josephine to lower her voice.

"What did they wish for?" Josephine asked, her heart's thrum suddenly in her ears.

"Not they. *She.* Your mother."

"My mother," Josephine repeated, her voice hushed. "So she won? She won the game here?"

Her mother had had no shortage of acquaintances but few real friends, and she'd always been quiet, bordering on secretive. Josephine had long since given up learning anything new about the woman who loved and raised her. But now it thrilled her to know that her mother had been here, in this house. That some strange thread connected them, even after all these years.

"Yes. Your mother played in Tadhana's coronation game. I suspect it's because of that wish that Tadhana came to Carigara and brought us all with her. They had a strange relationship. Love, hate, something in between. I don't know. Tadhana won't talk about it. I don't know what your mother wished for. I just know that it changed her life."

Josephine fell quiet, her head a knot of thoughts. Her mother had been in this house. She'd walked its strange halls, played the game and won. She'd gotten her wish, whatever it was, and it'd changed her fate.

"My mother . . . was born poor. The daughter of a fisherman. She talked about how, once, she was so hungry she tried to eat sand," Josephine murmured. "But then she met my father, and everything changed. Even his parents supported the marriage, despite her background. And he adored her." She had never questioned why her father had married her mother. She had always thought it was a true and genuine love, the type that people wrote fairy tales about. But Hiraya nodded, her face grim.

"Alejandro was born shortly after they married, wasn't he?" Hiraya asked.

Josephine blinked. She hadn't thought about it. But now that she did, it made sense. Her father had grand aspirations and a good Catholic background. And a child out of wedlock would have thrown a dark cloud over it.

Still, as Josephine looked again at the flowering trees, the walls of the house, their bleak and hollow windows, she could almost *see* her mother, young and willful, storming the halls. Of course she'd come and won the game. Her mother's face was a gossamer blur in her memory, but she still remembered how fearsome her mother could be. How stubborn and clever and ambitious.

Hiraya laid a soft hand on Josephine's, her face inscrutable and dark. "You should know that for all the people who come here, hoping for their perfect future, it's not a guarantee that anyone will get anything at all. Not every game has a winner. Sometimes, everyone loses."

But Josephine barely heard her. If her mother had won, *she* could win. She could follow in her mother's footsteps. She could be brave enough to change her fate.

"It's a game of tagu-tagu, isn't it? I just have to find the hiders, or outrun my pursuers, and I win. I can have the life I always wanted?" Josephine asked.

"Yes. I'll call out to the spirits, and they'll tell you precisely what you'll need to do to change your fate. You just have to win. And to be honest . . . I hope you do win. You deserve a future where you're happy, Josephine."

"But if I lose—" Josephine murmured.

Hiraya interrupted her before she could finish the sentence. "Do you want to see the source of our power? Our altar, where we call the spirits?"

Before Josephine could answer, Hiraya was pulling her up, her fingers intertwining with hers, tight and insistent. Despite her exhaustion, a twisting curiosity and a quiet pleasure filled her. Hiraya cared for her. She'd never felt so wanted, so explicitly loved.

"Why do I always want to say yes to you?" Josephine asked, her words wine-soft, her eyes bourbon-hooded.

Hiraya fanned a hand across her own face, her smile bashful behind her splayed fingers. "Do you really? Or is that the drink talking?"

"Both, perhaps," Josephine admitted. "I'll follow wherever you lead. I doubt I could find anywhere on my own anyway." Josephine grinned and resisted the urge to take Hiraya's hand and kiss the golden rings on her fingers.

"Wonderful, wonderful. It's close. It's dark, but it's close. You're not afraid of the dark, are you?" She leaned a little closer to Josephine, and Josephine shifted from side to side, heat threatening to overcome her.

"I wasn't in Carigara. But the darkness here feels different," Josephine admitted.

"I know. It's blacker here, isn't it?" Hiraya took her by the hand

and led her back down the stone path, toward the door they'd entered. They passed back into the house, so much more stifling than it'd been an hour ago now that Josephine had tasted fresh air.

Hiraya held her by the hand, her fingers tightly wound around Josephine's. She led her through the rooms and corridors quickly, far more quickly than she had when she was guiding Josephine to the garden.

But as they threaded through a dizzying array of twists and turns, Josephine felt unease growing at her back. Her shoulders tensed and she felt the skin on the back of her neck prick. She glanced over her shoulder, down the corridor they'd nearly reached the end of. Black shadows stared back at her, out of reach of the golden circle of light cast from Hiraya's lantern.

"Do your servants ever follow you, to attend to you?" Josephine asked, breaking the rhythm of their steps.

Hiraya's lips pursed in thought. "No, not really. There's usually one nearby. So if I call, they come."

"Ah."

Ah was all she could really manage. Because she was almost certain that someone was following them. Something tainted the scent of old wood and dust of the house. Like charcoal or burned meat. The servants she'd met so far all smelled like sweat and sweet, sickly rot.

"Don't worry. It's an old house. But there's nothing to be afraid of in the dark," Hiraya reassured her, and smiled.

SEVEN

IN half the time it took to reach the garden, Hiraya was pushing open the foyer door that Josephine had come through earlier that day. They stood together for a moment on the stone patio of the Ranoco house. The balete trees leaned toward the door from the edges of the courtyard, their thin aerial roots twisting and braiding in the breeze.

Was it possible for a forest to feel hostile? Predatory? Was it possible for a forest to stare? Josephine shuddered at the thought. She'd never felt more unwelcome.

"I've never seen a jungle like this," Josephine muttered. The goose bumps that sprang up on her arms punctuated the sentence, and she rubbed at them, trying to soothe herself.

"It's just a forest. Nothing scary about a few trees, is there?" Hiraya teased.

"I'm just being dumb," she agreed. "I just feel like everywhere I go, there's someone watching me." Even now, with the front door closed behind them, she wondered if their unseen stalker was still there. Leaning against the wood on the other side. Inches from them. Listening to their every word, counting their breaths.

Hiraya tilted her head, her eye catching the glint of light from the lantern. She appraised Josephine carefully.

"I used to be afraid of the forest, too. Aunt Tadhana used to tell Sidapa and me stories about aswang in the woods. In Carigara, you called witches aswang. But they're all manner of things, aren't they? Shape-shifting hunters, corpse eaters, baby killers. But no matter what story people tell, there's always one thread in common. They're all ravenous for human flesh. It used to terrify Sidapa and me, knowing the depths of depravity an aswang could sink into, driven by an instinct that dominates all else. You might want to take off your slippers."

"What?" Josephine asked, reeling from the jump in topics.

"Your shoes," Hiraya repeated. "Leave your shoes on the steps. It's a little muddy. You're more likely to lose them than keep them once we get to the side of the house."

Hiraya shucked her house slippers, and Josephine followed suit, not relishing the idea of standing in the mud. But she let Hiraya lead her onto the bare earth. It was soft here, but as Hiraya led them down the length of the house, the soil beneath her feet grew spongier and wet. Soon her toes sank into the mud, and its dirt clung to her skin. Intrusive thoughts of wriggling insects, hatching and squirming in the dirt beneath her, bubbled up, but she crushed the images down.

"Are there, then?" Josephine asked.

"Are there what?" Hiraya echoed.

"Aswang in the woods."

Hiraya laughed and rolled her eyes. "No, I don't think so. I've never seen one out there, anyway. Hiding among the trees, nibbling on stolen fetuses, digging up animal graves." She turned her fingers into claws and pawed at the air between her and Josephine, her grin cattish and teasing.

"Oh, shut up," Josephine muttered, swatting her hands away. She smiled, but she felt silly and childish for even asking. For even entertaining the thought.

"Don't feel bad!" Hiraya said, grabbing her arm and leaning against Josephine's shoulder. "I mean, you're not the first to think that. If anything, you're the hundredth. But I never understood the obsession with demonizing women. The pretty, unmarried women. The old women in the woods. Instead of the very real threat of jealous, lustful boys skulking in the shadows, trying to follow you home."

"I'd pick a pretty unmarried woman any day and any night," Josephine admitted.

Hiraya grinned up at her, her canines flashing. "I would, too."

They edged farther and farther back. Feet turned to yards. And yet the house marched onward, a wall of weathered stone and wood. But as the lantern swung back and forth in Hiraya's hands, the impressions of footprints on the ground came into view all around them. Deep prints, bare, not unlike their own. There were dozens of them. Whole trails, the feet belonging to scores of people, adults and children. They lay over each other, a marker of time.

Josephine's body tensed of its own accord. She felt eyes on her again. She was certain of it. But not from the jungle. She forced her gaze up toward the house, toward its wall of windows. The front of the house was neat. Massive, with a stone first floor and a wooden second. But on the sides of the house, all pretense of normal architecture had fallen away.

The wall's shape was irregular, with cancerous lumps of rooms protruding from its sides. Windows punctured it erratically, like termite holes. They were all dark, and yet she was certain she could feel someone watching her.

"It really feels like—"

"There's no one there, Josephine," Hiraya said, cutting her off. She tugged Josephine forward, insistent. "It's just us out tonight."

"Then who do all these steps belong to?" she retorted. Hiraya turned, and the light of the lantern sputtered with the speed of the motion.

"The servants. They garden, tidy, fetch wood. Build new rooms onto the house, expand it. They tend to the garden and keep it fertilized and healthy." Hiraya gave her a sympathetic smile and squeezed Josephine's hand. "Perhaps wine makes you paranoid."

Josephine grimaced, avoiding Hiraya's face. The servants. Of course. She'd forgotten the absolute battalion that the Ranocos kept in their employ. Of course they would leave prints. Someone here had to clear the yard, try to keep the ever-encroaching jungle in check.

"You must think me childish. Stupid." Josephine sighed.

"I think none of those things. It's been a long, strange night. Look, we're nearly at the end of the house. Just a bit farther. Shall we continue, or would you like me to take you to your room? It's at least midnight now, so . . ."

Josephine sighed again. "No, we're almost there. I think you're right. It's the alcohol. I don't usually drink, and I can't believe how massive this house is. It goes on forever," Josephine said.

"And that's just what you can see. It's so much more than its perimeter." There was an inkling of pride in Hiraya's voice. As much as she seemed to want to escape the Ranoco house, it was clear that she was proud, at least in part, of their legacy.

Far ahead of them, the roar of waves echoed. The ground beneath Josephine's feet turned firmer with each step. And there was the corner of the house. Its back wall abutted a steep cliff face so that a single tremor would assuredly drag some slice of the house off the stony edge, sending it crumbling into a watery oblivion.

Hiraya drew close to the edge, peering down at its sheer drop. She glanced over her shoulder at Josephine, her face golden and grinning in the lantern light. "We're almost there. You aren't afraid of heights, are you?"

"Not heights. Falling," Josephine said.

"At least take a look."

Josephine approached the cliff with mincing steps, still full of nerves, and peered over the edge. Without the sun, the ocean that had been blue and gorgeous when she arrived now stretched out into the horizon, dark and miserable. The waves beat against the black volcanic stone that surrounded the island in slabs and sea stacks, sending lacy foam spiraling upward.

Holding on to Hiraya, she inched closer. A stairway had been carved into the cliff's edge, working its way downward, almost into the water itself.

Years of climbing had worn the steps smooth, with grooves in the center of each. But they were still narrow, barely wide enough for someone to walk straight. It'd be so easy to miss a step, to slide on the slick rock, to fall and dash yourself against the crags that jutted from the ocean like so many brittle teeth.

Just looking at the drop was enough to turn her dizzy, and she withdrew, pushing a hand against her breast as she tried to steady herself. Her heart was a fluttering, terrified bird.

Hiraya wasn't smiling now. She only watched Josephine, her expression blank. But her remaining eye was hooded and judging, like a dagger of obsidian. "Are you going to run?" Hiraya asked, her voice soft. "I wouldn't blame you if you did."

Josephine sucked in her breath between her gritted teeth. Running was precisely what she wanted to do. But she stayed rooted in place.

"Somehow, I think it'd be wiser if I *did* run. Right through the jungle, right back to the boat. All the way home."

A smile cracked Hiraya's façade. "Maybe you're right. Maybe I'd go with you."

Josephine didn't smile back. She didn't like these stairs. The mud. The footsteps. The incessant insects that dogged her everywhere. The watchers she couldn't catch. The veiled servants. And the persistent feeling that Hiraya wasn't being honest with her. Had maybe *never* been fully honest with her.

"You can still go, you know, Josephine. I won't hate you. I won't stop you." Hiraya laid the lantern on the floor and she wrapped her arms gently around Josephine's waist in a loose embrace. She rested her chin on Josephine's shoulder, and her breath played along Josephine's neck, warm and rhythmic.

An involuntary shudder ran down Josephine's spine. Hiraya had never been so affectionate or intimate with her, and her hair smelled the way it had the night her parents died. Like santol flowers and oranges and earth.

"I can take you to your room and we can pretend like this never happened. You'll wake up in the morning and you'll wonder if this was all a dream," Hiraya whispered.

Her arms were a soft rope around Josephine's waist, and Josephine found her eyes fluttering shut. She hadn't been hugged so tenderly in years. Perhaps not since her parents had died.

"Is it important that I see it?" Josephine asked.

"It is to me."

"I won't fall?" Josephine pressed.

"Not if you hold on to me. And if you're very, very careful."

"That's not very reassuring."

But Hiraya was already pulling away from her, her hands gently tugging her toward the cliff's edge. Josephine let herself be led and watched Hiraya descend the first step. Now that she was at the top of them, she could see the steps all too well in the fleeting moonlight.

"It's so much worse up close. It's practically suicide," Josephine protested.

But Hiraya regarded the steps with a sort of apathetic detachment. "It's not nearly so bad. I go every few days. I could even do it blind."

As if to demonstrate, she descended another step without looking, turning back to peer up at Josephine with her free hand outstretched. "Take my hand. Put another on the wall. You'll be fine. You won't fall."

"You'll catch me if I do?"

Hiraya didn't answer, but it didn't matter. Despite the stupidity of it all, Josephine was desperate to impress Hiraya, to keep her close. To live for one more moment in the memory of that embrace.

"Did my mother ever walk down these stairs?" Josephine asked.

Hiraya tilted her head, her expression inscrutable. "Yes."

Josephine wasn't certain she believed her. In fact, she was certain that Hiraya was lying, and just saying it to coax her down the stairs.

But it gave her a kick of courage anyway. She took Hiraya's hand and squeezed tight.

They descended together. She clung to the side of the cliff and Hiraya in equal measure, refusing to glance at the ocean below. Minutes passed, or perhaps half an hour. She wasn't certain, but by the time she reached the landing, her fingertips were sore and skinned from the rough rock wall, and her calves trembled with the effort of keeping her on the slick stone.

"Here, we're here," Hiraya reassured her as the stairs stretched into the mouth of a cave.

Josephine gasped around a sob of relief. "I thought we might die. I really did."

"You did so well, though. I was a little afraid that you were going to slip and fall. I don't think anyone's ever survived the drop." Hiraya laughed as she glided into the cave, leaving the lantern near the entrance.

"What?" Josephine demanded, her mouth agape. "People have died, then? Going down it?"

"Oh yes. Several times a year. Just—" Hiraya lifted a hand and then let it bend nonchalantly at the wrist. "Right into the ocean. The rocks, you know, are what kill them. Or maybe the waves. The only beach is on the other side of the island, so there isn't much to hold on to, and the bodies don't stay for long."

"We could have *died*, Hiraya. That's insane."

"But we didn't! And no Ranoco woman has ever died descending those steps. And tonight you're a Ranoco woman, aren't you?" She flashed Josephine a toothy smile and spread her arms out to either side. "But here we are. It's lovely, isn't it? Almost as lovely as my garden. But don't tell Tadhana I said as much. She's weak, but I think she'd do her best to kill me for blasphemy."

Hiraya spoke quickly, her sentences interspersed with euphoric giggles, as if merely being in the room filled her with energy.

They stood in a cavern, its black rock riddled through with holes, like an anthill. Its cavernous ceiling reached high, and it seemed to have no end. Its back wall tapered into a dark tunnel that stretched farther than Josephine could see.

Tiny alcoves had been carved in the walls, and in their recesses lit candles rested upon thrones of melted white wax. Their light bathed the room in a golden glow that was reflected in the water-slick floors, so that everything shone. In the center of the room, a large altar dominated the chamber.

Josephine had seen countless altars like it before, during Holy Week. When the whole town would go on a pilgrimage of all the churches in the barangay. Among them would be ancient altars built into natural caves like this one. A holdover of a practice that existed long before the Spanish had landed on the shores of Cebu.

And yet this chapel was nothing like any Catholic shrine she'd ever seen. The wooden altar built in the center of this cave was carved from what looked to be the trunk of a balete tree. And at the altar's center was no Virgin Mary, no Santo Niño, no crucifix.

It felt sacrilegious, and yet something about it thrilled her. It felt like reaching back into the past, like seeing through the eyes of her ancestors before everything they believed had been crushed and ground away by friars and soldiers.

A strange bone tree sat at the center of the table. Its roots—ribs, perhaps—sank into the wood of the altar. Its trunk was a series of spinal vertebrae stacked together and held in place by blackened wax, colored rotting cloth, and rope. Josephine could not help but stare, fascinated, at the branches of the trees.

Thin bones of all types had been sharpened to points. Some she could recognize. The spiked ridges of a pig's spine, the chipped jaw of a dog. The narrow, delicate bones of a bird's wing. But others were thicker, more pronounced.

"Femurs. The bones of an arm, of fingers and toes," Hiraya explained.

The blood in Josephine's veins chilled. The bones were ancient, mottled brown and black. But her fascination gripped her. She couldn't turn away from this morbid statue, this thing that might have been pulled from the depths of her nightmares.

A sacred, hideous energy emanated from the facsimile of a tree. It inspired in her the same awe and dread that had filled her when she saw the parade of the crucified in San Pedro Cutud as a child. There, men were nailed to crosses and marched through the streets. Their sanctified suffering filled the air with a gruesome, divine power that told Josephine everything she needed to know about God. She gripped the crucifix at her breast. Its silver points dug into her fingertips. It hurt, but it held her in place.

She could sense Hiraya staring into her back; she could feel the Ranoco girl's restless energy. And she knew she hadn't yet discovered whatever Hiraya had brought her down to see. She stepped closer and saw that the makeshift branches of this graveyard tree were full of fruit, which were speared onto the sharpened ends of the branches. These fruits, almost husks, were no bigger than grapes. All of them yellowed and jaundiced and puckered.

"This is our family shrine. Our chapel. We come here to pray to the spirits," Hiraya explained. "Our tomb is at the end of the tunnel. But here, at this altar, is where we've built our traditions." Hiraya gestured toward the cave floor, and in the dim candlelight Josephine could see it shine. The stone had been worn away by years', maybe decades', worth of kneeling and prostrating.

Hiraya approached the altar and pointed toward a desiccated fruit, a little plumper than the rest. "This was mine."

Josephine blinked, not quite comprehending what Hiraya meant. But as she squinted at the shrine, at its tree and its boughs, she realized precisely what it was.

Those little golden fruits were eyes.

Her body reacted before her mind could formulate a single thought. She recoiled, pushing past Hiraya and stumbling back toward the cave entrance. She could almost feel the accusing, alien stare of those dozens of little desiccated eyes peering at her through their arcane crucifixes. But before she could flee into the black night, Hiraya was on her, her firm, calloused hands seizing Josephine's wrist, hard. In another second, her other arm encircled Josephine's waist in an unrelenting belt.

"Let go of me!" Josephine shouted, her voice feral with panic.

"Absolutely not. My God, Josephine, I can't help you if you fall. The riptides will take you if the rocks don't," Hiraya snapped.

Josephine sputtered and flailed, but Hiraya was so much stronger than her sleek figure implied.

"Hush, hush. It's just a small thing, a tiny sacrifice for a much larger gift," Hiraya murmured, and Josephine sobbed, twisting in Hiraya's arms to face her. Behind her, she could hear the crash of the black ocean. Another two steps, maybe less, and she would have plummeted into those waters. The blackness would have taken her. Her corpse would have never found the beach.

Yet she couldn't care less. All she could think about was Hiraya, the lattice of scars over her sunken eyelid. It was cruel. It was obscene.

"That's your eye, Hiraya. Your *eye*," Josephine hissed, and only realized that she was crying when the taste of her own tears wet her tongue. "How could that be a little thing?"

Hiraya smiled at her. But it was flimsy, as if she'd been asking herself that question for years. "I suppose it seems horrible to you, right? Terrible. To take someone's eye." Hiraya's hand drifted up to her empty eye socket. "I was terrified when I first learned what Tadhana wanted me to do. But you must understand. It's natural for us. Tadhana's eyes were taken when she was sixteen. Sidapa was next. But when Sidapa rejected her call, it fell to me. I joined my aunts in a sacred lineage. I shoulder the burden of this family. I decide its future. I sacrificed my eye for my family's future."

Josephine shook her head. Hiraya's words all sounded familiar. She knew intimately the pressure of adhering to tradition, of being forced into a role to protect a family legacy. And yet to demand something like *this*? It went beyond anything acceptable.

"But your eyes are so . . . so much a part of you. It's not like a lock of hair or a tooth," Josephine said, her strength returning. Hiraya withdrew from her now that she was steady, turning her back to Josephine. Instead, she approached the altar, laying her hands on either side of the ivory tree and its stolen fruit. Her hair spilled over her shoulders, haloing her face, hiding it away.

Josephine was almost certain she could see Hiraya's shoulders tremble. As if she were barely holding herself together. But when Hiraya spoke, she spoke smoothly, her voice riding along the crest of the waves behind them.

"It's the significance of the sacrifice that makes it so vital. I didn't want to give it up. I . . . I wanted to keep it. Stupid and childish as the thought is. But it's what connects us to each other . . . and to this island and its spirits. Without that sacrifice, we wouldn't be able to facilitate the game. The herbs we'd pick during Holy Week would just be weeds. The ointments we make would just be coconut oil and dull, dim wishes. We wouldn't be able to read the future in your moles or the entrails of a sow. We'd never be able to grant anyone the future they desire, and we'd live and die on this island alone."

Hiraya peered over her shoulder at Josephine, her face half-veiled by the locks of her hair. What little of her face Josephine could see was unreadable, and Josephine's heart broke. She hated this. She hated how far away Hiraya felt, how alien and lonely her gaze was. It was the stare of a woman who'd spent her life never quite trusting anyone, and it killed Josephine to be on the other end of it. She stepped forward toward Hiraya and the altar. "Don't you dare say that. How could you even think it? You're so much more than . . . than wishes, and whatever it is Tadhana asks you to do."

"Am I?" Hiraya whispered. She lifted a hand and cradled the air beside a withered fruit. Its dried skin was a little less browned than the rest. A sickly yellow to their almost blackened leather.

"I was born because of a dream. All the Ranocos were. Everything we are stems from the first woman on this island. She made this island a sanctuary. She opened her arms up like boughs to the women the world cast away. She ensured that we'd never go hungry, that we'd never have to live in fear. And she paid every price to make that a reality. She struck the first deal, laid out the first dinner. She made the very first sacrifice. And it is my duty to maintain the dream she built."

Hiraya's voice grew quieter and quieter with each passing word, until silence totally overtook her. She turned back to the altar, her hands on either side of it, her head bowed forward, her back hunched.

"It's not my dream," she admitted, her voice small. "It's not what I would have chosen for myself. Some part of me is still living with you in Carigara. I dream of the nights we were young, and the world was so big, so full of choice. But I wouldn't have allowed a piece of my body to be torn away if I didn't believe with my whole heart and soul in the women who came before me. I've seen precisely what the power of sacrifice can do. The course of an entire life can be changed with one decision. One offering to this altar.

"Tell me, honestly, that you wouldn't give up everything for your mother, your father, your brother. That you wouldn't give up everything, even the future you wanted, if it meant you could have saved them."

Josephine flinched as if the words were a blade. The gaping void her parents had left in her life was one that would never truly heal. She felt their absence every day. And she knew that the little things she did, the way she clutched her mother's rosary and pondered what her mother would do, were all just tiny, desperate ways to resurrect her mother, to pretend for a little longer that she wasn't gone—not entirely.

She desperately tried to remember her mother's face, the way she sounded, the way she stood. Even with the blur of time, she knew that her mother would have easily made that decision. That she'd sacrifice anything to see the future she wanted molded into reality. But she wasn't her mother. She loved her family, but if they asked her to tear herself apart on an altar, she wasn't certain if she could do it.

"I love my family. My parents, Alejandro. And I'd do anything to keep them safe. But I don't know that I'd want to be part of a family that demanded so much from me. I'd question . . . if they were really my family at all. What type of mother would ask her child to tear herself apart on an altar?"

Hiraya winced, her eyes wide. And for a moment, beneath the disappointment, Josephine could see something new in her. *Envy.*

"I understand," Hiraya murmured. "Then what is it you *really* wish for, Josephine? You can't tell me that there isn't a future you've been longing for."

The cavern was quiet, save for the sputtering flames on the wick and the crash of the ocean at the cave's mouth. She knew the answer. It was the dream she cradled in her heart, born the moment she sat in the pews of her church, watching the priest solemnly read from the Bible over her parents' caskets.

"I want to go home, and for it to feel like home. I want to feel safe and happy again. The way I did before Eduardo destroyed my family."

"That is a lovely dream. And it's not unreachable," Hiraya said.

But now it was Josephine's turn to roll her eyes. "Oh, I'm sure. I'd only need Marcos to be tossed off his throne and for Eduardo to keel over. But what do you want, Hiraya? Be honest with me. Really, truly honest."

"I . . . I want—" Hiraya stammered as she lifted her head. But she didn't look at the altar before her but instead at the long black tunnel at the end of the cave that led to her family's tomb. She stared into the darkness for a long moment, as if she could see something in the shadows, hidden behind the glow of candlelight. She wet her lips and tried again, turning away from it to face Josephine. "I want . . . to be free. I want to choose where I go, what I do, who I love. I want a normal life. I want Carigara, and mangoes so tender you can cut them with a spoon. I want sunsets on the boulevard and bickering over what channel on the radio to listen to. I want . . . to be normal."

"I can give you that. All of that. Why play this game at all?" Josephine asked, her voice hitching. It was such a small, mundane future. It'd be so easy to achieve. Just take the boat back to the mainland and start a new life on new ground, far away from this place.

"I know you would, if you could. But it's never that easy," Hiraya muttered. "I wish it were that easy. This game is my only chance to grab hold of a future where I'm not a facilitator of this game but my own person. Not a Ranoco. Just Hiraya. Just me. But every dream on this island, every wish, is molded from sacrifice. You have to remember that, Josephine. During the game. Happiness demands suffering. It demands pain."

She reached for Josephine's hand, her fingers splayed. Her jaw was clenched, her singular eye wet and glassy with tears she could barely hold back. And without hesitation, without a second thought, Josephine took her hand. The moment she did, Hiraya pulled her closer, drawing her into an embrace that felt tight and desperate. Josephine knew without a doubt that that was the first time Hiraya had ever admitted the dream she yearned for out loud. And from the way Hiraya shook in her arms, she knew that it was a wish that frightened her.

"I'll grant that wish for you," Josephine murmured into Hiraya's hair. "Just come back with me. You don't have to win a game or ask the spirits for any favors. I'll bring you all the mangoes you want. I'll find you ice cream and little bags of soda. I'll give you a garden you can tend to, one that's yours and yours alone. Just . . . say yes."

"You're so stupid," Hiraya whispered, her voice shaking. For a moment, she sounded like Sidapa had when Josephine found the younger Ranoco sister in that room of masks. "As if it were that easy, to leave everyone behind. You couldn't do it; admit it."

Josephine hesitated. Hiraya was right. If her brother needed her, she'd stay with him. Even if he didn't want her to.

"Maybe you're right. Maybe I couldn't. But . . . seeing you like this . . . if you stay here, you're sacrificing more than your eye. You're giving up your entire life, your chance at happiness. Any future you ever hoped to have that wasn't already premade for you."

"It's not that easy. It's not just packing up and leaving and saying goodbye. I have to win. It's my only way out. And you should try your best, too," Hiraya said. Hiraya dragged herself away from Josephine and held her gaze. The tears were drying on her cheek, and she swallowed, as if trying to compose herself. "Tomorrow, we all get the chance to change our fates. And it's worth it, I promise."

Josephine tilted her head. There was a fanged desperation in Hiraya's voice, but Josephine nodded. "Just . . . don't do anything too crazy, okay? But I still believe I can talk Alejandro into coming back to Carigara. And if I'm lucky, maybe I can still talk you into it, too. Without having to win a game." She smiled, but Hiraya didn't return it.

"I hope you're right," Hiraya murmured. But she seemed wholly unconvinced, her face grim. "But your brother has a weight on him. You can't underestimate how badly he wants to win this game. How badly he wants the future he's been chasing for years."

A silence fell between them. Josephine knew that Hiraya was right. There was a desperation in Alejandro that she hadn't seen before. A haunted look that hollowed out his once-handsome face. There'd been too many failures in Manila, too much taken from him. He couldn't even see hope in the revolution playing out in the highways, in the protests. He'd already given up on justice. But spirits? Would he go that far?

"Why wouldn't I let him have it, then? Why wouldn't I play to let him win? Or you?"

Hiraya shook her head, her brows furrowing. "Don't. Don't even think like that. If you throw the game and let someone else win, there is no sacrifice. The spirits won't accept a fake game, and no one will win. Everyone must do their part. But . . . we can talk more about it tomorrow, at dinner, when everyone else is here. Tadhana will explain the game and the rules in full. But you should spend tomorrow thinking, really and truly, about how much your future is worth. How much you want it, how much you deserve it. Because you do deserve it, Josephine. You deserve to be happy. Let's turn in for the night."

Hand in hand, Hiraya led her back to the entrance of the cave, where the tides had risen. Its waters were nearly flush with the entrance, and yet the water still swirled and gurgled, ravenously clawing at the lip of the tunnel. Hiraya placed a hand on the small of Josephine's back.

"It always seems like it'll flood, but it never does. It just fills in the cracks, washes out the filth," Hiraya reassured her. "Don't be frightened." She pressed Josephine toward the stairs, and Josephine realized that she'd be the first to go up.

She took the first step and hated how slick it was beneath her feet. But Hiraya's hand was reassuring on her hip. "I have you. Keep going."

Josephine was scarcely listening. She clung to the edges of the rock wall and flinched at the spray of water as it hit the back of her legs. She ascended the first step, then the next. Hiraya's hand was firm. A promise of safety, however flimsy. But it made things easier, and, shaking with fatigue, she soon reached the top of the stairs and dry land. She sighed, and her tired eyes rose to the Ranoco house and its windows, her gaze drawn in like light into a black hole.

Someone was watching her through the windows. She knew it.

"There's someone there, isn't there?" she muttered, weary and spent. She expected Hiraya to dismiss her again, but Hiraya nodded.

"I feel that way, too," Hiraya admitted.

Josephine glanced at her, searching her face. She couldn't pinpoint it precisely, but it felt like something had changed in the way Hiraya carried herself. As if some part of the façade she wore had been peeled away in that cave.

"Are we being watched?" Josephine asked, her voice quiet.

Hiraya's gaze lingered on the windows of the house, her single eye squinting. She hesitated, as if she could see something in the shadows that Josephine could not.

"Yes. Though often what's watching us are the insects, hiding in their crevices. There are so many of them on the island. Bees, beetles, centipedes. More than you can imagine. But let's talk about those things later when the sun has risen. I'll take you to your room."

Hiraya lifted the lantern again, her smile warmer than its light, and offered the crook of her elbow. Josephine took it, leaning against her, and she could feel Hiraya leaning back, her shoulders soft. Insects were a part of life in the Philippines. If that was all, she had nothing to be afraid of.

Instead, her head filled with visions of a possible future. It was so easy to imagine Alejandro back home. The two of them back in Carigara, brave and uncowed by the wet-eyed stare of Eduardo and his sons. Living testament to their parents' legacy that Eduardo's intimidation couldn't crush. But now her dream had a new layer. She could envision Hiraya with them, too. The three of them restoring the del Rosario manor, filling it with laughter and life. Would it really be as easy as winning a game of tagu-tagu? What sort of deal had the first Ranoco woman made that laid the foundations for such a trade?

In silence, they made the long journey around the house, back toward the front door. Their feet sank into the wet dirt, Josephine's mouth filled with the taste of petrichor and earth. The song of insects accompanied their squelching steps.

She tilted her head toward Hiraya and leaned into the moment, seeking whatever crumb about her strange, reclusive family she'd give her.

"Now that we're both Ranocos . . . will you tell me about the first Ranoco woman? Your 'primogenitor of eccentricity and strangeness,' I think you called her," Josephine said, her voice quiet, "the person who made this house?"

The question felt like it was treading on hallowed ground, and Hiraya sighed. "I don't know her name. It's lost, like many things, to time. But she was born in Biliran, centuries ago. She was a *babaylan*, a shaman, in a village along the coast. She was renowned for her ability to speak to the *diri sugad ha aton*, to those who live in the roots of the balete trees, in the places between the realms of the living and the dead.

"But then the Spanish came, and they sowed the seeds that turned her town against her. They called her a witch. An aswang. They tortured her, and she managed to escape to this island. They chased after her, but they couldn't find her. It was as if she had vanished. People believe she made a deal with the Engkanto of this island. One that promised her, and all the daughters who followed after her, immortality, safety, sanctuary. But it's just a story."

Hiraya shrugged, her reverent tone turning almost flippant. But the mask had fallen too late. Josephine knew that Hiraya believed every word of the story, from start to finish. And so had every other

Ranoco woman who'd been born and raised and had died in this house. They had to if they were willing to sacrifice themselves at the Engkanto's altar.

But now she understood the heavy air of melancholy and dread that clouded everything on this island. Even after all those centuries, it seemed the very land still remembered that final death hunt.

Josephine and Hiraya fell quiet as they passed through the doorway into the house, as if they were teenagers sneaking in. They slipped through the halls, the sound of their feet quieted by the dull carpet runner. She wanted to enjoy it for just a little longer, but the corridors felt like a throat around her. The thick, dust-choked air the last fetid breath of a corpse, caught in a lung, never to be exhaled. She didn't think it was possible to miss the feeling of paranoia the forest inspired, but now she desperately wished she were back in the muck, mosquitoes and gnats biting at her ankles.

"I don't think I like this house at night. It feels . . . different," Josephine whispered, feeling foolish even as she spoke.

She could hear the smile on Hiraya's face. "You'd have to be unhinged to like this house during any time of day. But you should enjoy the house while it's peaceful. Tomorrow night, you'll wish it were this quiet. This still."

They emerged into a grand corridor, and the rooms here were a little more uniform. "This is the guest hall. Alejandro's room is here." Hiraya laid a hand against the frame of a door, well scuffed and chipped, as if someone had tried to cut at it. "The one beside it is Gabriella's. But I chose this one for you."

She led Josephine toward the end of the hall, where a large window peered out into the night sky. "You'll have a balcony and fresh air. So it won't be as stuffy. And the sunset from this room is truly lovely."

Her voice was warmth and honey, and Josephine felt herself thaw as she watched Hiraya unlock the bedroom door.

"Are you playing favorites, Miss Ranoco?" Josephine asked, grinning.

"Oh yes. You're absolutely my favorite. Alejandro second. Gabriella very last."

Josephine winced, but she wasn't in the least bit surprised. "Gabriella can be a little prickly, but she's not a bad person. She can be kind, and sweet, and thoughtful."

Hiraya shrugged. "I'm sure. But she hates me, and she always has. So she gets the honor of that very bottom tier."

Josephine couldn't conjure a single word in argument. Hiraya was right. Gabriella, like most of Carigara, had always harbored a strong mistrust of the Ranoco women and, for whatever reason, a particular distaste for Hiraya. And if she were in Hiraya's shoes, she wasn't certain if she'd be half as graceful about it.

Hiraya pushed open the door, and Josephine stepped inside. The room was spacious and not unlike her own room back home. The familiarity was comforting after the strangeness of the house and its labyrinth of corridors. Between the door and the bed was a little sitting space, complete with two chairs and a table. And by the door was a terra-cotta pot, a metal *tabo* dipper, and a vase of water.

A bed stood against the opposite wall, its foot aimed toward the door, with her suitcase beside it. To the right of the bed was the balcony, its sliding windows closed. Hiraya lit the lantern on Josephine's nightstand, casting everything in a soft glow.

"It's perfect. Thank you, Hiraya. I could fall asleep just looking at it."

Hiraya beamed. "I'm glad it's to your taste. Sleep well. Come for breakfast at your leisure at the banquet hall. I trust you'll be able to find it with enough effort. Oh, and remember to lock your window and doors."

There was a firmness to the last statement, but a smile accompanied it, and Josephine chuckled. There was no one else on the island save the Ranoco women, the servants, and the three guests. And, she supposed, the countless insects.

"You sound like my mother," Josephine murmured. "Is a *sigbin* going to crawl through my window and chew on my leg if I don't?" She flashed Hiraya a toothy smile. Sigbins, like so many Filipino monsters, were bloodsucking animals that haunted the night.

"*Sigbin, kapre, tiyanak* . . . who knows what could be in the dark? Better safe than sorry."

Hiraya left the room with a wave, and Josephine leaned against the frame of the door. She watched Hiraya vanish into another room, pausing briefly at a door. She looked back over her shoulder at Josephine.

"Josephine? Thank you. For coming. For hearing me out. For . . . being my sister, for a little while." She was gone with a flick of her long skirts before Josephine could respond. But Josephine lingered against the doorframe looking after her, her body heavy with the last fleeting touch of wine and bourbon, exhaustion, and tingling adrenaline. She stared into the dark, letting the day wash over her and feeling the ache at being left alone again.

Carigara had been painfully quiet and monotonous. There she'd spent whole weeks barely noting the rise and fall of the sun. It'd been a hollow existence. And now there was so much happening.

The day had curved in so many strange directions, like a tempestuous fever dream she had no control over. But Hiraya made it softer, easier to consume. Every step of the way, Hiraya seemed to be there. An anchor in otherwise lonely seas, while Gabriella and

Alejandro murmured secrets on the dance floor or slipped into dark alcoves. And Hiraya had shown her the most vulnerable places of her heart and home.

As she stared, consumed by thoughts, into the space where Hiraya vanished, something flickered and thrummed at the end of the hall, at the edges of her vision. She blinked, the exhaustion in her limbs fading as she twisted her head to stare down the long corridor. The only source of light was the lantern on her bedside table, which pooled around her ankles, golden but dim. But she was certain that she'd seen something move in the shadows.

She gripped the doorframe with tight fingers. In the darkness, she could just make it out. The silhouette of something, just a little blacker than the rest. As she stared, the details swam into view.

Arms, legs, a head.

"Alejandro?" she called.

Or she tried to, at least. But her voice was a hoarse, dry whisper, crackling at the end. She knew even before she called Alejandro's name that it wasn't him. The figure was too slight. The way it stood was too rigid. But not unfamiliar.

"Sidapa?" she asked hesitantly. The name elicited no response. The figure at the end of the hall remained still, hands hanging at its sides. Josephine was certain that the figure was watching her. Pulling her apart with its unseen eyes, vivisecting her for some unknown purpose.

Nerves shook Josephine's voice free from the vise of her clamped jaw. "Sidapa? Are you okay? It's late, isn't it?" Josephine demanded, her nails biting into the wood.

The figure didn't respond. It only stepped backward, out of reach of the pale light that came from Josephine's bedroom. In moments, the dark consumed its figure. No matter how much Josephine squinted or stared, she couldn't see a hint of the figure any longer.

But Josephine was certain that it was still there. That it'd been just out of sight all along, following her since they met in the room of masks. And maybe even longer. When was the first time she'd felt eyes drilling into her? The moment the house reared up before her, when she crested the jungle trail? Had it been in the trees, stalking her from a distance, waiting for her to finally, finally, be alone?

She dragged her hands away from the door. Anger crept through the fear, growing roots. She was so sick and tired of being played with. Of being *watched*. Josephine spun and grabbed the lantern from her bedside table. It swung dangerously, its flame sputtering.

But in a second, she was back at her door and out of it, walking fast toward where she was certain she'd seen Sidapa at the end of the hall, the lantern aloft. The lantern's light flooded the surrounding hall, but its flame only stretched a yard or two out. And beyond that, darkness.

"Sidapa?" Josephine demanded again. Her voice had found its edge. Her free hand clenched in a fist; her teeth met each other in a grimace. Silence and the low groan of the ocean crashing against the cliffside answered her. She could hear it even here, through the open window at the end of the corridor.

"Just talk to me. If you have something to say, please just say it."

Down the hall, a door clicked shut. She hadn't even realized it'd been open, cracked open just a few inches, so whoever was inside could peer out. So that they could stare at her from the cover of darkness.

"There you are," Josephine proclaimed as she pushed open the door, her lantern aloft, a triumphant, wild grin on her face.

The grin froze on her face as all her bravery and indignant rage calcified and cracked. She'd seen witchcraft before. She'd been to a healer a few times, to have oil-soaked herbs pressed into her scalp when the nightmares of her parents and Eduardo were most persistent. But this?

Intricate bamboo mats had been woven and nailed to the wall, imitating the natural walls of a nipa hut. And nailed to those mats were dozens, if not hundreds, of ragged cloth dolls. Each a different color, some with bright floral patterns, others with the silken transparency of piña silk. Some were yellowed; others were rotted so badly they'd fallen from their nails and to the ground, where they lay upon piles of others at the bottom of the wall, their limp figures slowly being devoured by black beetles.

They looked like *haplit* dolls. Poppets used to curse whomever they were meant to represent. But these dolls didn't seem to be meant to carry out a curse. Instead, they seemed more like a macabre collection, with a rough symmetry to the room of masks she'd stumbled across in the morning. But if that room had been full of the death masks of the Ranoco women, then this room . . .

Are these all the people who've played the game? Josephine thought, staring open-mouthed at the walls.

The room smelled of metal, of rotting meat, of burning hair. The stench of it was so strong that it filled Josephine's mouth with bile. And yet there was nothing there but the dolls and the beetles and moths slowly devouring their cloth. Their heads were full of tufts of black hair, their bodies run through in a thousand different ways. Some had their cloth necks torn open, so that the dried grass that filled them jutted through the cut, the stalks stained dark rust. Dozens of others were missing limbs. Another doll was in pieces, each piece nailed to the bamboo matting. Another was just a smear of ragged cloth and black.

But the room wasn't complete. There were swaths on the wall where empty gaps waited for their own idol. And yet, judging by how old the dolls were, it was clear that it'd been a few years since anyone had added to it. This was the work of a Ranoco woman who'd long since passed away.

Hiraya said the game has been going on for generations. But why make them like this?

Josephine swallowed, her tongue thick in her mouth. The flame in the lantern shook, throwing long, sputtering shadows on the wall, though there was ample kerosene sloshing in the canister. She shut the door and turned back down the corridor, toward her room, not wanting to spend one more moment in that room.

But the hall was so much darker than when she'd left it. The open window, which had previously let some of the dim moonlight in, was shut. The hall was black. She hadn't heard the window close, but how could she, with her heart pounding in her ears? She lifted the lantern up, to try to see who had closed the window, which was just a few feet away from her own room.

Her body trembled, but she edged down the hall to her bedroom. She was aware of each creak and groan of the house. Of the feeling of being watched. And still she crept down the hall until she was in front of her own door.

It was open.

Had she left it open? She'd left so quickly she wasn't sure. She wet her lips and slipped inside, shutting the door quietly behind her. The key was still in the lock, and she turned it. To be safe, she jostled the knob, and the lock held.

She turned and let the light of the lantern fill the small room. No one hid in its corners. No one watched her from her bed. It'd felt so safe before, when Hiraya first brought her here. A sanctuary.

If she'd just closed the door after Hiraya left, if she'd just gone to sleep, it would have still felt like that. But she refused to let the fear take her.

She dragged one chair from the sitting area and propped it beneath the knob. It felt ridiculous to guard herself against Hiraya's sister. Sidapa had always been . . . eccentric. But she'd never been a threat. She'd never meant harm.

But Josephine couldn't forget the night that Hiraya and Sidapa had come to her house. That night the Ranoco family had fled Carigara for good as their house went up in flames. Sidapa had been bloodstained, almost catatonic, but covered in kerosene. Hiraya had been rough with her, but nervous. Almost . . . frightened. Maybe there'd been a reason for that.

EIGHT

S HE undressed swiftly, shucking dirty clothes and laying her
mother's earrings and hair comb on the table. Every part of
her felt disgusting. She'd trekked miles and hiked through muck
and sea-soaked tunnels barefoot. But the vase of water and the
terra-cotta bowl were the best she could do.

She dipped the *tabo* dipper into the clear water and washed her
hands and her face over the pot, scrubbing the last vestiges of her
mother's lipstick away. Every time she closed her eyes, her mind
filled with images of the bone tree, of yellowed withered eyes, of
rotting, red-stained dolls. She turned to her feet. The thick muck
came off in pieces, and she scrubbed until her feet burned red. Her
skin was covered in insect bites. She hadn't noticed before, but they
must have been nibbling at her the entire time she was outside. She
grimaced at the thought of their alien black legs scrambling along

her skin, their sharp, cruel jaws biting into her. The room was quiet. The door was locked. The windows were locked.

It's just a house, she thought. *It's just a game.*

And yet the desperation in Hiraya's voice as she described her wish ricocheted around Josephine's skull. Hiraya wanted so desperately to be free of this family, of this house, and the work that went on here. There was a reason for that. A reason she'd let Josephine glimpse by bringing her down into the altar room. But one she hadn't yet fully unveiled.

The Ranoco women were secretive. But Hiraya seemed desperate for Josephine to understand her. To help her escape.

She pulled on her nightgown, its hem falling to her knees. But over her bare skin, it felt flimsy.

The lock, the chair. She was fine; she was safe. There was no reason to think she wasn't safe. But as she turned back to the room, she could see the telltale sign of termites embedded into the walls and floor. Hairline fractures and holes pocked the dark wood, haloing her bed. She was certain that she could hear something behind the wood panels. She leaned her head close to the bed and held her breath.

A gentle scratching came from the other side. The sound of insects crawling through the wood. Thousands of them slowly hollowing the house from the inside out, just beneath the house's skin.

Or maybe not. Was it the sound of waves that she was hearing? Or the way her teeth ground between her clenched jaws? She prodded at the holes and tried to feel something beneath them. A squirming, a twitching. But the tunnels remained hardened, empty veins piercing through to an unseen heart.

Gabriella was right. This place was more than odd. In the dark, it was a nightmare that tucked its ugliness beneath its wood, in the folds of its rooms. Hiraya had to carve out a place in its body to try to create something lovely. But even then, the garden was surrounded on all sides by looming rooms and dark, watching windows.

She settled onto the bed, pulling the thin quilt up to her neck, and breathed deeply, trying to steady her thoughts. She'd hoped the bed would smell of Hiraya, but it didn't. It smelled like an amalgamation of people. And though her body was electric with dread and worry, in moments sleep stole over her like a thief, wrapping her in a thin, restless haze.

She swam at the edges of consciousness and dreams. They mingled together in vague images and thoughts, not coherent enough to take shape, each tainted by shadow and the stench of burning skin.

But permeating every image was a soft, rhythmic clicking. A barely audible *tick-tick-tick*. Her eyes opened half an inch. The room was pitch-black, the lantern's kerosene long since spent. Her body was heavy beneath the quilt stretched over it. No part of her would move. Not a finger, not a toe.

A cold sweat broke out over her as she blinked awake. Her eyes strained to their peripheries, and she glanced toward her door. It still seemed shut. So was the window. But the sound continued.

Tick. Tick. Tick.

Like someone tapping.

The smell of compost and earthy rot filled her mouth. Beneath the bed came the sounds of bones cracking and popping. Then something wet and soft.

"*Ah,*" Josephine sputtered. She choked around a sound that had meant to be a scream for help. She struggled. Her hands convulsed with effort, her fingertips scratching at the thin sheets beneath her.

The quilt at her side tightened, pulled taut by something

persistent and heavy. From the edge of her vision, a head lifted itself up, its face covered with long curtains of black hair, obscuring the mottled, discolored skin of its face.

It hid beneath my bed. How long was it waiting for me to fall asleep? The panicked thought jolted through her, filling her with horror. Josephine's mouth spasmed around another aborted scream. What came instead was a pathetic wheeze.

The thing, the creature, pulled itself onto her bed with arms that were too long, its nails biting into her calves as it dragged itself onto Josephine's legs. The full weight of its torso bore down on her. But where its legs should have been, something steaming hot and soft stretched instead.

Her mind filled with images of glossy ribbons of pink and gray tumbling over each other in knots. She knew what monster had crawled from beneath her bed and now dug its claws into her skin.

An aswang. Not just a witch, but a monster, twisted and cursed to spend its nights hunting for flesh. Leaving its legs behind in some hidden nest, its organs trailing out of the raw edges of its torso. A creature capable of shape-shifting, of using every type of blasphemous sorcery.

Tears streamed down her temples and her body shook as the aswang dragged itself higher up her body.

Now that it was so close, she could see that its black hair was coarse and brittle, like the bristles of a tarantula. Not a pure black but edged with gray. These bristles pierced through the quilt and pricked her, sending the patches of skin it touched into an itching, burning fit.

Its hot breath bathed her face. Its human eyes, if they could be called that, had been scooped right out of its head, leaving scarred hollows in its skull. But it watched her with countless others.

All across the creature's arms and chest were the cold, obsidian eyes of a beetle. Black and soulless and eternally watching, like God's own ophanim angels, if an angel could be crafted in the fires of hell.

The aswang opened its thin, wrinkled lips, and Josephine stared in horror as its tongue extended outward, unfurling and hardening like the tongue of a mosquito.

It licked Josephine's cheek before dragging the tip of its tongue lower, toward her sternum. Her negligee did nothing to hide her collarbones, nor the golden expanse between her breasts. The aswang teased the sweating, glossy skin where her ribs protruded, and Josephine's body shook with panicked gasps.

Her nanny told her when she was a child that aswang only ate the unborn fetuses from their mothers' stomachs. They'd pierce the belly with their needle-ended tongue and suck the baby up in a slurry over several visits until there was nothing left but the dregs of the child, which would be passed and left in the woods without a grave.

Josephine had never even come close to having a child. But it didn't seem to care.

"*Francesca . . .*" the creature whispered, its voice distorted and trembling, as if whatever part of it was human were buried in the very pit of its chest.

But the word made Josephine freeze. Francesca. That was her mother's name.

The aswang's tongue lapped over the beads of her rosary and came to rest over her breast, over her quivering heart. And gently, gently, it pushed. It stung like nettles at first. And then came the burn.

Josephine screamed as her nerves turned white-hot and blinding.

She screamed a hoarse, whispering scream, until there was no air left in her lungs. Until her throat felt like it was tearing. Until unconsciousness snapped her into the stygian black.

She dreamed of being devoured alive. Of being split open, the empty cavity of her chest filled with insect eggs. She dreamed of being buried and being birthed between the roots of the balete tree. Naked and riddled full of holes, where black beetles and bees made their homes.

She dreamed of her mother, lying in this same bed, caught in the same nightmare thirty years ago. She dreamed of her mother, stabbing back, a fruit knife in her hand and hate in her heart, as she killed the beast that would have killed her.

NINE

February 24, 1986

THE buzz of flies above her started her awake, her heart thrumming in her chest. Her negligee clung to her skin. She jolted to a sitting position, her shoulders steel rods after the paranoid nightmares that had haunted her, and her hands roved across her chest and neck, expecting blood.

There was no one in the room save half a dozen flies, bloated and fat, spiraling above her in lazy circles. Her quilt, which should have been bloodstained with the trailing of the aswang's innards, was clean. The balcony window was shut, the copper hook on the window undisturbed. The door to the room was still blocked by the chair. The key was still in the lock, unmoved.

No one had come in. No one had left.

She put her feet on the ground and felt herself shake, despite the heavy heat of the new morning. That *thing* had come from beneath the bed. She didn't want to look. But she had to. She had to prove that it was all make-believe. A nightmare born of wine and a whirlwind of strange, unsettling events. Sucking in a breath, she lowered herself to the floor and peered beneath the bed.

There was nothing but shadows, dust, a dead insect. And, faintly, scratches. Dozens of them, crisscrossing, right beneath the bed's center.

A cat, perhaps, had done it. A cat or rats. Or a monster with too many eyes and a mouth that had wanted to split her apart and devour her while she was still living and warm. A monster who had known her mother's name and said it like its heart was breaking.

She clumsily untangled herself from the sheets, the quilt dragging behind her and falling to the ground like a runaway bride's veil. The thin, dust-clouded mirror against the wall showed her a haggard face, with dark shadows beneath bloodshot eyes, a body untouched by the bristles of a monster. The hangover clung to her like a low-beating crown, and she scowled at her reflection.

There, a few inches below her collarbone, was a mark. She leaned closer to the mirror, pulling the neckline of her nightgown low. Right above her heart was a red circle. It radiated outward in a gradient of pink and red.

She touched it tentatively, and winced at its tenderness and warmth, and felt stupid. She *had* been bitten in her sleep, but not by an aswang. Just another one of the countless, incessant insects. The sensation of the bite, and the events of the day before, had concocted a nightmare that had felt terribly, terribly real.

But the scratches beneath her bed? Had the creature made them? She wasn't sure. But whatever *had* made them was long gone. Perhaps it'd slunk into the termite holes in the wall above her bed. The line between reality and dreams lay wreathed in a thick mist of doubt. Perhaps there was more than one way in and out of this room, hidden behind a secret panel or the armoire. In a place like this, she'd never know for certain.

"Pull yourself together," she muttered to her reflection. But she didn't like the sound of her own voice. It sounded fragile, teetering on the edge of tears. Not like a grown woman who was determined to corner her brother and force him back home, or a grown woman who had promised to save the woman she'd quietly been in love with for the better part of a decade.

She could still smell that monster's breath, the warmth of its innards on her legs, its blood sinking through her nightgown. She could still hear its rattling, inhuman voice dragging the name of her mother through its monstrous lips.

She pressed her hands over her face and tried to push it all out of her mind. When she won, when she was living her new life, she'd go to confession. She'd see the local grandmother for cleansing. She'd drown herself in holy water and purge every part of this place away until it was nothing more than a strange memory she'd convinced herself she'd exaggerated. She'd look back and see it for what it was. The long, winding nightmare of a silly woman from a rural village who'd had too much to drink.

She opened her suitcase and laid her outfit on the bed. From the case she withdrew her mother's lipstick. She rolled the cool metal tube between her fingers, then uncapped it. Gently, she applied it across her lips. Her mother had come to this house. She'd slept in one of these beds, maybe even *this* bed. She'd played the game and won. She could do what her mother had done. She could carve out a future of her very own, one of her own choosing. She just needed to make it through the day.

A sharp knock bounced off the door. Twice, firm.

"Josie? You're up, aren't you?" Gabriella's voice floated through the door as if it weren't the crack of dawn.

"Gabriella? Yes, sorry, wait one second."

Jarred at the sudden intrusion, Josephine scrambled for clothes. Sitting on top of her clothes was a book of matches that she'd never seen before. They were old and faded, but she tucked them into the pocket of her long, flowing skirt and pulled on a thin white blouse. She tucked the blouse quickly into the waist and fluffed her hair, glancing briefly in the mirror.

There was no salvaging it. The hair on the crown of her head stuck out at odd angles, and she cringed at how rough she looked, even with her mother's lipstick. But she could almost feel Gabriella's impatience radiating through the door. She pulled the chair from against the knob and opened it to the smell of meat and eggs, and the face of Gabriella.

"Did I wake you?" Gabriella asked as she breezed past Josephine into the room. She held in both hands two lavishly stacked plates, which she laid out on the small sitting-area table. She glanced at Josephine's hair, her unevenly tucked shirt, before taking stock of Josephine's face. "I did, didn't I? Sorry, darling. I know it's early."

"Oh, don't worry about it. I was awake, just trying to get the sleep of my eyes." Josephine straightened her skirt. Of course Gabriella was awake, combed, pinned, gelled. She'd fastidiously avoided any offer of wine all night, and she'd gone to bed much earlier. Gabriella's face was bright with rouge, her lips a morning-dew pink. Beneath the aroma of breakfast was the soft chemical bouquet of flowers wafting from her collarbone. It shook her that Gabriella could be so neat, so pretty, in this place. As if the house hadn't laid a hand on her.

"You couldn't sleep, either, then?" Josephine asked, settling at the table.

Gabriella nodded. "Oh God, no. Not in this wretched place. It creaks and groans. The moment dawn broke I went to breakfast. And *that* took ages, even though we didn't make it very far." Gabriella glanced toward the chair, still stationed near the door. A single eyebrow quirked up. "I see I'm not the only one who's paranoid." She laid the heavy plates of breakfast down and pushed the chair back against the table.

"Oh well. You're going to think me childish, but I thought I saw something in the hallway. So I . . ." Josephine waved her hand at the door. "Silly, right?"

"Not silly. Smart," Gabriella reassured her. "Everything about this place is creepy. If I didn't have Alejandro, I don't think I would have slept at all. How was your night, darling?" Gabriella asked. "I felt so bad leaving you alone with Hiraya, but Alejandro was insistent. You know how stubborn he can be."

Josephine grimaced. She didn't want to contemplate what Alejandro insisted upon. But she forced her mind away from it. So much had happened the night before, and she'd barely had any time to process it, much less make it palatable to Gabriella.

"It was good to catch up with her. We spent a lot of time talking," Josephine stated, hoping that would be enough to sate Gabriella's curiosity.

"Mm-hm?" Gabriella hummed as she sat down at the table. She leaned back against her chair, her gaze patiently on Josephine's face, her hand folded across her fork.

"It was a busy night, actually." Josephine sighed as she sank into the chair opposite Gabriella. She stared down at her plate. Gabriella's bore a generous cup of garlic rice, golden pork tocino, runny eggs, and sausage. Her own plate was nearly identical. But where Gabriella had meat, Josephine had mangoes. It was a small kindness. A gesture that sent a wave of surprise and remorse through Josephine.

Years ago, they'd been best friends. It'd been Gabriella's shoulders she leaned on, her shirts she'd stained with tears, in the wake of her parents' deaths. And when she lifted her gaze back to Gabriella's face, she could see the same face that had cared for her when she'd needed her. Even now, it shocked her how easy it was to talk to Gabriella. The letters they'd exchanged over the years felt stilted, but now that they were face-to-face, it felt natural to talk to her. As if nothing had changed. But something had. *She'd* been the one to put a knife in Gabriella's back all those years ago.

"Hiraya took me to visit her garden. And then we walked around the outside of the house. Just a brief tour." She didn't want to fill in the gaps. The confessions, the secrets, the altar. They'd both bared their souls to each other in those twilight hours. She knew that Gabriella wouldn't like any of it. Worse, she'd look for the hidden motive behind all of it. She'd never trusted Hiraya or her family. And after everything Josephine had seen in this house, and what lay beneath it, she could scarcely blame her.

"Wasn't it strange to spend so much time with her? After all this time." Gabriella jabbed her fork into a bit of tocino, scrutinizing it. Her nose scrunched, but she popped it into her mouth. "The meat here is gritty. Like it has sand in it. And its taste is a little off, too. A little sour."

"You should stop eating it. But yeah, it was awkward at first," Josephine admitted. "Then it felt like nothing had changed between us. I suppose that's the magic of childhood friends. Thank you for getting breakfast, by the way. I'm not sure if I would have found my way back to the dining hall on my own."

"Well, someone must make sure you eat. And that you take care of yourself. You look so thin; it goes way beyond chic. It's concerning." Gabriella stared pointedly at Josephine's neck and wrists.

Josephine fought back the urge to sink her hands beneath the table, to hide her hands in her lap. She'd been steadily losing weight over the years. Without anyone else in the del Rosario house, it was easy to carve pieces of herself away.

Gabriella took one of the small buns on her own plate and put it onto Josephine's. Josephine opened her mouth to protest, but Gabriella hushed her.

"Please? For me? It's one roll. Anyway, I'm nauseated as it is." Gabriella laid a hand against her stomach, massaging the soft crest in circles. But she did it in such a slow, methodical way it was clear that she wanted Josephine to notice, to ask.

"Because of . . . the house?" Josephine asked, her voice hitching.

Gabriella hesitated. Conflicting emotions flickered across her face. "Maybe. But . . . I think, perhaps, I might be pregnant."

"You're what?" Josephine sputtered, leaning forward. She'd never once thought that her brother would have a child, that Gabriella would become a mother. That they'd do both together.

"I don't know for certain!" Gabriella protested, shifting uncomfortably at the disbelief on Josephine's face and her raised voice. "It's just a feeling. But even if I am, it wouldn't be so terrible, would it? You'd be an aunt. We'd practically be sisters."

She smiled, but it was wilting. Josephine blinked and shook her head, trying to shed the shock. "No, of course it wouldn't be terrible. It'd be a blessing. You'd be a fantastic mother. I—I would love that, actually. I've always wanted to be an aunt. I just never thought Alejandro would get around to having a child."

She took Gabriella's hands, clasping them together in hers. "I can't believe it. You're going to be a mom? Congratulations."

The words still didn't feel real on her lips. But with each passing moment, she felt herself warming to the idea. She'd never wanted children herself, but the thought of a new del Rosario coming into the world sparked an excitement and joy in her that she'd never felt before. "Are you . . . are you coming back to Carigara? You have to. Manila isn't a place to raise kids."

Gabriella brightened and looked away, practically beaming at the floor. "I've been thinking about it, a little. I think you're right. I think Carigara would be the right place. I think that this might be the best thing that ever happened to me. That this is my purpose in life. I just hope I can be a good mother to them."

"To *them*?"

"Oh." Gabriella looked startled. Her blush deepened. Josephine had never seen her so bashful, so vulnerable. "I had an amazing dream last night. It was so surreal, and yet so vivid. I'm certain they're twins. Girls. Beautiful, clever girls."

"If that's true . . . that'd be wonderful. You'll be a perfect mother, Gabriella. I've known that since we were kids. They'd be so lucky to have you. And . . . and of course I'll do anything I can to help. I can't say I have a maternal bone in my body, but I'll do my best to help however you and Alejandro need it."

Tears welled in Gabriella's eyes and she nodded. "Thank you, Josie. I know we haven't been exactly close these past few years. But knowing that there's someone waiting for me back in Carigara, that there's a whole new chapter of my life out there . . . I'm just so excited."

Gabriella closed her eyes and dabbed away at her tears, and the cheerful expression on her face melted away. When she opened her dark eyes again, she was composed and serious.

"But before we go even one step further, I think we need to clear the air."

"Ah," Josephine murmured, her heart falling. She could see from Gabriella's stare that this was precisely the look she used in her business deals. Gabriella came from a long line of accomplished business owners, and if she hadn't tethered herself to Alejandro, Josephine had no doubt that Gabriella would have had phenomenal success in Manila. But no part of her wanted to be at Gabriella's negotiation table or to have to dredge up these old memories.

Gabriella paused, then stabbed at the pile of sticky, yellowed rice. "Hear me out before you shut me down, okay? I don't like Hiraya. I didn't like her when we were children and I like her even less now. I know you think I'm superstitious, or judgmental, but Hiraya and her family have always been secretive. And there wouldn't be so many dogged, vicious rumors about them if there weren't a grain of truth to them."

Tension fell over the table. She'd expected Gabriella to dive into the heart of the matter, and it startled her to see Gabriella take the flank instead. But she wasn't surprised. "Where's all this coming from? She was there for me when my parents passed. The way you were there for me," Josephine said.

"It's more than that, isn't it?" Gabriella replied, taking a bite. She chewed slowly and stared Josephine down. But Josephine said nothing. She sat rooted in her chair, her back straight. She'd never told *anyone* how she felt about Hiraya. But Gabriella was perceptive, and she knew her well.

Gabriella sighed and rolled her eyes. "Oh, do we really have to pretend? You've always loved her. Whenever she wanted to play that dumb little game of tagu-tagu as kids, you were first in line. And then again, during the fiesta. She came back to town and then . . . you didn't show up. You followed her to the beach instead. You traded a promise for a chance to spend a few hours with her."

Josephine swallowed. This she'd been expecting. And yet the anticipation didn't make it hurt any less. "I don't know what to say . . . other than that I'm sorry. I know I promised I'd be there to see you in the procession as Reyna Elena. I know how much it hurt you that I wasn't there to see you dance."

"I was so worried when you didn't show up. I thought something happened to you. But then someone told me you spent the whole day with her on the beach. I felt so stupid when I realized that. I watched for you, and then I waited for you, and you never came. That hurt, Josephine. I feel like . . . you'll always choose her."

Silence fell across the table as disbelief, guilt, and bitterness twisted in Josephine's heart. It was true. The day she'd seen Hiraya, she'd been on her way to see Gabriella. A parade of dancers and musicians had filled the street with color and sound. A river that flowed toward Holy Cross church's auditorium, where Gabriella would have performed as the Reyna Elena of the Flores de Mayo fiesta. The queen of the Santacruzan procession, a role unofficially reserved for the prettiest girl in town.

But when Josephine saw Hiraya across the street, she hadn't thought twice. She chased the Ranoco girl to the sea, and she missed the entire procession, Gabriella's dance, the feast. And when Gabriella left the next day for college, there'd been a wound in their friendship that had never quite healed.

Josephine wet her lips with her tongue. After all these years, she should apologize. Across the table, she could see the hurt still displayed plainly on Gabriella's face, undisguised. She'd laid her bleeding heart on the table for Josephine to crush or mend.

Softly, Josephine placed her hand on Gabriella's. Somehow, that one act of vulnerability hurt her in a way she couldn't quite describe. It was painful to admit that she'd been wrong, and that she'd known she'd been wrong for years. "You're right. I broke a promise to you, and I know I hurt you. I wish I could take that pain away. I . . . ran after her because I'd wanted to see her for so long. And I thought I'd never see her again. It's not an excuse, and I was selfish for doing it. I'm sorry for taking our friendship for granted, and I appreciate how much you've been there for me over the years. You were there for me when my parents died, and you were there for me years after, when the entire town started to treat the del Rosario name like it was cursed. You never left my side, and now you never leave Alejandro's side. And . . . I'm sorry for never saying so."

Gabriella sighed, like a weight was coming off her shoulders. Her dark eyes, once like flints of obsidian, softened, and she was the girl that Josephine had known her whole life. Sweet, and clever, and perhaps too forgiving.

"I know. If I'm being honest, I'm jealous. I know that there's a Hiraya-shaped hole in your heart, and that I'll never be able to fill it. And I should be happy that you love someone as much as I love Alejandro. I think you could do so much better. Doubly so if the revolution in Manila fails, and Eduardo and his sons continue their dynastic reign of corruption in Carigara. But . . . I'm happy that we're still friends. And that we're going to be family. Now it's your turn."

"My turn?" Josephine asked, her head tilting.

"I know you've been angry at me for years. Maybe since the night of the fiesta in Carigara all those years ago. You can't pretend with me. I was there when your parents died. I washed your hair when you could barely get out of bed. I dried your tears when you felt alone. For years, we were inseparable. And then, in high school, it felt like it all changed. You drifted away from me. And . . . even if you picked Hiraya because you love her, maybe there was another reason. Or am I reading too far into things?" Gabriella smiled, but it was thin and translucent. She knew she wasn't wrong.

Josephine swallowed. Hiraya was right. Gabriella had a way of seeing through the smoke, of cutting straight to the point. She was too good for Alejandro. She was too good for her, too.

"I—" Josephine's voice failed her. She tried again. "You're right. I didn't want to see you dance. I didn't want to see you, beautiful, shining, the Reyna Elena of the fiesta, Carigara's princess. Not because I'm jealous, or because I felt like you didn't deserve it, because you do. I just . . . didn't want to celebrate the fact that you were leaving me."

"Josephine." Gabriella sighed, taking Josephine's hands and pressing her thumbs softly into her palms. Her fingertips were silky, uncalloused, so unlike Hiraya's. "Why didn't you come with me? If not to Santo Tomas, then one of the dozens of other colleges. My aunt would have happily housed you, too. We could have studied together, explored the city, *lived*."

Josephine pulled her hand away. "How could I possibly leave the del Rosario house after everything Eduardo did? Just . . . leave it to the maids and his greedy, grubbing hands? They'd find a way to take it. Or maybe they'd vandalize it, or steal from it, or do anything they like, because I wouldn't be there to protect it. I can't leave that house, when it's the only part of my parents that is left. Even if . . . it's all falling apart. Alejandro took our entire inheritance with him when he last visited, and I haven't seen my allowance for months."

Gabriella blinked, and then her brow furrowed. "He hasn't sent you . . . anything?"

"No, not a cent." Josephine sighed. "I knew that he lost a significant amount of our inheritance after his campaign in the barangay failed. But he said that he had a business idea that would mend it. That he'd make back all the money he lost."

Gabriella nodded, but Josephine could almost see her closing off, her eyes darkening. As if she knew something Josephine didn't. "Ah. I see. Things have been difficult. The economy is unstable, and somehow we just keep betting on losing dogs. It's been weighing on him so heavily," Gabriella murmured.

"He seems tired," Josephine agreed. "He's been distant, in what few letters I've gotten this year. He looks like—"

"Like he's given up," Gabriella finished. "I hate seeing him like this. I hate seeing *you* like this. I don't know what Carigara's done to you. But . . . I'm coming home. I think we all should. Even if it's not perfect, we'll be better, happier, together. Like we used to be when we were children."

"Do you really think Alejandro will come back?" She wanted more than anything to hear Gabriella say yes. But Gabriella stared down into her dark coffee as if she could see a future she didn't like in that obsidian mirror.

"He seems . . . frightened to come back. I think he thinks it'll put you at risk. Or maybe he's afraid that if he goes back, it's like he failed to live up to his father's legacy. I don't know. Alejandro's not much younger than your father was when he died, but to hear him talk about him . . . it's like he's a giant. I don't know if he'll ever escape that shadow. But if I win the game? That's my wish. I'll wish that we can all go back to Carigara. That we can all have that happily-ever-after. And . . . even if I don't win, I know that the protests in Manila are going to change things for the better. No more midnight calls at his apartment, no more debts, no more worrying. Everything's going to be all right." Gabriella smiled with a warmth that felt like childhood, with a tenderness that thawed.

"I hope so," Josephine murmured, basking in Gabriella's warmth. She really, really hoped so.

TEN

THE conversation flowed languidly between Josephine and Gabriella, and they fell naturally to well-loved topics. Gabriella delighted in hearing about the scandals their old classmates had gotten into over the years, all the gossip she'd missed in Carigara while she was away. And Josephine couldn't help but find herself grinning as Gabriella spoke about her college escapades.

"It was . . . so nice to finally catch up," Gabriella said as she set her empty coffee cup down. She glowed, and Josephine found herself nodding. She hadn't known how much she'd truly missed Gabriella. She hadn't wanted to let herself believe it was possible that their friendship could ever be repaired. It'd been easier to pretend it was long past saving. But now she was grateful that Gabriella had never truly given up.

"Thank you for coming. For bringing breakfast. For talking

with me," Josephine said, knowing even as she said it that those words fell short.

"Well, I'm just getting started. Now I have to track down your brother." She stood, and they bid each other farewell. Gabriella vanished down the hall, far more confident in navigating than Josephine was.

Gently, Josephine left the plates outside the door, and almost instantly the fat flies that seemed to infest every part of this house descended, desperate to gorge themselves on the scraps. She watched them for a moment, disgusted, as they crawled over the edges of the egg before turning away. She needed fresh air.

But getting outside wasn't easy. There were four carpet runners that ran the length of the house. Scarlet, cerulean, emerald, gold. She stood on an emerald carpet now, peering down the hall, letting her gaze skate over the maid as if she weren't there. Emerald meant guest rooms, guest baths, guest parlors. Scarlet was entertainment. Cerulean, the Ranoco family rooms. Gold, the servants'.

But there was no fast indicator for *exit*. She unmoored herself from the little pier of her room, hesitant to let go of familiarity. Once she started wandering, she knew she'd be well and truly lost. And yet staying in her room seemed so much worse.

She opened the door across from her room, trying her best to follow the edge of the house, as if that might lead her outside quicker. It didn't. The turns and endless doors frustrated her at every new corner. Room after room of old books, stacked junk, and half-finished crafts greeted her. Each one was empty, and yet she never felt alone. The heavy feeling on her shoulders, of some unseen person's stare, was her constant companion.

Josephine glanced over her shoulder into the room she'd just passed. An empty armchair stared back at her, dusty, its lap filled with yellow newspapers. No one was there. But the feeling didn't fade, no matter how far she spiraled into the house.

It was with bone-deep relief that she found the grand staircase that marked the house's entrance. The three-tiered chandelier hung above the stairs, glowing in the midmorning light, its necklaces glittering like dust-choked stars. From the walls, the thin, aging corpses of taxidermied insects watched as she descended the stairs.

She pushed gently against the grand entrance door, and it opened into warm air and birdsong. "Ah, Mother Mary," Josephine murmured, leaning into the sunlight. The world outside the walls of the Ranoco house was bursting with life. The shrill scream of insects, the cacophony of birds. From an open window above her, she could hear the radio.

"I cannot in good conscience recognize Marcos as commander in chief of the armed forces. I call upon everyone who is imbued with a sense of justice and respect for the law to disobey the orders given to them . . ."

The creeping dread that had stalked her through the house faded in the fresh air, eaten away by the sunlight and the impassioned words of the priest on the radio.

She hated Marcos, his wife, and the army of cronies he'd amassed. For years, he'd been untouchable. Marcos had tortured, killed, and vanished countless people over the past two decades of his tyrannical rule. But now the people were turning against him.

They believed in a better future. And after the conversation with Hiraya last night, she was starting to believe a better future might wait for her, too. One where she and Alejandro could live with their heads held high in Carigara. One where she'd no longer have to bite her tongue against Eduardo or endure the heavy stares of her neighbors. Perhaps Hiraya would join them there, too.

She slid on the shoes waiting for her outside and stretched her arms up, letting the beams of light warm her skin. Gnats swarmed her in a loose cloud, but she paid them no mind as she headed through the courtyard gate.

Even the balete trees, which had seemed so intimidating when she arrived here yesterday, seemed softer. Just trees, full of vines and birds, their branches filled with gardens of ferns and orchids. A thin path had been worn through the grass and wild plants that surrounded the house, snaking around it to the side. Last night, she and Hiraya had probably walked this very path to the cliff. But now that it was light, she could see that it was well worn indeed.

Josephine followed it, her shoulders finally loosening and curving as her arms swung lightly at her sides. Everything Hiraya had told her last night felt like it was touched by a dream. The fog of wine and bourbon hadn't helped. But if she could see that cliff, if she could see those stairs, she'd know that it was all real. That everything Hiraya promised was grounded in hundreds of years of rituals and sacrifice. But the farther she went down the trail, the more the feeling she was being watched returned.

It was as if the house itself were watching her, sullen that she'd escaped its maw and now wandered unrestricted outside its grasp. She ignored it, and in no time at all she found the earth beneath her feet turning to mud, and she was at the broad side of the house again.

She shucked her shoes and carried them, then hitched her skirt up. But as she drew closer to the edge, she trod across a new set of footsteps pressed deep into the earth, still fresh. They led to the cliff, and to Alejandro, looking out over its edge.

His pants had been rolled up, and mud stained his ankles. He seemed out of place there. Too metropolitan for the rough ground, with his slick hair and the black cigar smoke that wreathed his head like a dark halo. Even from a distance, she could see that he was deep in thought, his hands clasped behind his back, in a pose that reminded her all too much of their father.

She slogged gracelessly toward the edge to join him. Her arrival hadn't been quiet. The ground had squelched with each of her steps, but he didn't glance at her. She let her gaze fall to the black, thin stairs, and immediately regretted it. The stairs were there, but narrow, and the fall below was unforgiving. They'd been real, after all. And now she couldn't believe that she'd ever gone down them and survived.

Neither one of them said anything for a long moment. She could feel the gulf that absence and diverging paths had dug between them.

"Gabriella's looking for you," Josephine said, breaking the silence between them.

Alejandro sighed. "I know. That's why I'm out here. She hates the mud. But even at the edge of the world, it seems like I still can't escape you."

"I'm surprised you're even out here," Josephine murmured, ignoring her brother's barb.

"I don't know why. Something about this place, the cliff. It felt like I needed to come here. But now that I'm here, all I see is that black, ugly ocean." His voice was heavy, and he flicked at his lighter, lighting another cigar.

"Those things will kill you, you know," Josephine chided.

"At least I'll die doing something nice." Alejandro chuckled, taking a long drag.

"Gabriella would hate to hear you say that. She very much wants you alive. Ideally, in Carigara." She let the comment hang in the air, but in her periphery she could see her brother flinch.

"I already told her that's not happening. I'm not going back. I can't go back," Alejandro said.

"Would it really be so bad to come back?" Josephine asked.

"That's not an option," he repeated, his voice flat, before lifting his chin toward the stairs at their feet. "What's down there?"

Josephine hesitated. It had felt like a secret when Hiraya had shown her. And while she couldn't bring herself to lie, she skirted around the truth. "It's like a chapel. One of the old, pre-Spanish ones."

"Of course they've hidden it away someplace like that. Mother told me when we were kids that the Ranocos had an old shrine. I wonder if she knew it would come to this." He sucked at his teeth, and Josephine glanced at him from the corner of her eye.

"Why would she ever think we'd come here?" Josephine asked.

"Mother was hell-bent on keeping us away from the Ranocos. She'd rage at me whenever she caught you spending time with Hiraya. As if it was my job to keep you two apart. But after she was done yelling, she'd get sad. Almost . . . resigned. As if she knew it was inevitable that you two would be inseparable. Maybe she knew we'd come here, to the Ranoco house. Maybe she knew that this was the only way I could make things right. Maybe I'm full of shit and trying to find meaning in the memories they left behind."

She knew that her mother hated the Ranocos, or at least pretended to. But her mother had never spoken to her about it, never told her why. Perhaps she'd been too young. For a brief moment, she wondered what secrets about the Ranocos her brother might know that their mother had passed along only to him.

"There's more than one way to make things right . . . It doesn't have to be in Manila. I . . . just really wish you'd come home," Josephine said, her voice quiet, nearly consumed by the waves.

He laughed and flicked at his cigar, sending a small cascade of sparks over the cliff. "Is that all you got? I thought you'd come out swinging."

Josephine's face burned. He knew just how to goad her. "Fine. Fine, if you want me to say it, I will. As insufferable as you are, I miss you. And the del Rosario house needs you. *I* need you. And I know you've been trying to build a legacy out there in Manila, but you don't need to keep chasing Father's dreams. You don't have to live under the shadow of his ghost, pretending it's him wearing your polos and slacks. You never smoked, and now you're always lighting his favorite cigars, like they're candles on a grave you haven't left behind. You aren't him and you never will be, and that's okay. So, please, please pick the future you actually want. One where you might actually find some crumb of joy, because after all these years you deserve it."

Alejandro nodded, as if that was the hit he'd been expecting. He took a slow drag of the cigar and breathed out a dark cloud of smoke. It rested along his shoulders, it cradled his hair, it stroked his cheek. He seemed to lean into it, his eyes turning half-lidded and dim. She knew even before he spoke that his mind had already been made up, and she had lost.

"I'm not going back to Carigara. Not now, anyway. Not until I've accomplished what I've set out to do. I didn't crawl through glass and filth for the past decade, fighting every step of the way, just to give up now. I'm going to win tonight's game of tagu-tagu. And when I do, I'm going to build my campaign again, and I'll aim higher than barangay council. And this time I'll win. Not for Father. But for me, and you, and our legacy."

He turned to look at her, his face solemn. "I'm proud of you, Josephine. I don't think I've said that enough. Maybe ever, actually. But you've done a good job taking care of the house for as long as you have. But it won't be your responsibility anymore. This summer, I'll be selling it to fund my campaign."

Silence and shock gagged Josephine for a moment. For a few seconds, the only sound was the crashing waves against the cliff and the quiet burning of Alejandro's cigar. And when her voice returned to her, it didn't sound like her own. It was tight and trembled in her mouth, full of disbelief.

"You—what?" she stumbled.

"Don't worry. I know you have this idea that the del Rosario legacy is that house. But it isn't. It's our actions. It's the life we live. But I know that house means a lot to you. So when I've won the election, once I've made all the money back I've lost, I'll buy it back for you."

He spoke clearly, with all the assurance of a man who'd long ago made the plan and was simply conveying a fact.

"Where will I live, then?" Josephine demanded. But even as she said it, a soft dread settled over her shoulders.

"Do you know Roberto, the doctor? He wrote me a few weeks ago, asking about you. Well, he's written more than a few times, actually. He's made it clear that he's very happy to pay a dowry, and you'd get his name, a well-established house, and the protection from Eduardo and his boys that come with it."

"You expect me to marry him?" Josephine asked, her voice dropping in disbelief. A nightmare of a life flashed before her eyes. Of white wedding dresses and silent evenings, of stilted kisses and beds that felt too full. Of aging slowly beside a man she knew she could never love. "He's fifty years old. He's a womanizer."

"He's an intellectual. Now that his late wife has passed, he needs someone to care for him. Keep the house, make sure the staff stays in line. And he likes you. He thinks you're beautiful."

"Alejandro," Josephine pleaded. "You can't be serious."

"I know you might spend the rest of your life hating me. That I've spent the past decade failing you as your older brother. But Roberto can keep you safe. For now, he can do what I can't. But when I win this game, when I come back successful, I'll make it up to you. I'll buy back our house. And I'll come back to Carigara. And we can live the lives we were always meant to. You just have to wait for me for a few more years."

He lifted his hand toward the sky, staring at the gap where his ring finger had once been. In the light of the day, she could see the rough, angled chop, the hard callus of the healed skin over the bone.

"I can't keep putting you and Gabriella at risk. I risked everything when I ran for barangay council. I risked you. I risked Gabriella. And I paid only the first drop of blood for it. When I run again, they'll do whatever they can to take the house. To hurt the people I love most. But if you're hidden away, if the house is gone, then I'm the only one they can touch. It really, truly is for the best. Even if you don't want to see it."

"There has to be another way. The people in Manila will overthrow Marcos. Gabriella can—"

Alejandro laughed, the noise a harsh bark. "No, Josephine. Gabriella *can't*. If I let Gabriella or her father throw more money at me, what do you think would happen? More debt collectors. More made-up fines. It doesn't matter how the people in Manila protest, how they scream and beg for justice. Nothing ever changes. More people will die, and Marcos's wheel of tyranny will keep on turning."

He heaved a great, heavy sigh. "It's not what you want. But you'll get a new name. A family that you can sink into, hide yourself in. And at the very least, you can live like a normal woman. With a doting husband, and children, and a house to care for."

"I don't want to marry Roberto," she retorted through a clenched jaw. She felt feverish and sick. But even as she said it, she knew that this was always the way her life was heading. Roberto had known it, too. Perhaps he'd known it the moment she'd turned twenty, and he'd been biding his time, circling her like an aged and patient vulture.

"It doesn't matter. I already accepted the dowry. The wedding's set for May, before the rainy season. I'll ask Gabriella to help prepare. She'll like that, I think. Though I think she'll hate the idea that I'm asking for a wedding for you and not her."

"You can't just accept a dowry on my behalf without asking me. You can't just marry me away like I'm a *thing* to be bartered and sold. You can't just give up."

He turned to Josephine, facing her for the first time. But Josephine couldn't bring herself to face him. She stood staunchly in the mud, facing the ocean, struggling to hold back the flood of tears.

"Josephine." He sighed, grasping her shoulders and forcing her to turn to face him. She hated the hot tears that were beading in the corners of her eyes, and she forced herself to stare at him, unblinking.

"I know you hate me now. But everything I'm doing is for the best. I'm not selling you; I'm protecting you. And I'm so far from giving up. This is the first time in years I've felt like I have a chance to make things better. And I promise you. You hate me today, but one day, we'll be in Carigara together and you'll be happy I did this."

He laid his hand on her cheek. He'd never touched her like that before. He had never been so gentle with her. She hated the foreignness of it even more. It made it feel final, and she slapped his hand away, pulling away from him.

"I won't go through with it, you know. I won't marry him," she insisted.

"The money's already spent. And I can't pay it back. They'll take the house. It's the way it has to be," Alejandro said, his voice gentle, as if she were being a child.

She turned back toward the sea. She couldn't let herself breathe. If she did, she knew she'd break down. And she didn't want him to see her like that. Not when it was so obvious that no matter how much she begged or screamed, he was never going to change his mind.

She could feel Alejandro staring at her for a long moment. She could feel the exhaustion in that gaze.

"I'm sorry it has to be this way," he said, finally. "But you'll see that this is really for the best." He turned and walked away, leaving her at the edge of the cliff.

ELEVEN

S HE stayed rooted in that spot until the mud around her ankles stung. Until insects landed on her bare arms and nibbled at her flesh, thinking her dead or perhaps just easy prey. She'd never felt so helpless, so lost. Tears streamed endlessly down her face, wetting the collar of her blouse. They blurred her vision, turning everything gauzy and dreamlike.

If she lost this game, if she listened to Alejandro, she could see the way her future would unravel. She'd go back to Carigara, to Roberto. She'd be swept into his arms and into his house, where she'd spend her life in an unending cycle of bed, kitchen, market. Perhaps she'd skirt by without a child to show for it if she was lucky. If God and the angels all smiled down on her and let her escape into the grave unscathed. Roberto was old; his sons and daughters were all her age. But even old men could sometimes spit in the face of biology and good sense.

I can't live like that. I won't.

She needed to win. She couldn't let Alejandro take the del Rosario house and sell it, as if it were nothing more than walls and wood. She couldn't let him take her future.

She followed her brother's footsteps, walking beside them, refusing to let hers overlap with his. She didn't want to touch him, not even this trace of him. With every step, her heart splintered and crumbled with bitter grief.

The earth beneath her feet firmed, but Alejandro's step shot off, past the front door, headed toward the other side of the house. She watched them vanish, trying to see if she could see the shadow of Alejandro in the distance. But the encroaching balete trees had already consumed him, their darkness shielding him from her view.

Exhausted and filthy, she stepped inside, almost relieved to be enshrouded in the house's walls. The daylight and fresh air no longer had any charm for her, but the foyer offered no direction or purpose.

When she'd left Carigara, she hadn't expected her life to spiral so far out of her own hands. She'd thought she'd come here and wrangle her brother home. That she'd somehow convince him to leave his life in Manila behind and come back to the del Rosario house. Now, in the darkness of the house, she felt stupidly naïve.

If she lost this game, the rest of her life would be carved in a stone that would mark her grave.

JOSEPHINE UY.
WIFE OF DOCTOR ROBERTO UY.
MOTHER.

And nothing else. Her identity before him would be erased, consumed by his accomplishments and her new matrimonial role.

She needed to win. And to do that, she needed to understand the game, this house.

She stood at the center of the room she was in and breathed deep. Hiraya had already given them some inkling of what to expect. Tagu-tagu was a game of hide-and-seek played only at night. But in this version, the four of them would be split into two pairs. Each pair would have the aswang and the prey. The aswang's role would be to hunt down the prey through the house, and the prey's role would be to elude the aswang until dawn.

It was an easy enough concept, but success would be dictated by luck and knowledge of the countless rooms and corridors. She couldn't let things boil down to luck. She had to be proactive.

And there was so much about this house to learn. Everything she'd learned from Hiraya felt incomplete, as if the Ranoco girl was showing her only a glimpse into the secrets of the house and her family. Sidapa was even more secretive, and Josephine shuddered to remember her staring at her down the hall the night before. If that figure in the blackness had even been Sidapa.

She'd use what little time she had left to unravel the Ranoco house the best she could. Starting with the nearest room. She pushed open the door and took stock of it. Old antique furniture stood gathering dust, pressed against the walls. Chairs, end tables, piles of upturned lanterns, discarded in a pile on the floor. She could see bits of shattered glass among the debris, which had been pushed to the side instead of cleaned up. A cemetery beetle scuttled over the shards, unperturbed by their sharpness. Faint scratches and scuffs covered the floors and walls, but that was an almost constant theme in this house.

Josephine opened the next door, trying to add it to the catalog of her memory. A lounge, a bedroom, another storage room. She went through each one, trying to commit them to her internal image of the map.

And yet she was startled when the next door opened into another great hall. An aorta of the house, with a dirty blue carpet runner extending down the length of it. The carpet marked her place as somewhere in the Ranoco family hall.

Josephine hesitated and glanced at the doors on either side of the hall. There'd been many, many women in this house, if Hiraya's story was anything to go by. But one of them was surely Hiraya's.

Her heart twisted and softened and filled with want. If there was one solitary place she could find comfort in the wake of her brother's declaration, it was in Hiraya's arms. Hiraya, who had never been bound to the conventions of traditional society, who scoffed at the idea of marriage, would know all the right things to put her at ease. Or at least make her feel like she wasn't alone and doomed.

Gently, she tried a knob along the hall. Locked. So was the next, and the next. But perhaps that was no surprise. These were the personal rooms of the Ranoco women. She'd be intruding, it'd be beyond rude to just barge in. And yet . . .

The next knob she tried jiggled, and slowly it turned. She hesitated before she pushed the door open. She really, really shouldn't.

"Hiraya?" Josephine called quietly. There was no answer within, and she pushed the door in farther.

It was a bedroom, larger than the one Hiraya had given her. Across from the door was a large open window that overlooked the cliffside, with a view that looked all too familiar. It only took her a moment to realize that this was the bedroom beneath hers.

The walls here were made of teak, a sultry orange-brown. But where the rest of the house felt like an old spiderweb spattered with hollowed-out swathing bands of silk, full of clutter and dust, this room was immaculate. Not a hint of dirt, no undue mess. The bed with its thin mattress was neatly made. Against the wall was a rough portrait of the island the house sat on. The island itself was distant, as if the painter had envisioned it far away, a distant memory. She'd endured enough tutors as a child to recognize an untaught hand, but it was clear that there was passion in the stroke, a raw talent that could have been nurtured if the artist had been raised anywhere but this rock sequestered from the rest of the world.

Josephine stepped inside the room, taking stock of it. It *smelled* of Hiraya. That sweet, floral, earthy scent. Santol and honey. What would it be like to lie in Hiraya's bed? What would it be like to lay her head where Hiraya laid hers, and dream the same dreams the Ranoco girl did?

She couldn't let herself think on it. Instead she drifted toward the vanity. It sat against the wall, so its mirror offered a full view of the room, but what drew Josephine to it was the photograph pushed into the edge where the mirror met wood.

The photograph's colors were dull, the image grainy, but she knew the moment in time precisely. It was of her, Gabriella, Alejandro, and Hiraya, sitting in the Sacred Heart school courtyard. They were grinning at a camera the nun had wielded all those years ago, their hands wrapped around lunch, practically swimming in school uniforms that were too large for them. They'd been so young then. So happy. It comforted Josephine to know that this brief blip in time, those fast, young years, had meant just as much to Hiraya as it had to her. There were no pictures of her family, of Sidapa, Tadhana, or her mother on the vanity.

The rest of the vanity was scattered with golden jewelry that looked decades old. Each piece glistened as if oiled. But beside them were pressed flowers and a stack of unused paper that Josephine recognized as the same type that had been sent to her with Hiraya's invitation.

Half a dozen balls of parchment were in the bin beside the vanity, crumpled and tossed away. But she could see her name written on one of the sheets. Gingerly, feeling guilty, Josephine plucked the paper from the bin.

It read:

Dear Josephine,

I miss you more than words can describe. I often think of you and wonder if you think of me, though I suppose you'd be better off if you didn't. I know you are deeply unhappy, as am I. I think we could save each other from our twin miseries. Even though you have no reason to come, even though it might put you in grave danger, it would mean the world to me if you would. Please save me. Please let me save you.

The letter remained unfinished, but she recognized it immediately. It was an early draft of the succinct letter that Hiraya had sent her. But the desperation in it had turned the script heavy, the loops dark and thick.

"What in the world do you mean, Hiraya?" Josephine whispered.

Behind her, the door creaked. Josephine glanced into the mirror, her heart leaping into her mouth at being caught. But the face in the crack in the door wasn't Hiraya's. It was a black face covered in cascading hair.

Sidapa.

The door clicked shut, and Josephine jolted toward the door after her.

Last night, she was certain it'd been Sidapa who was staring at her from down the hall. It'd been Sidapa who had led her to the room of dolls. She was sure of it now. Sidapa knew something.

Josephine threw open the next door just in time to see the door at the end of the hall close. The door was unlike the rest in the Ranoco family hall. It was made of dark, heavy wood. The edges of it seemed to be scorched, and she could almost taste the faded stench of something burnt. She licked her lips, tasting the residue of an old fire. A heavy padlock lay on the floor beside the door, cast away like an afterthought. Once it had kept this room closed. For a brief moment she hesitated outside the door as warning bells rang in the back of her head. There was a *reason* why they'd kept this lock on the door. But she was so sick and tired of half-truths, of hints and meaningful pauses. Of having to read between the lines. And she'd drag the answer out of Sidapa.

She pushed open the door and stepped inside, steeling herself to finally confront the younger Ranoco sister. But Sidapa was nowhere in sight.

It was a room as big as the bedroom Hiraya had given her, its ceiling low enough she could have stood on tiptoes to grab the rafters if she stretched. But unlike the rest of the rooms that filled the Ranoco house, the rafters were unpolished and raw. Between these pillars of wood were all sorts of magpie knickknacks and heathen fetishes, tied there with ragged strips of cloth and twine. Amulets, the glossy gold melded into strange shapes. Old herbs tied into bundles, the leaves covered in fungus and mold. Wasps' nests, the paper torn open to reveal cells stuffed full of beads and colorful glass.

This room of fetishes didn't disturb her, though they were strange and ungodly. It was what lay beneath them that sent her skin crawling. A terrible fire had blackened half the room. Greasy soot coated every part of the back wall and most of the floor, reaching up toward the rafters. The trinkets that had hung there had been burned away, leaving nothing but a void behind, as if the black maw had consumed them in some ugly sacrifice. There was no furniture to speak of at all, save for metal cuffs driven into the floor, clearly meant to bind someone's ankles and wrists in place, pinning them to the ground.

The door behind her shut slowly, clicking into place with a somber finality. But Josephine didn't turn around. She could hear Sidapa breathing inches behind her, her breath irregular and strained. It'd been silent a moment ago—she was certain that Sidapa wouldn't have had the time to bridge the gap. And yet there she unmistakably was, just feet from her. The sound of her ragged breaths mingled with the buzz of flies, and Josephine realized the room crawled with insects. Beetles scuttled along the cracks in the tiles. Flies drew halos along the rafters. She could feel their countless eyes on her, watching.

"You're such an idiot, Josephine. I begged you to stay away. And here you are, in my room. Why couldn't you stay away?" Sidapa exhaled. Her breath rattled as if she was trying to loosen her voice from her chest. Even speaking seemed to pain her.

"Sidapa?" Josephine asked. The name trembled on her lips.

Sidapa ignored the question, but Josephine could feel her edging closer. The only light in the room was a lantern near the door. Its dim glow turned Sidapa's silhouette long and reaching, its blackness mingling with Josephine's shadow, consuming it. Sidapa was so close, but Josephine couldn't bring herself to face her.

She didn't want to see her face.

Josephine wet her lips with her tongue. She swallowed hard. "It's not really a bedroom, is it?" There was no bed here. Or, if there was, it'd long since been burned away.

"No, it isn't," Sidapa answered, and took another step closer, her feet dragging on the floor.

"It's a prison," Josephine said, her shoulders tight and square. "It's a cell."

"Yes," Sidapa said.

"Why would anyone keep you here? Why would someone lock you away?" Josephine pressed, and again Sidapa paused. She was closer now. But the question seemed to light something in Sidapa's chest. A bitter anger.

"Because they wanted to make me their heir. Because I failed to kill Tadhana and my mother in that fire all those years ago. So they brought me here. Into this room. Into this cell. Before I was too strong to escape and try again."

Josephine shook her head. The memory of that night, the fear in Hiraya's eyes, the blisters on Sidapa's fingers, flashed through Josephine's mind. She'd been certain that it'd been a hateful, religious zealot who'd torched the Ranoco house in Carigara. But it'd been small, mousy Sidapa who'd set the blaze.

"I would have killed to have the life you have outside these walls. Why are you even here, Josephine? *Why?*" Sidapa demanded.

Josephine didn't have an answer for her. At least not one she knew Sidapa would like. "Why don't you leave, then? Why don't you just go? You and Hiraya both, you act like you're stuck here . . . but there are boats. You can see the mainland from the shore. It's a mile away at most."

Sidapa exhaled and rasped, and it took Josephine a moment to realize it was a bitter laugh. "Leave? *Leave?* Christ, you idiot. Do you think I'd be here, in this maze of insect-riddled halls, if I could leave? I spent a year of my life in those chains at your feet. Do you think I had a choice?

"I hurt my mother badly. But she was still strong enough to keep me here for the last year of her life. She was strong enough to feed me the raw meat from the kitchen, slathered in the honey she had Hiraya steal from the bees that nest in the balete trees. Did you know, Josephine, the bees here don't make honey? Not the way they do in Carigara. The bees on this island feed on carrion. They vomit the meat up in their nests and mingle their honey with it to create a sort of sour paste. Bloodied meat and sour, rotten honey—that's all I ate for a year. Until my hunger was a prison."

A wave of nausea rolled through Josephine's stomach. She'd seen the fat, ugly bees on the island. She'd watched Alejandro and Gabriella slather honey onto mangoes, lick it from their fingers. But now, at least, Sidapa's emaciated body made sense. They'd been starving her for a year. How could a mother do that to their child? How could Hiraya let it happen? Did she know Sidapa was in this prison of a room the entire time?

"Why would Tadhana and your mother torture you like that?" Josephine murmured. "How could they?"

"Oh, do you think they worked alone? That Hiraya is completely innocent? Don't let your crush make you so stupid. She brought me all those trinkets in the rafters. The bottles of oil, the golden amulets with clumsy protection spells. Shiny things, interesting things. Things she thought I might like to look at while I was chained to the floor. But when Tadhana demanded she hold my head down so she could pry out my eyes, Hiraya did it."

A finger dragged itself along Josephine's back. The skin caught on the cloth of the blouse, tugging at it roughly.

"No," Josephine protested. "She wouldn't. Not Hiraya."

Josephine breathed through her mouth. Everything smelled of smoke, of burning hair, of charred meat. She couldn't even conceive of what Sidapa was telling her. She'd seen the damage done to Hiraya's eye. Hiraya even admitted it'd been Tadhana who'd done it to her. But would Hiraya really do the same thing to someone else? To her own little sister, who'd spent her childhood clinging to Hiraya's skirts, chasing along in her shadow?

"She would. She did. And now she thinks she can escape by playing the game, by following the rules. And she's tricked you into thinking you can escape, too. That there's a happily-ever-after waiting for you with the dawn. But there isn't. This house doesn't play fair."

A long pause stretched between the two of them, and Sidapa seemed to struggle with herself for a moment. Her soft voice found a hardened edge, as if the memory still wounded her.

"I refuse to play the game anymore. I tried to escape once, thinking that death would set me free. I set myself on fire and burned there against the wall. And still, *still* it wasn't enough. Because here I am. The spirits refuse to let me go. I am the matriarch until another succeeds. But you, Josephine, you might end this misery once and for all. If you refuse to play by the rules. If you listen to me for once, and not my sister."

Josephine stared at the blackened floor, the pale outline of what might have been a body, a little lighter than the rest. The smell of burning that had followed her through the house—it had all come from this place. Her mind reeled. She couldn't accept a single thing Sidapa had said.

"Are you dead?" Josephine whispered. Her mind was static. She could feel Sidapa at her back. She could taste the smoke that rolled off her. She could almost see her blackened fingertips, twitching at her hair.

There was no answer. The heavy presence at her back fell away, and the room felt emptier. She hesitated before turning around. The spot where Sidapa had stood was smeared by soot-coated footprints. Blackened handprints covered the door and knob, thick and stinking of smoke. Josephine squeezed her eyes shut, relief washing over her in a wave.

She was here. She was really here. But how much of what she said was true? Did Hiraya really hold her down? Did she really die here?

Even as she thought it, she knew in the pit of her stomach that it was true. She fled the room, desperate to escape the lingering smell of burning and misery, her head tangling over dozens of unanswered questions. She needed to talk to Hiraya.

TWELVE

THE farther she wandered from the rooms, the more the stench
of smoke fell away from her. The soot that stained her clothes
dimmed and grayed until it vanished completely, as if it had never
been there at all. She rubbed at where the spots had been, as if she
could bring them back.

"She was there. I know she was there. I didn't imagine it," Josephine muttered to herself. From the cracks in the tiles, insects
with black, intelligent eyes watched her. Mocking her strained
voice, her gritted teeth. She ignored them. *She'd seen Sidapa in that
terrible room.* She was certain of it.

The Ranoco house was more than just a maze. It was a Japanese
puzzle box, and each secret she uncovered only seemed to reveal a
dozen other new ugly questions. What was the grave danger that
Hiraya had tried to warn her about in her discarded letters? Why

had Sidapa been chained up for a year and forced to endure that gruesome ritual? How much was Hiraya hiding from her?

Was this the reason why her mother hated the Ranocos, why she had been desperate to keep her from Hiraya? To shield her from the truth of what they did to those chosen daughters? Or was it something else entirely?

As much as it wounded her to think it, she was certain that Hiraya would have held her sister's head down. She'd seen the pained reverence with which Hiraya regarded the bone tree in the altar room. But how much further would Hiraya go?

She prodded at her own face, sinking fingertips into the shallow fat of her cheek. She clawed and massaged at her own temples, then worked her fingertips into the roots of her hair. Nothing felt real. Her own body felt ephemeral and dreamlike. And yet she had skin. She had flesh. She had hair. A nagging voice in the back of her head rolled over the possibility that she might be insane.

Not for the first time had she thought she was losing her grip on reality. There'd been long stretches of days, perhaps even months, when she wandered the empty rooms of her family house, feeling like she, too, had died on the day they massacred her family.

Delving deep into the house, Josephine worked through each room until she found the main foyer. The windows were open to let in the warm light, and she leaned against the first one she could find, inhaling a chestful of fresh air. She gasped and chewed on each breath as if she were drowning.

The morning had given way to midafternoon, and in her absence, the pretty blue had dulled to a weathered pale gray. Clouds formed on the far-off horizon, over the heavy boughs of the balete trees, thick with the potential for rain.

But as she stared out into the sky, her gaze avoiding the trees, she felt a desperate itch to find Hiraya. She needed Hiraya to parse out what was fact and what was fiction. To pin her down and demand full, unbridled honesty. No more half-truths or little omissions.

From down the hall came the heavy sounds of knives on wood and metal scraping against metal. Dinner was being prepared; the soft cacophony of its making competed with the birdsong and the croak of unknown insects.

The kitchen—at least someone would be there. Someone who could point her in Hiraya's direction. Josephine released her grip on the windowsill. She followed the dingy golden carpet toward the servants' wing, guided by both it and the sound of cooking.

Both led her to a heavy door at the end of the hall. Josephine tried the handle, but it didn't budge. That made sense, she supposed. Perhaps they didn't want guests underfoot while they made dinner. She knocked, knuckles rapping hard against the wood. "Excuse me? Is Hiraya there?" she called.

The rhythmic sound of chopping ceased and was followed by rustling that, even through the door, sounded irritated. "No. Go away," a male voice said. The sound of chopping resumed.

"Um, excuse me? I just wanted to see—"

"I'm making dinner. Christ, always people banging on my door. Week after week, just pounding. Do I need to repeat myself? I'm busy," the man shouted, irritation bleeding through his voice. The sound of his chopping grew heavier, more aggressive.

Josephine gaped at the door, the dread that had dogged her momentarily replaced by indignation. "Well, excuse *me*. Sorry to disturb you," she muttered, turning from the kitchen, wearing the offense on her face. She couldn't blame him for not wanting to entertain her, but would it have killed him to at least open the door and reject her to her face?

And yet his gruffness soothed her. It was an anchor in all this madness. Something human and real. She wasn't alone. That rude man was here, too.

But as she turned down the corridor leading toward the banquet hall, she found Alejandro instead, peering at a painting of the jungle that surrounded the house, its focal point a balete tree and a woman lying among its roots. Josephine paused at the threshold, frozen in place as a love song crooned over a radio in a nearby room. Alejandro held the remains of the cigar between his fingers, the ash falling to the floor, its herbal scent filling the hall. A day ago, she would have been relieved to see him here. She'd spent years wanting to see him, to have to make idle chatter. But the wound he'd left her on the cliff still throbbed, and she clutched instinctually at her blouse, forcing her fist into her heart, as if that might stymie the sudden pain.

"Are you lost?" he asked, taking another drag from the cigar. He didn't look at her.

It took her a moment to find her voice. Even looking at him was hard. But still, she found herself stepping toward him. He was still her brother, even if he meant to marry her off. He was still her family, and he felt safe and familiar in this strange house with its stranger secrets.

"No, I was going to the dining room to find Hiraya." She left out the questions she wanted to ask. She wasn't certain if she was sane yet, and she didn't need Alejandro questioning it, too.

"Ah. It's a little early to eat, isn't it? Though you must be hungry. You've scarcely eaten anything since you've arrived."

His voice was soft, as if the conversation earlier hadn't happened at all. He laid his free hand on his stomach and sighed. "Maybe that's for the best. I think last night's dinner turned my stomach. I've been feeling sick for hours now. Like something's crawling around my gut."

"Ah," Josephine murmured, her shoulders rounding. An instinctual familial concern washed over her before she could quash it. "Have you tried tea yet? I'm sure the butlers will bring you some."

"I hate the butlers and maids," Alejandro muttered, and took another long drag of his cigar.

Josephine chuckled. That little tender spot in her heart twisted. It seemed that even after all this time, he could still make her laugh, just like when they were children. "They're awful, aren't they?"

"Creepy little ghouls skittering all over the place. Worse than the bugs." Alejandro grimaced, and then a thin smile broke out over his mouth, as if he could feel that old fondness, too. They held each other's gaze. This moment—Josephine knew that this moment could mean something. She might bridge the gap that had been growing between them since their parents died. She might convince him to come back home and at least try a life where they were once again family, not beholden to fear or the lofty goals their parents cast on them, even in death.

"Alejandro—"

But Alejandro interrupted her, as if he'd expected her gambit. "If you're looking for Hiraya, she's with Tadhana. But she told me we'll be having an early dinner before the game starts."

"Oh," Josephine said, the hopeful sentence dying on her lips. Alejandro nodded, and she could see him closing off. His body tightened, and the light in his eyes dimmed. The brief moment was lost.

Josephine mirrored his nod and tried not to feel her heart sinking. "I see. Have you seen Tadhana, then? I haven't seen her since we arrived."

"No, and I'm honestly glad I haven't. She was creepy when we were kids and I somehow doubt that time added anything to her charms. Have you thought more about what we discussed? A season, perhaps, for the wedding. The colors, the venue. I'm sure Roberto would be happy to let you take the reins. He'd honestly probably prefer it."

"Because he's done it all before," Josephine retorted, saying what her brother wouldn't. Her hands flexed at her sides, and it was only through substantial effort that she kept them from balling into fists. "I don't want to marry him. There has to be another way."

Alejandro sighed and turned away from her, back to the painting. He took a deep drag of his cigar and let the smoke fill the air, haloing his head in a thin gray mist. With his free hand he massaged his temple, as if talking with her was giving him a migraine.

Josephine rolled her eyes at his back. She was so sick of him treating her like an inconvenience. As if she were still his little sister instead of a grown, intelligent woman capable of making her own decisions.

"I wish you could see that this is all in your best interest, Josephine. You might not be happy, but at least you'll be safe. And the sooner you accept the situation, the better. You can kick and scream and throw all the tantrums you like. But this is happening."

Josephine swallowed, indignation and anger building in her chest. She chose her words carefully in case there was still some chance she could salvage this. She hated his attitude but, still, she was sure there was a way to mend the bridge he seemed hell-bent on burning. "There has to be another way, Alejandro. With the protests in the street, there's a chance Marcos—"

He lifted his hand, cutting her off. His face had darkened into a scowl, and Josephine relented. The mere idea that the people might succeed, that the Philippines might change for the better, seemed to enrage him. Tender pity twisted her heart. Marcos and his cronies had broken her brother so badly that he couldn't even entertain the idea of hope.

She let a fraction of vulnerability soften her voice, and she stepped toward him, out of the safety of the doorway. "Please come home for a few months. Not even a year. I'm not asking you to give up on your dreams. I just . . . miss you. I barely see you."

But her words seemed to roll off him as if she were a stranger to him. "I can't. Just stepping foot in Carigara—it's like admitting defeat. I can't."

"Please, Alejandro," Josephine repeated, her words firming. "You have to see that this isn't healthy for you. Trust me, for once. Give me a chance to show you that there *is* hope. That things can be better. You can't let Eduardo run you out of your own town forever."

It'd been only a few hours since she'd last seen Alejandro, outside the house. But in that short time, a sickly pallor had fallen over him. A sheen of sweat had broken out over his face. His hands shook, and the cigar in his hand twitched like an angry, dying sun.

"Josephine. This isn't a discussion. It's not a debate. And the faster you understand that, the faster you accept it, the happier you'll be." He pronounced each word fully, quietly. The cigar burned close to his fingers, dripping fire-flaked ash at his feet. But he didn't seem to feel the heat. He turned to face her.

"Do you think it's been easy shouldering all of this? Maneuvering our family through the absolute carnage our parents left for us? I've killed myself trying to become a man that Father would be proud of. Someone who could protect you. I've risked everything trying to carve out a place of justice, of integrity. I've broken myself on the wheel for the smallest scrap. And what have I gotten for it? A mangled hand, an empty bank account, and a sister who won't do as she's told."

He gritted his teeth and pressed the cigar against the wall, crushing out the flame before letting the butt fall to the floor. He hadn't raised his voice at all, and yet each word seemed to fill the hall.

She should have recoiled, and he seemed to expect her to. But she stared at him, her breath caught in her throat. And yet, as anger and resentment boiled in her stomach, she snapped back. "I know what you've lost, and I'm sorry. But that doesn't mean I should be damned to live my life at your whim. I deserve more than that, and I refuse—"

"So where will you go when the house is sold? Because the house *is* being sold, whether you like it or not," Alejandro retorted.

"I'll—" Josephine stammered, "I'll stay here. I'll stay with Hiraya. She invited me to stay here for as long as I like."

"You'll stay with that witch over my dead body," Alejandro spat, his mouth twisting in disgust.

In the background, the soft, melancholy love song had ended. The garbled voice of the radio host cut in and out, and the room filled with a voice that made Josephine's blood run cold in her veins.

President Ferdinand Marcos, his voice tinny and full of fury as he lambasted his detractors and the rebel troops. "*My political opponents are saying that the president is incapable of enforcing the law. They repeat that once more and I will sic the tanks and the artillery on them. We'll wipe them out,*" Marcos promised. "*If they think I am sick, I may even want to lead the troops to wipe out these rebel groups. I can tell you I am as strong as ever. I am just like an old warhorse smelling powder and getting stronger.*"

The recording cut off, followed by the chatter of the radio hosts, speaking fast about the latest statement from the president. Josephine flinched. Hundreds of miles away, and Marcos was still ruining her life.

"Goddamn him. Goddamn you. Why can't you understand that I'm only trying to do what's best for you?" Alejandro asked. "Don't you hear what he's saying? Whether you want to admit it or not, Marcos has waged war on us. We are *always* a foot away from that open grave he put our parents into. And every time I try to save you, you spit in my face. What more do I need to sacrifice, Josephine, before you understand what's at stake? How much more of myself do I need to peel away before you realize I'm trying to *help you*?" His voice reached the rafters; each word he spoke came with a rain of spittle.

"I couldn't help but overhear. I'm not interrupting, am I?" Hiraya stood in the doorway opposite them, fully made up, her hair braided high, her lips painted red. Her gaze slipped between Josephine and Alejandro, the edges of her mouth lifting into a smile that was equal parts intrigued and amused.

Alejandro dragged his hand through his hair with a sigh, trying to tame the rage on his face, the resentment and bitterness in his eyes. But there was no bringing back the charm he'd inherited from his father.

"No, no. Just a little argument between siblings. I hope we didn't disturb you?" He glanced at Josephine, and she knew he was trying to goad her into apologizing as well. But she remained stony and silent, glaring at him, and Hiraya waved away his apology.

"No worries. That isn't the first scream this house has heard, and I doubt it'll be the last. Besides, Josephine's quite right. I'd love for her to stay. And I promise not to initiate her into the Ranoco coven. Unless she wants to be initiated, of course."

Relief swept through Josephine at the assertion. Hiraya hadn't just been making hollow promises in the moonlight with a wine-drunk tongue. She'd meant it. She'd really meant it.

Hiraya glanced toward Josephine, her head tilting, her mouth twisting into a vulpine smirk. She strode across the hall and looped an affectionate, familial arm around Josephine's waist. Her hand came to settle at her hip, and Josephine felt a chill run down the length of her spine. That hand might have held Sidapa down by the temples. It might have done so much more.

"Marcos has no sway here. She'll be safe, and she'll be treated like one of the family," Hiraya chirped, as if she couldn't feel Josephine stiffening beside her.

Alejandro stared at Hiraya; his bloodshot eyes narrowed, and his face twitched.

"She will *never* be a Ranoco," Alejandro said, each syllable dripping venom as the anger crept back into his face.

"Oh, why not? It's no different than taking some random man's name, is it? At least she likes me," Hiraya said. Josephine's brows rose. Had Hiraya been eavesdropping all this time, around some unseen corner? How could she possibly know about the conversation she'd had with Alejandro by the cliffside?

"I would rather die than take Roberto's name," Josephine said, steeling herself, holding her brother's gaze. She didn't know what secrets Hiraya held, what terrible things she'd done. But she knew she'd rather be here, with her, than with Roberto. And at least she could escape the Ranoco house. She could find a job and save up enough money to take back the house that her brother was all too willing to sell.

"It's not your choice. And after this game, Josephine, I'm taking you back to Carigara. I don't care if I have to drag you," Alejandro pronounced. His veins bulged in his temples. He seemed so unlike the man he'd been on the cliff, as if he were someone else entirely.

Hiraya sighed. "Oh, don't be so stubborn. Perhaps it won't even matter. Perhaps you'll win, Alejandro, and this whole conversation will be moot. Shall we make our way to the banquet hall? Gabriella will be there shortly."

Without another word, Hiraya led Josephine by the waist out the door. Alejandro, after a long pause, followed them. His feet dragging on the carpet, his gaze burned holes into Josephine's back. Beside Josephine, Hiraya seemed to delight in the hatred she'd inspired. She hummed a low tune as they maneuvered through the halls. As if everything she'd hoped for was going perfectly to plan.

THIRTEEN

THEY arrived in the banquet hall, the air around them still choked and stiff. But that eased once the doors opened to a new height of decadence. Hiraya had spared no expense or effort this late afternoon. Fragrant garlands stretched across the table, mingling the scent of sampaguita flowers with the heady aromas of meat, fruit, and wine.

Hiraya led them toward the table, and Josephine allowed a servant to seat her, her body rigid with the awkwardness of the ritual. Across the table, Hiraya stared at her. Her face was no longer smug but serene, and Josephine stared back. There were ten thousand questions she wanted to ask her.

But now wasn't the time to ask. They weren't alone. Tadhana sat at the end of the grand table, her gnarled hands folded and resting on its glossy surface. Time had been exceptionally cruel to her. She was no older than Josephine's mother and should have been only fifty. But she looked now to be in her late eighties. A bright red shawl was laid around her thin shoulders, meticulously woven with geometric patterns that had managed to survive Spanish influence.

Once she'd been a strong, stout woman with an intelligent, expressive mouth and a hardened jaw and handsome cheekbones that Hiraya shared. Now Tadhana's lower jaw slanted high, betraying the teeth she'd lost. Her meager hair lay in lank gray streaks across the soft, liver-spotted skin of her scalp. She was no longer the woman that Josephine's mother might once have loved.

Tadhana smiled down the table at her, and Josephine disliked the look immensely. She could only think of Sidapa's face and Sidapa's dark, soot-stained room.

"There the del Rosario siblings are. How you've grown and grayed. I hope you've found our home to your liking," Tadhana purred.

Josephine hesitated and instinctually glanced at Alejandro. Her brother was pale, his collar damp and heavy with sweat. He didn't seem inclined to answer. During the short walk from the corridor to the banquet hall he had deteriorated to a frightening degree, and he listed forward, leaning toward the table.

Tadhana chuckled, her smile losing its edge. "Don't be so demure with me. Not today of all days."

The door opened, and a flurry of skirts announced Gabriella rushing through the door. Like Alejandro, she was pale, with a sheen on her forehead as if she'd been ill. Was it morning sickness, Josephine wondered, or the same bug that had gotten to Alejandro?

"I'm sorry, am I late?" Gabriella asked.

"Gabriella, there you are, my darling. Already wilting, I see. What a shame, what a shame," Tadhana chirped.

"Aunt Tadhana. What a surprise. I didn't think we'd see you

tonight," Gabriella stammered, her face reddening beneath her makeup.

"Oh, I couldn't miss tonight. A fine feast. Finer company. And, of course, the ascension of my young niece, who will finally take the role of the Ranoco family matriarch."

Josephine winced. She didn't like the way Tadhana spoke about Hiraya as though she were a chess piece she could move. Tadhana tilted her head as if she could see Josephine's grimace.

"Little Josephine. Even without eyes, I can tell you're just like your mother. I can sense you have her stubbornness. You see what you want and you go after it," Tadhana murmured, the dark, empty sockets of her eyes fixated on her. "You've even chosen her chair. As you get older, you'll see that everything runs in circles."

"I'm my mother's child. But I'm very much my own person," Josephine retorted.

"Oh? I suppose that's true," Tadhana said, and grinned. "I suppose we'll see just how different you are."

More dishes came through the opposite doors with each passing moment, ferried by veiled servants. Soon the feast had been fully laid out, at least twice the size of the night before. A large, soft lechon was set in the center of the table, with two petite bodies on either side. *Piglets of the sow,* Josephine thought grimly.

Tadhana nodded. "There we are. What a fine feast our chef has made. I'm happy you three have joined us in our home. And I'm beyond thrilled that you would join us tonight in a tradition that extends back centuries."

"It's early for dinner, isn't it? It's still light out," Josephine said.

Tadhana laughed, the wrinkles scoring her leathery face deepening with the movement. "The game begins the moment the sun sinks and may go as far as dawn. You'll be thankful that your stomachs are full before the end of the night, I promise you." She lifted her hands toward the grand spread.

"Please, eat. We offer you the bounties of this island. The flesh, the fruit, the honey, the wine. Everything born of this soil," Tadhana said.

Hiraya was the first to pluck from the spread, tearing off a generous section of skin from the fattened lechon at its center. Alejandro followed next, cutting into the white skin beneath, his knife sinking deep. Despite his sickly pallor, he cut a generous chunk from the sow's piglet.

Josephine tore her eyes away. It was hard to focus with that thing in front of her, but the same thoughts kept rolling through her head. Had Tadhana really bound Sidapa in that terrible place? Had Hiraya really held her down while her eyes were torn out?

"Is Sidapa going to join us for dinner, then? Since it's a special night," Josephine said, her voice shaking. She needed to know the truth.

Tadhana chuckled and popped a succulent piece of meat between her lips. "No, I don't think so. She's dead. Has been dead now, oh, seven years? Isn't that right, Hiraya?"

Hiraya stared at the food in front of her, her head bowed. Josephine couldn't see her face, but she could see the way her shoulders were hunched and squared.

Josephine's body turned rigid in her seat, and her gaze flitted between Tadhana and Hiraya. "She's dead?" she repeated. "How?" She forced her face into a mask of surprise, as if this were the first time she'd heard the news.

"Killed herself. Poof, right up in flames. A selfish waste. Years were spent preparing her to inherit the house and all its duties. And so it all fell to Hiraya."

A wave of cold certainty washed over Josephine. So it was true. Everything Sidapa had said was true. Tadhana had ripped out her eyes, and Hiraya had held her down. But if a family could be so cruel they'd starve their sister, their niece, and tear out her eyes, what would they do to friends? To her?

Hiraya straightened her back, and when she looked up at the table it was clear that she'd curated a perfectly obedient mask. But Josephine could still see the tendons popping in her neck as if she wanted to scream. Instead, Hiraya's hand flitted to the pocked skin near her eyes. "I'm not fully suited to it, though." She smiled, but it didn't reach her intact eye.

"No, no. We could only take one eye. And even then, the spirits didn't much care for Hiraya. Won't bend to her, barely whisper to her. Sidapa, though. She was strong. But we make do." Tadhana nodded sagely, though she wore the disappointment unabashedly on her face.

"You . . . took it intentionally?" Gabriella demanded, her mouth falling open. "You blinded her intentionally?"

"It's no different from circumcision, tattooing, piercing. A bit of modification, and all for the best. To improve the function of the body," Tadhana retorted.

"What could you possibly improve? She's *blind* in one eye," Gabriella said. "It's demented. It's *cruel*."

"It's not," Hiraya replied, her voice quiet but firm. "I did what had to be done. And it's over now."

"Blindness is inherent to our practice," Tadhana explained. "It makes that practice stronger. Connects us to the other world. To the black winds that are rooted in this house's many corners. It allows us to perform miracles. When this is over, Hiraya will fully inherit the role and the last eye will go. And then she will truly be ready to succeed me."

Josephine caught the smallest flinch on Hiraya's face, but it smoothed away quickly, as if Hiraya was terrified that Tadhana might see even a hint of weakness or doubt.

"You can't take both of her eyes. Just so she can commune with a spirit? It's ludicrous," Gabriella said, her voice sharp. Her gaze swung toward Josephine and Alejandro, demanding an ally.

"It's how it's done, Ms. Santos," Tadhana stated, her voice hardening. "It's how the games can be played at all. Otherwise, it's all for naught. And you wouldn't have come here if you didn't believe your wish could come true."

Tadhana leaned back in her chair. "For centuries, the Ranoco women have worked our craft in this house. Here we found a refuge from those who hated and hunted us. And we've only known this peace because of the Engkanto we are bound to." She lifted her hand broadly, sweeping outward, as if encompassing the house and the land it sat on.

"Our Engkanto, the spirit of this island, has given us everything we could have ever wanted. Our daughters are beautiful and cunning. We've never wanted for anything. The earth is fertile and tender, and we are never, ever hungry. And in return, we offer the Engkanto a parade of sacrifices. Our servitude, our sight. But the best of those offerings is this game.

"You can call me crazy all you like, little Miss Santos. You can spit on my feet, like your mother did when you were just a child, when she was teaching you to hate me. But this is the nature of the house, the nature of our family." Gabriella glared at the old woman, but she clenched her jaw, holding her tongue.

In silence they began to eat, and the mountain of food at the center of the table began to fall apart. The lechon reduced itself to bones, the vegetables and fruits mere scraps and puddles of soy sauce and vinegar, pink and yellow pools of juice. The oceans of rice trickled to thin alabaster rivers.

"Josephine, you don't care for meat, do you?" Tadhana asked, interrupting the quiet.

"Ah. No, I don't," Josephine said, flinching, in midreach for a new handful of rice. Immediately, all eyes were on her again.

"Then have honey on your fruit, at least. It's a Ranoco specialty. The bees are raised here, unique to this island. They can be found nowhere else. So their honey is a delicacy. A once-in-a-lifetime experience," Tadhana pressed. A servant strode from the wall and placed a glass pitcher full of the honey beside Josephine. The liquid within was thick and golden-red, like the color of rust. It smelled of the earth and sweet rot.

Nausea blossomed in the pit of her stomach. Hadn't Sidapa told her that the bees fed on rotted flesh? Hadn't it been what they fed her, keeping her alive on only that and raw meat?

Josephine glanced at the pitcher, then Hiraya, who held her gaze. Josephine's mouth ran dry. Tadhana was playing a game. Hiraya couldn't warn her, couldn't do anything more than stare. But Josephine could read her well enough to know that Tadhana was weaving a web around her. But to what end, she wasn't sure.

"I would, but I'm allergic to honey," Josephine said.

Alejandro lifted his head, his brows arching high. She wasn't allergic to honey, and he knew it. But she shot him a pleading look. He kept his silence, taking another sip of his wine. Despite everything that had transpired today, he was still her brother, and he was still on her side.

"Is that so?" Tadhana asked. Her voice was quiet. She stared at Josephine with her hollowed-out sockets, her fingers thrumming along the table.

Josephine didn't answer. One lie already felt like one too many, especially to Tadhana. But Tadhana didn't say another word, and they sat in tense silence until a bell rang deep in the house.

"It's nearly dusk," Hiraya announced. "It's time to draw roles."

Tadhana leaned back in her chair. "Excellent. Then let me explain to you all the nature of the game." She rolled her wrist, her bones creaking as she did so.

"The game is simple. You will be split into two pairs. In each pair, someone will be the aswang and someone will be the prey. It is the aswang's goal to find the prey before dawn. It is the goal of the prey to survive until dawn."

A servant came to stand at her side, a lacquered box in his hands.

"One at a time, reach inside and take a coin," Tadhana instructed.

They exchanged glances, but Hiraya reached in first, confident. She withdrew a coin and held it tight in her palm. Alejandro drew his, then Gabriella, then Josephine. All at once, they opened their palms, revealing the coins to the table.

Gabriella's and Hiraya's coins both bore the image of a cemetery beetle. She and Alejandro had coins engraved with the image of the carrion bee. She glanced at Alejandro, and Alejandro held her gaze. His shoulders fell.

"I'm sorry, Josie," he said, as if it were a foregone conclusion.

Josephine's jaw set. "I'm sorry, too." She wasn't going to let him win. "There's no way I'm marrying him."

"So we have our teams. I will face off against Gabriella," Hiraya explained. "And Josephine will compete against Alejandro. Next, we'll draw for what role we'll play. Just like the game we played earlier, we'll pick wooden blocks from the cup. If you draw a black block, you'll be an aswang. If you draw a white block, you'll be the prey."

The servant presented the cup to Hiraya. She plucked a wooden diamond and opened her palm to the table. A black diamond lay on her palm. "I will be the aswang, then." She glanced at Gabriella, who glared back.

"This feels rigged," Gabriella muttered. "Why couldn't I draw first?"

Hiraya laid the cup out in front of Josephine.

Josephine stole a glance at Alejandro, who stared, fixated, at the cup. She couldn't read his expression as she dipped her hand into the narrow confines of the bamboo container. She didn't want to compete against him. She didn't want to hunt him or be hunted by him. She just wanted things to go back the way they were. Before he'd gone to Manila.

The diamond pressed hard against the skin of her palm, and she held it, enclosed, over the table.

"Go on, then, show us," Alejandro pressed.

She unfurled her hand, presenting to the table a white diamond.

"Well, that's all you really need to see, isn't it? Our aswang, Hiraya, will hunt Gabriella. And Alejandro will hunt Josephine." Tadhana grinned broadly at the players, her toothless mouth a black crescent. "The hunt will continue until daybreak. And the hunted must survive or find Sanctuary. Neither may leave the grounds of the house."

"And what is Sanctuary, then?" Josephine asked. She recalled the reverence with which Hiraya had once laid her hand against the bark of the santol tree when they were children.

"You must discover it yourself. But I assure you, you will know it when you find it," Tadhana said.

"It seems the hunted have the easiest role, then. There are ample places to hide here." Alejandro lifted his hands, gesturing broadly at the house. "How are we meant to find our prey?"

"You'll find that the servants will make your hunt much easier. As the night trails on, they'll join the hunt. Hunters need only follow the mobs to find their prey. But in the final two hours, in the twilight before dawn, the servants will turn against both hunters and hunted," Tadhana said.

Alejandro nodded. "So we drag our prey here and we've won, then? Or is it as easy as finding them?"

"Oh, love, no. For an aswang to win, they must kill their prey." Tadhana chuckled, as if his naïveté tickled her.

A brief silence fell over the table, and Gabriella laughed. The forced, polite laugh of someone trying to save someone else from an awkward faux pas. "You're joking."

"Am I?" Tadhana retorted, her lips crumpling upward in a foul, mocking grin.

Gabriella's smile faded, and she turned to stare at Hiraya. "If you don't tell me that she's joking . . ."

Hiraya met Gabriella's gaze, her jaw set. "That is the nature of the game. That is the nature of aswang."

"So you're going to try to kill me? That's what you're saying?" Gabriella stood abruptly, the chair's legs scraping across the floor.

Hiraya pulled another sliver of white meat from the lechon. "The scale is equally weighed. Your future, your happiness, weighed against the risk of your life. All you need to do is survive."

"It's so easy for you to say, isn't it? You aren't risking your life. Even if you lose, so what?" Gabriella hissed.

"If I lose, I die," Hiraya murmured. "We're both risking the same thing."

"I'm not hunting my sister. I'm not . . . I'm not dying here, either," Alejandro muttered, his bloodshot eyes flicking between Hiraya and Tadhana. "You never told me that the game was murder."

Tadhana hissed through her narrow lips. "No, no. It's a possibility that no one will die. That the hunted will both escape, that the aswang will survive the games and the servants, even if they arrive empty-handed to the new day. It's possible that whatever blood is lost will be blood wasted. But I suspect that tonight will have its winners and losers. And that those losers will be obligated to pay the cost of the winner's future."

Alejandro settled back into his chair, his shoulders squared and defiant. But in the short amount of time while they all ate, it was impossible to ignore how sickly he'd become. The light caught the damp saliva accumulating at the corners of his mouth and the sweat coating his forehead. His dark irises floated in the pinkening sclera, and if they'd been anywhere else Josephine would have demanded that they go to the hospital.

"Fuck your game," he declared. "I'm not playing."

"You will. Just you wait." Tadhana chuckled. "But you're free to try and leave. To brave the forest and try to row to shore. No one has ever survived the journey down to the beach. Once the game begins, and it *will* begin, the Engkanto won't let you go so easily."

"So we've no choice. We've no choice but to play," Gabriella murmured, her face pale. She groped for Alejandro's hand, leaning close to him. "I don't want to do this, Alejandro. I want to go home."

He held her hand and kissed her knuckles, his face drawn and dark. "I'm sorry I brought you here."

Hiraya dragged her fingertips across the rim of her wineglass, causing it to sing a discordant, eerie note. "The stage is set. All the choices we've made in our lives so far have led us to this moment. We may as well play, and play to win."

"Shut up, Hiraya," Gabriella snapped. "Don't even get me started. How is it fair that you get to play at all? This is your house. How can I expect to hide from you and survive?"

"I suppose it's a bit unfair," Hiraya agreed, a bitter smile lifting the edges of her lips. "You'll just have to try very hard."

"You're a miserable bitch," Gabriella spat, leaning across the table toward Hiraya, the tendons of her slender neck taut as her jaw clenched. "And I hope you die here."

"And I hope you don't. But I suspect you will." Hiraya sighed. "Maybe if you're lucky, we both will."

Tadhana clapped, dragging the table's attention back to her.

"You hate each other—wonderful. It doesn't matter. But dusk is here, and the game must be played. The aswang will stay in the dining room and recite the tagu-tagu rhyme three times. And in that time, the hunted will hide or run. The game will continue until dawn, or until the hunted find Sanctuary, or until all the hunted are dead. There will be no more questions, no more arguing. I expect a good game out of the four of you."

Hiraya folded her hands in her lap and began to recite the old childhood rhyme, her voice loud and crystal clear, so that it bounced through the halls. And yet despite the cheerful tune, she looked miserable.

"*Good night to all the lights, the moon is silvery bright—*"

The rest briefly exchanged glances. It felt too sudden. They'd only learned the true nature of the game minutes ago, and now they were expected to run or die.

"Oh Lord, shut up. Shut up, Hiraya, *shut up*," Alejandro groaned as he leaned forward, his hands pale, his short nails digging into his scalp as he pressed the palms of his hands as hard as he could against his ears. As if that might block out the sound.

Josephine clenched her jaw. She couldn't understand what miserable spell was being woven at the table. But she could see the way her brother shook, and the smug, knowing grin on Tadhana's mouth.

"Gabriella, let's go. Now." Josephine stood, and the chair scraped backward. She could feel the eyes of the servants against the wall, staring at her through their veils.

Gabriella gaped at her and Alejandro, her gaze swinging between them, wide-eyed. "You can't be playing their hideous game. It's insanity—you have to see that."

"Do you think that they'll just let you sit there?" Josephine demanded as she grabbed Gabriella by the wrist and tugged her out of the banquet hall doors. Gabriella was right. This was all insane. But she wasn't willing to sit at the table and lay her throat bare like a lamb for the slaughter.

She glanced over her shoulder. Tadhana grinned back at her, her arthritic fingers steepling. And Hiraya stared back at her with her single black eye, her gaze softening, as if she wanted to tell her something but couldn't.

Josephine slammed the door shut behind her, the sound mimicking the pounding of her heart. They couldn't afford to be slow. The song was short, just a nursery rhyme. And in no time at all, the game would begin.

FOURTEEN

THEY sprinted through the rooms, Gabriella trailing just behind her. In the hour they'd been in the banquet hall, the
house seemed to have changed. The lanterns on the wall were all
lit. The walls groaned as if the house were stretching, waking up.

*All these lights. Is this the Engkanto's doing? Or were the servants
pretending to be utterly incompetent all this time?* Josephine wondered.
The servants moved like tin soldiers when in the presence of the
Ranoco women. But she could scarcely imagine them scuttling
through each room, lighting each lantern by hand.

She chose her path carefully, trying to recall the way she'd come
with Hiraya after dinner the night before. Far behind her, she could
hear doors slamming open. Alejandro's pained, enraged shouts
echoed out behind her, the words blurred and indistinguishable.

Is he screaming for Hiraya? Or for me?

After passing through a dozen rooms, she realized she'd been this way before. The musty tomes that lined the walls marked this room as Hiraya's great-aunt's personal library. She tossed open the next door and found that it was full of glinting copper knickknacks. Hiraya had guided her so carefully along this path after last night's first dinner. She'd taken her time, making sure that Josephine had time to soak in the path. And now Josephine suspected that Hiraya had foreseen all of this—from the path that she'd take to her role in the games.

Maybe Gabriella was right. Maybe the game was rigged. There'd been layers of deceit from the start. Hiraya had known the nature of the game from the very beginning, and she'd never warned her of just how deadly it would be.

"Josephine—Josephine, wait." Gabriella gasped as she tugged at Josephine's hands, turning to an anchor that forced Josephine to a standstill. "I need to catch my breath." Gabriella bent forward at her waist, sucking in air while one hand massaged a stitch in her side. "I really need to rest."

Josephine nodded and tried to suppress the panic and irritation that threatened to blossom in her like a thorned flower. She dragged her hands down across her cheeks, a rush of words spilling out of her mouth. "Do you really think . . . Alejandro will come for me? Do you think he'd really—"

"Of course not," Gabriella snapped. But then she paused, a dark shadow passing over her face. "I . . . don't think so, anyway. Ever since dinner last night, he's been acting odd. He had nightmares the entire night. Dreams of rotten food and mazes, and . . . and things he didn't want to share with me. Things he said would scare me. And each hour, it seems like he gets sicker."

"Did he dream of aswang?" Josephine asked, brows rising. Was it possible she and her brother had shared the same all-too-real vision?

"What? No, insects, I think. That's all he'd say. Insects."

"There're so many bugs here. They're everywhere," Josephine muttered. If she focused her eyes on the cracks in the wall and the wooden floor, she could see them now. Ants, termites, flies. There was no room that was truly empty.

She sighed. "Don't hate me for what I'm about to say, but I think it's a good idea to split up."

Gabriella balked, her mouth falling open. "That's the dumbest possible thing you could've said."

Josephine held up her hand and nodded. "I know. I *know*. But consider what Hiraya said when she first found us. She said she heard the house creaking. That it led her right to us. If there are two people running in opposite directions or on different floors, you have double the chance of surviving. And in that time, we can both split up and find Sanctuary, whatever and wherever it is."

Gabriella flinched and sighed, as if the plan physically pained her. "Oh God. You're right, aren't you? She's going to track us like a dog through the halls."

"She is. She wants to win, Gabriella. But if we can find Sanctuary, we can avoid anyone dying tonight. Once we think we've found it . . . let's meet up in the foyer and go together. Okay? One hour before dawn."

"You won't leave me?" Gabriella asked, her gaze hard on Josephine's face. "I know how you feel about her."

"I'm not leaving you to die, if that's what you're asking," Josephine retorted, her brow furrowing. "We had a falling-out when we were kids. But I still love you."

Relief flooded Gabriella's face. "Yeah. Of course. I know that.

It's just . . . nice to hear you say it." But the thin smile on her face gave way, and she stepped closer to Josephine, taking her hand. "I know you trust her. Or maybe you just want to trust her. But you're right—Hiraya's desperate. And desperate people do terrible things. That goes for Alejandro, too." She drew away from Josephine, grabbing the handle of the door next to her. But before she slipped through it, she peered over her shoulder. "Don't get caught. And I'll meet you at the foyer."

"One hour to dawn," Josephine repeated. "I'll be there."

They shared a tense smile, and Gabriella shut the door quietly behind her. Her footsteps faded away, and Josephine found the steel bar of nerves in her back unraveling, just a bit. If Gabriella could bury herself deep in the house and bide her time, she'd survive. Even Hiraya couldn't explore every nook and hall.

In a distant room, she could hear the chime of clocks all together. It was still early, and she had plenty of time.

Strengthening her resolve, Josephine turned to her right, only to choke on her own shuddering gasp. The door stood open, and in its frame was a maid. Her gloved hands clutched at the wood, entrenching herself like a spider grasping the edges of its web.

As Josephine stared at her, she became certain that she knew the woman's silhouette, the thinness of her arms, the narrow, birdlike box of her shoulders. It was the maid she'd seen crouched at the roots of the balete tree. Perhaps she'd been in the dining room as well, embedded in the line of servants against the hall.

"Damn you. Did you follow us here?" Josephine demanded. But the maid kept her silence. Instead, her gloved fingertips dug deeper into the wood's smooth frame, as if she was holding herself back. As if she was moments away from leaping at Josephine.

"You can't touch me. Not yet, can you? And you can't tell him where I am." She didn't expect the maid to answer, and edged away from her, toward the next door. "The game's just started. I still have time."

Josephine slipped through the door of the next room and shut it behind her. This next room offered little but a thin Oriental rug and a few chairs. She grabbed the nearest chair and jammed the top edge of the wooden seat beneath the doorknob. A chair barricading a door hadn't saved her from nightmares of an aswang, but against a much more tangible threat she hoped it'd do the trick.

Josephine rushed through the next handful of rooms, pausing once when she heard the echo of her brother's footsteps. She knew them well. They were a little different from when they were children. They'd grown heavy, and they dragged, as if he was struggling to walk straight. But unmistakably it was her brother. Not quite far enough for comfort. But even closer she could hear the chair she'd placed beneath the doorknob falling to the ground with a distant clatter.

She stopped in her tracks and turned to stare over her shoulder, the way she had come. A rash of goose bumps had broken out over her arms. A moment passed, and she could hear a door open, then shut. Then another. Each one growing closer and closer, until she could hear floorboards moaning under the weight of someone creeping across them, methodical and slow.

Josephine rushed to the door of the next room, her hand grasping the knob. The door behind her opened, its ancient hinges creaking. The hairs on her neck stood on end. The door she'd just passed through minutes earlier cracked open just a few inches. The veiled face of the maid peered out. But she came no farther. She stood in the doorway, watching her. Waiting.

"Stay the hell away from me," Josephine warned, her lips pulling back to bare her teeth. The maid stared through the crack in the door, her thin fingers creeping inward to grip the frame. Without another word, Josephine pulled open the door to the next room and shut it quickly behind her. She needed to concentrate. The house was hard enough to navigate with her full attention, without adrenaline and fear spiking her nerves. She worked her way through the house, taking familiar turns, using landmarks she'd seen once and stored away in her memory as if they were life preservers. Right at the bust of José Rizal. Go straight beneath the archway, beneath the yellowed and dust-coated capiz shell chandelier. Down the narrow spiral stairwell. Through the door, barely wide enough to fit her shoulders.

She passed a window and saw that the sun had already begun to sink, though it was only just past six p.m. On the far-off horizon above the canopy of balete trees she could see dark clouds, thick with rain and lightning, filling the air with electricity and tension. One hour had passed, eleven more to go.

FIFTEEN

S HE reached the landing and followed her wine-hazy memory
through the hall. Each step drew her deeper and deeper into
that first game of tagu-tagu she played with Hiraya as a child. It felt
so innocent then, as she dove and scrambled beneath the ferns,
desperate to beat Alejandro and win Hiraya's approval.

But when her mother had called them to the house from the
edge of the woods, she'd been furious. No, not furious. *Horrified.*
Horrified that her children had been caught in the snare of the
Ranoco game. That, giggling, they pantomimed a death hunt she
had managed to survive.

Did you really kill someone, Mom? Josephine thought, the idea
burning at her heart. She'd always admired her mother's ambition,
her fearlessness. Her clear, sharp eyes that seemed to always look
forward, never back. But would her mother go so far as to kill for the
future she wanted? Was she so desperate to escape the life she had?

Is Alejandro?

At the end was the ornate door covered in carved flowers and trees, stained dark like a camphor chest. From behind it came the soft song of water spilling. She had no idea how she'd found it again, but she pushed open the door into Hiraya's hidden garden. The subdued steel gray of a coming night stretched overhead. But storm clouds rolled over the horizon, thick and heavy with rain.

Josephine sucked in a deep, soul-restoring breath, filling her chest with the scent of brine and flowers. The air here was so much different from the rest of the house. Fresher, freer. She could feel the hard metal of her tense muscles unwind, if only a bit. This was the one place where things felt safe. Where she was certain that the maid who had dogged her through the house wouldn't venture.

But as her eyes fluttered open, she craned her neck to find the garden's keeper. Hiraya was nowhere in sight, and only stony Daphne, caught midtransformation, occupied the quiet courtyard. Josephine stared up at the statue's determined eyes, their edges crinkled with fear. Finally, she understood why Hiraya had chosen Daphne to stand guard in this garden. She represented precisely what this house demanded—the ultimate sacrifice for a future of your own choosing. And for Hiraya, freedom from a fate that had chased her all her life.

Behind her, the door opened, and Josephine spun, her skirts whipping around her knees. Hiraya stepped into the garden, her hands clutching her skirt. "Josephine, you're here. I'm—I'm—" Hiraya choked around the rest of the sentence. She wet her lips, and Josephine could see the way her eye glittered, wet with tears that threatened to spill across her lashes at any second. "I'm so, so sorry," Hiraya whispered, her voice hitching.

Despite everything, Josephine felt her heart twist. Her hands were heavy and fisted at her sides; she was clenching her jaw so hard that she was worried her teeth would break. But she'd never seen Hiraya, always confident and mischievous, reduced to something so utterly pathetic and lost.

"Hiraya . . . you let me come here, knowing what this game is. You set me up to potentially die. How could you?"

"You have every right to hate me. You should hate me. But . . . please believe me when I say I wouldn't have invited you here if I didn't think you could win. That we could both win." She reached for Josephine but thought better of it, as if she didn't deserve to touch her. Her hands fell limply to her sides.

"How?" Josephine demanded. "Tadhana was perfectly clear. You only get the future you want if you kill Gabriella. And Alejandro only gets his future if he kills *me*."

"What Alejandro wants and what's good for him are two entirely different things. You just need to survive and win, Josephine. And you can do that. You can elude your brother for a night, can't you? And I . . . well, I can get the future I want, even without killing Gabriella. Besides . . . what's your other option? Go home, let Alejandro sell your house, go to bed with an old man, and have children he'll never see grow up?" Hiraya replied, her voice quiet.

Josephine balked. It was true, but how did Hiraya know it? Hiraya hadn't been there when she had that cliffside conversation with her brother. It'd just been her and him and the gnats and flies.

"How do you know that, Hiraya? Have you been spying on me?"

"I—" Hiraya stuttered. "Not intentionally. It's the insects. Sometimes I can hear them in my head. Whispered fragments, ugly demands. It's been that way ever since Tadhana took one of my eyes. And there are so many of them—they see everything. Sometimes they tell me what they see." She flinched and dragged her hands over her face. "I know I sound insane. But that doesn't matter! What matters is that it's possible for you to win, and for Alejandro to survive."

"And Gabriella?" Josephine retorted.

"Gabriella, too. We just need to play the game carefully. I would have never asked you three here if I didn't have a plan. If I didn't think we could all live. If I didn't think I could offer you a better future than the one your brother has in mind for you."

"Okay, fine, then. I'm listening. What's your grand plan?" Josephine demanded.

"I can't tell you yet," Hiraya murmured.

"No more secrets, Hiraya. No more lies. Tell me the truth."

"I would if I could! But I'm terrified of being overheard. The servants, the insects, they're always watching. Always listening. And if they hear—we'd lose. We'd lose everything. But ask me something else. And if I can tell you, I will. I'll be as honest as I can. No more smoke, no more half-truths. Just . . . please, try to trust me," Hiraya pleaded.

"Then tell me. When I was a child . . . there were rumors about your family. Terrible rumors. People said the Ranocos were shape-shifters. Murderers. Corpse eaters, baby killers. They said your family bewitched men and flung curses."

"And . . . do you believe them?"

Josephine chewed viciously on her lip for a moment. But then frustration bubbled out. "Not all of it. But most of it."

Hiraya nodded, but she didn't seem angry. Instead, she sighed and tugged at her necklace, her fingers running over the gold beads. "I am many of those things. But when we were just kids in Carigara, when we first met, I wasn't any of it. It's only when I was forced back here, into this house, that the rumors became true."

"And Sidapa?" Josephine demanded. She pressed a hand against her chest. She wanted to know the truth of what she'd seen in that room. She didn't want to believe that Hiraya had truly held her sister down while Sidapa's eyes were taken.

Hiraya squeezed her eye shut and grimaced, as if trying to close off an awful memory. "When you first told me you saw Sidapa, I knew you were going to ask this question. I knew she'd tell you everything. She hasn't spoken to me in years. I really think she hates me."

"So it's true," Josephine persisted, her voice shaking. "Everything she said. About the room, about you."

Hiraya nodded. "Tadhana forced Sidapa to consume a seed, the fruit, that our mother carried until she died. That seed—it's what all aswang carry. It's the source of our curse and blessing. It's generally passed down from eldest to youngest, but Sidapa . . . Sidapa was gifted. The Engkanto chose her over me. But Sidapa hated the spirits, the fruit, the role she'd have to play, and she refused to incubate the seed in her body. She burned herself alive, trying to destroy it."

Hiraya's voice slowly grew more monotone as she spoke, the color draining out of it. As if she was dissociating from the memory even as she recited what happened. "If it were so easy, there'd be no aswang left, I think. But Tadhana took the seed from Sidapa's body. And then she had me consume it instead. No one wants to be an aswang. And I cried for days, months, maybe years. I tried to vomit it out; I thought of killing myself. Sidapa always seemed so timid when we were kids. But of the two of us, she was always braver."

She smiled at Josephine, but it was a gnarled, ugly thing, full of teeth. *This is the smile of an aswang,* Josephine thought, and she reached instinctively for Hiraya's face, stroking the flyaway locks framing her cheeks, as if that might bring some humanity back to it.

"Oh, Hiraya. I'm so sorry." Josephine's voice was softened by the hurt she could sense, embedded deep beneath Hiraya's façade. She'd never known how dark a sadness Hiraya carried, how she'd suffered here on this island, all alone.

Hiraya squeezed her eye shut, as if she hadn't expected such tenderness in the wake of her confession, but she leaned her face against Josephine's hand.

"No. Don't be sorry. Don't you ever apologize to me. I wish I'd been as strong as Sidapa. I wish I'd had the strength to tell Aunt Tadhana no. But I didn't. I thought it was my duty, my fate. And now it's here." She took Josephine's hand from her face and pressed it below her breast, at the end of her sternum. An unnatural heat radiated outward, and Josephine, for a moment, thought she could feel a throb. As if there were two hearts nestled in Hiraya's chest.

"I don't want to be this way anymore. I love my family. I know they sacrificed so much for me, that everything they've done, they've done because they thought they were protecting me. But I don't want to be the monster chained to this house, luring people in. I don't want to hurt anyone ever again."

"You're not a monster," Josephine protested, driven by instinct, though so much of what she'd seen said otherwise. But Hiraya barked a laugh that was so vicious Josephine flinched as if she'd been struck for her stupidity.

"I am, Josephine. And you know it, too. Only a monster would bring you here. Only a monster could put you and everyone who was ever kind to them at risk, in a desperate gambit for freedom."

Her expression softened into something Josephine was certain was genuine. "You've no idea what you mean to me, Josephine. You have every right to hate me. But you've always been sweet to me. You're the only one to show me a true and tender love."

Josephine's mind filled with images of the dolls with their tufts of stolen hair. The room full of soot, Sidapa's silhouette burned into the ground. The wretched metal tree and its ungodly fruit. She'd peeked into the dark corners of Hiraya's inheritance, and still she found herself gravitating toward the Ranoco girl, who'd been held here against her will her entire life. Even if she'd known the truth from the start, she would have come here to try to save her.

"I don't know if it's in me to hate you," Josephine admitted. "But you said there's a way for us to all survive? Tadhana and my mother both survived."

"Yes. Tadhana had a weak spot for your mother, I suspect. Maybe it's in our blood."

Hiraya sighed, her gaze lingering on Josephine's face. "It's possible for all of us to survive. But, for now, you must run. Eventually you'll have to fight, I think. Alejandro and the house won't let you hide forever. And as for me, I think I have a plan for Gabriella. One that will let us both see dawn."

Josephine breathed a sigh of relief. "Promise me you won't kill her. That you won't hurt her."

The softness in Hiraya's face drained away and her mouth pressed into a thin, hard line. "Even if I don't kill her, the house and its servants will try."

"And if they do, that's her blood on your hands. You should have never brought her here. So promise me, Hiraya. Promise me she'll be okay," Josephine repeated.

Hiraya paused and nodded, glancing furtively at the darkened window. "But your brother is . . . more complicated. The meals here, the meat, in particular . . . it's washed with our blood and seeded with a curse. When he was chosen to be a hunter in tonight's ritual—"

"With blood? A *curse*?" Josephine sputtered. The dreams Alejandro had been having, the ghastly pallor of her brother. It clicked together in Josephine's head, but she pushed the thought away. She didn't want to believe it. But Hiraya continued as if she hadn't heard her.

"That curse will twist him, at least until dawn. He'll play as if he's an aswang. As if he's starving, until he's half feral, until all he can think about is feeding."

"You cursed him?" Josephine demanded, refusing to be ignored.

Hiraya grimaced. "Yes. Well, not me. Tadhana did, when she bled herself and had it rubbed into the meat. But her curse wouldn't work if there weren't something for the spirits to cling to. There have been countless Alejandros in this house. People full of desperation and fear. This house, this game, is a relief to them. It's a place where things are simple. They live if they're strong, perish if they're weak. If he didn't want to take part in this game, if he wasn't willing to sacrifice for it, then that curse would have never rooted in him the first place."

Her face grew deathly serious, and she took both of Josephine's hands in hers. "If you want to survive in the face of his hunger, you need to want to win. You need to want to survive. Or he'll eat you alive."

"Alejandro would never hurt me. He'd never—"

"He would. I promise you, Josephine. He would. It's not what you want to hear, but you asked me how you could survive. How we could *all* survive. This is it. You need to be able to defend yourself. Not just against Alejandro but the house itself. Even now, he's hunting through the house for you. I . . . can hear his hunger. He's stalking around on the second floor."

Josephine buried her face in her hands and sucked in the wet night air. How could any of this be happening?

"Fine. Fine. I will win this game . . . and we're all going to get out of this alive. Just tell me what I need to do."

Hiraya smiled, light filling her eye. "You'll need a weapon. And they're everywhere. There are rooms with weapons hidden in compartments or hung on the wall. But if you're trying to be quick and efficient, just go to the servants' wings. To the kitchen."

"But the servants. Someone was following me. She trailed me all the way here," Josephine protested.

"I'm sure. You'll just have to be fast and take advantage of their sluggishness in the early hours. Soon they'll be just as dangerous as Alejandro. Maybe more so if they gather in large enough numbers."

Hiraya lifted her chin upward. Josephine followed Hiraya's gaze to see two servants on the balcony above them. A man and a woman leaned over the railing to stare down at them, their veils long rivers of white.

"Dear Lord, I hate them," Josephine muttered, her eyes narrowed. She felt braver at a distance, but she could feel their eyes on her, intent and obsessed, and it made her skin crawl. She couldn't stay here forever, in this little paradise of fresh air and soft comfort. Even this place wasn't safe. Nowhere in the house was.

"I hate them, too. I don't know if I'd survive a lifetime with them, staring at me from the corners. Always watching."

"We'll get out of here. We'll win," Josephine retorted, leaning forward. "You wouldn't abandon me. I won't abandon you. And somehow we'll both find a way out of here. Back to Carigara."

Hiraya gazed at her for a moment, her eye wide with confusion.

But it lasted only a second and a small, painful smile lifted her lips, its edges crumpled as if she wanted to hide it.

"You mean it, don't you? You're not lying."

"I'm not," Josephine said. And she wasn't. In the pit of her stomach, she knew that if Hiraya was left here alone, she'd stay here with her. It was better to die in this house, with all its hunger, than live as the bride of a man whose touch withered her soul.

"But what happens if I fail? What happens if Alejandro catches me?" Josephine asked, quietly. Hiraya seemed so sure that she'd win, and yet Josephine could sense the evil and violence of the house all around her. If she made it through this, she had a feeling it'd be a miracle.

"Then if you lose, but you make it to dawn alive . . . I'll stay here with you, too. We'll survive in this terrible place together."

Hiraya looped her fingers around the rosary hung from Josephine's neck and tugged Josephine toward her. Heat rose into Josephine's face at the petal-softness of Hiraya's lips, at the feeling of Hiraya's hands tracing along her ribs.

Hiraya tasted as she smelled—of flowers and fruits, intermingled with the soft rot of wet roots that had just begun to decay. Josephine could have buried herself in the soil of that kiss and let herself be consumed by it, because she was certain in the end she'd find a way to grow. To become the person she was always meant to be.

She would find a way to save Hiraya. And when dawn came, they'd leave this place together.

SIXTEEN

JOSEPHINE closed the garden door behind her and followed the golden carpet runner toward what she hoped was the foyer and the front of the house. All around her, she could hear the patter of dozens of feet, of distant doors opening and closing. The house was so much louder than before.

Her ears strained to catch the sound of her brother's familiar footsteps, or for the door behind her to open and close. She thought she could hear him if she held her breath. The thud of footsteps like distant thunder, rhythmic and frantic, a stride that had been embedded in her heart since childhood. Doors opened and slammed, marking his path. It sickened her to think of her brother twisted by the Ranocos' curse. She was certain that Hiraya had exaggerated the depth of its influence.

When Alejandro finally found her, they would talk it out and come to terms. No matter what, he was still her brother. She knew he wouldn't hurt her. No matter how badly he wanted to follow in their father's footsteps, no matter how long he'd been chasing that dream.

She curved through rooms until she'd nearly made it back to the foyer. Outside each door she hesitated, listening to see if she could hear breathing or soft, barefoot steps moving sluggishly across the ancient tiles and dull rug. Some telltale signs of the servants.

There was nothing, not for a dozen rooms. But as she reached the door before the foyer, she leaned her head against the door and held her breath in her clenched jaw. Just beyond it, she could hear something. Not shuffling, but thumping. Her hand hesitated at the doorknob. She could try to find another path, perhaps. But she knew she'd never find another way back to the kitchen. And every passing minute only cut her time shorter.

The servants frightened her, but they couldn't touch her. She needed to remember that. She pushed open the door and peered through the inch-wide crack and wished immediately she hadn't.

Beneath the glow of the chandelier, dozens of shadows intermingled with one another. The servants stood in loose knots in the entryway. Most stood in place, listing to one side and then the next as if they were on board a ship rocked by an ocean. But some seemed weaker, their spines curving like sad question marks toward the ground, their hands groping for the earth, as if they were mere moments from falling apart. But the thumping—the thumping came from a thick man standing in the far corner. He seemed healthier than the rest. His shoulders were squared, his thick calf muscles pushed against the cloth of his pants. He banged his head against the wall in rhythmic, hard blows, over and over without pause. As if he didn't feel pain. But the other servants ignored him, caught in a lifeless malaise.

Josephine swallowed hard, her mouth dry. There were too many of them. She'd have to push her way through. Gently, she stepped into the foyer, hoping her entrance was quiet enough not to disturb the group.

It was not. Her soft, subtle movement drew their attention immediately. Their heads snapped toward her like sharks tasting blood in the water. Josephine froze, her hand coming to grope at the knob behind her, ready to run. But no one approached her. Their pale veils fluttered with labored breaths. They salivated, so that the veil stuck to them, creating yellow smears across the cloth.

Behind her, the door of the room she'd just passed through opened. She glanced over her shoulder to see the maid who had stalked her all the way to Hiraya's garden. The woman slid into the room, her movements stiff but so much faster than before.

There was no going back.

From just past the servants in the foyer, Josephine could hear the clamor of the kitchen, though dinner had long since ended. The sound of metal hitting the chopping board. The metal clang of a frying pan being struck by a spoon. It sounded like a safe harbor in the storm. And if she was ever going to make a run for it, it was now, while she was still safe. While they still couldn't touch her.

She barreled through the servants, her nose filling with the stench of their earthy musk, as if they'd been born in the soil and bathed in it. In the corners of the room, in their shadows, she could see the creep and skitter of insects. Their hands reached up, brushing against her wrist and waist, but their fingers remained lank and fangless. She held her breath, and the man banging his head against the wall turned toward her. The cloth over his forehead was tacky and dark, with blood both clotted and fresh. He groaned, a wordless, almost animal-like noise.

But even if the servants couldn't hold her down, that didn't stop them from following her. Their bodies were the sauna heat of a fever, and they trailed after her in a gruesome procession she knew she couldn't outrun forever.

Josephine broke into a sprint, not caring about the sound of her feet slamming against the tile, nor her breath ricocheting off the halls, just moments from becoming a scream. The sound of metal and cutlery grew louder, coming from a door at the end of the hall.

Josephine pulled and twisted at the knob, but it refused to give way. She could hear the metal of the latch jostling in place, keeping the door locked.

"Oh, Santo Niño, *please*. Please open up!" she cried, pounding on the door. Tears threatened to spill from the edges of her eyes. The servants drew closer yard by yard, funneled into the corridor. She didn't want to die here, crushed by their vile bodies.

The door cracked open, just enough for her to look through. A tall man stared down at her, his thick brows creased, a butcher's apron tight against the broad, jutting peak of his stomach. "Brought them all here, huh? Not the best maneuver," he muttered, his voice gruff. She recognized his voice as the one who'd told her to leave the kitchen hours ago. He pulled back his teeth and glowered at her, revealing a row of rotting, scarlet-stained teeth. The telltale sign of betel nut chewing.

"Please let me in," she begged, and grabbed at his apron, clenching it in her fists. A touch of scarlet slick smeared across her fingertips, but she didn't care. He sucked at his narrow, deteriorated teeth and glowered at her, as if she didn't have a horde of servants only a few yards away from her, filling the hall with their wretched stink and the sound like marbles coming from between their gritted teeth.

"I'm not meant to let you in. It's not in the rules, per se. But it's always been one of those unspoken understandings." He stared down at her, taking stock of her.

"Can't you—can't you make an exception?" The panic in her chest turned her voice thin and desperate. He sighed, a deep, bottom-of-the-chest sigh.

"I shouldn't. I really, really shouldn't. But both the girls like you. It's rare for them to ever see eye to eye on anything."

He stepped back, pulling the door open, and she slid inside with an exhausted, grateful gasp. But he held the door a little longer, his hand firm on the handle.

"Go on, then, go," he growled at the throng of servants. They'd come no closer since he'd opened the door, as if the very sight of him was enough to root them in place. He spat on the floor in front of them, his saliva red-tinged and flecked with remnants of tobacco and betel nut, and the servants recoiled, sliding back toward the foyer.

"I hate how they skulk around, and they hate me, too. But they need me, you know. They need the butcher. I keep their ladies fed and happy," the man muttered, full of vexation, and shut the door and its latch. Josephine trembled, still shaken by the servants' pursuit. She had no idea if he was talking to her or not, but she nodded anyway and trailed after him like a lost dog.

The walls in the kitchen were made of stone; in the entrance beside the door hung a line of scarlet-stained aprons. The smell of cooking meat mingled with the harsh stench of copper, and it hit her in a wave. She gasped and breathed through her mouth, steeling herself. She didn't want to offend the chef. Not when it'd be so easy for him to kick her out and deny her a chance at a knife.

But he didn't seem to notice her discomfort. He tromped back to the kitchen and took his place at the counter in the room's center. His hand returned with a familiar grace to the handle of a large butcher knife. No part of him was refined, and yet his hands were long and elegant, and they moved in a rhythmic, satisfying dance as they chopped.

Without looking at her, he lined up the blade against a rib cage. The skin had already been peeled back, and Josephine found herself transfixed by the slab of meat. Wet markets were a daily occurrence in Carigara, filling up the open plaza near the pier. You couldn't go a yard without seeing the bodies of pigs hanging on rusted hooks, their heads there beside them, staring out into the milling crowds.

The cycle of meat, from piglet to corpse, was nearly every child's first exposure to life and death. Even her own family had a few fat sows in the backyard, kept contained in a concrete pen. And yet it was because she was so familiar with it that Josephine realized that there was something *wrong* with the slab of meat on the butcher's table. It didn't have the oblong chest or the flat shoulders of any pig she'd seen.

No. She recognized the contours for what they were. A human figure reduced to its barest parts, all pink and white and anonymous. Josephine's hand flew up to her lips, her knuckles forcing their way into her mouth as she stumbled backward, her back hitting the wall. Her eyes bulged as she stared at the corpse, even as her legs weakened and failed her. She slid down the wall, clutching her mouth now with two hands. As if that might somehow keep the scream from escaping. Her breath wheezed and whistled out between the gaps in her fingers, a pathetic mewl of terror and shock.

The chef didn't lift his head. He kept his eyes focused as he lifted the butcher's blade and brought it down.

"I—I think I'm going to be sick," she gasped. She twisted to the side, her throat gurgling.

"Don't you dare—" the butcher growled.

But it was too late. The remnants of her dinner flooded over her lips and spilled onto the warm stone floor.

When she opened her eyes, she could feel him glowering at her. His glare burrowed into the pool of half-digested fruit before flickering to Josephine's sweating face. "Disgusting. You vomit on the floor of my kitchen? After I'm good enough to open the door to you? I don't know what they see in you."

His lip peeled upward, and he slapped the flat edge of the butcher blade against the island's wooden surface, twice.

"Get over here, clean this up," he demanded.

A servant tending to a wok on an antiquated stove on the back wall turned toward Josephine. Her veil was short, falling just below her chin, likely to keep it from dipping into a pan. The dress didn't rise high enough to cover her neck, and Josephine gawked at the exposed skin there.

The veins and arteries flanking her trachea were engorged, and circular scabs riddled it. As the servant drew closer with a rag, Josephine could see black veins sprouting from those barely healed wounds, like corrupted roots.

Josephine scuttled away, still on the ground, away from the servant who mopped up her vomit. She took shelter in another corner, where a traditional broom made of the midribs of palm leaves stood. Its bottom was stained gray and red with dust and dried viscera.

"Just one look at meat and you're sick to your stomach," the chef muttered, packing his lip full of betel nut and tobacco. "If the clean bits make you sick, I wouldn't look around. Have a bit of decorum, eh? A bit of restraint. My sous chef has work to do. She can't constantly be tending to you." He waved the butcher knife around the room, pink rivulets running down its dark blade, and for the first time Josephine realized how far the kitchen stretched behind him. Its doorless rooms sprawled, dominating this section of the first floor.

From the rooms closest to them came the sounds of servants at work. It jarred Josephine how nostalgic the rhythm of it was. She'd grown up hearing the clatter of pots and pans. It'd been the ever-present soundtrack of her childhood, starting at dawn and ending only at dusk. But here the familiar noises of cooking, which had once been comforting, had become rotten and cruel. Her stomach twisted at the sound of meat slapping into a bowl, the slice of a sharp knife against something sturdy.

He was right. Looking would be a mistake. But she couldn't help herself.

It's a slaughterhouse.

She could barely comprehend what she was seeing, but those three words ran in circles around her brain. The stone floors were coated in pink water. Near the drain were three more servants, all women. Their dark skirts were bunched in their laps as they kneeled on the floor, their feet wet and scabbed. Their backs were hunched, and their hands moved quickly. It almost reminded her of when all the girls and servants would gather in the shed to winnow the rice. But this was no pile of grain.

She could see through the gaps between the servants the figure of a nude person. Its feet twitched as the servants did their arcane work, their hands moving rhythmically. Periodically, insects would hit the floor, then vanish into the cracks in the tiles.

"You're . . . you're a murderer. You bring people here and you

224

kill them." Josephine's voice shook as she tore her gaze away from the twitching feet.

The chef blinked at her accusation and pushed the tip of the knife into the wooden block in front of him as he thought. "A murderer? I suppose I am. But that man"—he lifted the knife and jabbed it toward the body the servants were bent over—"stopped being a man a long time ago. He was dead long before he ever came into my kitchen. Now he's just meat. A breathing, walking steak."

"You're going to eat him, aren't you? You're going to kill him and cook him." It wasn't a question. It was a statement that dripped judgment and disbelief and venom. But if the butcher cared at all about the edge in her voice, he didn't show it in his face.

"Soon enough, once the scullery maids get all the remnants of rot and insects out of him. Every single person in this house is filled with the bugs. With the exception of me and the ladies themselves, of course. Your pretty little friend is incubating more than just babies in that gut. And that boy who's tearing apart the house trying to find you, he's absolutely choked with them. He was a fan of my lechon. Just couldn't stop gobbling it up."

The butcher grinned as if he was proud of his work. "I can only put the tiniest of seeds in them. Little worms, their eggs pearly white. But just a sprinkling—that's all it takes to make sure the game kicks off right. The bigger eggs, well, that's not my job. I'm a butcher, not a farmer."

"None of that makes sense. Not a single word of it," Josephine whispered. She'd seen insects everywhere. Fat flies, ugly bees, cemetery beetles. But to know that they were crawling beneath the skin of the servants disgusted her in a way that nothing else had. And to know that they were in Alejandro? That they'd hatched in his stomach and were wriggling their way into his flesh?

"Why . . . why fill them with insects?" Josephine whispered.

"That's what old Tadhana tells me to do. She says the bugs want to be in the bodies—in someplace warm. And once they're inside, they fester. They grow. They take on their true form, working their way through the veins, turning everything inside black. Then, bit by bit, they eat the meat. And when they're done chewing away like the parasites they are, we get the dregs. I season the meat with their eggs, make it presentable, and serve it up to the next batch of players. And so the cycle repeats."

"You can't be serious," Josephine hissed. With a visceral disgust, she recalled how Gabriella chewed on the tocino and complained of its grittiness. Of Alejandro's stomachache, his bloodshot eyes, the sweat on his ashen face. "Every servant . . . is crawling with insects? You've been feeding Gabriella and Alejandro insect eggs?"

The chef nodded. "Sure have. Adds that special island flavor you only get here. It's hugely popular until people figure out what the secret ingredient is. But the only thing you really need to know is if you win, you get to leave, and your perfect future's waiting for you. Or you lose, and you get added to the cycle."

For the first time, she felt her blood boil. She wanted to kill him. How could he be so blasé about such inhuman cruelty? She breathed through her nose and tried to compose herself.

"Can you give me a knife, then? Something I can defend myself with," she said.

"Sure, can't deny you a weapon. Not allowed." He waved toward the wall, where knives hung by the dozens. Most were clean, but others were bloody and left to rust. "The ones used for the hunts, I never cook with them. I like the stains on them—sort of a souvenir, you know? Memorabilia. I'm a fan."

Josephine didn't reply as she approached the wall of blades. The ones that were bloodied were the largest, their old stains soaked to the hilt. She didn't let her gaze linger on them. She plucked a small knife from the wall, so inconspicuous it could have easily been hidden in a sleeve. A fruit knife, used to peel things so much softer than human skin. The chef quirked a brow but said nothing to dissuade her. She was certain it meant nothing to him at all who lived or died. For a brief moment, as she looked at the blade, she wondered if she really had it in her to kill him. He was twice her weight, easily. And he'd clearly had years of taking apart human bodies.

But beyond that, she realized, no. She didn't have it in her to kill anyone. She wasn't like him. She wasn't like Tadhana.

"How can you live like this?" she murmured, clutching the knife. "How can you live with yourself?"

He rolled his eyes, but he seemed unperturbed, as if he'd heard the accusation a thousand times before. "Easy for you to pass judgment, isn't it? You've no idea what it's like to be an aswang. You've never felt the itch to follow the mourning crowd to the graves. To struggle against the impulse to dig your hands into the freshly turned soil, to eat the cold flesh, the congealed blood. But here? It's ethical. You offer your bodies and friends for a chance at a better future. It's a fair trade."

He gestured toward the man in the wet room, his feet still twitching.

"The maidens downstairs seed them with the big eggs, the beetles and centipedes and roaches, and it gives them five, maybe ten years to live. By the time they reach the end of their lives, they're vacant. The bugs have hollowed them out." He tapped his temple. "The servants will start moving on autopilot. Like drones in an anthill, piloted by the colony inside them."

"Downstairs? There's a downstairs?" Josephine pressed. She hadn't known that there was any more to the house than its sprawling two stories. But a secret floor might house Sanctuary.

"Sure, but I don't know if it's a place for you. Not with how late it's getting. But if you're insistent, the stairwell is near the center of the house. I don't know much beyond that. Not my job, not my business."

The scullery servants shifted in the wet room. In unison, the three of them lifted the corpse they'd been working through and laid the body out in front of the chef. The chef stared down at the fresh corpse, sizing up the muscles as if it were a prime piece of meat.

Without a word or a thank-you, Josephine turned to leave. She couldn't stand to see this body turned to meat. Even if it meant braving the servants outside the door. The chef chuckled, and she could almost feel his amused eyes on her back before the soft *thunk* of the knife began again. She'd heard that sound when she'd first arrived, and now it sickened her to know that the lechon at the dinner table had come from this kitchen.

"Good luck, little lady. You'll need plenty of it," the chef called as she slipped out the door. She could feel the grin in his words as he stared into her back.

SEVENTEEN

THE corridor was blessedly empty. She leaned against the kitchen door to steady herself, her body shaking with nerves and anger. But footsteps, heavy and familiar, drifted down the hall. She'd heard those steps countless times throughout her childhood. She could place them anywhere. Alejandro, still somewhere in the house's tangle, but close.

"He'll be here soon," a voice sighed in her ear. Josephine froze as cold fear ran down the length of her spine like liquid mercury. Her mouth filled with the taste of smoke and the sulfurous odor of burnt hair.

"Sidapa," she gasped.

"*Hide.*"

The single word filled Josephine with electricity. It freed her from her paralysis, and she snatched the knob of the first door she saw. Barreling inward, she gasped as her body slammed against a wall. She was in a closet. Scarcely a closet. It was a space just deep enough for her to turn around in. Just wide enough to hold her shoulders. She spun to face the hall.

Sidapa stood in the doorway, inches from Josephine, blocking her escape. She wore no mask this time. No hair spilled across her face. No shadow obscured her features. But Josephine desperately wished that anything, anything at all, could have spared her from the sight.

What little flesh and skin that had survived Sidapa's immolation had become a calloused charcoal over bones that, here and there, peered between the cracks. Bits of ivory in a nightmarish landscape that clung to its structure only through some unholy will.

But Josephine stared, transfixed, at Sidapa's eyes. Her sockets were empty, shallow grooves. But around those empty sockets inhuman eyes pocked her cheeks, the corners of her lips, her forehead, bulbous and shiny. The eyes of a spider. They did not blink, and in the dim light Josephine saw the open-mouthed horror on her own face reflected in the black orbs.

In the corner of her eyes, she caught sight of the gaping hole in Sidapa's chest. This was how Tadhana had stolen the seed that she'd forced Hiraya to consume.

Before Josephine managed to utter a single word, the door slammed in her face. Josephine shook around a stifled sob. Something pressed against the backs of her arms and her spine, dried and crackling. The smell of an old fire filled the space, and Josephine held her breath just to stop herself from breathing it.

"You are so, so loud. He'll hear you. You don't want that, do you?" Sidapa whispered into the conch of her ear, her breath cold. There was no space for Sidapa in this room; there was hardly enough space for Josephine. But thin arms encircled Josephine's waist. Then another set of hands covered her mouth, firmly. Josephine clamped her mouth shut. Sidapa was *dead*. And yet she felt so real. She could feel her pressed against her back; she could feel her breath rasping against her ear.

Josephine trembled in Sidapa's many arms. But she didn't dare move. And now she could hear Alejandro's steps on the tile in the corridor. But with him came the sound of a radio, its speakers whining and squealing like a sow. It wasn't on any channel, but just above the shrill noise Alejandro muttered as if he heard a broadcast tuned only to his own ears.

"This is it. I can't believe they think there's a chance he'll ever leave . . . He's a murderer. He's a killer. Flowers and prayers aren't going to stop him. But if I can win, if I can expose him . . . I just need to do what Dad couldn't. I can't let anything stop me. I can't just run away . . ."

Alejandro's words were slurred, but there was no mistaking the desperation in his voice. Something hard hit the floor and the radio was violently silenced. "Goddamn him . . . Where are you, Josephine?"

Josephine squeezed her eyes shut.

If he found her now, she'd never be able to fight him. Even with the fruit knife clenched in her fist, even if she was faced with death, she wasn't sure she could ever turn the knife on her own brother. She could hear him taking a deep drag on his cigar, the sweet herbal smoke mingling with Sidapa's sulfuric stench.

He breezed past Josephine's closet and headed directly to the kitchen. He pulled at the knob, and when it didn't open, he knocked hard against its wood. "I can hear you in there," he called. His voice was impatient but measured.

The old metal of the latch clattered, and the door creaked open. "Can I help you?" the chef asked, his voice gruff and short.

"I'm looking for my sister. Have you seen her?"

The butcher said nothing. A long silent moment passed, and Josephine was certain that the two of them were staring at each other, waiting for the other to break. Her heart pounded in her chest. She hadn't been kind to the chef, and she was certain he'd betray her. If he did, she was doomed.

Alejandro spoke again, his voice lowering. "Is she in there?"

"There are sisters in the kitchen, I'm sure. But not yours."

"Well, to be safe, I think I should look around," Alejandro pressed.

"Nope, not allowed. It's one of those unspoken rules. No hunters, no hunted. No guests. Just the kitchen crew, and the ladies, if they so choose."

Josephine hadn't thought it possible for the butcher to be gruffer, but his voice was the low roll of thunder, with Alejandro's demands sliding right off him.

"So she really isn't in there, then? It's against the rules for you to help her, I bet. I'm sure Tadhana would hate to hear how you're ruining the game." Alejandro's voice was strained, as if he was speaking through a clenched jaw with bared teeth.

"How many times do you want me to say it? *She isn't here.*"

The door shut with finality, and the locks relatched. Alejandro's feet scraped against the tile, as if he was turning to face the corridor as she'd done moments before.

Through the door she heard him exhale and imagined his face wreathed in cigar smoke.

"You again. Ugly fucks," Alejandro muttered. His footsteps retreated down the hall, but not very far at all. Only a few yards. He scarcely sounded like her brother. He sounded rougher, impatient. Almost cruel, his voice wet and thick.

"Stay still," he muttered.

A brutal crack, like the sound of lightning, filled the hall. Something heavy and soft thudded to the floor. Alejandro grunted, and then came another crack, another soft thud. Two more swings, and Alejandro was gasping for breath, exhausted.

There was the faint, familiar click of a lighter. She was certain that he'd lit another cigar, and for a moment he seemed to stand there, smoking and contemplating.

"Midnight's almost here. And you might have eluded me for now. But can you keep this up until dawn? I don't think you have it in you," Alejandro called. "You've always been weak. Always waiting for me to come home. Never willing to build anything yourself."

Josephine shrank back against the wall, against Sidapa, who was steadfast behind her. Her grip tightened around the hilt of the knife. But he didn't come any closer. His soft murmurings seemed to be reserved for a version of her that he kept in his head.

His ragged breaths faded, along with his footsteps, and Josephine squeezed her eyes shut. Like petals falling from the pistil of Josephine's lips, Sidapa's hands and arms fell away into the dark without a sound, as if they'd never been there at all.

Josephine was alone. She could sense the absence in the space around her that Sidapa had once filled. The stench of soot that Sidapa carried with her everywhere was gone. Josephine let loose the breath she'd been holding in her chest. It trembled with the start of a dry sob. But she steeled her nerves and eased open the door a fraction of an inch to peer outside.

The corridor was silent, but it wasn't empty. The dim lanterns on the wall cast shadows that curled and entangled themselves with strange shapes on the floor. Josephine stepped into the hall, for a moment not quite comprehending what lay in front of her.

A maid stared up at her from the floor. The once-pristine white of her veil had turned into a slickened ruby, blessedly hiding her face, though the wet cloth gave vague impressions of her broken features. Two other servants lay in a loose knot behind her, limp. Bright red halos pooled beneath their heads on the tile. A trail of blood and smeared footsteps showed where her brother had gone.

Somehow those smears of blood, those approximations of his footprints, were so much worse. Far worse than the servants and their splayed fingers and open palms. How could her brother do this? She'd never seen him lift a violent hand. It didn't make sense. This wasn't him. Whatever curse had laid its roots in him, it was twisting him. Turning him into an ugly facsimile of her brother.

"Oh, Alejandro. How could you?" she whispered. Grief laid its hooks deep in her. It felt like she was losing her parents again. Like the last vestige of her family was being torn viciously away by forces outside her control.

"Get it together. Get it together," she murmured to herself, forcing her spine to straighten. She swiped at her cheeks, throwing the tears that stained her cheeks to the floor. She didn't have time for this. She couldn't stay here. More servants would come, after all the noise Alejandro had made. She couldn't let herself get cornered. She wouldn't let herself die here. All she needed to do was make it until dawn.

Edging around the pools of blood and tangled limbs, she refused to look at the remains. Beyond the long corridor, the foyer opened before her, empty and cool. A flash of movement on the second landing caught her attention, soon accompanied by sprinting footsteps.

Gabriella, her skirts hitched high enough to show the tension in her calves, ran full tilt through the second-floor landing. Her eyes were the bright circles of a hunted deer, catching the dim light of the lanterns.

She vanished around the corner, and moments later Hiraya came hurtling after. But, as if she sensed Josephine, she slowed. Their eyes met briefly, and Josephine stared Hiraya down.

You promised is what she wanted to shout. But Alejandro was too close, and instead she gritted her teeth, holding on to the hope that Hiraya had meant everything she said. That this was just part of a greater, innocuous plan.

The sound of their steps vanished into the house, but Josephine stayed rooted there for a moment longer. Hiraya had promised her that Gabriella would live through this. That she wouldn't kill her.

Forcing herself past the staircase, Josephine kept to the first floor and plunged deeper into the house. She had no idea how far the rooms and halls sprawled to either side. If Sanctuary was anywhere, it'd be where the house was oldest. A place that would have seen the very start of the games, through the decades and centuries, through the fires and plagues. And surely that would be at the house's foundation. In its basement.

Throughout the house, clocks chimed. Midnight.

EIGHTEEN

TRADING the yellow carpet runners that marked the trail to the servants' quarters for cerulean blue, Josephine moved with light, precise steps. Occasionally, she heard a clatter above her as Gabriella and Hiraya ran through the house in a frenzied game of cat and mouse. But what terrified her were the rooms all around her.

The dragging sigh of steps on the tile. Doors creaking open, items shuffled and moved. All around her was *noise*. All around her were the servants, already scrounging for her. The farther she delved into the corridors, the more rooms stood open.

It's just a matter of time. I have to be fast, Josephine thought. If Alejandro didn't find her, the infested servants certainly would. She darted past each open door, trying not to catch the attention of anyone who might linger within.

From a distant room, a radio crooned a love song.

She couldn't help herself. She leaned against the side of the corridor, her temple against the wall as she listened to the old song. It was a song of joy, of despair, of finding friendship and community at your lowest point. It was a bittersweet melody in this house, where friends had been turned against each other.

She peered inside the open room where the radio played, halfway expecting to see her brother leering at it. But the radio lay tossed to the floor. A servant crouched over it, balancing on his knuckles like an ape. He seemed intent on the song, his hidden face bent close to its mesh speakers.

She hated how almost human he seemed. The chef had said that the servants were practically drones, and yet this one rocked to the beat, as if he knew precisely what it was. As if he recognized it, and it comforted him.

But the moment Josephine tried to withdraw, his head jerked up toward her. Without a moment's hesitation, he unfurled, his spine still nearly bent at the waist. A complete departure from the stiff, almost mechanical movements that had marked the servants in the hours and days before.

He leapt toward her, his long arms reaching and grasping at the air, as if possessed by a wild, insatiable hunger. Josephine stifled a scream as she shot down the hall like hell itself was on her heels. She couldn't let him lay a single hand on her. If he did, she doubted she'd be able to get away.

She turned a corner, nearly tripping over herself. A scream pierced through the ceiling, full of anger and desperation, only to be followed by another violent clatter. Somewhere overhead, Gabriella and Hiraya were at each other's throats. But she could scarcely worry about their fight. Behind her, the man's feet slapped on the tile, an uneven cadence as he dived after her, filling the hall with animalistic grunts.

Doors opened behind them like a series of dominoes as servants alerted to the chase came careening through the house, joining the hunt. They hit the walls in their fervor, quickly righting themselves to sprint after her. But together they became a blackened, howling river. How much longer before they caught her? Before they dragged her down to join them in their strange, parasitic web? Even if they didn't catch her, Alejandro would certainly hear their thunder of footsteps.

"Left, left," Sidapa whispered into her ear. Josephine could feel Sidapa's jagged fingers digging into her shoulder blades, as if she were clinging to her back.

But without hesitation, Josephine took a sharp turn left.

She could hear the radio playing still. The music had cut to a clip of a protester screaming, *"We will not run! We will not surrender! We will die here, for our country, for our brothers and sisters—"*

Near the end of the hall stood Sidapa, her back to Josephine. It was Sidapa, but locked into the moment Josephine had last seen her. Tender in her youth, just on the cusp of adolescence. Thin and delicate and clearly uncomfortable in her own body. Sidapa before she'd been starved and tortured.

She turned to Josephine. Her eyes were gone, and Josephine knew that this was a vision Sidapa had conjured. A sign. The girl pointed to the open door and turned to look again at its floor, as if contemplating its contents, immune to the horde hot on Josephine's heels. The room seemed scarcely any bigger than the narrow closet Josephine had hidden in. But as she neared, she could see that it was a cupboard with a hole where its floor should have been.

This is the way to the basement? This pit?

Little Sidapa stepped forward and vanished into the floor.

"Sidapa!" Josephine gasped, panic twisting her voice. For a moment, she'd forgotten that the Sidapa she'd once known was gone. But as she reached the closet, in the dim light she found that there was more than just a hole. There was a ladder pressed against the rock. Rusted and ancient, reaching into the blackness below.

She couldn't see its bottom. She wasn't certain how deep it went. But her pursuers were only a few yards away, and she scrambled down the rungs.

As she sank into the ground, the light in front of the closet was blotted away. Sidapa was no longer below her. It'd just been a soft illusion. Instead, the monstrous figure of Sidapa she'd seen before outside the kitchen stood at the door, no longer young and birdlike but blackened and disfigured. Through Sidapa's legs, Josephine could see the servants sprinting toward the closet. Their veils were twisted around their faces or thrown back, revealing their mottled and scab-pocked faces. They'd taken on an unnatural pallor, so that their veins could be seen through their skin. A network of blackened roots that seemed to pulse with malignant life.

The insects that possessed them had turned them violent and vicious with bloodlust, but the door slammed shut in their faces, cutting them off from Josephine.

Bodies crashed against the door, as if the servants hadn't slowed at all. As if they'd been willing to break their necks on the wood if it meant catching her. Josephine grimaced and braced herself for the door to break as they pounded and tried to claw their way inside.

The door held, even as the copper knob shook and trembled in its mooring, refusing to turn. Dozens of fingertips probed at the crack at the bottom of the door, scratching and wriggling as they tried to reach her.

Without wasting another moment, she sucked in a steadying breath and shut her eyes as she descended into the dark.

The rock walls scraped against her arms, threatening to tear the cloth of her blouse. Condensation slickened the metal bars, making each rung precarious. With each foot she descended, dread slowly settled on her. No human was ever meant to slide down this narrow hole, into the space beneath the house.

A dark thought wormed its way inside her brain. *What if this ladder is bait? Something to lure the desperate into the island's bowels, where whatever waits below—*

She didn't finish the thought. She was trapped now. Up wasn't an option. She could only go forward and hope that Sidapa had saved her, not damned her.

With each rung, her skirts turned heavier with moisture drawn from the rock. Above her, the knocks against the door had slowly dwindled to nothing. As it quieted, she could hear the scrape of something heavy against stone. Something was down there, far below. She continued down despite it, until her foot touched firm, blessed ground.

Breathing a sigh of relief, she made a sour face at the dank air. It tasted stale, full of minerals and mold. But there were signs of life here. She stood in a dark little alcove that seemed to be half cave, half cellar. Its walls were mostly smooth, as if someone had carved them away. And farther along a sloping, curving tunnel, she could see a flickering pool of light. She edged toward it and saw that the walls were cracked through with holes. Some were barely large enough for her to sink her fingertips into, others large enough that she could walk through with a bent back.

She'd seen something like this before, as a child. An old farmer had pulled up a thick, old shrub to plant pineapples. In the crater where the plant had once been rooted was a torn-open anthill. Tunnels and strange chambers sprawled before her, as if planned with inhuman intelligence. From deeper within the cave, the scraping continued, just loud enough to distinguish itself from the steady drip of water.

Josephine crept closer, steeling herself as she rounded the bend into the entrance of a small carved chamber. The ceiling sloped upward by a foot, though still low enough that Josephine could have raised her hand and touched it with her palms flush. A lantern hung at the edge of the room, the flame low and sputtering.

But the three women scarcely seemed to notice her shadow that leapt in the dying light. They were consumed in their work, their hands moving in a soft rhythm, as if they were sowing seeds in fresh soil.

A man lay between them. He was naked, spread-eagle, and Josephine tore her eyes away in embarrassment. A burlap sack covered his face, and if not for the slight movement of cloth, she would have thought him dead.

"Hello?" Josephine whispered, but no one responded. She wasn't sure they knew she was there. She crept forward, drawn by a morbid curiosity.

What little remained of their hair fell in thin curtains around their swollen, cauliflower-like ears. The skin of their faces hung in loose sheaves, heavy with age. The effect was that of a melting portrait. But their dirty bodies were covered in thick, almost armorlike calluses. As if they'd spent years on their hands and knees, crawling through this place.

"This isn't Sanctuary, is it?" Josephine murmured. The lanterns cast long, dancing shadows into the center of the cavern. But she could see where the shackled man had been wounded, and she knew immediately that he'd played the game and lost.

The gray women bent over him as if they were farmers tilling a field. They plucked their seeds from the basket at their sides, which gleamed white or glossy brown. Josephine squeezed her eyes shut.

Did Sidapa bring me here on purpose? Did she want me to see this?

"Josephine?"

Hiraya's voice floated down from above, and Josephine's eyes flew open. From the next chamber, she could hear Hiraya descend.

Hiraya emerged into the seeding chamber, her lip bloodied and her blouse torn, as if someone had grabbed at her neck and instead found the collar of her blouse. Josephine froze. If Hiraya looked like this, then she knew Gabriella looked far worse.

"Gabriella—"

"She's fine," Hiraya interrupted, lifting a hand. "Alive and well. I promise. I caught her briefly, but it was like trying to pin down a feral cat. She's vicious."

"If anything's happened to her," Josephine warned.

"It hasn't. I swear to you. She's got a few bruises at most. As you might expect, she didn't want to talk to me at all. Every time she sees me, she tries to murder me or run. Usually both, in that order."

Yeah. That sounds like Gabriella, Josephine thought.

Hiraya's gaze drifted over Josephine, taking stock of her dirtied clothes and haggard face.

"The more important question is, are *you* okay? When I heard the servants clawing after you I was terrified. I was worried that—" Hiraya stopped and swallowed, blinking hard. Her eye was shiny with tears she was barely holding back. "I don't want to see this house take you."

Josephine balked. "Am I okay? You know what I saw in the kitchen. I've seen the servants, their real faces. And now this place?" Her voice jumped through the room and echoed through the stony corridors, surely loud enough to penetrate the swollen ears of the seeding women. But none stopped their work.

Hiraya flinched at Josephine's voice and dragged a hand through her tangled hair, the braids now half undone, pulled apart by Gabriella's hands. "I know. I know exactly how it looks. But I sent you to that kitchen for a reason. You asked me to tell you the truth. The *whole* truth. And . . . this is it. I knew our chef would send you here. I needed you to see it for yourself. I needed you to understand why I have to escape. Why losing isn't an option for either of us. I can't stay a Ranoco if this is what it means. I can't live the rest of my life perpetuating this."

Josephine fell silent, her fists clenched. She couldn't argue with that. She couldn't think of a worse prison. "And your plan will get us out of here? All of us. You can escape this place for good?"

Hiraya's head dropped. "Those insects are the Engkanto, the spirits of the island that have a hold over the Ranoco women you can't understand. It's the Engkanto's fruit that's rooted in my body. And so long as the fruit is in my flesh, this house is my prison. And I have to play by its rules."

"Sidapa spat out the seed, didn't she? She rejected it."

Hiraya's voice cracked as she laughed. "Yes. She was young and stupid enough to think she had a choice. She thought there'd be an easy way out. But it doesn't matter if you rip it out of your own stomach. It doesn't matter if you set it aflame. The roots are in you until it finds another host. I'm sorry, Josephine. I'm so sorry. I wish I hadn't brought you here. I wish I'd never led you into this death trap—"

Josephine cut her off. "But you meant it, didn't you? When you said we could escape. There's a way to end this once and for all. No more blood. No more death."

Hiraya nodded. "If we can end this game before dawn, yes."

"Then what I'm competing against isn't really Alejandro, is it? It's the insects. That's what's possessed him."

"Yes. Those insects arrived centuries ago, when they settled into the black holes of this island. Tadhana communes with them. Sidapa could, too, however briefly. And now they speak to me in broken fragments. They're waiting until I'm fully sanctified. If I lose this game, the servants will take my remaining eye at dawn and I'll be the new successor, no matter what. The Engkanto *must* have its host. It needs someone to feed it."

"Then we won't let that happen. But can't we at least free him?" Josephine asked as she gestured to the man between the bent women, whose tireless hands continued to poke and prod. "There's no reason to keep him here. There are enough servants above. At least save one person."

Hiraya flinched. "I'm sorry. He's not mine to take. The seeds are all almost planted. Soon they'll take him into the gestation chambers so the eggs can incubate." She lifted her chin toward the long tunnel behind Josephine. "And then he'll be birthed and join the rest of the servants."

Above them was the sound of scuffling and footsteps on the ladder. They stilled and turned silent, but Alejandro's voice floated down.

"There you are, Josephine. I've been looking all over for you."

NINETEEN

JOSEPHINE crushed her knuckles to her lips, as if that might undo all the noise she'd made. Had her conversation bounced along the walls and worked its way up, past the closet door, straight into Alejandro's ears? Or was it not the conversation but the bestial servants she'd left behind, hands bloody from clawing at the door, desperate for the quarry that had eluded them? It didn't matter now. He was here.

Hiraya stepped back toward the wall, as if she might vanish into its cold stone. "I know you think you might be able to talk this out with him. I promise you, you can't," she whispered to Josephine, her one eye half-hooded, her voice slung low so that he couldn't hear her whisper. "I'll try to keep him occupied. So run. Please, run."

Josephine's gaze darted from Hiraya to the exit. The pile of bodies he'd left behind told her Hiraya was right. But she couldn't go back the way she had come. Alejandro was already descending the ladder, his footfalls steady and inevitable. She had nowhere else to go but through the tunnels that stretched out all around her. The one closest to her was large enough to fit her if she crawled on her hands and knees.

The misshapen figures of the women made sense to her now. Their calloused limbs, their hunched backs. How long had they been here before their flesh had molded itself into something more suited to this dark, twisting place? Or had they been born in the catacombs? Not quite human, not quite insect, but an abomination between them.

Josephine didn't dwell on it. She threw herself toward the closest tunnel, falling on her hands and knees, with no light at all but the lantern behind her. She scrambled forward on her palms, the rocky wall brushing against her back and sides, the hard rock floor rough on her hands. It took only a few yards for her body to blot out the light behind her, leaving only a black abyss ahead of her.

Moments later, Alejandro's bare feet hit the floor and there was a beat of silence, followed by a shuffle as he entered the chamber Josephine had been in. "Hiraya? *You.* You've done something to me, haven't you?"

"I've no idea what you mean," Hiraya replied, her voice saccharine and smooth.

Now that he was closer, Josephine could hear the strain in his voice. A feverish tremor shook it and turned it watery and rasping. But it was still her brother's voice, and that made her heart shudder in her chest.

"I've been having thoughts. Thoughts that aren't mine. Sick, twisted thoughts. I've had moments where I feel like I've passed out, where I've fallen asleep standing up. And when I wake again, I'm standing in an entirely new place. I woke up like this, covered in blood."

"Ah, that. I suppose there might have been something in the food," Hiraya admitted. "Maybe all the rumors your mother spread about us were true. Maybe you should've never begged to play this game in the first place."

There was a clatter, then a rough crack as something hit the wall. Josephine jerked in surprise in her narrow cave, but a long moment of silence followed the harsh noise.

"Are you done, Alejandro? I know you can't touch me. They won't let you."

"So you know what's happening to me," he murmured, his voice shaking with hate.

"Maybe. But whatever it is, I know it will only get worse as time passes."

"Where is she, then? I know you're playing favorites. You were talking to her. Were you helping her cheat?"

"She is my favorite, and it's not even close. But we were only chatting. Conversation isn't considered cheating," Hiraya replied, her voice clipped.

"Hmm. Aren't you the rule keeper? I hope you haven't led her to Sanctuary with all your conversation."

"This is not Sanctuary by any stretch," Hiraya retorted.

"Sanctuary . . . no. You aswang love your graves, but this isn't it. There's only one way she could have gone."

"Alejandro, wait—"

"Don't you fucking touch me. That's against the rules, too, isn't it? All your little schemes collapse like a deck of cards if you break a rule now, Hiraya. So think very, very carefully about your next move."

A long stretch of silence filled the chamber. And finally Hiraya broke it.

"Try to fight it, Alejandro. I know that you're in there, somewhere. You're stronger than Tadhana's blood. You're stronger than *them*. And she's your sister."

"Oh, big talk from Hiraya Ranoco. The insects told me *precisely* what you did to your sister. Didn't she beg you to let her go, help her run? And instead, you bullied a weak, tortured girl and held her down as that old witch clawed out her eyes and sealed them shut. You might as well have set fire to her flesh yourself. Did you know that, Josephine? I bet she didn't tell you all that."

"Alejandro, listen to me. They're trying to poison you against us—" Hiraya pleaded.

He ignored her. The soft shuffle of his steps approached Josephine's tunnel, and she scrambled forward on her hands and knees, keenly aware that the surrounding rock walls grew tighter and lower with each passing yard.

Behind her, she could hear her brother grunt as he fell onto his hands and knees. "There you are. C'mon, Josephine," he called, impatience infecting his voice. The sweet smell of his cigars filtered into the tight space, nauseating in its strength.

She picked up the pace, her head bowed to avoid the crudely carved walls. And still the rock peeled away at her. Her head filled with warning bells as the walls crept in closer all around her. They brushed against her shoulders, tearing at the delicate cloth. Her skirt became a noose around her waist. With an angry, desperate hand, she folded the long cloth into her waistband and kept crawling.

"Josephine. You can't keep going. You'll get stuck." Alejandro's voice floated through the cavern several yards behind her. It was so easy to hear the worry in his voice. The brotherly concern. But instead, it spurred her on.

She could hear the sickness beneath his words, and something strange. Now that he was closer, his voice bouncing along the walls, she could tell that it wasn't just her brother speaking. Beneath his voice, she could hear dozens of smaller whispers, blending like a foul chorus, echoing everything he said. They were forceful, insistent. Hungry.

She knew that he and whatever spirits rode along in his throat and beneath his skin weren't worried that she'd get stuck. They were worried that the tunnel would become too tight for Alejandro to follow her. And once that happened, how could they possibly drag her out? She pushed forward until she was almost on her belly, and Alejandro's breathing behind her became labored and irritated.

"Got you."

A hand snapped around her ankle, pulling her back. She screamed; she couldn't help it. The noise ricocheted off the walls, only to smother in the narrow tunnel as Alejandro pulled her back half an inch.

He'd gotten so much closer than she expected, and his hand was hot and persistent and strong. She kicked in a violent lash, her knee and calf and toes scraping painfully at the rock as she twisted her leg around like a hurricane.

Alejandro dug his hands into her tendons, but his hand was slickened by the damp of the cave and the sweat condensing in his palm. She wrested herself free, and like a frog that had escaped its child captor, she pushed herself forward with a shot of adrenaline terror.

"Josephine! Josephine," Alejandro shouted, his voice losing all its sympathy, all its worry, so that there was nothing but anger and hate in it instead. "Why are you making this so hard? It'd be easier for everyone if you'd just die."

She scrambled away from the noise of Alejandro's reaching,

scratching hand. Farther and farther in until it was no longer possible for her to retreat. She inched along, her entire body aching, until she collapsed with exhaustion on her face. She let herself rest in the dirt, her cheek pressed against the earth. Behind her, Alejandro worked his way slowly back, grunting and hissing as his body scraped across the ground. It was a process that took minutes, and as he left, relief and panic washed over her in waves.

He was right. She shouldn't have gone in so deep in. If she'd been wise, she would have waited just out of reach. And then, when she was certain he'd gone, she could work her way backward the way Alejandro had. Now that wasn't an option.

She shifted from side to side and found that her arms were almost perfectly pinned to her sides. She could scarcely lift her legs off the floor. There was no going back.

Her body trembled as her heart ricocheted in her chest. Was she going to die here? Stuck, wedged between the rocks, in a place so dark that no one could ever find her? Would she suffocate? Would she starve? The heat of her body warmed the surrounding air so that it felt like she was baking.

In bursts, she worked her way forward, her body scraping along like a worm in the dirt. Inch by inch. Yard by yard. At some point she'd begun to cry, and she hated herself for it. Not because it felt weak, but because it turned the dirt against her cheek into something slimy. Snot trailed down into her mouth, made all the viler with the grit of stone. She needed every drop of water. Every iota of energy. And here she was, wasting it on tears.

"Keep going," a soft voice whispered in front of her, in the black shadows that stretched endlessly ahead. "You're almost there."

Sidapa. She was almost certain that tiny voice was Sidapa. Or perhaps she was going insane, desperate to hear anything other than her own panting breaths. But it worked. The encouragement spurred her, and she pushed forward, her body burning. Her ankles hurt in ways that she hadn't been able to fathom. Her shoulders screamed. But air pushed against her face, hotter than her own breath. She couldn't turn her head toward it, but this new, novel touch was the beacon of hope she needed.

It took minutes, maybe an hour. Time meant nothing in that narrow, miserable crevice. But the space around her scalp opened, and a tremor of exhilaration filled her as she lifted her head up a few inches. Her chest and neck burned, but she craned her neck anyway, thrilled to have the freedom to do it. She pushed herself forward until she was spilling over the edge of the tunnel, her body ablaze with scrapes and bruises, and fell into something soft and squirming.

Josephine gagged on the musk of earthiness and rot. And yet she sucked the next breath in, filling her chest with it. She had thought she was going to die in that tunnel, crushed under the earth, unbirthed and caught in a trap of her own desperate design. And now, even this filthy pocket of earth felt like a haven.

She counted her breaths, forcing them in and out in long, steady measures even as her skin crawled with the feeling of life all around her. Her hands shook as she scrambled for the thin matchbook in her skirt pocket. She hesitated, then struck a match against its rough paper. It refused to light, and she cursed aloud.

On the third try, the match lit, and its small flame cast a flickering pool of radiance around her. She dropped it immediately. Across from her, a creature with a carabao skull stared back at her from the wall, its yellowed jaws inches from her face.

A pitiful whimper escaped her. But the skull didn't move in the blackness, as far as she could tell. The small, cramped hole she found herself in remained silent save for her heavy breathing and the sound of larvae wriggling over one another.

Her frayed nerves had been through enough, but she forced herself to strike another match, and this time she kept her hand steady.

She sat on a throne of crushed larvae, with more spilling across her lap and legs with each passing moment. There was no escaping them. They cascaded from the walls and dirt and root-entwined ceiling in an endless number, dripping into her hair. But she focused her gaze on the effigy across from her. It was a carabao skull; she'd been right about that. It was bound to the wall, roots tying it in place. The skull's lower jaw hung open, revealing another set of bony jaws within. A dog's, perhaps, so many were its teeth. Then another, perhaps a cat, tucked into its mouth, and another still. A nesting doll of mouths.

The makeshift effigy of a shape-shifter, of an aswang. She didn't need to be an *albularyo* to know that this was a black magic, a cruel curse. She lunged at the skull. She tore at it, crushing the smallest in her hand, and it crumbled as if it were centuries old. But the fangs of the cat and the dog bit into her palms as if it were a beast fighting back. The roots clung tight to their prize, but Josephine tugged one skull out of the other until they sank into the rotten womb around her. Until there was nothing left but the carabao skull, staring at her with hollow eyes.

"God damn you. God *damn* you," Josephine snarled, hacking at the roots that kept the skull tethered to the wall with the fruit knife she'd taken from the kitchen. This effigy, the insects, they were all tied together. She knew it. They hid in the walls and beneath the very ground she'd walked on. This was precisely what Hiraya had hinted at the night before. These spirits in insect form had made servants out of Hiraya and all those who'd come before her. And through the Ranoco women, the spirits had lured countless people onto this island.

And now they had Alejandro. She knew that the maggots and larvae that writhed and bit at her exposed calves wanted so desperately to worm their way into her, too. But she wouldn't let them win. She wouldn't die to these ancient parasites.

She stood and forced herself to think, her body shaking with exhaustion and nerves and anger. There were so many insects here, and beneath her feet was a bloated firmness. From its stench, and that miserable first meeting with the maid, she knew precisely what she stood on. The discarded bodies that hadn't been dined on, the bits of viscera that had never made it to the dinner table.

It was a burial pit for all those who'd come before her and lost.

But there was something beyond the heat and scraps of their rotting bodies. There was a soft breeze that teased at the flyaway hairs at the top of her scalp. She lifted her head and stared toward the ceiling. If she kept her breath caught between her lips, she was sure she could hear the wind.

She dug her hands into the wall, ignoring the slick and slime. Beneath the maggots were dirt and roots. All the better to cling to. She pulled herself up, her arms screaming with exhaustion. She pushed through it until her hands found the crevice she'd fallen from. It was narrow, but it was enough to be a foothold.

Her groping hands found another hole of similar size and shape, then another. She'd been unlucky. There were half a dozen tunnels that were far larger than the one she'd found herself almost lodged in. This strange insect womb, this gestation chamber, was riddled with human-sized holes. She was struck by a vision of those who'd played the game and lost, squirming on their faces beneath the house through these tunnels, desperate to feed the millions of hungry mouths that waited for them below.

She climbed the walls like a ladder, and her groping hands found the thick roots of a tree above her. Her nails threatened to pull from their beds, the varnish long since chipped and ruined. But she clung and pulled, until the warm breeze of the island filled her mouth, and the top of her head was pushing past the sticky, knife-like grass. The verdant blades clung to her, slicing paper-thin cuts into her once-delicate hands, across her cheeks and temples. She relished it. She was almost out.

She dug her hands into the soil, pulling herself over the edge, eating dirt and bits of root as she did. With only her elbows and hands, she dragged her lower half up. The ground felt sweet, and she lay face down in it, sobbing into it as her body screamed with fatigue.

The balete tree that overlooked the burial pit sighed down at her, its leaves rustling, as if disappointed to lose her. Josephine pushed herself to her knees, her head hanging forward, and breathed deep. All manner of filth covered her. There was no escaping the stench. But she'd never felt so alive. Through tear-blurred eyes, she lifted her face to the skies and stared up at the moon, mostly hidden by a scattering of thick, angry storm clouds.

The Ranoco house reared up before her. She was still on its grounds, though near its side, where she'd seen the countless footsteps the day before. The countless barefoot prints. She glanced toward the forest's edge and saw that the balete trees stretched across the courtyard, almost in a perfect line. Beneath them were half a dozen more holes, identical to the one she had crawled up from.

TWENTY

Y OU can't stay here," Sidapa murmured, her paper-dry voice almost consumed by the wind and the rustle of the balete tree's aerial roots.

Josephine froze where she sat, too exhausted to move or run. Behind her, the grass rustled and crunched beneath the weight of a body that hadn't been there moments before. She could almost envision Sidapa behind her. Her body blackened, her arms folded in on her narrow chest.

"You're an aswang, too, aren't you? Just like Hiraya," Josephine murmured.

"Yes. Maybe. I don't know. I spat out the seed, but that hunger still infected me. Or perhaps it's the curse of the Engkanto, torturing me. Keeping me hungry, incapable of leaving on my own."

"What do you want from me?" Josephine whispered. "Why have you been haunting me?"

A low groan pushed past Sidapa's lips, like a soft, lonely howl carried across a night sea. "I want what you and my sister want. I want to choose my fate. I want *freedom*. While this house and its garden are here, I can't have that. No matter what Hiraya might be plotting. Not while there are still people to feed the trees and new insects being born endlessly from those trees."

"You make it sound like a factory."

"Not a factory. A *farm*. You were called from a field far away, but you are still livestock. If you lose, your body feeds the insects, the trees, my sister and my aunt, and whatever cursed girls my sister has. Not even your soul will escape. Once they put your body in the soil, it stays here until it becomes part of the Engkanto, twisting into one of the insects that haunt this house."

Josephine reeled, and she felt herself edge closer to the brink. She couldn't contemplate that her soul might be caught here, that she'd never have a chance to see her parents in heaven. That the insects that crawled and writhed, with eyes that seemed oddly intelligent, had once been people like her. She'd break if she thought about it. So, instead, she laughed, and the noise was like the shattering of glass.

"And you want me to destroy it? Sidapa, I'm barely surviving. These insects, those servants. Alejandro. They're tearing through the house for me like the dogs of hell."

"And if you give up here, they'll consume you. The heart of this house is where it's weakest. If you set that heart ablaze, you will survive."

"And if I can't? If they find me first?" Josephine shot back.

"Then I'll try to save the next player. Someone stronger, smarter. Someone who can set me free."

"The Ranocos . . . might be the most cursed women I've ever met," Josephine muttered.

Sidapa rasped, and it took Josephine a moment to realize she was laughing. "You don't know the half of it. Or maybe you know too much."

Josephine wished she could forget half the things she'd learned tonight. But instead she dug her fingertips into the grass and steeled herself for what came next. "Tell me what I need to do. To save you and Hiraya. To put a stop to this farm once and for all."

"Find Sanctuary," Sidapa instructed.

"That's what everyone keeps saying. Problem is, I've no idea where that is," Josephine spat. A long, tense silence stretched between them. Sidapa turned deathly still, her whole body locked in place, as if something kept her from speaking. That valley of quiet stretched, filling with a desperate electricity, and for the first time Josephine sensed that Sidapa had more in her than whispers. Her burnt lungs were filled with screams, with a voice that wanted to be heard, but something kept it all bound and quiet.

"I don't know where it is, do I?" Josephine repeated, this time glancing at Sidapa from the sides of her eyes. Where there should have been a girl, there was only a misty, ungodly black. Josephine's eyes jolted forward again. But Sidapa said nothing.

Josephine chewed at her lip, her brow furrowing as she dug through her memory. She'd seen many rooms, but none that struck her as Sanctuary. "Libraries, rooms full of junk, studies, a bath. If I've seen it, it surely wasn't in this house. Not in those cramped, claustrophobic rooms."

The realization struck her like a slap. She blinked and twisted her face toward the sea, toward the cliffs. "Not the cave on the cliff side? That's not in the house. That's cheating."

Sidapa sighed, her shoulders sloping in relief, like something had unshackled from around her neck. "All I can say is that this house has one goal. And that's to eat. The fewer people that win, the better. A winner happens once every dozen games. And the winner is almost always someone who will return and bring others with them. Someone who can ensure there's a second meal."

"It's rigged," Josephine muttered, peering off toward the far side of the house, toward the cliff. Now that she looked closely, in the near blackness she could see glimpses of gray. Like wraiths in the fog haunting the path. There were dozens of them, if not more. They'd gathered there to ensure that no one came close to the cliff.

"How can I possibly get past them?" she demanded, feeling the ugly taste of despair in her mouth. But Sidapa was an obsidian mirror, unrippled and unperturbed.

"Go to Hiraya's room and leave through her window. From there, you'll have to climb down. That will offer you some means to avoid them. Doors to lock and bar. A chance to hide. If you go straight to Sanctuary across the field, you'll never survive."

"I can't navigate that house. I only found Hiraya's room by chance."

"But I can." Sidapa leaned close to Josephine and recited instructions, whispering in Josephine's ear in measured, even sentences about the precise door Josephine would have to enter, the turns she'd have to make.

Josephine's mind spun, but she clung to every word, desperately attempting to commit them to memory. It felt like her last chance. The slick rope of salvation, cast out to sea, even while the waves fought to drag her down.

"Wait until the moon sinks behind the clouds, then run," Sidapa finished. And then, with a shallow sigh, her body collapsed into the shadows beneath the tree.

"How easy for you to say," Josephine muttered, her jaw set. Her body burned from crawling through the cave. And she could feel something like panic or madness biting at the edges of her brain, turning her skin into static, making her hands tremble and her teeth chatter. But she rolled her hands into fists, clenching them tight so they couldn't shake.

She couldn't count how many servants lurked in this house, how many haunted the surrounding grounds. It would take just one mistake, one stroke of bad luck, to end everything now. She sat in the darkness, her chin tilted up to the sky. The moon stared back at her, silver and apathetic. Minutes passed before it slid behind the clouds and the courtyard was bathed in the true pitch black of night.

She rose and stared toward the house's door. There were servants scattered here and there. But she had no choice but to run. She sprinted, rivulets of hot tears pricking at the edges of her eyes. Above her in the windows, the servants turned toward her, for a moment frozen in place. Then they tore away from the windows in a single-minded pursuit to cut her off.

They knew the house just as well as Hiraya and Sidapa. Perhaps even better. But this house was riddled with holes, secret passages, and hiding places. She had a chance. She just had to be clever. She made it to the front door untouched, unchased. The dark of the night had played in her favor.

But the entryway stood open. Pressing herself against the stone wall, she crept closer and peered inside. A single servant stood within, facing toward the rightmost corridor. He was injured, his right leg broken, so that it bent at an odd angle. But he scarcely seemed to notice. He limped down the hall away from her, as if he didn't feel the pain. He was fixated on his patrol.

Biting her lip, she crept into the foyer. The entire house was full of noise, like it hosted some violent, debaucherous party. Above her, furniture fell to the ground and splintered. Uneven, discordant steps filled the adjacent rooms, as if servants were running in circles, tearing apart the house with their bare hands. They were frenzied and desperate. Dawn could be only a handful of hours away.

Had anyone been caught yet? Had everyone survived this far? She couldn't let herself think of the possibility that they hadn't. Holding her breath, she slipped through the door closest to her before the limping servant at the end of the hall could turn and find her. The door opened to a narrow, misplaced bedroom. It made no sense here, on the first floor so close to the entrance, but there was no logic to this house's design.

In the room beside her, she heard a door open, then slam. There was a brief shuffle of paper and furniture, and then the slow thud of footsteps headed her way. Josephine darted toward the door on the opposite side of the room, the door Sidapa had promised would be there, and opened it. She crept into the semidarkness of a study and closed the bedroom door behind her. Less than a breath later, someone entered the bedroom she'd just been in. She had a minute at most to hide before they grew bored with searching the bedroom and came into her study.

Josephine ground her teeth as her eyes flitted around the dim room. There wasn't much here. A chair, a table with a thin tablecloth, and a series of bookshelves pushed almost to the corner of the back of the room.

She dashed toward a bookshelf and forced her body into the meager crevice between it and the wall. One shoulder pressed against the room's corner, the other pressed against the end of the bookshelf. This was the best she could do.

The door to the study swung open, its ancient knob hitting the wall with a clatter. Josephine pressed herself against the wall, sucked in her stomach, and held her breath. Her rib cage felt too large, her skull too forward sloping. A single glance—a step too deep into the room. That was all it'd take for her to be discovered.

Her fruit knife hung heavy against her upper thigh in the pocket of her skirt. The intruder moved in the doorway, lingering there. And for a moment, Josephine harbored the naïve hope that he'd simply close the door and walk away.

Instead, the servant fell forward, face first, toward the floor. The sound of his skull hitting the ground drew a gasp from her. But in the distance, thunder rolled and roiled over the ocean. Just enough to blur her mistake, turning her shocked inhale into something that might be mistaken for the wind of a storm building in the distance.

On the tile, the servant moved. He lifted himself up on his hands, his legs splaying like a cricket's, and scuttled across the floor like an insect. Josephine recoiled in disgust.

He clawed his way beneath the table, knocking over the chairs and tearing off the tablecloth. The dingy white cloth caught on his arms and for a moment it dragged behind him. He seemed utterly oblivious to it. The display would have been comical if not for his head tilted up at an impossible angle, as if the bones of his neck had all snapped. His veiled head tilted this way and that, erratic and desperate to catch any sign of movement.

The lantern hanging on the wall sputtered out, turning the dim room black. Did he even need light? But a crash upstairs drew the servant's attention, and he scuttled out the way he had come, still dragging the tablecloth behind him like a cape.

A long moment passed before Josephine allowed herself to exhale. She peeled herself out of her corner and felt her body shake with a barely contained laugh as tears poured down her cheeks. She'd never seen something so ridiculous. He'd really devolved into the bug that infested his body. Would he climb walls next? The thought tickled her. It threatened to overwhelm her, and she chewed at her own tongue, letting the pain ground her to the moment. She needed to stay sane for just a little bit longer. That was the only thing that separated her from them.

Edging her way through the study, she opened the door to a hallway marked with a cerulean rug. Hiraya's room wouldn't be far now. But as she stole down the narrow corridor, she squinted and stumbled over bits of splintered furniture and scattered clothes. The lanterns, which had been bright when she'd first entered the dining hall, had grown dim. Soon they'd all sputter out, and she'd be forced to wander the halls blind. In the far distance, a radio crooned a song. The same radio she'd heard before when she spoke with Alejandro, though it crackled now, as if it'd been abused and left half-broken.

"Now I've got to know what is and isn't mine / If you received my letter telling you I'd soon be free . . ."

Yellow ribbons flooded the streets in the wake of Ninoy Aquino's assassination. His death had been a blatant murder by Marcos to stop his fiercest political opponent once and for all, though Aquino was riddled with lung cancer and months away from death. But in killing him, Marcos had martyred him. Now yellow was Josephine's favorite color and she knew, somewhere in Manila, a crowd of people all dressed in yellow were fighting against impossible odds, against a parasite that had killed countless citizens and would consume the rest of them if they let it.

The song was filled with hope, and Josephine let it soothe her as she worked methodically through the hall. Sidapa had been explicit. Josephine couldn't deviate, couldn't attempt a shortcut. Doing so would mean she'd lose the path entirely.

It was such a simple thing to ask. But Josephine's heart lived between her teeth, and she shook with nerves as the house groaned and rattled around her. Every time a door banged open, too close for comfort, she pressed herself against the wall or slid into open rooms, hiding in the dark shadows of their doorways.

Every few minutes, a servant lurched through the hall, their veil dampened and stained yellow and scarlet. Most threw themselves into the adjacent rooms, only to vanish into a new tangle of corridors. But not all of them. A woman burst through a doorway beside her and hit the floor as if she'd been thrown there. With disjointed limbs, she crawled across the carpet, passing Josephine's door.

Josephine swallowed her scream as the servant scurried past. The woman's veil intertwined with her long hair, her legs stretched like a roach's across the threadbare carpets as she scurried.

Josephine stayed rooted to the spot until the woman vanished around a corner, and only then did she creep back into the hall. The deeper she went, the more turns she took, and the more certain she was that the servants were multiplying.

"I'll kill you, you heinous bitch!" Gabriella's shouts echoed from down the hall, muffled by doors and walls.

"Gabriella?" Josephine whispered, her heart filling with a wild panic.

Hiraya had promised that she wouldn't kill Gabriella. But that wasn't the scream of someone in a tense conversation. That was the scream of a woman who intended to go down fighting, filled with a bloodcurdling hatred that Josephine had never heard before. Without a second thought, she abandoned the corridor and ran, chasing the sound of Gabriella's voice.

TWENTY-ONE

G ABRIELLA'S screams and curses filled the corridors, and Josephine ran with the full force of her damaged, bruised body. Behind her came the stirring of servants alerted by her foot-falls, who'd seen the flash of her body through the doorways. Or perhaps they'd heard Gabriella's shouts and knew that somewhere a hunt was reaching its brutal end.

She tore open door after door, letting them slam against their old copper hinges, dark wood moaning in protest. Gabriella screamed once more, her words unintelligible, but the sound of a struggle grew louder and louder. Furniture crashed; wood thudded against something soft, followed by soft grunts of pain.

Servants shot out of the rooms behind her, filling the hall. But they didn't pursue her with the dogged passion she expected of them.

Josephine glanced over her shoulder and wished immediately

she hadn't. In the dark, she could see little save for their twisted and stained veils, floating over bodies clad in black. They stared back, their hands twitching and clawing at their chests, the walls, the floors. They wanted to pursue her but couldn't.

She leaned a heavy hand against the wall and stared at them for a moment, trying to understand. Then the answer struck her like a punch in the gut. Hiraya had lied to her. She'd said that the servants were just as much of a threat to her as anyone else. But Hiraya's mere presence seemed to repel them, keeping them back. Whatever dark magic kept Sidapa chained to this place also protected the Ranoco women. A symbiotic relationship laced with blood and sacrifice. But that protection seemed to be a tenuous thing at best. They prowled and reached and probed, as if, at any moment, whatever protection Hiraya had would fall away.

The closer to dawn, the more dangerous they become. Even the Ranocos aren't safe forever.

Josephine turned away from them and ran. Sticky scarlet pearls were scattered across the floor, catching the last threads of light from the lanterns. Josephine's heart sank.

No. No. I can't be too late. Hiraya wouldn't— She refused to let herself finish the thought.

At the far end of the corridor, a door stood open. In the nearly complete darkness, she could see the feet of someone laid out across the floor, bare and covered in dried blood. A soft murmur came from the room. A woman was speaking in dulcet, venom-laced tones, in stark contrast to the screams moments before.

Josephine steeled herself. She wouldn't let Hiraya break her promise, even if it was one that Hiraya had never intended to keep. The Ranoco house had seen too much death, had claimed too many lives. She crept forward and froze in the doorframe.

It wasn't Hiraya speaking. It was Gabriella. She straddled Hiraya's waist, one hand keeping Hiraya's wrists in place over her head. Her other hand clutched a knife, which she held with its point balanced on the ground beside Hiraya's good eye. She leaned over, nearly lying atop Hiraya, speaking quietly to her.

But Hiraya could scarcely fight back. Her face was coated with scarlet, blood pooled at her side. And Gabriella's colorful dress, once so fashionable and chic, had turned an ombre of red and brown with Hiraya's blood.

"I always knew you were a vicious little viper," Gabriella whispered across Hiraya's lips. "You might have fooled Josephine. But I know *precisely* what you are."

"Are you still mad . . . that Josephine chose me over you?" Hiraya laughed, the noise a rattling, pained thing. "I was never going to kill you. But you seem more than happy to kill me."

"You're such a lying bitch." Gabriella sat up and lifted the knife, her knuckles white, her mouth twisted with two decades of resentment and bitterness.

Josephine moved on instinct. She grabbed the first thing she could find, a copper candlestick holder on a table near the door, and swung it like a racket against the back of Gabriella's head. The impact made a dull sound, and Gabriella listed and collapsed to her side, dazed. Josephine dropped the candlestick holder on the floor.

"Gabriella," Josephine gasped, as if she couldn't quite comprehend what she'd done.

"Josephine?" Gabriella asked, turning to stare at her with eyes that weren't quite seeing. "What are you doing?"

But Hiraya was already scrambling to her knees, taking the candlestick holder and hitting Gabriella once again on the head, more firmly, knocking her out so she collapsed to the floor.

"Hiraya, no!"

"I'm not—Christ, I'm not going to kill her. Why does everyone think that? No, don't answer that . . ." Hiraya sighed as she rubbed her neck. Gabriella's handprint lay against her throat, angry and red.

"Why wouldn't you just tell her that? Why were you chasing her around the entire house?" Josephine muttered, rolling Gabriella onto her back. She was breathing, but Josephine could feel a wet spot on the back of her head.

"She'll live. I know the difference between stunning and killing," Hiraya said, moving to kneel beside Gabriella. Her face was intent, her gaze dark on Gabriella's unconscious face.

With shaking hands, Hiraya parted Gabriella's lips. Then she began to gag, her chest heaving, tears streaming from her eye. She opened her mouth wide, and for a moment Josephine glimpsed rows of teeth between her lips, like the nesting doll of mouths she'd seen beneath the roots of the balete tree. Beneath her dark skin, Josephine could see Hiraya's veins swell and blacken, tracing down her throat like roots, slinking down past the neckline of her blouse.

Is it a trick of the light? Have those teeth always been there? Josephine thought as her mind flashed back to the kiss they'd shared in the garden. *No,* Josephine decided. This monstrous side of Hiraya had always been just beneath the skin, waiting to be peeled away. She could see it now, not just in the teeth but in the dilation of Hiraya's pupils, in the desperate, eager shaking of her hands. She was hungry for this. Hungry in a way that only freedom could sate.

A thick, bulbous lump rose from the base of Hiraya's throat, climbing upward toward her mouth. It emerged from between Hiraya's lips, which had split and torn. In the dim, reflected light of the room, Josephine could see that a translucent pink membrane stretched across something round and hard. A placenta, wrapped around something the size of a large egg, the capillaries of the membrane throbbing with an unnatural life.

This was the seed. The fruit that Hiraya was cursed with, Josephine thought with horror. The shock of the situation fell away, and without a second thought she grabbed Hiraya by the shoulders and hair, pulling her away from Gabriella.

"What are you doing? Don't you dare touch her," Josephine warned.

Hiraya choked and gagged, but the seed sank. She slapped Josephine's hands away, hot tears at the corners of her eyes as the seed sank back down her throat. When it was gone, Hiraya exhaled, as if the effort had pained her.

"Goddamn it, Josephine," Hiraya rasped, glaring at Josephine for the first time with anger as she tugged her hair out of Josephine's hands. "It has to be this way. This is the only way we all survive this. I need to take her place. She needs to take mine."

"What?" Josephine demanded, her hands clenching into fists, her voice rising. A few silken threads of Hiraya's hair trailed between her fingers. "You can't just make her an aswang."

"I can. I think. I told you I'm bound to this place by the fruit, the seed, that I inherited from Sidapa. But why couldn't I pass it on to someone else?" Hiraya retorted, but her voice had lowered in the face of Josephine's anger and her own uncertainty.

"You can't trap Gabriella here. You can't damn her to this house," Josephine protested as she crouched beside Gabriella, laying a protective hand across her chest, blocking Hiraya from her.

Hiraya stared at Josephine in frustration, her jaw set. "I know it makes me a monster, Josephine. But I can't live here for another year. I can't be chained to this house and its hunger, this legacy of blood, for the rest of my life."

"There has to be another way," Josephine insisted.

"There is. I kill Gabriella and ask the spirits about the path to a future where I'm free." Hiraya laughed, the sound a pained bark. "I don't think you'll like that option much better." She grinned at Josephine, and Josephine tried to catch sight of those teeth again. Those sharp, jagged teeth. But all that was left was Hiraya's usual bitter grin.

Josephine fell silent, her eyes on Gabriella's placid, blood-splattered face. Beyond the tears in her clothes, she looked untouched. In stark contrast, Hiraya looked exhausted and miserable. Her body was battered and bruised, her arms cut, and a bloodstain blossomed at her side. But despite all the scrapes, Josephine was certain that if Hiraya had wanted to kill Gabriella outright, instead of capturing her, she could easily have done it. It was the nature of the curse that had been foisted on her.

"Fine. Give it to me," Josephine said, holding her stare.

"What?" Hiraya asked, her head tilting, her face twisted in confusion.

"Give me the seed. I'm not going to kill my brother. And you're not going to kill Gabriella. We're all going to live through this. I just need to go to Sanctuary and ask the spirits for a future where I live a happy life without this seed, with all of you."

"I could never do that to you," Hiraya exclaimed, leaning forward, her hands on her knees. "I would never risk you—"

"You can and you will, Hiraya Ranoco," Josephine said, cutting her off. "You know I'm right. You know this is the best option for all of us."

Hiraya blinked at her, her mouth forming soundless words of protest. She bowed her head, her body trembling, as the first pained sob escaped her. "I didn't mean for all of this to happen. Like this."

"Hey, c'mon," Josephine whispered, taking Hiraya by the shoulders and forcing her to look her in the face. Hiraya stared through the knotted locks of her hair, her eyes shiny and wet. "It's just for a few hours. Just until dawn," Josephine reassured her.

"Josephine," Hiraya whispered, "I'd never forgive myself."

"That's fine. I'll forgive you. But we're wasting time. Dawn's close. I need you to do this, and I need to get back to your room, and the balcony—"

Light returned to Hiraya's eye, once she seemed to realize Josephine knew where Sanctuary was. She nodded, her jaw setting. "It will . . . hurt."

"Fine. Just . . . tell me what to do."

Hiraya guided her onto her back, her face reluctant. "Open your mouth, and keep it open," Hiraya whispered.

Josephine didn't like that instruction, but she did it as she watched Hiraya straddle her stomach and felt a heat build on her face. There was nothing romantic about the room or the circumstance. She could hear the house groaning around her. But still, her body felt like it was on fire as Hiraya leaned over, her mouth coming to line up with hers.

She held her mouth open even as Hiraya's mouth widened, and widened, and widened, until she was like a snake above her, and she could see something fleshy and red and gleaming working its way up the back of her throat. She stared up at Hiraya, even as Hiraya's hot, wet tears fell across her cheeks, as if she were the one who was crying.

Hiraya pressed her lips against Josephine's, her mouth overlapping hers, her hot breath filling Josephine's mouth. And for the first time, Josephine felt regret—regret and fear and second thoughts. But instead, she held Hiraya steady over her, her hands firm and comforting on Hiraya's sides as something living pressed against her lips and pushed deep inside her mouth.

It tasted horrible. Not the earthy sweetness she'd come to expect from Hiraya. And it pressed inward, threatening to suffocate her. Josephine breathed deep through her nose and endured, even as it descended into her throat. Impossibly large for her throat, and yet still somehow it fit, descending, stretching her skin until she felt like her body would break.

Hiraya was right. *It hurt.* But she endured because it was a temporary thing. Because she knew that it would free Hiraya from this house for good. And she knew that she was strong enough to save herself.

Hiraya lifted from her, her face full of concern, her mouth red where her lips had split at the sides. She set her trembling fingers on Josephine's cheeks.

"Are you okay? Are you okay?" Hiraya whispered, her voice thick and shaking with new tears.

Josephine lay beneath her for a long moment, staring up at Hiraya's beautiful face. Her body was nothing but soreness and pain. But more than that, she could feel a new heat in her chest, where she could feel the fruit lodging. She could almost feel it weaving a web beneath her sternum, creating new synapses and tendrils to lodge it in place, like a spider nestled between her lungs.

Her body felt too full and profaned. But still, Hiraya was safe. She was clean now.

She lifted a hand to Hiraya's cheek, wiped away the tears that were streaking there. Hiraya buried her face against Josephine's hand, kissed her palm, and wept.

"We'll fix this," Hiraya whispered. "We'll get it out of you. I won't let you live like this."

"I know," Josephine whispered back.

Hiraya lifted her head and turned to stare down the dark door-way beside them. Fear wrinkled her face, and Josephine scrambled up despite the ache in her mouth and throat and chest. Despite the foreign heat that threatened to overwhelm her.

The lights in the hall were gone now, and the corridor was pure black. But Josephine didn't need to see. She could hear the rhythmic stride of someone walking toward them, his gait smooth and unhurried. She knew that stride, and it terrified her.

"He's here. *They're* here. Dawn's too close. You have to go. Now," Hiraya demanded as she ran for the door. She fumbled for its lock. It slid into place with a soft, metallic click.

A moment later, the knob jostled, and a knock came from the other side.

"You're always playing favorites, Hiraya. That's not very fair. And now, look at that: it looks like you can finally be punished." Alejandro's voice pressed through the wood. But with it came the whisper of dozens of other voices, feminine and masculine, young and old. They were so much louder now than when they were in the cave. It sickened Josephine to hear Alejandro's voice in their chorus, nearly lost to their bitter snarls.

Hiraya didn't answer Alejandro, or the voices that chided and hissed through the door. Her hands wrapped around the copper knob, and she turned to stare at Josephine instead. "You have to go, Josephine. I've lost too much blood. I don't know how long I'll be able to hold him here." She spoke fast, her words desperate and pleading.

The door shuddered and bucked as Alejandro kicked it. Hiraya flinched and pressed her shoulder against it.

"I can't leave you," Josephine retorted, her hands balled into fists. "And what about Gabriella?"

"You have to leave me. Find the future that saves you. Saves us. But you can't die here. Not at his hands. I'll keep Gabriella safe. So don't worry about us. Just *go*." The door shuddered again with another kick. Hiraya grunted and leaned her back against it, her whole body weight pressed to the wood.

"I'll fix this," Josephine promised, and kissed Hiraya's forehead. She could see the Ranoco girl wilting as scarlet trickled down her blouse, pooling at her feet. But she smiled at Josephine despite the pain in her face.

"I believe you. Go."

Alejandro threw his entire weight against the door, and its copper hinges began to whine and break. Soon it would fall away entirely. Without another word, Josephine took the only other door out of the room, slipping into the blackness of the halls.

TWENTY-TWO

BEHIND her, she could hear the creak of the door of the room she'd just been in. The fruit knife bounced along the top of her thighs in her pocket. How feeble it was, compared to whatever tool he'd used to bludgeon the servants outside the kitchen and now used to beat down the door. She knew that soon enough the door, held closed by an anemic Hiraya, would give.

Josephine fled, twisting down a corridor she hoped would take her back to the path that Sidapa had marked, her skirts fluttering at her knees. It was a hopeless effort. She was lost.

A shadow in the center of the hall twitched and flickered, and Josephine stopped in her tracks. Though it was almost pitch-black, she could see the shape twist. She held her breath and tried to stand still, but it was far too late for that. The servant whipped toward her in a spasm of violent energy.

Josephine threw herself against the wall, stepping out of his way so that he stumbled past her, falling to the floor in a heavy tangle of limbs. His hands twitched; his limbs jittered. In seconds, he'd be on his feet again, his clawed fingers reaching for her. She ran past him, tripping and stumbling over the debris scattered along the floor.

It was too dark—she could barely see anything. The house seemed to breathe foul life all around her, its walled body convulsing with endless parasites that wanted nothing more than to consume her. What was real and what was imagined? In the darkness, she couldn't tell.

Far behind her, Hiraya shouted something unintelligible. But a crack, followed by a stifled thud, sent a cold shudder down the length of Josephine's spine. Alejandro had broken through, and he had wasted no time with Hiraya. She was certain that he'd find her soon enough, too. Panicked, she turned toward the closest door and threw it open. But this room, filled with old, rotting clothes, was already occupied.

Three servants stood within; their veiled faces all turned toward her. Josephine gasped and stumbled backward into the corridor, slamming the door shut a little too hard. She flinched at her mistake, then turned to flee down the hall.

Behind her, the door of the room full of rotting clothes swung open, and she knew without looking that the servants were on her heels. Behind them came the thud of other doors slamming open, their heavy metal knobs hitting the wood with dull thunks.

Hands and feet slapped against the tile behind her. At first, just a few, but in moments there were dozens. A horde at her back. The farther she went, the more doors opened, the more the servants seemed to spill out of the walls, out of twists in the corridor. She was slowly being surrounded. Soon she'd drown in their limbs, in their clawing hands.

She tried to swallow a whimper of panic. At the far end of the hall, she could see a door crack open and swing inward. She expected to see another sliver of gauzy white staring out at her, ready to cut her off. But there was nothing. Just a small, empty room with a lantern lit within.

A thrill of hope lanced through her, and she ran for the door. The moment she entered, it shut quietly behind her, its lock sliding into place, dragged by some unseen hand.

"Sidapa?" Josephine gasped, still trying to catch her breath. The room remained quiet and still. But she was certain that Sidapa had had a hand in luring her here, and she whispered a thank-you as she took stock of her surroundings.

She was in Hiraya's room. The capiz windowpanes were open to reveal the predawn skies, darkened by thick, raging clouds. A harsh wind buffeted her face, but she leaned into it, sucking in the fresh air. Even breathing felt wrong with the seed inside her. It felt like she carried a stone in her chest, heavy enough that she couldn't fill her lungs.

The storm had grown fiercer over the ocean, and she could see rain pelting down in sheets a mile away from the island. A radio cracked with electricity on Hiraya's bedside table. President Marcos's voice cut in and out, tinny and distant.

"There is no way under which I can step down or resign from the position of president. If necessary, I will defend this position with all the force at my disposal."

A gruff voice cut him off. *"The Air Force, sir, is ready to mount an air attack."* She recognized it as belonging to one of Marcos's generals. *"That's why I come here on your orders, so we can immediately strike them."* She could hear the hunger in his voice, the anticipation.

There were so many civilians in Manila, coalescing in the state capital. Had things gotten so bad that Marcos was willing to bomb the heart of their country? Would anyone survive the night? If she survived until dawn, would her home still be whole and waiting for her?

She had no time to contemplate it. The low, guttural groans of her pursuers grew louder with each passing second. A minute later, the bedroom door thudded and groaned beneath the weight of a dozen bodies pressed against it. Their hands scratched furiously at the door, as if they could feel the dawn stirring on the edges of the horizon. As if they knew that soon she'd be out of their reach for good.

Josephine dragged the narrow bed from its post against the wall and pushed it against the door. But the cot and its frame shook and shuddered with each blow. The old copper hinges of the door whined. Whatever meager barrier she could make, she knew it wouldn't last long. She grabbed the photo of Hiraya, Alejandro, Gabriella, and herself from the mirror and shoved it into her pocket. One keepsake, one fragment of her life before this nightmare.

She rushed to the balcony and leaned over the ledge. The wind tore at her hair, causing her eyes to water. Her heart sank when she realized what she had to do. The drop to the ground itself wasn't far, a yard at most. But the sliver of land between the house and the cliff was a narrow strip she would just be able to walk on. And the black ocean that stretched below her promised that a single mistake would be an inescapable death.

Gritting her teeth, her mind reeling with the insanity of the situation she found herself in, Josephine hitched her skirt high. She tossed her legs over the sill and tried not to see how bruised and damaged they were. If she survived this, she was certain she'd carry scars for the rest of her life.

Sucking in a breath, she steeled herself for the drop. She needed to be perfect. She needed to be precise. One false move, one panicked spasm—that was all it'd take. Behind her, the lock of the bedroom door cracked open. The bed moved half a foot. She glanced over her shoulder to see a tangle of hands clawing through the gap.

Josephine jumped and winced as she landed on the soft, wet earth. She gasped for breath, her whole body shuddering as she clung desperately to the house. The open air was nauseating, and she leaned her head against the stone wall. The panic that had followed her from the pit beneath the roots of the balete tree hadn't left her. She could still feel it buzzing in her brain, in her veins. She was so close to losing it.

But she swallowed the despair and bitterness welling in her throat. She couldn't stay here. It wasn't safe. All around her, she could see footprints embedded in the earth. She wasn't the first to step along this ledge. It would be only a matter of time before the servants found her. She forced herself to move, treading over footprints, toward the stone stairs Hiraya had led her down. She leaned heavily against the house, her shoulder scraping its lichen-spotted stone, and took comfort in how it scraped at her. It hurt, but it was so much better than the void beside her.

The wall stretched unbelievably far in either direction, and each step she took along the length of it was filled with suffering. But she limped on, keeping herself steady, until she reached its end. She breathed a deep sigh of relief as the thin ledge grew large enough for her to stand comfortably, and peered around the corner of the house.

How she'd struggled just to reach the other side of the courtyard. If she squinted, she was certain she could almost see the balete tree whose roots she'd emerged from, a distant figure in the pre-dawn mist. But between her and that tree were countless servants. Some still stood, wandering in loose patrols, leaving in their wake trails of footsteps. But others had given in to the malevolent spirits that possessed them, and scuttled and squirmed along the ground.

She wanted to laugh, though she knew that was her mind breaking. Her only blessing was that the servants' heads pivoted in sharp, mechanical motions toward the house, the forest. Every-where but the black ocean behind them.

They didn't expect her to come this way. But behind her she could hear the clatter of the open capiz window being jostled. Glancing over her shoulder, she could see the first servant pushing her way over the windowsill. The woman stretched toward the earth with her hands, as if she had no fear of falling into the abyss below. Three more veiled faces peered out over the edge, their necks craning.

Josephine jerked her head forward and squinted until she found the outline of the stairs that Hiraya had led her down the night be-fore. They were glossy and shiny with rain, and Josephine jolted toward them. They would lead to Sanctuary. And if she made it there, she would be safe. That was the promise.

None of the servants in the courtyard noticed her as she stole across the few yards between the house and the stairs. She steadied herself at the top and descended slowly. She twisted her body to-ward the cliff face, grabbing hold of the sharp rocks. The ocean stretched to her right, its waves crashing against the black rock below. Its white crests reached for her in splayed fingers of foam.

As stupid and suicidal as this was, hope ignited in Josephine's chest. She could see the soft glow of flickering light from the cav-ern's mouth far below her. The candles were lit, and their light stretched outward onto the rocky landing like the soft rays of a new day.

A spray of pebbles rained down above her and Josephine flinched as she clung to the cliff wall. Moments later, a woman plunged through the air, her skirts flapping around her chest, her veil a long scarf that trailed like the tail of a comet.

Josephine gasped as she watched the servant plummet into the ocean below. She couldn't help herself. She stared into the churning waters, and an instinctual hope that the woman would survive twisted in her heart.

A long moment passed, but the servant bounced up again to the surface, her back toward the heavens, her head dipped below the ocean. The waves ferried her limp body, throwing it against the stone, and the tide kept her anchored there, against the blackness.

Another spray of rock came from above, and Josephine lifted her gaze upward. Above her, half a dozen of her hunters stared down. From this angle, their veils haloed their heads, and for the first time she could see their faces. These were the faces she might have seen if she'd walked through the marketplace. The faces of grandmothers and students, of fishers and farmers. The faces of people who could have been her neighbors. They all stared back at her with wide, terrified eyes, as if some part of them were still alive. But now they were simply passengers, staring through while something wicked and cruel worked their limbs.

She wanted to scream. But the servants above her were already clambering toward her. They didn't bother to work their way along the ledge, like she had. Instead, they descended in unison and scuttled down the cliff like insects, their movements fast and jerking. But their soft, human bodies were as fallible as hers. Their fingertips slid against the slick rock, and they tumbled and pirouetted off the cliff edge, bouncing off the stairs in front of her and plunging into the ocean below.

One caught the edge of the stairs as he fell, but the force and speed of the fall fractured his hands. A second later he, too, fell into the water, joining the others in the swirling waves. Josephine crushed down a wave of despair, refusing to look into the waters below. She couldn't bear to look down at the breaking waves. Above her came a continuous rain of pebbles as more servants from the house scrambled over the balcony's ledge and toward the cliff wall—all of them lured by Josephine's presence, all of them whipped into a frenzy by the fast-approaching dawn.

It'd taken her half an hour to climb down the stairs the night before, but now Josephine practically ran down the stairs. She fixed her gaze on the warm light far below. She chased it until her shaking legs and fingertips brought her to the last step. A single lantern sat near the cave's mouth, a warm beacon. She let herself bathe in its light, her eyes squeezing shut in relief.

TWENTY-THREE

THE cavern was precisely as she'd seen it the night before. The lit candles, the macabre altar at the center, with its dozens of staring, withered eyes. But as Josephine bent to take the handle of the lantern, something new caught her attention.

Clothes lay scattered like breadcrumbs at the entrance of the tunnel that led to the Ranoco family tomb. A blouse, a skirt, undergarments, a pair of threadbare slippers, led into the cave at the back of the chamber, as if someone had stripped naked as they walked through the narrow tunnel. She recognized the clothes instantly.

She leaned down to pick up the blouse with two fingertips. Sea spray soaked it, but at the edge of the collar were flecks of scarlet, still wet and vivid. She stared down the winding black hall, where the golden light of candles and lanterns wouldn't touch.

These are Tadhana's clothes. Why is she down here? Josephine mused, her heart sinking.

"Tadhana, can you hear me?" Josephine called, still clutching the shirt. Her words echoed back at her from the depths before tapering to silence. There was no sound of footsteps, not even a whisper of the old woman's voice. But the crash of ocean waves filled the cave, echoing off the walls. Even if Tadhana called back, she doubted she'd be able to hear her.

She clutched the shirt tighter and took one hesitant step forward. "Are you okay?"

The question felt stupid the moment she said it. Of course Tadhana wasn't okay. She'd been unhinged at the table, and somehow she'd scrambled down a cliffside of stairs in the dead of night to go crawling naked into the Ranoco family tomb.

Tonight of all nights, when everything was coming apart at the seams.

Josephine pressed the blouse close to her chest and edged closer to the entrance. Roots penetrated the ceiling of the cave, though that should have been impossible. The house stretched above, and no tree could reach so deep. But here they were, knotting along the walls, thicker than her arm.

Frustration bubbled up in her as she stared down the rocky corridor. She let herself come to terms with the fact that she'd been wrong. The altar room wasn't Sanctuary. She wasn't safe, and she hadn't won. But she was close. There was only one other place it could be. Aswang, so inexplicably tied to graves, had made their own family tomb Sanctuary. She could feel her new heart in her chest pulling her forward. It yearned for whatever lay at the end of this dark tunnel.

With the lantern in one hand and Tadhana's shirt in the other, she pressed inward, fighting against every instinct that told her to run. The entrance by the sea seemed so much safer than the black tunnel that stretched beyond the circle of light the lantern offered.

She walked forward with leaden feet, propelled by the deep desire to see this through. To win the game for Hiraya, Gabriella, Alejandro, Sidapa, and herself.

The lantern caught the thick webs that hung in drapes from the ceiling, pulling them from their anchors. The dusted silk melted away against the hot glass. But the spiders didn't scuttle off to hide in the crevices of the volcanic rock. They nestled deeper into what remained of their webs, stretched between the branches and nooks of the balete roots. Their stillness unsettled her. They seemed too confident. As if they knew she could be no threat to them. As if they knew she was *part* of them.

Between the crevices of the roots, which grew thicker with each passing yard, were piles of offerings. In the circle of her lantern's light, she could catch the gleam of fruits and meats left as tokens to the spirits here. Some were fresh, others so old that they'd become misshapen, fuzzy masses of sickly green and blue. But insects coated all of them.

She hated this place, and the fattened insects with their grim intelligence. She pushed herself forward down the narrow corridor, the lantern swinging wildly. Bugs crawled through her hair, fell onto her shoulders, skittered down the back of her blouse. Her body itched with the unwanted touch of beetles and centipedes and spiders, real and imagined.

Midstride, the path beneath her gave way. Josephine gasped as she tumbled forward, her body rolling down a flight of dark obsidian stairs she'd missed in the darkness. The lantern flew from her hand and rolled a few yards away, its flame guttering.

Exhausted, pushed to her limit, Josephine lay face down on the floor for a long moment, her body full of searing pain. She forced herself to her knees, tearing the last few insects out of her hair and off her clothes. But as they scuttled into the dark, Josephine tilted her head up toward the high arched ceiling of the chamber she'd found herself in. Her fear shrank in the face of awe and disbelief.

The entire room glowed, as if the night sky and its Milky Way had been contained in a single room. Hundreds of candles covered every surface, settled on dried-wax bases that were inches thick, as if a candle had been burning in the same place for hundreds of years. When she was young, she'd looked up at the golden rafters of the church, at the stained-glass windows, and felt certain that she was in a place touched by the divine. She hadn't felt that way in a long time, but she felt it here as she marveled at this sacred chamber carved into the heart of the island from the blackened stone.

She was deep within the island, surely at the very center of the Ranoco house, dozens of feet below the surface. But despite that, a massive, ancient balete tree filled the cavern's center. A tree that had never seen the light of day.

Its tendril-like branches reached into the earth below and up, creating a spiderweb of wood and leaves, with the twisting, knotted trunk at its center. Its canopy stretched so wide that Josephine was certain that the balete trees that surrounded the Ranoco house all stemmed from its branches.

At the center of its massive trunk, a woman stretched, half-merged with its wood. Her skin was leather-brown, and the vines of the tree wrapped around and pierced her, pinning her to it.

Vines had forced her rib cage open. The bones cracked and stretched so they extended outward like wings caught just before flight. In the woman's hollow torso, dozens of fruits glowed glossy in the candlelight. They filled the space between her ribs like pomegranate seeds. At the feet of this crucified woman, Tadhana prostrated herself.

Josephine drew unsteadily to her feet. It disturbed her to see the old woman like this, naked and kneeling before the woman, her forehead pressed against the corpse's desiccated feet in an inverse of the respectful *mano* gesture. The ridges of Tadhana's spine pushed against the blurred tattoos on her back, creating a strange topography. Somehow she'd escaped unbitten, whereas Josephine's body crawled with rashes and swollen wounds.

"Tadhana?" Josephine called. But her voice came out in a soft whisper. She lifted the shirt and approached the old woman. The divine awe that had swept up Josephine only mounted. But dread mingled with it and grew stronger with each step. She felt as if she were approaching the stray dogs around the village, who'd grown hungry and lean with the famine and recession. And starving, dying dogs were vicious things.

But as she edged closer, she could hear Tadhana murmuring to herself. Josephine could recognize pieces of Bisayan, which sounded almost like a prayer. Words that had almost been lost when the Spanish had come, and now sounded foreign and strange to her ears.

Josephine peered over Tadhana's head toward the trunk. The pierced-through woman wasn't alone against the tree. An entire family of bodies was sunken and interlaced in the hollows of the trunk. Some were as old as Tadhana; others were only children. Among them was a woman who looked almost precisely like Hiraya, if Hiraya ever saw middle age. They shared the same cheekbones, the same broad nose. But this woman's skin was blackened, her arm missing.

But interred beside this burnt body was another. So much

darker, charred and desiccated. Josephine recognized her the moment she laid eyes on her. This body wasn't cocooned in the tree like the rest. Instead, thick rusted nails had pierced through the body's blackened limbs, keeping the young woman in place against the tree, which had refused to accept her. Her eye sockets were empty. There was no mistaking it. This was Sidapa's body. She'd been here, beneath the house, all along.

But as Josephine stared at the charred corpse, Tadhana grew silent and straightened her back. She tilted her head up, her empty sockets fixated on the face of the woman whose chest was full of gleaming fruit. Even now, it seemed like she could see, though her eyes were surely in the altar room, skewered upon the iron tree.

"Oh, Josephine. There you are, love. No longer a del Rosario but a Ranoco woman through and through. I wonder if that was Hiraya's plan all along."

There was a sickly sweetness in Tadhana's voice, laid over something smug and coy. But Josephine didn't take the bait.

"You're the last person who's going to make me doubt her. I know precisely what you did to Sidapa, what you want done to Hiraya. And just because I have this *thing* in me doesn't mean I'm anything like you."

Tadhana laughed, the sound a wheezing, dying death rattle of a noise. "Oh, of course not. You're so different. *You* won't feel hunger rise in your gullet when the sun sets. You won't feel your mouth slicken and dribble when a corpse is laid out before you. You'll be the one to resist the call of the Engkanto, the shadows of the tree, the call of the insects."

Tadhana laid a tender hand against the roots of the trees. "No. You'll succumb like the rest. This is fate. You were brought here for a reason. It takes a certain intuition to speak to the spirits of the land. To navigate this house and learn its secrets. You could sense Sidapa and the spirits from the start, couldn't you?"

Josephine said nothing, though she realized it was true. She'd felt unsettled by the insects the moment she left the beach and let the jungle fold itself around her, and that unease had only grown the longer she spent in the house. But Sidapa? Sidapa she'd felt the moment she crossed the threshold into the Ranoco house. She had followed Josephine throughout the house, haunting her and guiding her through its depths.

"You don't have to say anything," Tadhana said. "But I know it's true. Hiraya might have conspired to escape, but the spirits conspired to bring you here. It's a fair trade. I'd trade my dud of a niece for a young woman with true intuition in a heartbeat. It's a rare, delectable thing. You might even be better than me, once you're initiated. Once your eyes are laid out on the altar."

"You're crazy if you think I'll let you take my eyes," Josephine hissed, her hands clenched fists. "We're all leaving this place. Hiraya lost the game, but I've won it. And Alejandro, so long as he survives—"

"Oh, Josephine. You are a *delight*. When I first met you, you were just a tender babe. You entranced me. Would your delicate shoulders crack and crumple at the loss of your parents? Or would you persevere?" Tadhana sighed.

Josephine's mind raced. Puzzle pieces clicked into place. The long divination sessions Tadhana had with her mother beneath the full moon. The sheer devotion Tadhana and her mother shared with each other, which had continued right up until her mother's death. How many times had Tadhana read her mother's future and seen an immovable death in the cards? And yet they'd kept it a secret. From her, from everyone.

"Are you saying you knew this would happen?" Josephine whispered, staring into the back of Tadhana's head. "You knew my parents would die? You knew when you saw us all those years ago. And you let it happen?"

For the first time, Tadhana seemed to deflate. Her shoulders slumped by inches, and her voice dropped low.

"Do you think I didn't try to save her? There was no spirit, oil, or amulet that could keep her from dying. Her fate was cemented when she came here so many years ago. She and I, we were both chosen to be aswang in that game. And like you, she resisted the call of the game at first. She didn't want to play. And then she let herself succumb to it when she realized what she could have. And she got precisely what she wanted: fame and fortune in equal measure. Fortune when she married your father. Fame when she died."

"You're lying. My mother would never have hurt anyone. Not for money, not for fame," Josephine retorted, but even as she said it, she wasn't sure. Her memories of her mother were like faded photographs. Each year, they grew a little dimmer, more distant. Who had her mother been? What would she have done? It frightened her to think she might never have known her at all.

Tadhana clucked her tongue, impatient. "Oh, come on. Don't you speak to your brother at all? I sent him a letter detailing precisely what future his mother sought and how she claimed it. How a single night turned her from a provincial girl to a socialite, as beautiful and cultured as Imelda Marcos. How it changed her fate forever. Didn't he tell you? He practically begged for an invitation to the games. He was certain that it was his only chance to overcome the fate that life had written for him.

"Then Hiraya insisted we invite you. A game isn't a game unless it has enough players. And I agreed, though I thought her love was writing your gravestone's epitaph. And yet . . . here you are. Maybe you have something of your mother in you after all, and my bitterness made me too shortsighted to see it. I suspect the spirits always knew you'd overcome their challenge and arrive in this place, ready to ascend and tend to them."

Tadhana straightened her back, her bones cracking like broken shells beneath a boot. She tossed her head back and took a pair of old, rusted shears from between the roots of the trees. Her old hands gently cut her long steel gray hair from her scalp, so the thin locks fell like rivulets onto the ground. "Oh, Josephine. It's time for me to die. I'm tired of this body. It falls apart with each passing year. Even meat tastes like rot for me now. But I can't leave this place with that fruit still rooted in me."

Tadhana pressed a knotted, arthritic hand into her chest. "It always has to be two in this house. One to hear the insects' song, to follow their will. The other to breed more daughters and carry on the tradition. Sidapa would have been their host, their song seer. Hiraya the mother, the *sirena* that would lure men onto the rocks and bear the next generation. But when Sidapa refused the seed and destroyed her body, she ruined everything. She kept me from death and she left Hiraya in limbo, successor to both roles. But you've come to save me, haven't you? Fine intuition, clever and stubborn. And Gabriella? I thought her meat, tender and soft, when she first arrived. But no, she was always meant for this place. She was always meant to be your sister. The mother."

Tadhana pressed her fingers into the space beneath her ribs with both hands. Her fingers were thick and arthritic with age, but Tadhana kept them straight, forcing them into the sagging skin.

"Tadhana, stop, you're hurting yourself!" Josephine cried out, more on instinct than anything else. Everything the old woman had said to her was vile and twisted. And Josephine was certain that if she'd ever seen evil, she'd seen it in this old woman. But still, it pained her to see her hurting herself so viciously.

Tadhana grunted with effort. Around the old woman's waist, Josephine could see her dark blue veins turned thin and fine, like cracks in porcelain, and bit by bit Tadhana split apart.

Horrified, Josephine stumbled backward, but the transformation had already begun. Tadhana collapsed forward onto the roots of the trees. Her intestines, still half moored to her lower body, trailed after her.

"Tadhana, please," Josephine warned. "I don't want to do this. I don't want to fight you."

Tadhana said nothing. Her arms extended inch by unnatural inch. From her wrinkled, loose skin, black bristles erupted like the fine hair of a tarantula, covering her.

"Please," Josephine repeated. Segments of Tadhana's skull collapsed inward. In these concave dents, fresh eyes blossomed. The eyes of a spider, set like a halo on Tadhana's head. These faded and split and turned bulbous, morphing into the eyes of countless insects. Her lips split apart and extended, like an imitation of a spider's mouth. Her bristles shifted to scarlet armor, then to a heavy exoskeleton.

Aswang were shape-shifters, cursed to tear their bodies apart and twist them into new shapes. But Tadhana had clearly lost control of herself. The creature she became was a chimeric monstrosity. A strange amalgamation of shiny, armorlike scales, black bristles, and too many eyes. A monster that Josephine almost recognized, as if it had visited her in her nightmares. As if its hot breath had whispered her mother's name in the dark of the night, pained and lonely. Tadhana clawed at the roots and turned toward Josephine using her strange, spiderlike arms.

For a long moment, Josephine could only stare at the old woman's half dozen eyes, at her hideous, unearthly body. There was a malicious intent in those black pearls.

Run.

Her mind filled with the word, as if it was being screamed by dozens, hundreds, of voices. Josephine sprinted as fast as her torn and bruised legs could take her, toward the obsidian stairs she'd fallen down minutes ago.

Tadhana scarcely seemed surprised. She lunged across the floor with her arms. And though she had only her twisted arms to propel her, she moved quickly, like a serpent darting through graveyard grass. She chittered in an unknown, abominable tongue, older than Bisayan, older than any language known to man.

Josephine mounted the first stair, and Tadhana's vise grip of a hand snatched her ankle, pulling her back. With a gasp, Josephine stumbled forward on her hands and knees, trying to climb up the stairs like a dog while kicking viciously with her caught leg. But Tadhana was strong, and with her free hand she grabbed the back of Josephine's skirt and pulled her back into the room, tossing her in a heap onto the floor.

"Tadhana, don't do this," Josephine gasped as she scrambled to get back on her feet. But Tadhana's hands were ferocious and unrelenting. She grabbed at Josephine's neck as if she were a viper, forcing Josephine back onto the ground.

"Please don't," Josephine repeated, her voice a thin scratch in the narrowing passage of her throat. But Tadhana moved as if she couldn't hear her, dragging her split torso over Josephine, letting her innards rest on Josephine's shaking rib cage, like the monster that had haunted her the night before.

Tears welled at the corners of her eyes, spilling over the edges. She could see herself reflected in Tadhana's halo of eyes. Her face appeared distorted and stretched along the glassy mirror.

With a low chitter, Tadhana leaned over Josephine, her gnarled, bristle-covered fingers reaching for Josephine's eyes, as if she meant to tear them out by hand. But as the twitching black fingers reached for her face, Josephine knew precisely what to do.

She reached for the fruit knife in her skirt and plunged it upward into the soft, delicate underside of Tadhana's chin. The reaction was immediate. Tadhana screeched, her hands clutching at her throat to try to stymie the thick, viscous blood pouring from the wound.

The moment Tadhana slid off her, Josephine sucked in a breath of air. It strengthened her, and she was able to scramble away as Tadhana clawed at her again, trying to pin her down.

Not this time.

With all the strength she had left in her battered body she swung at Tadhana again, slicing wildly as she scrambled and tore her way out of Tadhana's reaching, grabbing fingers.

Scarlet arcs stained the cave's floor, coating both Josephine and Tadhana. The old woman, twisted and malformed as she was, had become even more hideous beneath Josephine's violent attack. Despite that, the old woman crawled. She dragged herself with her hands and elbows onto the roots of the ancient balete tree. Her bristle-coated body slowly contorted until she was an old woman again, though she'd left her legs behind, still neatly folded.

Josephine watched her go, knife still clutched in her hand.

"Please," Tadhana begged. "Open for me. Take me in, Mother,

please." Her voice rasped and broke. And as if the tree could hear her, its tangled trunk seemed to unravel for Tadhana. Its branches withdrew to create a crevice. Without another word, Tadhana slipped her broken, battered body into the alcove. But for a moment, Josephine could see that Tadhana wasn't alone. Within the wooden nook, ancient leathery arms and shards of sallow faces peered out, their bodies embedded into the wood. But Tadhana purred and sighed with relief.

"Oh, Mother, Mother," Tadhana murmured. She nestled her face against the face beside her, buried in the wood. "I *missed* you. I missed you so much. Let me be with you again. Let me come home."

The vines and wood refilled the space slowly. But they didn't build their lattice around Tadhana. They built through her, thin vines puncturing her body like needles through cloth. They sewed her into place, and Tadhana's purr became soft whimpers and gasps. The vines pulled apart her chest, her ribs splitting. There in the middle was Tadhana's heart, somehow still beating. Nestled beside it was the fruit, so much redder than Tadhana's blood that spilled from her wounds, nourishing the tree.

"It belongs to Gabriella now," Tadhana whispered. "Take it." The halo of spider eyes melted away, replaced by the hollowed-out sockets of Tadhana's eyes and her soft, wrinkle-lined face. Her ragged breathing tapered to nothing. Her white-tinted, ancient heart slowed but continued to beat. The fine white filaments that kept the fruit in place, anchored in Tadhana's chest, snapped one by one until it fell. It bounced across the roots and rolled, landing inches from Josephine's feet.

Despite the gore it'd been nestled in, it glowed in the candlelight, ruby and succulent. This was the twin of the fruit nestled in her own chest. But she knew precisely what she had to do with it. She had to destroy it. But before she could move toward the fruit, before she could lay her hand on it, a new gaze lay heavy and malicious on the back of her neck.

He'd finally found her.

TWENTY-FOUR

February 25, 1986

S HE turned toward the stairs. A man stood at the top of them. His white button-up shirt was stained yellow with sweat, brown with dirt, and an ombre of pink and scarlet. The buttons near his neck were missing, as if they'd been violently ripped, and scratch marks scored his chest. Hiraya had given him a fight. In one hand, he carried a hardwood *bahi* cane that he tapped against the side of his leg, rhythmic and threatening.

She knew him, though she couldn't see his face. An intense, malevolent smoke wreathed his head, so thick it utterly obscured his features. The smoke writhed and twisted in an angry mass, but in the candlelight Josephine could see faces bubbling up from the black. The faces of the old and the young. And sometimes faces that weren't human at all and never had been.

"Alejandro," Josephine murmured. His name felt heavy and thorned on her lips as she tried to comprehend what evil had dug its claws into her brother. She wasn't certain if her brother was there at all or if he'd been utterly consumed by the spirits that had laid their hooks deep into his flesh.

"Josephine," Alejandro answered, his voice mingled with dozens of others. In the cavern where he'd chased her through the tunnels, those voices had once been weak. But now they overlapped Alejandro's voice like a discordant chorus, leaving his voice a whisper crushed beneath them. "I've finally caught up to you. I'm so happy you made it so far."

She took a step back, her eyes darting from side to side. The cave had been carved into the heart of the island with no means of escape. There were only the obsidian stairs behind Alejandro, and he descended them as if he knew it. As if he had the leisure of an endless day, as if he'd already won the game.

"The game is over, isn't it? I won. I found Sanctuary. You're too late," Josephine shouted, knowing that it was with the spirits, the Engkanto, that she really spoke. "So let him go." But even as she said it, she knew that they wouldn't. Not willingly. She'd seen what this house did to its losers. What it needed to do to them to survive.

The black-haloed creature that had enraptured her brother hesitated at the bottom of the stairs, and the smoke vibrated with what Josephine was almost certain was laughter. "You have won, haven't you? You found Sanctuary, and breath still rattles around in those lush pink lungs. Let me divine the future for you, then, as a reward for all your sacrifice." He took another step toward her, closing the gap. The familiar perfume of cigars lay heavy in the air between them. But there was a sickly earthiness to it now, the rot gnawing away at benzoin and smoke.

"You dream of a home that your brother returns to. A house where you and he can build your family legacy. One so great that

Eduardo will never think of laying a hand on your family ever again. One where Roberto is a distant memory, left to be forgotten, and you are free to love and lie with whomever you like." He reached for her, as if to touch her cheek, and she recoiled as if he meant to strike her.

He let his hand drop. "Here's precisely what you need to do to claim that future, Josephine del Rosario. Give up." Alejandro gestured broadly to the cave around them, to the house that rested on heavy foundations above them.

"The Ranoco house is yours to inherit. A grand estate that will only grow grander, beneath your hand. And your brother"— Alejandro laid a hand against his own chest—"will attend you and Gabriella. And when you die, when your body is interred into the great tree, we will be together. Forever." There was no hint of her brother's voice in the mocking divination, just the ugly mob, their voices whispering and overlapping as they painted a new blackened future that was hers alone to claim.

"That's not the future I want at all," Josephine shouted back, horrified. And then a dark, terrible realization fell across her. This was the miserable truth her mother had met in this very same house. The spirits promised a future, and they twisted it to their own designs. There was no kindness in this place. No fair trades. No sacrifice worth the pound of blood each game clawed from them.

"It is as we promised," the spirits sighed, but she could hear the softest amusement beneath the proclamation. "*We* make the game. We decide its rules. We present to you your prize."

The insects chittered in the tree. The ants and spiders and centipedes had taken on a smoky, blackened effect, like the halo of smoke around her brother's head.

They were all connected. They'd never been apart. The insects beneath the balete tree. The insects that squirmed, birthed, from the bodies of the servants. The fat, ugly flies that had followed her from the beach up to the Ranoco house. They'd all been part of one hideous network. And even now she wasn't sure if she'd seen the heart of it or if this black smoke and the tree that sprouted in the chamber were just more facets of the monstrosity that had flourished and crept up from the darkened crevices of this island.

"The servants will take your eyes when you're ready to ascend to the house. And I—I will take Gabriella her fruit." He reached for the fruit that had spilled from Tadhana's chest. Dried blood was encrusted beneath his nails, flaking away from his skin.

Without hesitation, Josephine grabbed hold of his wrist, clinging to him as she peered up into the blackened smoke that obscured her brother's face. "Alejandro, I know you're still in there. I know . . . I know the last thing you want to do is condemn Gabriella to this place. Listen to me." She raised her voice, so her words rose over the chorus of spirits.

He tore his hand away and she stumbled and fell to the ground, her fingers scratching at the cave floor. But as he turned away from her, she forced herself back up to her feet and scrambled to him, grabbing the back of his shirt and clinging to him, burying her face into his back.

She felt like a child. This was so much worse than when her brother left her for the first time. Worse than the ten thousand needle pricks of his letters, where he'd grown distant and quiet over the years, the gaps between them deepened by the words left unsaid. Worse still than him condemning her to a life with a man she knew she'd never love. This time she felt like he was really, truly leaving her.

"Let him go. Please. None of you wanted to die here," Josephine called, though she knew that trying to reason with the hellish choir was hopeless. "Don't take him, too. Give him back. Alejandro, please come back," she said into his shoulder. "Please don't do this. Don't leave me alone."

He paused. She could feel his muscles spasming as if something desperate in him was trying to keep his legs from moving. From ascending the stairs, from leaving her one final time.

"Josephine, I—" His voice cracked, lifting over the chorus and sighs and hisses of the blackened spirits that contorted around his head in a halo.

But hearing her brother's voice lift above the others lit a spark of hope in her chest. He *was* in there. They might have rooted in him, but he was still alive. There was still a chance that she could save him. That they could both get out of this.

She took hold of the chance with both hands. "I know . . . I know you think that there's nothing for us out there. That there's no hope left in the world. But . . . we don't have to save the world. We don't have to be Mother, or Father. We don't have to do anything but survive and try to be happy. To carve out our place in this world. Let's just go home, Alejandro. Let's be a family again."

Tears wet the planes of Josephine's cheeks. She could taste the salt of them on her cracked lips. But the blackened shadows around his head convulsed, and for a long, long moment he stood rooted in place. When he spoke again, his voice mingled with the voices of many, though she could hear the desperation in his words.

"There is no future in the Philippines for me. If I go back to Carigara, Eduardo will do whatever he can to kill me. If not with a shot to the head, then with debts. With rumors. With an endless parade of indignities. There is no life for me outside these walls."

"But you'd steal away Gabriella's future? You'd condemn your children to this house and its depravities to spare yourself the indignity?" Josephine retorted. "Look at that fruit, Alejandro—look at it. See it for what it is. See what it is they want you to do to her."

"My children? Gabriella . . . she's—" He paused, his head bending, as if to look at the fruit in his hands for the first time. It wasn't some beautiful thing; it wasn't a gift. It was a mottled placenta, wrapped around something full of demonic desire. Not power or freedom, but a chain he'd clamp around the throat of the woman he loved and their children for the rest of their lives.

"I—I—" Alejandro murmured, his fingers flexing, his wrists cracking. The blackened halo tightened around his skull like a swarm of disturbed bees emerging from a nest.

"*Shut up.* Goddamn you, shut up," the chorus howled, drowning out his voice. Alejandro dropped the fruit and it rolled to the ground as he bent over at the waist, his hands tearing at his own shirt. He groaned, then screamed, as if he were tearing himself apart.

"Alejandro?" Josephine whispered. But she regretted uttering his name the moment it left her lips, because he swung at her, his hand coming to clutch at her throat, and threw her to the ground. She scrambled to her feet, but he was already on her again, his body so much stronger than it should have been, his hands so much faster.

He grabbed her by the back of the shirt and tossed her back to the floor. Josephine, heart pounding in her ears, scrambled back up to her hands and knees. But before she could stand, Alejandro brought the hard cane down upon her spine with a cruel arc.

Josephine screamed, the noise ricocheting through the cavern, and collapsed onto her stomach. She tasted blood in her mouth. Had she bitten her lip? Had she broken her teeth when she hit the ground, or were there rocks in her mouth? She wasn't sure. She had no time to contemplate it.

"Don't you *dare* interfere. Don't try and command us," the chorus bellowed.

Alejandro kicked Josephine onto her back. Through tear-blurred eyes, she stared up at her brother and the mass of black that covered his face.

He kneeled, as if he meant to grasp her by the throat again. And she let him, one hand coming to rest on his wrist that grabbed her throat, the other reaching into the black halo that surrounded his head. She found his cheek, coated as it was in insects, and laid her hand against it. He was warm and alive, and the tears that had pooled in Josephine's eyes cascaded in thin rivers down her temples. The insects that writhed on his face bit her, but Alejandro froze beneath her touch.

She wanted to tell him she was sorry he'd suffered so much and for so long alone in Manila, with the weight of their family's legacy crushing him. To tell him she loved him. But she could tell by the deep, bone-rattling sob that shook his body that he already knew.

The ants and beetles writhed and dug their pincers into her, attacking whatever inch of bare skin they could find. But she refused to let go of him.

"Josephine—" His voice trembled and shook, and he pried his hand away from her throat. "You have to . . . you have to destroy the fruit. Cut through it—destroy the core," he murmured, doubling over as the blackened cloud around his head buzzed and screamed, trying to drown him out.

Taking the opportunity, she sprang for the fruit knife that lay discarded on the cave floor. She held its tip against the fruit and pressed. The skin was tough, like a membrane, and she brought her whole body down against it. The placenta around the seed broke, revealing tender flesh that reminded Josephine of a newly ripe mango. She tore it apart with the knife. Its sticky juice covered her fingers with a delicate peach pink. But at its center was a small leathery seed, mahogany brown and elegant in its symmetry. From it emanated thin tendrils of black smoke.

The bright seed in her chest shook, full of fear and revulsion and hate. It burned so hot it hurt. She tried to steady her hands, to let the knife's tip align with the pit. But she trembled, as if some force within her conspired to stop her.

"I can't. It—it won't let me," she whispered.

Alejandro laid his own hands against hers, his palms hot, his hands warm and familiar and comforting. "Together. Push," he wheezed as the blackened halo contorted and whirled, enraged at his betrayal.

Josephine took the bloodied fruit knife and placed its tip against the core. Together, they bore their weight down on the pit, until the horde that infected Alejandro began to scream and cry and weep in a thousand voices, as if she brought down the blade upon their very immortal souls.

The core cracked open and a black mist lifted from its broken shell. It emanated malice and hate, and Josephine watched, sickened, as it rose to the ceiling.

Alejandro went limp, and the haze that surrounded him dissipated, dividing into dozens of distorted bodies that vanished into the high ceilings of the cavern above.

She scrambled for him, taking him by the shoulder. "Alejandro?" she asked, almost too terrified to know what voice she'd hear from him. But when she turned him over and let him rest in her arms, horror froze the breath in her lungs.

The spirits and insects had feasted on his face. But it was still the face of her brother, and she spilled kisses onto his hair, wet tears catching along his blackened locks like dewdrops.

"Alejandro," she murmured. Grief spread through her, breaking her heart and filling her body with sorrow so deep she felt she might drown. Every mistake she'd ever made, every chance she'd missed to bridge the gulf between her and her brother, burned in her heart.

"Josephine," Alejandro murmured, his tongue fattened and clumsy in his disfigured mouth.

"I'm here, I'm here," she wept. "Don't try to speak. I'll get you out of here. We're going to survive this, you and I." She cradled him, and he licked his cracked and bleeding lips.

"I've been thinking about it. Going back to Carigara does sound nice."

"Alejandro," she murmured, tears springing hot in the corners of her eyes. Her heartbeat was loud in her ears, almost loud enough to drown out his rasping, ragged breaths. "Save your energy."

"It's a good house. Good for a family. Have Gabriella move in, okay? Tell her I told you so. Tell her I love her. That I love them."

"Shhh, of course she knows that. Of course she knows," Josephine sobbed.

Clumsily, he reached for his pocket, but his fingers had lost their dexterity. "Can you?" he murmured.

She reached into his pocket and found a small box. Its velvet had been worn away by the years and countless days spent in Alejandro's pockets. With trembling hands, Josephine opened the box. In it, their mother's engagement ring glistened. Bright white and polished, like a star captured in gold.

"I thought—I thought I had to wait until the perfect moment. I wanted her to be safe. Wanted to make her proud. I think I waited . . . a little too long. Give it to her, won't you?" he rasped.

"She'll love it. It's perfect," Josephine murmured between tears.

His swollen eyes fluttered shut, and Josephine clung to him even as he grew still and his labored breathing turned to nothing. She bent double, her whole body racked with sobs, and buried her face in his chest. Beneath her cheek, she could feel his heartbeat slow, then stop.

Beneath the smell of earth, she could smell her brother. He smelled like the old wood of their house. Like the flowers that their mother had planted in their yard. Like the sunshine they'd played in when they were children, the ocean he'd taught her to swim in. She clung to him until a warm, soft hand came to rest on her shoulders.

"Josephine?" Hiraya murmured. "He's gone. I'm sorry."

"Is that—? No . . ." Gabriella's weak voice followed, and Gabriella, bloodstained and shaking, came to kneel opposite Josephine. She laid a trembling hand on his cheek and gently pushed a lock of his black hair away from his brow.

"What have they done to you?" Gabriella whispered, and folded into him, her arms around his chest, her face in the crook of his neck.

Swallowing her own tears, Josephine lifted Gabriella's hand from her brother's shoulder and slipped the ring onto her finger. Gabriella lifted her head, and another pained sob escaped her as she took her hand, clutching it, and buried herself back into Alejandro's side.

Hiraya encircled her, resting her head against Josephine's back. "We'll give him a proper burial. We won't let the spirits have him."

"I'm . . . I'm stuck here, aren't I? Forever," Josephine whispered.

Hiraya didn't answer, and Josephine lifted her head to look at her. Hiraya was battered, bloodied. Her face bruised and her nose broken. Tenderly she stroked Josephine's face and tucked the tear-sticky locks of her hair beneath her ear.

"I'll stay here with you. We'll build a life here. Something better, something kinder. I'll have Gabriella taken to shore. She, at least, can escape this place. And with only one Ranoco woman . . . no, one del Rosario woman, then perhaps this house will die. No more daughters, no more chains."

Josephine laughed, the sound a joyless, borderline hysterical bark. She gestured toward the woman at the center of the tree, her body crucified, her chest split open. New seeds were growing there, as if she were a garden. "Look at her. Even if we destroy this fruit, she'll grow another one, won't she?"

Hiraya lifted her head toward the original Ranoco woman and the bright scarlet seeds that blossomed within the space of her ribs. Some were fully ripened, others no larger than the pit of a mango. It was enough to feed a dozen new girls.

"*Give it to me.*" Sidapa's voice cut through the room like the wind that follows a scythe. When Sidapa spoke, it'd always been in her ear. But now that wheezing whistle of a voice pierced through the grim silence of the room.

Josephine lifted her eyes up toward Sidapa, nailed to the tree. She should be dead, every part of her looked to be dead, and yet Josephine could see the slightest, most imperceptible movement of her chest, as if she still breathed.

"Sidapa?" Hiraya murmured, her eye wide. She stared up at her sister in shock, though Josephine suspected that this wasn't the first time she'd seen her sister stretched out on the tree, nailed to its wood. "I thought—I thought you were dead. Tadhana told me you died when you immolated yourself. If I'd known—"

"Take me down. Pull me off," Sidapa wheezed, her voice quiet.

Josephine hesitated. And then, with shaking, unsteady hands, she grasped Sidapa's shoulders. "It'll . . . it'll go through you."

"I know. It's the only way," Sidapa muttered.

Without a word, Sidapa leaned forward, toward Josephine, and Josephine began to pull. Softly at first, then firmly. Sidapa's body tore apart at the seams, and ash and bone fell to the ground. But still Sidapa dragged herself forward, ripping her body away from the tree, falling into Josephine's chest. She fell to the roots in a crumpled heap, missing a leg and a hand. For a long moment she was still, as if pain racked her shattered body. But she lifted her head with the sound of cracking bones and skin. Josephine kneeled beside her and realized that she was crying. She had felt Sidapa break in her hands. And still she had pulled.

"Tadhana nailed my soul and body to this place in the bitter hope I'd never leave. She wanted to punish me. But . . . I won't let them trap you both here, too. I won't let them win again. Give me the fruit." She lifted her head to Josephine, her empty eye sockets black voids. And still Josephine could feel the resolve in them.

Josephine pressed a hand against her chest. "I . . . I don't know how," she admitted. She remembered vividly the way Hiraya had straddled her, the way her jaw had become unhinged. She was certain she couldn't do that.

But Sidapa was insistent. She beckoned, and without a word Josephine leaned closer to her. Sidapa's burnt hand brushed against her lips.

"The fruit will resist. It won't want to let go. It will hurt," Sidapa warned. "I will steal it from you. I will take it by force."

Revulsion caused her skin to prick, but Josephine parted her lips and Sidapa reached into her mouth. She reached unfathomably far, as if she could pull Josephine's very heart from her chest. As if her hand weren't a hand at all, but blackened shadows and mist, her fingertips hooks that she laid into the flesh of the seed that had burrowed and threaded its way into Josephine's chest.

And then she *pulled*. Josephine desperately wanted to scream, to bite down on the hand in her mouth. But Hiraya held her and pleaded with her in whispers to endure. *Just a little longer. Just a little longer.* The scent of Gabriella's shampoo surrounded her, and her hands rested firm and comforting on her shoulders. It was the same way she'd held her when she'd learned her parents had died, and Josephine leaned into it.

But what kept Josephine in place was Sidapa's face. Blackened, disfigured, stoic. She'd endured so much for so many years, her body ruined, her soul trapped. And Josephine knew that if she stayed here, her fate wouldn't be so different. Her body would be just another corpse to join the dozens of other Ranoco women buried in its profane trunk.

Excruciating minutes, or perhaps only seconds, passed and she felt the fruit tear from its mantle and drag upward into her mouth. Onto her tongue. And there it was, scarlet and glossy, like a corrupted garnet in Sidapa's hand. Her chest felt empty, but she felt sanctified. As if she was finally herself again, not the vessel for an unwanted parasitic passenger.

Without hesitation Sidapa swallowed it, and Josephine watched in horror as it stretched and broke the skin around Sidapa's throat.

"It goes down easier the second time," Sidapa murmured after a long moment, her hand fluttering across her chest, her expression unreadable. Though Josephine knew precisely the pain. "Lay me on the roots of the tree. Make me kindling. Burn me, and this tree, and this damnable orchard once and for all. If we can kill the tree, if we can kill *her*, then maybe this will end once and for all." Her hand twitched toward the woman crucified on the tree.

"Sidapa! There has to be another way," Hiraya protested tearfully. "If it's a curse that's kept you here, then there's a way to undo it."

"Christ, Hiraya," Sidapa sighed, leaning against the trunk. "Do you know how hard it's been for me to do this? How much I've suffered? Those ritual nails . . . they're weaker now that Tadhana is dead. But to break our deal with the Engkanto? To destroy the fruits and the curse on me once and for all? It will take an aswang spitting back the gift. Refusing immortality. Refusing hunger. Set the fire, burn her and me both. And I think . . . this time I'll really be free." Sidapa grew quiet, her body exhausted, her battered body folding into the roots. But her head was tilted up to look at Tadhana's face.

Josephine forced herself to her feet and, in silence, took the lantern that had fallen to its side when she'd first stumbled down the stairs. Oil sloshed in its copper base. Not much, but enough. She prayed that it was enough.

She felt like a monster as she splashed the oil across Sidapa's chest and arms, her gaze flitting away to look up at the ancient woman embedded into the wood of the tree. She could see why so many women had fallen to their knees in front of her. Why they'd found solace in her empty gaze. But she could also see the ants that marched along the woman's body in thin lines like veins, the centipedes curled in the shadows of her ribs. These dark occupants watched Josephine with loathsome black eyes, full of patience and hate. They wore the woman's body like a skin and flaunted the fruit like the light of an anglerfish.

Weeping and whispering apologies, Hiraya laid soft kisses on

Sidapa's shorn scalp, but Sidapa said nothing at all. And when Josephine fetched a candle, breaking it from the heavy wax base, Hiraya moved only with the deepest reluctance.

Hiraya stared up at Josephine for a long moment, her face tear-streaked. "There's no other way?" she whispered.

Sidapa shook her head. "This is the only way."

Josephine kneeled beside Sidapa, the candle wax dripping across her knuckles. "Thank you . . . for saving me, Sidapa. I'm sorry I came. But I'm glad I did. I'm glad we could end this once and for all."

Sidapa said nothing, the exhaustion of wresting herself from the nails and taking Josephine's fruit too much. But her fingertips lay against Josephine's skirt, firm. Reassuring. They twitched as if beckoning the fire over.

Josephine tipped the small, blossoming flame against Sidapa's body. The fire crept along her almost instantaneously, working its way across her blackened skin to the tree and its roots, across the ancient mother's limbs. The flames licked at the fruits, tearing and eating away at their garnet skin. The ants between the woman's tendons were frenzied, scattering away in a wide, chaotic spread of black. Sidapa had been right—she was the perfect kindling. She stared up at the ancient woman in the tree, her white teeth bared in a ferocious, triumphant grin as the fire ate away at her one last time. "This ends it. I'll finally, finally be free of you."

They watched the tree burn until smoke gathered at the top of the cavern. And then, only as the heat grew suffocating, did they traverse the long tunnel back to the altar room. Josephine, with the help of Gabriella and Hiraya, lifted Alejandro and carried him on her back. She refused to leave him here in this lonely cave. She would bring him home.

The three of them limped along, the path a laborious blur as they fled the heat. Every part of Josephine ached. But she'd tasted nothing as good as the sweet sea air as they emerged into the altar room. For the first time she felt she could breathe.

Pale light filtered into the entrance of the cave, brighter than the dim light of the candles. It was dawn. Hiraya dragged her toward the landing, toward the stairs. The sun didn't wait for her. Dawn hid behind the clouds, and rain pelted the entrance, freezing after the hot flames that had threatened to scorch them.

But Hiraya refused to let her rest, as if she knew that once Josephine collapsed, she'd never get up again. She coaxed Josephine up the stairs, while Gabriella held Alejandro steady on her back as they ascended the cliff together. With Hiraya in front of her and Gabriella behind her, her grip firm, determined, Josephine had enough strength to endure the hike. Without them, she was certain she would have plummeted into the ocean below, where the bodies of the servants still lay, their veils tangled around their throats and limbs, staring up at the new day's sky with empty eyes.

The ground beneath Josephine's feet felt hot as she reached the muddy courtyard, as if the earth were on fire. And yet the heat felt soothing as the two of them limped to the front of the house and Josephine collapsed onto her back onto the dirt, laying Alejandro softly beside her. The balete trees above peered down at them, their canopies dark, their aerial roots shaking in a wind that Josephine could not feel. But there were no flies, no beetles. Just the noise of rain pattering down on their battered, bleeding bodies.

Hiraya lay beside her and, without a word, her hand came to reach for Josephine with tentative touches. Their blistered fingers intertwined, blood mingling with blood. Tony Orlando crooned a line of "Tie a Yellow Ribbon Round the Ole Oak Tree" from a radio on a distant window ledge, while a triumphant crowd cheered and sobbed. A reporter detailed Ferdinand Marcos's flight from the presidential palace by helicopter and Cory Aquino's triumphant rise in front of a gathered crowd in the early-morning hours. She'd be inaugurated by a provisional government.

Cory Aquino's voice cut over the music, her voice bright. *"The long agony is over. A new life starts for our country tomorrow. A life filled with hope, and I believe a life that will be blessed with peace and progress. We can be truly proud of the unprecedented way in which we achieved our freedom, with courage, with determination, and most of all in peace."* Josephine squeezed her eyes shut and prayed to every saint and god that it was true.

"Make a wish," Hiraya whispered. "You won."

"I wish . . . for a future where we're happy."

When she opened her eyes again, the flames had begun to lick through the windows of the house, chewing away at its old wood. It was a monstrous animal of a house. But even it could die.

EPILOGUE

November 1, 1991

JOSEPHINE leaned over her family's mausoleum altar and lit three candles. One each for her father, her mother, and Alejandro.

Across from her, Gabriella's hand lay heavy on Alejandro's name, the ring he never had a chance to give her himself a star on her finger. Her dark eyes wet with unshed tears. Five years ago he'd left them, and the pain had dulled for Josephine. But she knew that for Gabriella it would be a wound that would likely never heal.

"Mom! We brought gifts for Daddy," a bright voice called.

Twin girls darted toward the grave with garlands of sampaguita flowers in hand. Hiraya trailed after them with bags full of food in one hand and a soft-bristle broom in the other.

Gabriella lifted the girls so they could lay the flowers along with the other offerings. Gently they placed the bundle of flowers on top of Alejandro's favorite cigars.

Quietly, Josephine slid away from the grave to give Gabriella and her daughters a chance to spend time with Alejandro alone.

"Did you want to leave anything for Sidapa and Tadhana?" Josephine asked as she helped stretch out the towel on the mausoleum steps, where they'd eat. The whole town had gathered for All Saints' Day, and Carigara's cemetery had gained a distinctly festive air. Men played cards beside concrete tombs, and children ran between the graves, pelting one another with candle-wax balls. The whole town would be here through the night, eating and drinking, spending time with their loved ones. The atmosphere had changed so much since Marcos had gone. Things were far from perfect, but it felt like the country was finally healing.

Hiraya peered out over the graves and shook her head. "Sidapa would be annoyed, I think. And Tadhana . . . I think I need another five years before I can pray for her in a way that doesn't feel bitter. I'm just happy to have you, and Gabriella, and the kids. I didn't think it was possible to ever have a family again. To have any sense of normalcy. To be *happy*."

Josephine squeezed her hand. "I'm glad you came with me. The house is so much better with you and Gabriella and the kids in it. It'd be absolutely perfect if you two could stop bickering."

"I'll stop when she stops," Hiraya murmured, but she was smiling.

Josephine rolled her eyes. But the grin froze on her face when she saw Eduardo and his sons enter through the cemetery gates. They were thinner, their faces dark and hunted. When Marcos fell, they'd promptly lost their political dynasty. And their years of bullying and intimidation had made them unpopular in town.

Eduardo's gaze met hers and Josephine stared him down, her jaw clenched, refusing to be the first to look away. It was Eduardo who broke the stare, and he slunk into the maze of graves with his sons. She'd never forgive him for taking her parents from her. But there was satisfaction in knowing he'd never have the power to hurt anyone ever again.

Gabriella's daughters darted to the towel, their hands pawing at the bag. "Did you bring any snacks, Auntie Hiraya?" the elder of the twins asked.

Josephine lifted her off the bag, pulling her into her lap, grinning, Eduardo already fading into the background of her mind. "Come on, now, table manners. Let's say prayers for your papa first."

House of Monstrous Women would not exist without a good deal of suffering and so much more bravery. It's hard to be the woman who dives into the dark, chasing after a future that isn't guaranteed, the chains of obligation coiling around her ankles ready to pull her back when she dares to go too far. It's hard to be the woman already bound, clawing at the locks. Or the woman who has already accepted that life is cruel, and gently pads the shackles for her successor, so that her daughter's life will be a little bit easier.

This is the cycle that the Fama women have endured for generations. I am the first Fama girl to be born in the United States, though the chains still followed after me.

But Carigara, the home of my ancestors, came, too, in the stories my mother told. My childhood was filled with tales of the dark forests that surrounded her village in the Philippines. She whispered bedtime stories to me about the monsters who hid in the trees there. Creatures who sprung up between roots and who'd drag you into the spirit world if you were disrespectful or too beautiful. But the stories that fascinated me most were those about aswang. For some, aswang were monsters. For others, they were cursed people who were tormented with a vicious hunger, who spent their lives like wolves cloaked in the fleece of lambs.

The aswang sank their claws into me as a child and became more than monsters as I grew. In high school I saw myself in them as I struggled to blend in with my peers, failing to swim in the synchronized rhythm of normality no matter how I flailed. It was then that my mother added a new chapter to the story. She told me about a friend she'd had who the entire village thought was an aswang. Eventually the rumors and heavy looks became too much and her friend fled, reinventing herself in a new town, under a new name. It comforted me to know that there was always a chance for new beginnings. She even moved close by, an hour away, and she's still a family friend.

When I entered college, first tackling a degree in politics, my mother shared a new story. A story about death, and hope, and what it means to fight against impossible odds. She told me the story of the People Power Revolution and how it was born on the backs of those who'd sacrificed themselves to fight against a dictatorship. She told me about how, even in her rural village, she could feel the passion and electricity from Manila as the people swarmed the streets in peaceful protests. This inspired me to focus my major on Philippine politics, and I dove deep into political dynasties, which still grip the country today.

The last story my mother told me was after I passed the bar. I never wanted to be a lawyer, but I pursued it to make her happy. I was miserable. I saw my future shackled by forms and baked beneath fluorescent lights. For the first time in my life, my mother apologized, in her own way. She told me the story of the women of our family. How every woman had lived in quiet sorrow, sacrificing themselves for the betterment of the family. An act as hard as it was brave. And then she cried. She wasn't just crying for me but for herself, and all the women who'd come before us. She'd suffered so much to make my life easier.

Years of stories coalesced. I saw myself in the aswang, in the centuries of suffering of the Fama women. In the girl who ran away and wrote a new story for herself. From all this, *House of Monstrous Women* was born and the shackles that I'd shared with so many women were broken.

House of Monstrous Women is a story of darkness, and it is a story of hope. It takes many of its cues from real life. The political massacre that annihilated an entire family, the witchcraft and the family practicing it, all have roots in reality.

And in my opinion the Philippines has the most interesting traditional sorcery in the world.

ACKNOWLEDGMENTS

Thank you, *Tita* Ronilda, for going above and beyond. Somehow you managed to find not only an *albularyo* couple but a *mambabarang* who was more than happy to talk about how he gained his power from an *engkanto*, the price of such power, and how he used it to kill. I can't express how much I appreciate your arranging those meetings and everything in between.

And finally, where would I be without Dorian Maffei and Candice Coote? You both saw something in *House of Monstrous Women*, and I am so happy you did. Thank you for all the hours of work and love you poured into this book. Thank you for making my dreams come true.